15   10/08
19   3/14

22   3/18

Grimes

Grimes, Martha.
The Old Wine Shades

$ 25.95

The Old
Wine Shades

MARTHA GRIMES

The Old Wine Shades

A Richard Jury Mystery

VIKING

VIKING
Published by the Penguin Group
Penguin Group (USA) Inc., 375 Hudson Street,
New York, New York 10014, U.S.A.
Penguin Group (Canada), 90 Eglinton Avenue East, Suite 700,
Toronto, Ontario, Canada M4P 2Y3 (a division of Pearson Penguin Canada Inc.)
Penguin Books Ltd, 80 Strand, London WC2R 0RL, England
Penguin Ireland, 25 St. Stephen's Green, Dublin 2, Ireland
(a division of Penguin Books Ltd)
Penguin Books Australia Ltd, 250 Camberwell Road, Camberwell,
Victoria 3124, Australia (a division of Pearson Australia Group Pty Ltd)
Penguin Books India Pvt Ltd, 11 Community Centre, Panchsheel Park,
New Delhi –110 017, India
Penguin Group (NZ), Cnr Airborne and Rosedale Roads, Albany,
Auckland 1310, New Zealand (a division of Pearson New Zealand Ltd)
Penguin Books (South Africa) (Pty) Ltd, 24 Sturdee Avenue,
Rosebank, Johannesburg 2196, South Africa

Penguin Books Ltd, Registered Offices: 80 Strand, London WC2R 0RL, England

First published in 2006 by Viking Penguin, a member of Penguin Group (USA) Inc.

1 3 5 7 9 10 8 6 4

Copyright © Martha Grimes, 2006
All rights reserved

Grateful acknowledgment is made for permission to reprint an excerpt from "The Pauper Witch of Grafton" from *The Poetry of Robert Frost* edited by Edward Connery Lathem. Copyright 1928, 1969 by Henry Holt and Company. Copyright 1956 by Robert Frost. Reprinted by permission of Henry Holt and Company.

ISBN 0-670-03479-7

Printed in the United States of America
Set in Bodoni Book
Designed by Francesca Belanger

To Vicki

and in memory of Dodger

They don't dispose me, either one of them,
To spare them any trouble. Double trouble's
Always the witch's motto anyway.
I'll double theirs for both of them—you watch me.
They'll find they've got the whole thing to do over.

From "The Pauper Witch of Grafton" by Robert Frost

Man Walked into a Pub . . .

Prologue

(from *The Winds of Change*)

*T*hey sat in silence for a moment. Then Harry Johnson said, "If you want a story, I'll tell you a story—though I can't explain it, or tell you the end; there isn't any end."

"Sounds intriguing.

"Oh, it's intriguing, all right."

"Go on."

"It happened to a friend of mine. This person, who was the luckiest person I've ever known—you could almost say was hounded by good luck—lost everything overnight."

"Bloody hell. You mean in a market crash, something like that?"

"No, no. Not money. I mean he lost everything. He woke up one morning and found himself sans wife, son, even his dog. He did not know what had happened, and of course no one would believe him and he had no idea what to do. He considered going to the police, but what in hell would he say? They wouldn't believe him, I mean wouldn't believe the wife, the son, the dog had simply disappeared; well, you know how bloody-minded police can be—"

"I do indeed." Jury smiled in a crazy kind of way.

"Right. Families don't all of a sudden disappear—I mean, unless some psychopath walks in and murders them all. He told me he felt he was living in a parallel universe, that his wife and son were in one and he was in another."

"Then what did he do?"

"He hired the best private detectives. They found nothing, not a trace. There was simply no trail." Harry stopped, took out another cigarette, offered the case to Jury again, and Jury again refused. "That was a year ago."

"And—?" It struck Jury suddenly, the answer to the question he had glumly posed to himself earlier: what kept him going? Here was the answer: curiosity. He waited for Harry Johnson to fill in the blank after "And—"

Harry lit his cigarette, blew out a stream of smoke and said, "The dog came back."

Jury stared. "This is a joke, right?"

Unsmiling, Harry Johnson said, "No, it isn't. The dog just came back." They were both silent for a moment while Harry Johnson seemed to be collecting himself. "So do you want to hear the rest of it?" Dumbly, Jury nodded.

Man walked into a pub . . .

1

Harry Johnson lit another cigarette, flipped his lighter shut and said, "You're not convinced, I can see. I'm not joking."

Richard Jury just looked at him, and seeing the man was not about to back down from his improbable tale (for surely that's what it was, a "tale"), Jury could only laugh, turn back to the bar and pick up his pint. "Come on. 'The dog came back.'" He drank. "Wife, son, dog disappear, and the dog came back. After how long, did you say? A year?"

"Nearly. Nine, ten months, perhaps." Harry Johnson blew a big smoke ring and then a little one straight through it.

That really rankled. The man was clearly well off if that cashmere coat, that gold ring bore testimony; handsome—just the sort who made other men feel tatty; intelligent and well spoken. And besides all that he could blow proper smoke rings.

Intriguing, too, don't forget that. Even though Jury didn't believe him. "The dog came back, sure." Jury laughed again, a little too abruptly, perhaps, a little too indicative that Jury himself couldn't take a joke. Well, but that was the point, wasn't it? According to this Harry Johnson, it was no joke.

Harry Johnson smiled, set down his whiskey and got up. "Can you wait here a minute while I go to my car?"

"Me? Oh, sure, got all the time in the—" But Harry Johnson was gone before he finished. Jury looked down the bar, wishing the barman were up at this end so he could ask him about this fellow. The barman had called him by name, acted as if Johnson was often in here. But the barman was down there talking to a raucous couple with toothy smiles and hackers' coughs. There were times Jury thought the entire world smoked except for him, Killjoy Jury.

He looked down at his empty glass. Had that been number two? Three? Was he getting drunk?

The door to the pub opened and Harry Johnson was back with a dog on a lead.

He sat down and smiled and so did the dog. Sat down, that is, not smiled. It was a medium-sized dog, nothing special, a hound of some sort, the kind you'd pick out at the shelter to adopt, flop-eared, tan and white coat, immediately likable, the kind of dog you itched to scratch between the ears. It was sitting in its lopsided way, the way dogs do, and Jury reached down and scratched his head.

"Are you telling me this is the dog, then?"

"He's the one."

Jury looked from Harry Johnson to the dog. "What's his name?"

"Mungo." Harry held up his empty glass, and Trevor, the bar-man, came along, smiling, and refilled it. Jury declined, thinking he had drunk a great deal in a short period of time. "We've an excel-lent Batard, '85. Full and fat," the barman said. "You're drinking whiskey tonight?" There was the hint of a reproach in his voice.

"That's pretty obvious, Trev." Harry smiled, no slight intended. He said to Jury, "Trevor is the wine fellow. I mean *the* wine fellow. The expert. I'm not sure the others can tell the difference between a Pouilly-fussé and Pellegrino."

"Then they're the ones I should order from, not knowing my-self," said Jury.

Trevor said, "Come on, Mr. Johnson, we're not that bad."

"*You're* not, no. Maybe we'll switch in a minute."

Trevor shook his head. "Not after that single malt you're drink-ing." He slid his look over to Jury's glass. *That* wasn't even worth evaluation. Trevor walked off.

Harry laughed. "Wine is not something you fool around with, not where Trevor's concerned."

"So Mungo—"

Here the dog sat up a bit, alert.

"Showed up at your friend's place—wait a minute—the 'friend' isn't going to turn out to be you yourself, is he?"

"Good lord, no."

"All right, but remember, it's you who has the dog."

"I found Mungo sitting outside Hugh's front door. That's the friend's name, Hugh Gault. This was their home, in Chelsea, not far from mine, in Belgravia. He's a good friend of mine, Hugh, so I expect that's why Mungo was willing to come with me. I'd gone to the house to pick up a few books and things. Hugh is seriously thinking about putting the house on the market, but somehow I doubt he will. I think he's afraid that as soon as he's done it, his wife and son would turn up with no place to go."

"But he doesn't live there?"

"No. The whole thing nearly sent him over the edge. He's in a private clinic in Fulham."

"Psychiatric, you mean?"

Harry nodded. "All of this drove him into a deep depression. He's much better now."

Jury felt the dog edge under his bar chair.

"Anyway, Mungo was waiting there at the door, I don't know for how long. He looked worn out and hungry and after I let him in I went to fetch food for him. But what he did instead of eating was to go from room to room, sniffing, investigating, taking a long time at it. Then he attacked his bowl of food as if he meant to eat right through it and the floor. I gave him more, and he ate that, too. He drank a bucketful of water. Then I took him home with me. I live in Belgravia, or did I mention that?"

Not a shabby address, thought Jury, but then there was that black cashmere coat Jury couldn't stop coveting. "Is it possible your friend Hugh fantasized all of this?"

Harry Johnson just looked at him. It was a disappointed look. "And I did too? Fantasized Hugh and family? Don't be ridiculous. Is that the best you can do?"

Jury laughed. He was glad he hadn't told Johnson he was a detective with the Met. A detective superintendent, no less. And he certainly wasn't going to tell him now. Jury's question had been incredibly lame. "I take it that's a no?"

"Unless you think I'm fantasizing it too."

"It's a possibility."

"Oh, please."

"You could be winding me up."

"Why? Why would I walk into a pub and start telling a perfect stranger a story that isn't true?"

"I don't know. I expect I'll find out at some point. But go on." Jury looked down at Mungo, who'd crawled back out from under the chair and who raised his eyes when he sensed Jury's own on him. "How do you explain Mungo?"

"Coming back? Well, there've always been tales of animals finding their way home from long distances, these miraculous treks to find their homes. What was that book that was so popular when I was a teenager? *The Incredible Journey,* wasn't it?"

"But it took Mungo nine months?" He looked down; the dog was looking up at him in what Jury would describe as a beseeching manner.

"I still detect an edge of sarcasm. I doubt Mungo was traveling for nine or ten months, but as I don't know what had transpired in those months, I don't know how even to guess. But maybe they don't forget the way we do. There are times I can't even remember what street I live on."

Jury smiled. "Sorry about the sarcasm. Did the husband report this to the police?"

"Of course. You can imagine how Surrey police reacted to all of this: if the wife and boy were truly missing, then the prime suspect would be Hugh himself. But that's England's finest. No imagination, none at all."

"I'll drink to that." Jury held up his glass, and Trevor came down the bar. "Hugh went to Surrey?" His curiosity deepened with everything Harry told him. He watched Trevor fill his glass.

"Hugh? Not initially. I went for him. He got stuck on the idea that Glynnis and Robbie would be back and he wouldn't be there to see them." Harry went on. "They might have been murdered, they might have been kidnapped, or—as was the popular theory at the outset—unhappy wife leaves husband and takes the child with her. That was so ridiculous I couldn't understand how police held on to it."

"But it was a likely explanation. After all, the police didn't know the wife as well as you do." Jury had been about to say *It's the one I would have gone for* before he stopped himself. Instead he said, looking down at the dog, "So only Mungo knows."

"Whatever is known, right."

"You said at the outset you'd tell me the rest of it."

Harry Johnson nodded. "It was last year, in the summer, in July, I think. That morning Glynn—that's Glynnis—with Robbie and Mungo in tow, Glynnis set out for a look round the countryside in Surrey. She was viewing houses. They wanted a house outside of London."

"Second home? Weekend cottage sort of thing?"

"Not exactly—I'll get around to that later. Anyway, Glynn was to meet up with an estate agent who had a couple of listings she thought were worth seeing. They were about a half mile apart near a village called Lark Rise. She had appointments to see both houses, one still occupied and one empty. One she thought a complete toss, said it was too quaint and whimsical. She called the agent and told her what she thought and that she was then going to drive to the second house. The agent's name is Marjorie Bathous, and she's with a firm called Forester and Flynn. They're located in Lark Rise."

"But Glynn didn't call a second time. The agent calculated it would take only a few minutes to get to the second house, but was allowing time for Glynn to look around. That was a generous allowance,

she said, since Glynnis was the type who knew what she liked immediately, at first glance. Well, when she hadn't heard from her after an hour, she began to get concerned, thinking perhaps she'd lost
her way, or was having car trouble or something. When she didn't
hear after an hour and a half, she really got anxious."

"Didn't she try Glynnis's mobile phone?"

"She hadn't got the number. She said if there'd been trouble,
well, Mrs. Gault would have called her. So then this Marjorie
Bathous got in her car and drove to house number one. It took her
about twenty minutes from Forester and Flynn. When she got to the
first house, she called in. The couple there told the agent that yes,
they'd been there, even had had a cup of tea, but had left some time
ago. So the agent drove to the second house. What she thought she
might find was that their car had broken down, but if there had been
that kind of trouble, she thought Glynnis would have called her.
When she got to house number two there was no sign of anyone.

"That house was listed as available on a long lease, not for sale.
Anyway, there was no use asking at the door as the place was vacant. Still, she looked around the house and grounds for some clue
but found nothing.

"All this Mrs. Bathous could assume at that point was that
there'd been some emergency back in London; perhaps Mrs. Gault
had some sudden onset of illness, or her Chelsea house caught on
fire, then apologized for being so melodramatic, but none of that
could measure up, for melodrama, to the disappearance of a man's
family. She hadn't come to thinking in *those* terms because it was
utterly impossible. People don't disappear like—"

"People disappear all the time," said Jury, "although not wife,
child and dog all at once, I agree. Go on."

"The agent had been delaying a call to Hugh Gault, but now she
did call, thinking, as I said, there had been an emergency in London.
When she called him he was dumbfounded. Hugh called Surrey police. Can you imagine telling police your family has disappeared?
Just suddenly gone up in smoke? They quite naturally took the po-

sition that the missus had done a runner, not that anything had be-
fallen her and her boy."

"And Mungo."

The dog came out from under Jury's tall bar chair and raised his
eyes to look from one to the other.

Harry smiled. "Right. I keep forgetting Mungo."

Now the dog turned to Harry Johnson.

"Never mind," said Harry, roughing up the top of his head.

Jury hoped he hadn't really drunk up this last drink. Well, he
forgave himself for this apparent alcoholic thirst; after all he'd just
put one hell of a case behind him that had left him really knackered, among other things. He frankly didn't know if he'd find the
energy to get home. Take a cab, he'd have to. "Go on," he said to
Harry.

"The Surrey police came up empty, not surprisingly. But considering there was a nine-year-old child missing, they did make an
effort. Their forensics found evidence of tire tracks that matched
the brand of tire on Glynnis's car, but that did no good since the
agent knew Glynn had been at the house, the first house, anyway."

"What did they find at the second house?"

"Nothing. The ground was so hard where the car might have
pulled up that they couldn't get an impression of any tires at all, not
just Glynn's. Hugh was beside himself, of course, and convinced it
could only have been a kidnapping. I thought so too, except there
was no ransom demand."

Jury thought of the Flora Scott case, so recently resolved. "Is
there some reason there might have been one? I mean, are the
Gaults wealthy?"

"Not wealthy, but very comfortable. She inherited a little when
her mother died. Hugh's a professor at London University.
Physics."

"So your friend Hugh would not appear to have a motive?"

"Of course not." Harry sounded irritated. "Anyway, he was in
London; any number of people could testify to that."

"Yes, but that wouldn't necessarily stop him paying someone to do it. And if so, you bet he'd have witnesses, a raft of witnesses."

"That's exactly what the police said." Harry looked at Jury.

Jury laughed. "I'm a big fan of the Bill and—what's that other one?—anyway, I watch them all the time on the telly."

"But you don't know Hugh."

"You're quite right. What happened then?"

"Then came the private investigator."

"Who found nothing?"

Harry nodded. "And during this time, we drove to Lark Rise, to Forester and Flynn, where we picked up the keys to the empty house. They do that, these agents in the country, since the listings are some distance from each other. I'd say that's just asking for trouble."

For Glynnis Gault, it had been, Jury didn't say. "Then Mrs. Gault did go in the house?"

"The agent didn't know. If she didn't like the exterior, she probably didn't bother with the inside."

"Then your Glynnis is one woman in a million."

"Why do you say that?"

"Would any woman with a key to a strange house in her hand not use it? I'm sorry if that sounds patronizing. Perhaps I should say 'anyone.' It's just that I've found houses and what they contain to be far more interesting to women than to men."

"You think she went inside?"

Jury nodded. "Go on."

"The rooms were large, with very high ceilings, and the drawing room or living room was furnished with what looked like quite valuable antiques. There was a Russian bureau inlaid with silver, a Turkish rug of huge proportions and deep reds and blues. There were tea things set out, a silver tea service and cups and saucers and so forth."

"You mean in the way of Miss Havisham in Dickens? Didn't she keep everything regarding her near wedding exactly as it had been for years?"

Harry had lit a cigarette and was now exhaling. "No, I don't mean that." He seemed mildly annoyed that Jury was using fictional metaphor. He went on:

"The house sits about two hundred feet from the road. All of the front was overgrown—grass, hedgerow, shrubberies, very large trees front and back—a wood, actually at the edge of the gardens behind the house, all of it almost luxurious in its wildness. But it certainly wasn't anyone's idea of a country cottage. Hugh said he couldn't understand why the agent had even had it on her list of possible properties for Glynnis to see or that Glynnis would even bother going inside. It was quite an imposing place, but much too large."

"Well, I imagine she's not the first agent to show a client unsuitable property. Could it be someone was waiting for Mrs. Gault? What about the boy? And Mungo, here—"

They both looked down. Mungo looked up, again eying one and then the other. The look, thought Jury, did not appear to be *yearning,* but more bafflement or at leaset puzzlement.

"Had he or she or they really planned on taking all three?"

"Perhaps they had to; they could hardly let the boy go," said Harry.

"But they did Mungo."

Harry rolled his eyes. "I expect they thought Mungo wasn't about to write up a report on what happened."

"But an abduction doesn't seem very likely with whatever was going on in the house, anyway. So you don't know that there's any connection between the house and Glynnis and Robbie Gault's disappearance. It could be simply a coincidence."

Harry studied his drink.

"Who owns the house?"

"A man named Ben Torres. Benjamin della Torres, actually."

"Sounds aristocratic."

Harry shook his head, picked up his glass.

"Also sounds Spanish."

"Italian. He lives near Florence."

"You know a lot about this."

Harry nodded. "I had to, given everything that happened."

"Everything?"

"What I'm telling you." Harry smiled and looked at his watch. "Look, it's nearly nine. Would you like to get a meal? I know a terrific restaurant."

Jury looked at his own watch, astonished that he'd been talking to Harry Johnson for upward of two hours. "Why not? It's a good idea. What about Mungo?"

They both rose to put on their coats (Harry, cashmere; Jury, anything but). When Mungo saw this, he too got to his feet, tail wagging.

"Oh, Mungo's welcome to join us. I'll just ring the place to tell them we're coming." He pulled a cell phone from his coat pocket and turned away from Jury to make the call.

Jury knelt down and scratched around Mungo's ears. He wondered what the poor dog had been through. He wondered how an animal could have such a sense of direction to make a trip from God knows where back home. He wondered if "home" meant more to animals than it did to humans.

Harry flipped his cell phone closed. "Done. You'll like this place." Then he smiled down at Mungo. "Incredible dog. I just don't know what to make of him." He paused. "I don't know what to make of any of this, actually."

2

"The house itself—it's named Winterhaus, incidentally—I don't know where that German bit came from. I wanted to know more about the house itself. It struck me as a place that would serve as a setting for something."

They were seated now in one of those pleasant restaurants where the food and the service clearly took precedence over the packaging: no terribly modern blue Lucite or smoked-glass room dividers or etched wall sconces; no sumptuous, sinuous leather and bright white linens. Just a comfortable arrangement of tables far enough apart that you didn't feel the people at the next table were elbowing in on your conversation. Harry Johnson was obviously a long-standing diner here for the maître d' knew him by name and treated him as a valued customer.

They had ordered, or, rather, Harry had suggested the waiter order for them, just as he had told the sommelier to choose the wine.

" 'Something'?"

Harry shrugged. "I'm not sure what I mean. Melodramatic. An old man was passing in the road as we left the drive, a villager I supposed. We stopped to ask about the Swan, the nearby pub, and he told us it was down the road, then offered a bit of advice at the same time. His name was Jessup, he said, and he lived around there. He gave us a warning about 'that house' and said we should avoid the woods. If you can imagine." Harry laughed.

"Did you find anything dire in the woods?"

"No."

"What about the owner? What did he have to say?"

"He lives in San Gimignano, one of those little hill towns in Tuscany, one of the *casa torre*. It's full of towers."

"You've seen the town, then?"

"Yes. Well, we were looking for any clue at all. Hugh clearly wasn't up to it and so I undertook to go. The man wouldn't come to England—why should he? He'd put the house in the hands of an agent, so let her damned well deal with it."

"But couldn't this have been handled by telephone? Going to Italy seems a little extreme."

"Is going to Italy ever really extreme? And I'd never been there."

Jury laughed. "I see what you mean. Go on."

"The thing, the interesting thing is, regarding your point about the telephone is that he didn't want to discuss it over the phone. If I wanted to come to him, I was welcome."

The waiter was there with their salads, mostly new and trendy greens and Stilton cheese and walnuts in a citrusy dressing.

Harry went on. "Two days later I turned up on his doorstep. We had drinks, we had dinner at a little trattoria. I'd never eaten a *cappesante* like that before."

"I've never eaten it at all. Go on."

Harry smiled. "His story—and, incidentally, he didn't know my reason for wanting to hear it; all he knew was that I was interested in the house and wanted to know its history, as the estate agent knew sod-all about it. She didn't know much, Ben Torres told me, because he hadn't told her much; it didn't strike him as necessary to do so. But if I wanted to know before I leased the property, he was happy to tell me. I was presenting myself, of course, as a prospective tenant, or, rather, not presenting myself as anything else. I think he enjoyed the fact that I'd come all the way to Italy just to talk about this house. Torres's father was Italian; mother, British. He was raised in England and lived there until he was in his twenties. Hated it—so drab, wet and cold, and the people not especially warmhearted.

"His parents were divorced, his father in Italy, and that meant excursions to Italy a number of times to see his father, who lived in Siena. Winterhaus, the one that Glynnis Gault went to see, was in his mother's family.

"The last time he said he'd been at this property in Surrey was when he gave the listing to an agency two years before. Ben Torres said to me, 'Let me tell you a story. The place belonged to my mother's family. My mother died when she was barely forty, in London. It was completely unexpected. She hadn't been at all ill. I was sixteen. My father was living here at the time. They were divorced, had been for years. It surprised me they'd ever come together— they were so different. Sometimes I think that's what marriage is: a reconciliation of differences, and sometimes it succeeds. Not a grand vision, is it?'

"'At any rate, my mother—her name was Nina—had always liked that house in Surrey; she'd been a child there and found it mysterious. But then most children find mystery in things adults wouldn't give a toss for. More than once someone had made my mother an offer for the house—and if you saw it, you'd know it's quite a lovely site, even if it hasn't been properly kept up. But my mother wouldn't sell it, and not because she'd lived there as a child but because of something that had happened there and that she felt responsible for. I mean not that she'd done anything but that she didn't want to subject some stranger to the unhappy aspect of the house.'"

Jury lowered his fork. "'Unhappy aspect'?"

But Harry Johnson merely raised his hand to ward off questions.

"Torres went on: 'I myself was eight years old when she told me about it. Well, I'd kept after her and after her to explain what she meant. Finally one night, as she was tucking me into bed and was about to read me a story. She had the most beautiful voice. But I didn't want to be read a story, I wanted her to tell me one.'

"'"All right, Benjy, I'll tell you a story." 'She closed the book and set it aside. And she told me this story then and Lord knows how many times since, as I was always asking for it.'

" " "*A stranger was standing out there at the bottom of the garden. At first I thought he must be making a delivery or was perhaps an acquaintence of your father's. But he did not move from the end of the path. He was not a vagrant, that was clear from his overcoat and his hat.*" '

" " "*And his bowler hat.*" 'I said, "*You left it out.*" ' 'I would often interrupt in this way to ensure all of the details were included and even such commonplaces as weather and light, the slant of the sun, the turning leaves—all of these details had to be absolutely accurate, by that I mean always the same, before I would allow her to proceed.' "

Harry Johnson paused to have a sip of wine. Their dinners appeared as if by magic. Jury had ordered his dish because he wondered if its stunningly complicated name would turn out to be a simple dish. Whatever it was, it was good.

This "stranger" (Jury thought) would be the harbinger of bad news or would himself be the bad news. He would die, Jury was sure. "He was murdered, right?"

Harry opened his eyes wide with astonishment. "You're jumping the gun. Ben Torres would have your head on a platter for that." Harry laughed.

"Go on with the story. The stranger." (Who will, he added to himself, be murdered.)

"Ben Torres said, 'My mother made the correction about the hat. Then she continued:

" " "*He stopped there at the end of the path for some time. I don't know why I didn't go out and ask him who he was and what he wanted. I was afraid, a little afraid. I tried to read my book—I'd been sitting in the window seat reading, but I couldn't and when a slant of sun fell across the page, I looked again and he was gone. It was close to dusk. I was so relieved not to have to wonder if he would be there after dark and if he was going to try to get in the house. He was gone, thank heaven. But three days later he appeared again. At the end of the path in the same spot. I—'"* "Then she stopped and I said, "'You told yourself you had to do something.'"

"'"*Yes. The thing is we were there by ourselves. You were only eight.*"'

"Then Ben Torres, in telling me, became agitated, as if he still felt his mother's uncertainty and fear. "'So my mother did call the police station.'"

"'"*But what am I to tell them? Simply that a man had on two occasions stood just at the end of the garden path? Why would the police bother to investigate that? Still, I made the call, Benjy, and was surprised that they were so polite.*"'"

"England's finest," put in Jury and received a withering look from Harry Johnson.

"Ben Torres went on: 'The mystery of the stranger captivated more than frightened me, but, then, I was not easily frightened. My mother knew this. Still, she did not tell me the rest of it.'" Harry stopped to take another drink of wine.

Jury said, "Stop long enough to eat. This meal is definitely worth it."

"Oh, I've eaten it many times. It's delicious."

Jury liked that filling up on memory. His thoughts turned to that painting, *The Butterfly Eaters*, that he'd seen in Newcastle at the Baltic. Dining on illusion.

Harry continued. "He said: 'It was my father who told me the rest, years later. The house, my father said, had a sad history, a dismal history.'

"'*This is what that detective told your mother: There was a family who lived there, who had leased it, named Overdean. They lived there with their son, seven-year-old Basil. The boy and his mother were murdered in their beds one night. The father himself wasn't touched.*"'

"In such cases as this," Harry went on to say, "the crime always points first to a family member—in this case the father, who hadn't been touched despite the viciousness of the attack. There was no motive anyone knew of and his fingerprints were not on the knife; they'd been stabbed repeatedly. The knife appeared not to belong to the house. But all of that could be explained by the prosecution. Well, you know what police and lawyers are like—"

"I do indeed."

"—in the absence of any counterevidence, they could just say the father had wiped the knife clean of his fingerprints and could easily have brought another knife into the house—"

Jury interrupted again. "And then hung around in bed while his wife was being murdered. Please." The waiter had come to clear away their dishes. Jury's plate was wiped clean.

"That's exactly what I thought."

"He was convicted?"

Harry nodded. "The judge in this case seemed dubious about his guilt. He sentenced him not to life but to twenty years. He only had to serve ten; his behavior in prison was perfect. I think it was very flimsy evidence."

"It was certainly circumstantial. I'm surprised the defense wasn't able to drive a wedge of doubt into it."

The waiter returned with the dessert, a crème brûlée infused with lavender and glazed on top. "And what about the stranger? Mr. Torres hasn't explained him yet."

"Listen first to what his mother said about the house: 'She told me once, *"Benjy, houses are more than wood and stone and plaster. Houses breathe, too. I think they bear the imprint of all the people who've lived in them."* '

"Including Mrs. Overdean and her son? That doesn't strike me as very good storytelling, not to a little kid."

"I'm only repeating what Ben Torres told me. 'And the silent stranger in the bowler hat?' I asked my father.'

" ' "Your mother didn't know. Perhaps it was the father come back." '

"Dead or alive?" asked Jury.

Harry laughed. "Alive, I believe he said. It wouldn't be so surprising for him to come back to the house where everything had gone wrong, where he'd lost—" Suddenly, Harry stopped.

"Where he'd lost everything, you were about to say. Like your friend Hugh Gault. Except in his case, there seems no rational explanation for his wife and son's disappearance." Jury looked down when Mungo stuck his head out from the curtain of the tablecloth. "And his dog's."

Harry signaled to the waiter for coffee. "I asked Ben Torres, 'What about the stranger? Did your mother think he must be Overdean?' Ben laughed. 'I hardly think so. He would have been a bit too old, wouldn't you say? Overdean would have been long dead. No, that's quite impossible unless, of course, one believes in ghosts.'"

"And do you? Did Nina Torres?" Jury asked.

Their waiter filled their cups with coffee and set the silver-plated pot on the table. Harry shook his head. "I can speak with certainty only for myself. No, not for a minute. Mrs. Torres, though, sounded as if she might have. Hugh? Before this happened, I would say definitely not. But now he's searching for any explanation at all. It's all too depressing." He paused. "One thing that Ben Torres felt important: that I should stay away from the wood behind the house."

"Stay away how?"

"Literally. And this is interesting. He repeated the warning given us by this Mr. Jessup: to stay away from the wood."

"Why?"

"Torres didn't say why. He just waved the question away as if, you know, I were crazy for even asking it."

"And did you stay away?"

"It was the first place I went after I got back from Florence. Look, if someone pointed to a spot and told you to stay away, you wouldn't, would you? It's a challenge to one's curiosity."

"And what did you find? What danger lurked there?"

"None. Surrey police had combed that wood looking, I expect, for . . . remains." Harry picked up his cup of coffee and swallowed as if he swallowed the word with it.

Remains. A word that Jury had always hated—it was so distant, so clinical. "What about house number one? Wouldn't that be a likely place to search? No one even knows if Glynnis and her son ever got to the second house."

"No, you're quite right." Harry leaned back in his chair, his cup and saucer in his hands.

"It strikes me, you know, as a hell of an odd pattern."

Harry's frown deepened. "What pattern?"

"Well, surely you saw it. The Overdean woman, Nina Torres, Glynnis Gault. All were alone with their eight- or nine-year-old sons."

Harry leaned forward in his chair. "No, I didn't see it. I must be blind."

Mungo slid his muzzle out from under the table and rested it on Jury's shoe. Lazily, he blinked when Jury looked down at him. As if he couldn't be bothered. As if he thought the conversation was ludicrous. As if Jury were the biggest kind of fool.

Mungo yawned.

The wood's not it.

3

That's what it would be, a slap on the wrist delivered by an assistant commissioner or even the commissioner himself, for going into that Hester Street house without a warrant. Jury was surprised his hadn't been suspended as yet.

"I'll try talking them down, lad. You'll have me to thank for saving your job."

Was Racer kidding? Jury knew about how much the man would stand up for him.

"Thanks." He'd been sitting across from Chief Superintendent Racer (his boss, guv'nor, supervisor) trying to think of something nice to add to the "thanks" and coming up empty. He was more interested in the cat Cyril, who had flattened himself pancakelike to the floor and was snaking along to Racer's big desk while Racer babbled on, unaware. There was just enough room if Cyril could maneuver his body, all of it, to rug level and slip through the three- or four-inch space. Cyril liked occasionally to get his teeth around Racer's ankle and pull. When Racer yelled, Cyril would slip back through the opening and make for the door, trailing Racer's sputtered imprecations like a row of cans tied to his tail.

It was just something to do. Jury smiled.

As Racer's taking advantage of the present situation to lecture Jury was just something to do. In the pause while Racer was thinking up more things to say, Jury rose, asked, "Will that be all?" and started for the door. Behind him, CS Racer gave voice to either a yelp or a screech, and right away, Cyril shot out from under the desk to the door that Jury was holding open for him. They both missed the heavy paperweight that bounced off the rug behind them.

* * *

That night, after leaving the restaurant, Jury agreed to meet Harry Johnson the next evening at the Old Wine Shades and pick up the story where Harry had left it.

There was more, Harry Johnson had said, to come.

Jury had to admit he was curious about the Gaults and Ben Torres and their exceedingly strange tales.

Right now, late as it was, he thought he'd walk down to Lower Thames Street and then along the Embankment as far as Waterloo Bridge. Jury wanted to see how Benny Keegan was keeping. It was well after ten o'clock, but Benny did not exactly keep regular hours. His dog Sparky had probably saved Jury's life because he had led the others to him.

Sparky. Now, if it had been Sparky sniffing round that house in Surrey, he'd have turned up something. But he shouldn't be hard on Mungo; no, Mungo was far from dumb.

He watched the Thames and the glitter of lights reflected along its surface, cast by the National Theater and the South Bank.

Jury walked down the stone steps to the wide space under the bridge where several of the London homeless had set up house. Of course they had to take it all down in the morning and leave or the police would be all over them. But that didn't cramp their style; Jury got the idea they considered themselves quite fortunate to have this area under the bridge for their own, nights.

"Oh, Christ," said Mags (the first one he came to), "if it ain't the Filth again. I calls it police harassment."

Jury said, "Last time I was here was in January, Mags. Does that seem very harassing? It's March now."

"The Ides of." Her tone was churlish. "That fookin' Caesar 'ad 'is work cut out for 'im, din't 'e?"

"Well, I lay no claim to being Caesar."

"Good thing." Megs's laugh came from some deep and abiding resource within her body. It was hard to make the body out, given layers of skirts and shawls. She had made a fire in a big tin canister and was stirring something in a pot.

"So, it's gonna be onct every couple mumfs you come down 'ere? I'll go get me 'air done next time."

"You were never lovelier. Where are Benny and Sparky?"

"Up to no good, unlike the rest o' us law-abidin' cit'zens."

"When did you last see him?"

"'Bout fifteen minutes ago. Said he was goin' up t' that McDonald's near Charing Cross. He did good today wi'f his route."

Jury looked around. "Where is everyone?"

"Dunno."

There were ordinarily at least a half dozen here with bedrolls and blankets, and upward of a dozen who came and went at one time or another. It was (Jury had said) an "accommodation address," the accommodation being supplied by police who turned a blind eye as long as they were out of here the next morning with their blankets and bedrolls and pots and pans.

"Has Benny still got his same delivery jobs over in Southwark?" He nodded toward the South Bank.

"'Course. That lad don't know how lucky 'e is 'avin' a steady job."

"Oh, I think he knows." Jury turned at the sound of a bark, cut off as if the dog had sucked it back into his throat. A dead white blur ran down the steps. Sparky. He was followed by Benny, the second half of the team who had saved Jury's life.

"Hey, Mr. *Jury!*"

"Hi, Benny. How are you keeping?"

"Same old, same old," said Benny, hooking his thumbs in his jeans pockets. Benny liked American banalities.

Jury smiled. Bernard Keegan, boy of the world. Well, the boy was, actually. Benny had been on his own and on the streets for years; even now he was only eleven or twelve. "You deliver for the same people, like Gyp?"

"Tell the truth, old Gyp don't, doesn't, talk to me and Sparky like he used to do. He kinda keeps his distance. But he still gives out evil looks."

"You don't have to work for him, you know."

"Yeah, well, t' way I see it, if you give up because someone's mean to you, a person wouldn't get very far, and always would be subservant."

Jury knew Benny was especially pleased with "subservant." He liked new words (even if he didn't get them right), long ones you could "really get your mouth around" was the way he'd put it. It made a person sound more "edge-ecated."

They were sitting side by side on one of the cold stone steps. Sparky went around in circles.

"Why does he do that?"

"Oh, that's just when he gets excited. It's because you're here. Sparky always liked you."

Jury studied Sparky, who now had stopped circling and was sitting watching the two of them. "Tell me, Benny, when Sparky goes off on his own, do you think he takes in what he experiences?"

" 'Takes in'?"

"Understands, takes the meaning of?"

Benny looked at Jury as if the detective were loopy. "A course."

"Can he tell you?"

"Depends what you mean by 'tell,' don't it? He can bark, he can use his eyes, his tail, his whole self. Like that circlin' he was doin'. *And* you oughta remember it was Sparky got me out to that dock. It's a good thing I were lookin' for him, weren't it? He did that by runnin' back and forth on the dock and by barkin'. Sparky's got different barks, see. Mad, happy, dangerous—all different."

"You think all dogs are the same?"

"No. Just the smart ones."

"If Sparky'd been gone for a year, what would he do?"

"I'd never hear the end of it, would I?"

Jury laughed. "No, I guess you wouldn't." Jury got up. "I'll be going now. How's Gemma?"

"She's thinkin' of changin' that Richard doll's name. You know, the one dressed all in black."

"Why?"

"'Cause you come to see me and not her, I expect."

"Tell her I'll see her soon."

"Oh, I can tell her, but she won't believe me." This was uttered in a sort of *Best tell her yourself, mate,* tone.

"'Bye, Benny."

As he walked up the stairs, Mags's voice followed. "Back in two mumfs, you'll be."

4

"You are quite beyond me," said Lady Ardry, devouring yet another fairy cake as she sat across from Melrose Plant. Granted they were quite small (a staple of children's birthday parties), but still, this was her fifth, small or not, iced with buttercream.

She went on: "You've got too many things here to do."

"Since I never do them, going up to London won't make a difference, will it?"

"You haven't said why you're going."

Melrose turned another slippery page of his *Country Life*. "To buy a fresh pig, but not to worry; I'll be home again jiggedy-jig."

Agatha shut her eyes as if in pain. "There are times, Melrose, I honestly think you've never grown up."

Melrose made no reply; he just raised his teacup—again wondering why Martha, his cook, used this scalloped china. There was hardly room enough in the flowery handle to blow smoke through. He turned another page of his magazine to see, in the myriad overpriced property listings, that he could buy a hovel in Little Widehips located somewhere in England—was that the Devon coast? Or perhaps Cornwall? Or the Scillys? Why was it that estate agents always assumed you knew where these places were, as if Beekeeper's Cottage here in Little Widehips was located on the map in your mind? For all that, it could have been in Bermondsey or even Slough, which was probably the most depressing corner of England. Did anyone ever refer to "dear old Slough"? Melrose wouldn't mind letting—or even buying, if he could get it no other way—Beekeeper's Cottage, getting out of it after forty-eight hours, just so he could refer to "dear old Slough" and feel his eyes mist over. Or was it his ears? Agatha had been sitting there jamming like the Grateful Dead, at least making as much noise, and he didn't know what in hell she was talking about.

"What were you saying about Boring's?" he asked.

"I find it patently absurd that in this day and age a man would have membership in a men's club."

"That's what they're there for—men." Melrose scratched his ear.

"You know what I mean." She picked up one of the cream roses that Melrose knew were the very devil to make—all of that petal fluting. Meringue and strawberry cream. Why had Martha put one on the tray? Probably for him, forgetting that Agatha would vacuum up anything on the tray, yes, just as she was doing now.

"What is this?" She eyed the cream rose with suspicion. "It's hard, like meringue."

"Rigor mortis."

Quickly she set it down and Melrose snatched it up. He took a bite. "Um-um. Melts in one's mouth." It did, too. He took another mouthful and set the rest on his little plate. "Martha goes to quite a lot of trouble for you, Agatha. You really don't appreciate her."

"Of course I do. I'm often in the kitchen telling her how delicious things are."

"You're often in the kitchen, I know." He flicked over another page to be met with the rather bulbous eyes of the Honorable Judith Pudelthwaite-Duchamps. Judi was girl of the week (and where was the honor in that?), chosen for her title, her beauty and her dalliance with Renaissance painting, which she would pursue further at university. Only now she was in her gap year and intending to travel and visit the great museums of the world. Why didn't Judi make a stop at Agatha's cottage in Plague Alley? There were things that had been collecting there for at least as long as the Renaissance. That stuffed owl on the mantel, for example.

Oh, Judi, Judi, what you're really going to do is chase after boys and marry another "Honorable" and live on mummy and daddy's money and go foxhunting and have tailgate picnics at Newmarket and Wembley and do something or other with the Women's Institute.

"Melrose, what are you doing?"

"Thinking."

"Well, you do entirely too much of it. You were aimlessly looking off. Now, are you going to see Inspector Jury while you're in London?"

Melrose sighed in annoyance. "Agatha, you keep on demoting him. He's a superintendent. He's very high up the ladder."

"Well, he never corrects me."

"He doesn't need to." He didn't, except for the odd villain or two. It occurred to Melrose that Jury had fewer defenses in play than anyone he'd ever known.

"I can tell you this: Ruthven and Martha won't see much of me while you're gone, not with that execrable hermit you've installed out there." She tilted her head in the direction of the wide, deep lawn to the side of the house, where there sat, at a distance, the hermitage, a very fashionable installation in the eighteenth century.

"They'll be heartbroken. Since the hermitage was empty I saw no reason not to install him; there's one more upswing in our doddering economy."

"He creeps about."

"He's a hermit. They creep."

Agatha said, "Now that I think about it, I could do with a little trip to London. I need a few things from Harrods."

Unfazed by her plan, since he had no intention of including himself in it, he said, "Nobody actually needs anything from Harrods. I go to Harrods for the thrill of needing nothing it has on offer. For the thrill of being crushed in a busload of people who also need nothing. You've got to understand that with Harrods you're there because you're there. It's a destination place, you know, like Las Vegas or the La Brea Tar Pits. We've all known a Harrods moment. It's a Zen thing." He turned the page.

"You're not making any sense, Melrose." From the cake stand, she selected this time a small, nut-filled confection.

Her seventh? He was looking forward to his week in London. Right now he was looking out of the window to Agatha's left at Mr. Blodgett, his hermit, leering (as he'd been told to do). "Ah, look, Agatha!"

She turned to the window and dropped her pastry. "It's absolutely unbearable." She made a go-away, go-away gesture. But Mr. Blodgett stuck to his guns. He also stuck to Aghast (Melrose's goat). Now he was doing a little jig. Melrose smiled. It was a bit of cabaret. He waved in friendly fashion.

Mr. Blodgett occupied the little stone structure on the Ardry End grounds. He was much better than the first hermit Melrose had hired, as that one was always down the pub. Unfortunately, although Mr. Blodgett could revolt Agatha, he didn't keep her away.

Agatha also loathed the goat, and not even the two of them in tandem disgusted her enough to make her leave the fairy cakes. Melrose considered other possibilities to try at Ardry End. What about a theme park? A nature perserve such as the Duke of Bedford's at Woburn Abbey? Tigers? Lions? Chimpanzees?

He mused. Perhaps he would come up with something sitting around in Boring's, that London club out of some previous century. Yes, Boring's would definitely be on the list of Most Nostalgic Places in the country.

Ah, dear old Little Widehips!

Dear old Slough!

Dear old Boring's!

5

"I think it's disgraceful, me, you being punished when it was the only way of getting those kiddies out of that house." At the moment Carole-anne was sitting on Jury's sofa, applying nail art, little dibs and dabs of rhinestone and sequins.

"Pete Apted argues exigent circumstances."

"Who's he?"

"A barrister. Quite brilliant."

"What's 'exigent circumstances'?" She pressed another bit of rhinestone onto a nail.

From where Jury was sitting, it glittered in the lamplight. "That is a situation wherein the police find an emergency, say inside a house, husband battering wife and kids, something like that, a situation in which there is no time to get a warrant."

Carole-anne looked over at him, eyes wide. "Well, for heaven's sake, that's just what you found."

"Not precisely. See, the circumstances were known by vice. A colleague of mine had been trying to get into that house for months."

"You didn't know that."

Jury raised his eyebrows. "That's what Pete Apted said." Did he have, sitting across from him, a budding barrister? Good lord. Carole-anne arguing a case in court. The thought made him dizzy.

She waved the law away. Jury caught a glimpse of silvery bits, as if her hand were trailing stars. Carole-anne did not need body art; her body was already art.

"If the law's going to be that finicky, there's some of us never will be able to do what we think's right."

That from Carole-anne amounted to a philosophical position. "Yes, the law does tend to get picky at times." He thought for a moment. "I've been meaning to call Charly Moss."

"Who's he?"

"Not a—" But he caught himself before he said, *"Not a man, a woman."* He smiled. "Charly's a solicitor. One used by the able Mr. Apted." No use telling the truth. He'd be in for a merciless grilling.

She was finished, apparently. She held out her hands, the shocking pink nails studded with a selection of silvery things. "What d'you think?"

"Frankenstein's fingers?"

She threw a pillow at him.

6

As Wiggins stirred and stirred his tea, Jury told him the story of the Gaults' disappearance. Then, as in some religious ritual, Wiggins tapped the spoon three times on the edge of his mug.

"It's the strangest story I've ever heard. But why did this Harry Johnson tell you it?"

"We were sitting in the Old Wine Shades, that's a wine bar in the City, talking about narrative in dreams. I said that we always dream a story."

Wiggins shook his head. "No, I don't dream a story. I dream in symbols. Usually I can't say what they mean." That settled, Wiggins sat back and sipped his tea.

"You dream in symbols, yes, but the symbols take place in narrative form. Like this: let's say your symbol is a villain. There's your villain. Next, a victim. There's your victim. Then a pool of blood. You don't switch from one to the other without making the connection: the villain goes up to the victim and knifes her or shoots her and there's the pool of blood. Pool of blood being an effect. It's connected. They're all connected."

Wiggins thought about this, but gave no sign of agreeing.

Jury went on. "We're always waiting for a story, that we ourselves were a story."

Wiggins looked puzzled. "What does that mean?"

"That I'd had four pints."

Wiggins smiled. "All right. Now what about this Harry Johnson? How much had he had?"

"Whiskey, only two."

"Are you sure he didn't sit by you deliberately?"

"Why would he do that?"

"Maybe because he knew who you were."

Jury frowned. "He didn't follow me in; I'd had three drinks by the time he sat down."

"Maybe he saw you through the glass."

"Oh, please. Does anyone look at a pub through the window? No, you just go in."

"Then he went in and he recognized you."

"Wiggins, this is almost as improbable as the disappearance of Glynnis Gault and her son. In any event, what did he expect to gain by telling me?"

"That you'd investigate; that you might find them."

"If that's the case, why all this pretense?"

"Johnson might have thought it not such a good idea to intrude on a detective superintendent having a quiet pint."

Jury shook his head.

"Well, sir, you didn't tell him who you were; think about that."

Jury tilted his chair back, crossing his arms over his chest. "Okay. I've thought. What?"

Wiggins's sigh was slightly exaggerated. "For the same reason. If he knew who you were it would probably change the whole complexion of the meeting."

Jury chewed the inside of his cheek, annoyed not so much at Wiggins but at himself. He must be getting crusty; he was gearing up for redundancy, that's what.

"Mr. Plant called, sir."

Jury came off the dole and back to the working-stiff world. "Did he? Good. What did he want?"

"Just to tell you he'd be coming up to London this afternoon. And staying at his club"—Wiggins checked his notes—"Boring's. He says he's having dinner with someone this evening and could you get together with him tomorrow?"

"Excellent. It's just as well as I'm having dinner with"—he caught himself before he said "Harry Johnson"—"someone too."

"Isn't Boring's one of those men's clubs that still won't admit women?"

"Boring's will admit them on a certain day, but then they just try to stare the women down."

Wiggins was dipping another chamomile tea bag into his mug. "Don't you think that's a bit reactionary not to let women join?"

"No. It's a men's club. Let women go off and make a club of their own."

"There's the Women's Institute, I guess."

Jury shook his head. "That's not the same thing at all. That's an organization whose purpose is to concern itself with social issues. It's not a physical place where you can dodder around and drop in a leather club chair and have your glass of port and newspaper by a fire." Boring's was so pleasant, Jury thought he might join when they tossed him out of here.

7

Melrose Plant was standing in a late-afternoon shaft of sunlight, in which drifted a somnolent white moth. He had not recognized the little man at reception, but he didn't want to inquire after Buddings, afraid at what might have transpired there. But he told himself that at Boring's, the porters never seemed to die.

The Members' Room was exactly as he remembered it. Well, why wouldn't it be? He'd been here last year, hadn't he? He sat down in the same club chair he had occupied before and looked into what he could believe was the same fire. Nothing changed, time stopped; end of story.

"No," said Polly Praed, as they sipped wine and spooned up soup in Boring's dining room. "One dies. *That's* the end of the story."

Melrose shook his head. "Wrong. 'Change' is an experience in life. Death isn't."

"You're just doing semantics." She spooned up her mushroom soup.

Polly was certainly evidence of time's not changing. Same amethyst eyes, same unruly dark corkscrew curls, same ghastly mustard-colored suit. He had once told her that color played havoc with her pink-tinged porcelain skin. She had been unimpressed with Melrose's opinion of her clothes or anything else. Now, if it had been Richard Jury who had told her this, you'd never see her again in mustard-colored clothes.

"What are you writing now?" Right away, he cursed himself for bringing the subject up since he hadn't read her last two books. She churned them out nearly as fast as Joanna Lewes, Long Piddleton's

local author. Polly wrote mysteries—good old traditional manor
house, suspects-round-the-dinner-table-in-a-snowstorm-mysteries.
Melrose hated them.

"*The Monday Corpses.* That's my latest."

She really should do something about her titles. "Is this a se-
ries of Monday murders? Or will there be Tuesday corpses?
Wednesday?"

Polly frowned as Young Higgins removed their soup bowls.

Her tone disappointed, she said, "You could tell it's to be days
of the week, then?"

Only a dimwit couldn't. "Monday being a day of the week, yes.
You've got corpses you associate with a day of the week: Monday. I
assumed there'd be a bunch turning up—corpses, that is—on subsequent days. Either that or subsequent Mondays. "Isn't that how
your detective will find them?" Drat. Why had he asked?

Now she aimed her eyes at the plate of lamb Young Higgins had
set before her, Higgins himself having to lean briefly on the table for
support and covering the action by pretending to get Polly's plate in
line with the basket of rolls that were sending forth a warm rose-
mary scent.

"Are you all right, Higgins?" asked Melrose. "You seem just a
bit pale."

The porter stiffened his posture. "Quite all right, Lord Ardry.
Thank you for inquiring." And he shuffled off.

"Poor fellow looked as if he might have a stroke."

Polly watched Young Higgins out of sight. Her eyes were wide.
Then she leaned across the table and whispered, "Suppose somebody's poisoning him?"

Melrose looked at the ceiling. "My dear Polly, that is the most
lamebrained idea I think I've ever heard."

Undaunted, she went on: "No, but hear me out."

"Have I a choice?"

"No. Look around you at the other diners."

Melrose did so. What he saw was a surfeit of aged and aging

gentlemen with their big white napkins stuck in their collars and looking like so many dark-robed babies. "All right, I've looked."

"Wouldn't it be super if—"

"Polly, no one says 'super' anymore, if they ever did outside of P. G. Wodehouse."

"But wouldn't it be if one of them were a poisoner? Who'd even suspect one of them?"

"I would, as you've just pointed it out as a possibility." Melrose buttered his roll.

But Polly ignored that, too. Polly was just super at bending things to suit her fancy. The popular term was 'denial,' he supposed, but he never said it. He hated jargon.

She said, "Look, here's what—"

"Here's *what* what?"

"One of these old men could be Higgins's brother, who's trying to poison him, oh, say over Higgins's having inherited, I don't know."

"You really don't."

"Did you like my last book?"

Melrose feigned great concentration; since he hadn't read it, no amount of concentration would bring it to mind. "That would be the one where the protagonist—a well-drawn character, incidentally. Your protagonist is actually, well, quite finely nuanced."

Polly was pleased. "Yes, I thought his turning out to be the killer was quite a good stroke."

"You had me completely baffled!"

"Thanks. And what did you think of the black Lab?" She laughed.

The what? "Oh, the dog! Absolutely brilliant dog!"

Polly was laughing at her own ingenuity. "That scene where he was chasing the tennis ball?"

"Hysterical, wonderful. How many writers would ever think of that?"

"*Dog in the Manger*. I liked that title, didn't you?"

"Yes. There's a marvelous ambiguity in that title."

"What?"

"Hmm?"

"What ambiguity?"

Caught out. Why did he have to embellish? "The uncertainty, the inability to distinguish what is actually being said, the whole—" Melrose shrugged. "You know."

She frowned. "He's just a dog."

They ate in blessed (at least for Melrose) silence.

Then Polly asked, "Did you like the one before that one?"

Oh, *lord.* Now Melrose frowned, as if thinking up a liking for it.

"Were you surprised by the identity of the killer? I mean, that it wasn't Blake?"

"Blake certainly had me going for a while. Polly, I must confess that I didn't quite finish that one. What happened was that Ruthven was returning books to our library and packed yours up with the others. It was quite a parcel. I didn't even really know until I got back from Scotland—" That would distract her.

"What were you doing in Scotland?"

"Spot of fishing on the—*name of river, name name name!*—on the Ayr."

"Where's the Ayr? I never heard of it."

"Well, you wouldn't, would you? It's in County Ayr." That made sense.

"I didn't know you fished. I never heard you even mention it."

"Would one? I mean fishing is not all that newsworthy and I don't see you that often. The Ayr is specially good for trout."

"Oh." Another brief silence.

"My books—." She sighed and ate her roll. "Well, I can be a dreadful bore about them."

To Melrose the expression was so immeasurably sad, like a child whose crayon drawing isn't understood, that he reached across the table and put his hand over hers. "Polly, you are never boring."

"Thank you. Sometimes I think I would like to write nonfiction crime. A real case. Remember the body in the telephone booth?"

"How could I forget?"

"And remember the little typist who came to Littlebourne and was murdered and her fingers chopped off?"

"Oh, yes."

"And remember that art critic was murdered right out there in the Members' Room?"

"I do indeed."

Polly sighed. "Those were the days."

8

When Jury walked into the Old Wine Shades that evening at 7:00, Harry Johnson was already having a drink at the bar and Mungo was under the chair.

"Do you take Mungo with you everywhere?" asked Jury as he pulled out one of the tall bar chairs.

"No, not really. Except in this case I'm hoping the dog might, you know, come across with information or something." Harry raised his glass. "This wine is very good. Puligny Montrachet. What are you drinking?"

Jury nodded toward the glass of wine. "Some of that would be fine."

Harry Johnson raised a hand to the barman, who nodded. It was still Trev, but tonight he was joined by two others behind the bar. A much bigger crowd.

Jury said, "With all the wine on offer here, I still didn't realize we were in a wine bar."

Harry smiled. "The proprietor prefers wine *tavern*. It avoids all of the connotations of wine bar, the Hooray Henrys, the young business tycoons, dressed in power suits, pinstripes, mobiles glued to their ears and drinking wine out of a cardboard box."

Trevor set a glass before Jury as Jury said to Harry, "You know wine."

Harry said, "No, Trevor knows wine."

Trevor poured and said, "I'd say all the rest of the '66s are history. But this one is superb."

Jury tasted it. Trevor waited with what struck Jury as a winey grin.

"Delicious," he said.

Trevor nodded and went down the bar to serve other customers.

"You were talking about Hugh Gault. How did you come to know him?"

"Through mutual interests. Hugh's a physicist at London University. I'm a physicist, too. I read math and physics at university, but I don't work at it; I mean, I don't teach it. We're interested in quantum mathematics and string theory."

"Ah. That explains a great deal."

Harry nodded, missing the irony, and said, "I should say *super-string theory*."

Jury expected him to add something that Jury could acknowledge, at least enough to trip over. When he didn't, Jury said, "That clears up any lingering doubts."

Harry looked at him and laughed. "Sorry. Hugh and I like to argue. Einstein mistrusted quantum mechanics. Niels Bohr—you've heard of him?"

"You'd be surprised how little." Jury smiled.

"Quantum mechanics. The difference—if a difference is ever easy to explain, but I'll take a shot at it—is between determinism and indeterminism. Do you believe in fate?"

"Fate." Jury thought about this for a moment, quite seriously. "I don't think so, but—"

"Newton's mechanics?"

"Funny how long it's been since I dwelt on it."

"All I mean to say is that Newton believed if you knew everything in the present—every particle, no matter how many this meant—then you could predict the future. Quantum mechanics disagrees. You play snooker?"

"My God, you do dance around, don't you?"

"It's an analogy. If you feed everything into a computer, such as how hard you hit the ball, the angle of the cue, it would still be impossible to tell how each ball would respond to a collision. If there was some tiny alteration, like a bit of dust on one of the balls, it would throw everything out of whack."

"You know, I seem to recall something about chaos theory. The butterfly effect?"

Harry looked surprised. "You're a natural!"

Jury felt absurdly pleased with himself. This surprised him, since he didn't ordinarily try to impress people. Why should he want to impress Harry Johnson? Or perhaps he didn't. Perhaps he just wanted to keep up his end of the conversation before it turned into a monologue.

"Newton's universe was a clockwork universe. Determinism. Fate, in a sense. Not, however, that at noon tomorrow you'll meet the woman of your dreams."

Jury shrugged. "Then what good is it?"

Harry smiled. "The quantum world is *not* deterministic. You can't predict an outcome because you can't know both the position and the momentum of something at the same time. There's a measurement problem. Things change as you look at them. More specifically, when does the wave become the particle?"

Jury raised his glass, a signal to Trev, and shook his head at Harry. "Hocus-pocus?"

"Okay, I'll stop." But he didn't. "Gravity and electromagnetic force were a thorn in Einstein's side"—he turned to look at Jury—"but not in yours, I bet."

Jury laughed and got wine up his nose. "You could say that."

"It's quite fascinating that you can measure, for example, a subatomic particle by its momentum or you can measure it by its position, but not both simultaneously. Niels Bohr described wave and particle as the two aspects of a single reality. An unknowable reality."

"Unknowable? Then how does it influence what I do or who I am?"

Harry smiled. "You seem to have a grasp of the abstract. You haven't said what it is you do."

Jury debated, decided to tell him. "I'm a policeman, actually. Detective superintendent, to be precise. New Scotland Yard CID."

Harry's mouth literally dropped open. "Never!"

Jury smiled, rather glad he was responsible for that astonished look.

"I'll be damned. Well, then, you're just the person to hear this story. Maybe you'll come up with some explanation."

"I doubt it, but continue. You were talking about Hugh Gault."

"Yes. And the house. I drove there."

"Hugh Gault didn't go with you?"

"No. As I said before, Hugh was afraid that Glynn and the boy might call, or even turn up, and he wouldn't be there."

"When was this?"

"The next afternoon. The thing was, there'd been no time set for the two of them to return. She'd told their cook that if they weren't home by dinnertime, the day before, Mr. Gault should just go ahead without them. So there was no reason to get worried until that night, later. Glynnis hadn't called, though, and that disturbed Hugh. She was always so good about letting him know."

"But she had a mobile. You said she called the estate agent from her car."

Harry shook his head. "I'm betting a dead battery. Glynn could never remember to power up the phone. The battery was always going dead. She hates mobiles. Probably that's the reason hers is always running down."

"I'm with her on that."

Now, as if they had just been cued, three men at the bar pulled out their mobiles and proceeded to have three different, but equally loud, conversations.

"Christ," muttered Harry. "Let's go to a table."

Mungo, who'd been lounging under Harry's chair, pulled himself out from under and raised his baleful eyes to look into Jury's own.

As they took their seats in one of the stalls near the fireplace, Jury said, "Mungo has a very soulful look."

"That's just for show," said Harry.

"But I wonder if he doesn't really miss Robbie and his mother."

"I expect he does."

Jury looked down at Mungo, whose head was again resting on Jury's foot. "He doesn't strike me as a one-man dog. Did you take him to that house?"

"No, I didn't see how Mungo could help much with picking up a scent that was a year old."

"They can, you know. They're quite amazing."

Harry nodded and went on. "This house seemed implacably cold. It's the sort of cold that eats into you. I realize it had gone un- tenanted for a long while, but it still felt unnatural. They'd left the electricity on as they were trying to rent it. But not the heat. The house is too large for a family of three—"

"And a dog." Jury felt a brief push.

Harry smiled. "And a dog, yes. The architecture is basically Georgian. Large rooms, high ceilings, Adam moldings and chim- neypiece. I told you the place was empty of furnishings except in the drawing room. All of the pieces were antique and looked very pricey: Russian bureau, Regency commode and that gorgeous rug. Very posh. I was surprised the place hadn't been vandalized. The agent—Mrs. Bathous—had asked the owner to leave the drawing- room furniture, if he would, to give the place a little bit of a lived-in look. Surprisingly, he did. I wouldn't want those pieces just stand- ing around." He remembered something. "And Marjorie Bathous didn't understand the dregs of tea in one of the teacups. She hadn't put out the teacups. Minton, they were."

"Now, that's interesting. Someone had been drinking from one. That's curious. Would Mrs. Gault have done that? Filled the kettle and measured out tea?"

Harry shook his head. "I can't imagine Glynnis making tea there."

"It almost sounds staged. The setting, I mean."

"Staged? By whom? For what reason?"

"I have no idea. How about Glynnis Gault herself?"

There was silence as Harry looked at Jury, mystified. "You're kidding."

Jury laughed. "That's supposed to be my line, isn't it? Doesn't the scene look staged if you think about it?"

Harry drank off his glass of wine. "What this brings to mind is an analogy I read which compared Gödel's theorem to the actors in a play within a play, where what an 'actor' in the internal play said would be a commentary on his 'real' life. The real life in this case being the outside play, the fictive framework."

"Who is Gödel?"

"A mathematician who formulated a theory called 'incompleteness.' The theory of incompleteness. There's no proof that we know all that we think we know since all that we think we know can't be formalized, which is the incompleteness proof."

Jury thought about this. "If he's a mathematician, wouldn't that more or less work against logic? I mean mathematics insists on logic, doesn't it?"

"Absolutely. Gödel wasn't popular in the mathematics community when they finally worked out what he was saying. We're not machines; we have intuition. His detractors didn't like the idea of intuition where mathematics is concerned. Mathematics should be considered as pure logic."

Jury took a drink and wished like hell he had a cigarette. "Anyway, we were talking about Glynnis Gault's staging her own disappearance." Jury held up his hand. "Not that I think that; it's just an idea I tossed out."

"I don't get it; why would Glynn stage it?"

"Or someone else stage it?"

"It's monstrous. Why would she want to vanish in that way? And take Robbie with her?"

Jury felt a push at his shoe. He smiled. "And Mungo. It wouldn't be the first time an unhappy wife kidnapped her child for some reason. Custody battle it is, usually."

"Hugh and Glynn were happy; they weren't thinking about divorce."

"Not as far as you know."

"I know both of them very well; you couldn't be much closer than we were."

"Then let's say for the sake of argument, who knew Mrs. Gault was going house hunting besides her husband and the estate agent?"

Harry Johnson folded his arms on the bar and considered. "Their staff, I imagine. Certainly the cook, as she'd be getting dinner. The maid? Well, the cook probably mentioned it to her. 'Staff' is probably overdoing it in the Gaults' case as there were just those two."

Jury smiled slightly; for him, that would constitute "staff."

Harry went on. "Someone might have known she went to Surrey to look at houses, but exactly where in Surrey, I doubt. You seem to be looking for a killer."

"An abductor, anyway. Go on about the house."

"It sits back from the road, very long front garden and the woods around on both sides and the back. I thought it seemed awfully isolated, but that, of course, is what they wanted in a second home—peace and quiet."

"That's what people think they want, until they get it. What about Robbie? He'd be at a loss for friends, wouldn't he?"

"Unfortunately, Robbie was pretty lost anyway. You could say Robbie had already been kidnapped."

"What do you mean?"

"That's what I was going to tell you. Robbie was autistic."

"What a shame."

"He didn't have friends; he didn't make them very easily. Well, what can you do if you can't or won't talk? But he's a great reader. Actually, she might have taken Robbie along so as to see how he liked it. There's a school in Lark Rise for kids with autism and other speech and I suppose cognitive problems. That was what Glynnis wanted a house there for. She wasn't looking for a holiday cottage. They would live there during the school year. She didn't tell Hugh that, though."

"Why not?"

"Hugh didn't like the idea of Robbie's changing schools. He thought it would be too hard on him, and he had enough on his plate without that. They argued about that quite a bit. I think it was the only thing they *did* argue about."

"I see." Jury thought about this. "The first one, this cottage—"

"Lark Cottage. It was a small, neat-looking house in quite nice gardens. I didn't talk to the owner."

"What do you think it was that was so off-putting to Mrs. Gault?"

"Just a little too cute, too quaint. The kind of place tourists would think so typically English."

"There are entire villages that are that. Did she find Chipping Campden too quaint? Lower Slaughter?"

Harry laughed. "I don't know."

"Was Glynnis Gault a bit of a snob?"

"Not at all. Quite the contrary, I'd say. She was accepting of things almost to the point of naïveté. She was wearing a black suit she'd bought from Marks and Spencer when she left the house." Harry smiled at the thought.

"Then does this description of Lark Cottage, at least of her reaction to it, strike you as like her?"

"Since you put it that way, no, it doesn't sound like Glynn." He picked up the wine bottle, turned to Jury. "Are you saying maybe some other woman actually made the call?" Harry saw the bottle was empty.

"The telephone call? No, I don't think someone else made the call, although it's always a possibility." Jury paused. "Do you know of anyone who wished her harm?"

"Absolutely not. Glynn wasn't a woman to make enemies." Harry set the wine bottle down. "Look, I'm famished. Care to have dinner?"

Mungo came out from under the two stools as if the invitation were extended to him.

"Yes. Where?"

"I know a place." Harry rose, unhooked his coat from the back of the bar chair. "Then I can tell you about my cat."

"Cat?"

"Her name is Schrödinger."

"Good name for a cat."

"I think you'll like her."

Schrödinger's Cat

9

"Schrödinger's equation—" Harry began.

"I thought that was your cat's name."

"It is. My cat's named after the physicist Schrödinger."

"If I were your cat, I'd object." Jury felt Mungo twisting around on his feet as if he'd object, too.

"The Schrödinger equation is famous; it might be the greatest contribution to quantum mechanics besides Niels Bohr's."

Jury sipped a very good single malt. They had forgone the wine list in favor of whiskey. The Docklands restaurant was crowded with up-and-comers, you could tell, along with the chattering classes. "Am I going to like this?"

"You'll love it. There's a thought experiment in quantum physics—no, a hypothesis—and it's very interesting: you put a cat in a box along with a vial containing cyanide, together with a radioactive nucleus and a mechanism to trace the decay. Now, the nucleus has to decay; it's *when* the nucleus will decay that we don't know. But when the nucleus decays, it nudges the mechanism that releases the poison. The poison leaks out and kills the cat."

"I'm notifying PETA."

Harry winced. "You don't *do* it, for God's sake; you don't kill the cat. The point is this: you have only probability to go on that the nucleus will decay by a certain time. Nuclear decay is unpredictable. As I said, it *will* decay, you just don't know when; and, of course, you might open the box before the nucleus decays. But you don't know when or if the cat will die. Now, we know that the nucleus hasn't decayed, and the cat is alive only when we close the lid of the box. You could say that's our final measurement until we open it again. All we have to go on is wave function—the wave function of the nucleus—"

"What in hell's that?" Jury was feeling both relatively drunk and relatively stupid.

"It's hard to describe exactly. Say this: in classical physics—"

"Einstein," put in Jury, feeling better.

Harry smiled. "Good. In classical physics, an electron can be said to have a certain position. But in quantum mechanics, no. The wave function defines an area, say, of *probability*. An analogy might be that if a highly contagious disease turns up in a segment of the population, the disease control center gets right on it and tries to work out the probability of its recurrence in certain areas. The wave function isn't an entity, it's nothing in itself, it describes probability." Harry leaned closer as if he were divulging a sexy secret and went on: "So what we've got, then, is the probability of an electron's being in a certain place at a certain moment. Only when we're *measuring* it can we know not only where it is but *if* it is. So the cat—"

Jury waved his hands in front of his face as if clearing a space to breathe in. "Are you going to tell me the cat's both alive and dead at the same time?"

Harry smiled. "That's right."

Jury made a blubbery sound with his lips. "That's ridiculous."

"No, it isn't. You just don't understand. The decayed/undecayed nucleus is entangled with the live/dead cat—"

Mungo stuck his head out and looked, Jury could have sworn, balefully up at him. The dog pulled his head back under the tablecloth.

Jury laughed.

"What?"

"Mungo seems to be entangled with your zombie cat! The undead."

"He can't stand the cat; he never could."

"I sympathize." Jury lifted the cloth, said this, let it fall.

"To continue: Niels Bohr made it clear that, of course, the cat wasn't *literally* dead and alive at the same time, but *in the absence of measurement, there's no reality,* which is crucial. There's no reality without measurement, and to measure, one has to look. So that we can't speak of the cat as having any reality until we open the box and look."

"Kick the damn box; that'll tell you."

Harry shrugged. "Why do I feel my lecture is falling upon deaf ears?"

Jury smiled. "Well, drunk ears, anyway."

The waiter was there now, launching into his list of specials, a litany from which Jury could make out only two or three words that sounded familiar. "Salmon" was one. He ordered it, despite its sauce, its seasonings and other complications. "Fillet" was another. Harry ordered that. They both ordered the house salad.

They returned (all of them, if Jury correctly assessed Mungo's temperament) to the undead cat in the box. Jury said, "You know, you said something back in the pub about an objects' changing depending upon how we observed it. This Niels Bohr theory: it sounds like that. That we can't know if a thing exists until we see it. That's a lot like the tree in the forest falling."

"Something like it, yes. We can't comment on the cat's separate reality until we open the box. No, it's more that the cat *has* no separate reality until we see it; that is, can measure it."

Harry paused and drank some more whiskey. "Going back to Gödel: he was at Princeton with Einstein, who greatly admired him. Einstein couldn't have admired that many in his field. And he distrusted quantum theory. Anyway, Gödel proved the existence of unprovable arithmetical truths. Propositions both true and unprovable. When the physics community finally worked out what he was saying—and he said it in one well-turned sentence, as I recall—they couldn't believe it. When he said it, they didn't really hear it. Gödel was a young mathematician. But when they realized, well, as I said, they couldn't believe it. How could something be both *true* and *unprovable*? Truth posits 'provability,' doesn't it?"

Jury just looked at him, feeling thick as two planks.

"Of course it does. It's one of the most revolutionary theories in mathematics. The theory of incompleteness is what he called it. The incompleteness proof. A proof that, within a formal system, proves something unprovable."

Jury looked up from his salad. "That's paradoxical, isn't it?"

"You're absolutely right. Remember what's called the liar's paradox?"

"Vaguely."

"Take the sentence 'I am a liar.' That sentence is true only if it's false. If you say you're lying, then you're not, from which it follows that you are, and so on and so on. Of course Gödel is talking about arithmetical proofs. But that an arithmetical proof which should *automatically* be true—no. Gödel was talking about proving the unprovable. Proving that there were arithmetical truths that were unprovable."

Jury wondered how this was possible.

For a few moments they ate in silence.

"Hugh seems to think she—Glynnis—could be anywhere. It's like predicting the position of an electron. Until you measure it, it's nowhere. It doesn't have a definite position."

"In the world of Schrödinger's cat, maybe. But Hugh's wife isn't a particle."

"But that's the implication, isn't it?"

Jury thought about this. "This disappearance doesn't seem real, does it?"

"Perhaps not, but it happened," Harry said drily.

Jury said nothing.

"Hugh wondered a lot about that, I remember. I remember he shook his head and said, 'It never happened.'"

"What did he mean?"

"I don't really know."

"Perhaps with Hugh it was simply denial."

"Maybe." Harry seemed to be studying something not on his

plate but in his mind. "Upstairs there were four bedrooms, empty like the rest of the house. There were no outbuildings, no pasture or paddock, just the woods and the grass going down to them. Of course, we paid no attention to our Mr. Jessup's warning." Harry laughed. "It's just too much, isn't it? Anyway, the wood was quite pleasant with the light falling through the branches." Harry looked down at his plate. "I don't know why I noticed."

Jury smiled. "Because the world keeps turning. We're made to notice, Harry."

"There was nothing sinister, nothing menacing there."

"Why did he say that, then?"

Harry shook his head a little, as if clearing it. "Who?"

"Your visitor, Mr. Jessup."

"I don't know, couldn't even hazard a guess. I assumed he was just a screwball, a character with few social skills; instead of engaging in small talk, he handed out warnings. Thinking on it, though, we thought we would stop to see him and realized we didn't know where he lived. What he said was, 'It's been too many things happened there; the last was a woman and boy disappeared.' He put his palms together and shot one hand upward, and said, 'Like smoke, they did.'"

"And he said nothing at all except to warn you you shouldn't go tramping around in the woods?"

Harry shook his head, drank the last of his whiskey, left beside his wineglass.

Jury thought for a moment. "Where would Robbie have been when Glynnis was inspecting the house?"

Harry shrugged and pushed his plate back. "I thought about that. He was probably just tagging along with his mum."

"But perhaps not. You know how kids like to explore a new place. I wonder—" Jury sat back, let out a breath.

"Yes?"

"—if he saw something."

"Or if Glynnis did."

"If she did." Jury paused. "The agent must have shown the house to a number of people if it had been vacant long."

"Yes, but you know how estate agents operate in the country: hand you a key and let you get on with it. A peculiar practice, it seems to me."

"What did Hugh do then? I mean in the weeks and months that followed."

"As I said, he engaged a private detective when the police came up with nothing. Then he started coming apart. This puzzle—obsessed him."

"It would anyone, don't you think?"

"Yes, but it consumed Hugh. It was as if he stood in a burning building and couldn't move, as if he were waiting for the flames. It got so that he wouldn't leave the house, he was so afraid he'd miss the telephone call or the knock at the door. He told me he could swear he heard Mungo bark."

Weight beneath the table, Mungo rearranging himself.

"He'd only gotten worse; he didn't eat or sleep until his body knocked him out. I found him once by the fireplace and thought he was dead."

"No suicide attempts?"

"No, not Hugh. The cook and the maid stayed on even though he forgot to pay them. I paid them when I found out. They were devoted to the family. Gone now, of course."

Jury nodded, twisting his wineglass. No, he didn't want any more. He was whiskey and wine logged.

Harry leaned back, then forward and sighed. "And then he could no longer live by himself. I told him that. He gave me a blank look and said, 'But what can I do? What if Glynn and Robbie come back, what would they do if they came home and I wasn't here?' He seemed to regard his not being here as some sort of final, ruinous act—if he wasn't there, they would never see one another again."

"And it was 'when' they come home, not 'if'?"

"Yes. Hugh always thought they would."

"But he didn't believe it completely or he wouldn't have gone to pieces, would he?"

"You know it's strange, well not strange, exactly, but biblical or Greek, some act of God or the gods that is utterly unassailable and therefore unanswerable. Job. Oedipus Rex. Or something out of Shakespeare. I can't explain it, but, then, perhaps one isn't supposed to."

"That was Job's problem, as you said."

"Strange. Hugh had always been the coolest man I ever knew. I mean that not just figuratively but literally. He was self-reliant and self-contained and gracious—not in a superficial way, but gracious down to the bone. Even his anger was self-contained; he knew just how far he could take it before a relationship was irrevocably damaged. He always held the reins, had control of himself."

"Where is he now?"

"Stoddard Clinic. In Fulham. Actually, it is a pleasant place, very handsome, well cared for, expensive, obviously. There are few patients; it's geared to handle only a few. He's been there for about eight months now."

"Is he better?"

Harry shook his head. "He really couldn't be. Hugh's not psychotic, not mad; it's more like obsession. Like Othello, perhaps. Or Iago."

Jury smiled. "Not Iago. If revenge had really obsessed Iago, he could never have been as canny as he was. He would have taken a more immediate route to destroy Othello. He wasn't working at white heat. He wasn't caught up in his passions. On the contrary, I think Iago was dispassionate. I don't think any reason one could scare up would explain him any more than we can explain why Hamlet acted as he did. I think Iago ruined Othello because he could. Just that. Because he could."

10

"There's a house in Surrey I want you to check out," said Jury, looking across at Wiggins, who was ministering to his mug of tea. "The estate agent's called Forester and Flynn, and the agent handling the lease is a Marjorie Bathous. See what you can find out about it. The house is allegedly owned by a man named Benjamin della Torres." It occurred to Jury that if Winterhaus brought only a host of bad memories to Ben Torres, then why wasn't he selling it rather than leasing? But Jury supposed one could be addicted to bad memories as well as good.

"Just a tick," said Wiggins, extracting the tea bag from his mug. He then set about administering one of his holistic remedies. He put a couple of spoonfuls of some bizarrely blue liquid into the tea. Following that, three spoonfuls of sugar, which ought to undo whatever good the blue stuff was supposed to do, so what was the point?

Jury told himself he would not ask. "What's that stuff?"

"Oh, it's jojobu juice. Very good for the digestion." Wiggins stirred and smiled.

Jury crossed his arms and warmed his hands in his armpits. Or perhaps this attitude was a defensive measure taken against the jojobu juice. "It's blue like those awful blueberry iced lollies we used to eat when we were kids." Possibly, Wiggins still did.

With pursed lips, Wiggins slowly shook his head. "This tincture is good for you; iced lollies aren't. All sugar, they are."

This, coming from a man who'd added three teaspoons of sugar to his tea. But Jury let that pass. "I'm not contesting the nutrient value of iced lollies; I'm questioning the value of that stuff." Jury leaned his head to indicate the small bottle of blue liquid.

"You always do, sir. I've never known anyone so skeptical when it comes to what's good for your health. How often do I get sick compared to you?"

"Around five to one. You get sick five times more often."

Condescension ratcheted up several bars in the look and tone of voice Wiggins used. "Now, you *know* that's not the case at all."

"Ten to one, then. Ten for you, one for me."

Wiggins sighed and shook his head. Hopeless.

Jury sat considering, looking at Wiggins. "What do you think about the liar's paradox?"

"Don't think I know that one, sir."

"Well, listen: 'I am not lying.'"

"Never said you were, did I?"

"No, no. I don't mean *me,* personally. I'll change it: 'I *am* lying.' You see? The statement in and of itself creates a problem, doesn't it? Think about it. The statement itself."

Wiggins tapped his fingers on his Ed McBain paperback as if to summon support.

Jury sat forward, sighing. "Look, the 87th precinct isn't going to help you here. 'I am lying.' 'I. Am. Lying.'"

Wanting to indulge his boss in this quirky discourse, Wiggins smiled a bit. "Well, with respect, sir, I can't see the sense to it. I mean, if you're telling someone in *advance* you're lying—?"

To dramatize his frustration with his sergeant's thickheadedness, Jury brought his fist down on the desk. "Don't you see it's a *paradox*! If you *say* 'I'm lying' the very statement *itself means you aren't;* therefore, you're telling the truth!"

Wiggins pondered. Jury sighed. "Do you know anything about physics, Wiggins?"

"A lot. I keep telling you, that some of these, for instance, would be good for you." He held up a packet of black biscuits.

"Not *that* kind of physic. Not medicine. I'm talking about energy, matter, the study of their relation to each other."

Enlightened, Wiggins leaned back. "Well, I must admit, I was never good at math or science in school. Physics is harder still."

"Then you've never heard of Schrödinger's cat?" At the moment, Jury felt like the canary, what with Wiggins, the cat, sitting over there looking sure of himself.

"No." Wiggins drank his blue stuff. "Schrö—?"

"Schrödinger. See, this is a hypothetical cat we're talking about. Pretend you're putting the cat in a box . . ." Jury told him the rest of it as well as he could, and he thought he remembered pretty well.

Wiggins listened and chortled. Only Wiggins could chortle that way, a throaty sound, the way baboons might laugh. "Really taking the piss out, isn't he?"

"What? You mean Harry Johnson?"

"No, this other chap."

"Schrödinger?"

"Yes. That's pretty good, that is. Cat's dead and alive at the same time." Wiggins flapped his hand in a gesture of disbelief. "Join the circus, that cat should."

Jury was up and pulling on his jacket.

"Don't forget the guv'nor, sir," Wiggins called after him.

"He's in a right mood, he is." Fiona Clingmore sat zipping a large-grained fingernail file across her nails.

"When isn't he?"

Fiona pursed her lips. "Well, right before his club lunch, he feels pretty good."

"The question was rhetorical." Jury looked around the outer office. No sign of the cat Cyril. "Where's Cyril?"

Fiona shook her head. "Here, there, everywhere. Dunno." *Zip zip zip.* "Go on in." She yawned.

Racer glanced up, head in hands, told Jury to sit down and returned to contemplation of a pile of papers on his desk.

Jury sat. He scanned the ceiling molding for a sign of Cyril, who favored the cozy area between molding and wall designed for the recessed lighting. It was a spot he liked to catnap in. Jury didn't see him, which meant zip, as Cyril could be hiding anywhere, like the questionable cat of the equation. Cyril could be anywhere, anytime, too. The cat's dead, the cat's alive.

"Ever hear of Schrödinger's cat?" Jury asked.

The bald top of Racer's head came up, head still held between Racer's hands as if Jury had disturbed his morning matins. He tossed down his Mont Blanc pen, sat back and, having been reminded of a cat, sussed out the room's hiding places.

Jury said, "Schrödinger's cat is a famous thought experiment in quantum physics."

Racer glared. "Really? The CID could use a thought experiment on the Soho murder—that is, when you're ready."

"I take it that's a no about Schrödinger's cat. But let me explain." Jury did so.

"Dead *and* alive? A vial of cyanide? Have you completely lost it, Jury?" Composing himself (as best he could), Racer sat back with arms folded and said, "What are you doing about this Danny Wu case?" His crossed arms resembled a railway crossing sign.

"Waiting to be reinstated. I'm in a state of what seems to be semisuspension; neither suspended nor unsuspended. A little like Schrödinger's cat. So I'm doing nothing." Jury crossed his own arms.

"Oh, *don't* be dramatic. You think it's going to help your review? Sitting around reading textbook physics? Danny Wu's case needs sorting."

Jury considered. "The thing is, I didn't know it had worked into a 'case.'"

"Of course it's a *case*. What are you talking about? You've been on to him for years!"

"I've visited his restaurant for years, true."

Racer let his pen drop on the desk. "For God's sake, Jury, you know half the murders in Docklands lead back to him. He's with that gang that clinches knives in their teeth."

"No, he isn't."

"What? Of *course* he is!"

Jury shook his head, solemnly. "Danny Wu isn't a joiner."

"*Joiner?* For God's sake, we're not talking about the Boy Scouts or the Girl Guides! We're talking about the Triad. Worse than the Mafia."

"Whatever Danny does, he operates alone. Trust me on that."

"And this dead man on his doorstep?"

Jury shrugged. "Maybe forensics will turn up some DNA. Or maybe not." Jury flashed Racer a smile.

"I want you to stay on top of it. Go on." Here Racer gave him a backhanded wave.

Jury left, wondering why he'd come.

11

"That would be Young Higgins, sir," said the porter at reception, "who took the call."

Melrose read the message again, which he couldn't make head nor tail of and which was apparently from Agatha. That would account for the confusion he might, given any other caller, have blamed on Young Higgins (and his spidery scrawl).

And he hadn't been "out," either, an hour ago. He had been in the Members' Room, nearly asleep in a wing chair before a stout fire, a preluncheon whiskey in hand, reading Polly's book, which he had gone to Hatchards to purchase. He felt as if his eyelids were propped open. He had decided to actually read the book rather than chance comments at dinner as he had done the night before. Comments that could have applied to anything from Beano to *The Golden Bowl* about the unread last book was probably not a technique he'd want to try again, or at least not so soon.

This newest one was titled *The Gourmandise Way*, which wouldn't have irked him so much had it actually been a satire or a spoof of Proust. Only it wasn't. He would tell her that she simply couldn't keep making plays on Marcel's titles, that it wasn't very smart to call up a comparison, nor to lead the reader down the garden path—or *The Guermantes Way*—whereby the unsuspecting reader would think he'd got hold of a spoof. Yes, and most people would be delighted to read a send-up of Proust, since they'd always felt guilty, stupid and uneducated for never getting past that madeleine passage, which came around page thirty. Leaving only a few thousand pages to go.

Which was about where he was in her new book, on page thirty-six, leaving three hundred pages to read, worse luck.

Melrose did not like mysteries. With maybe two or three exceptions, today's mysteries were just too dumb to hold one's attention. In this one, the "gourmands" of the title ran an out-of-London, out-of-the-way restaurant that Melrose bet was modeled on Le Quatre Saisons, where he knew she'd eaten once. This chef in her book had devised an incredible meal for ten of his valued customers. They were gourmands one and all.

Gee, thought Melrose, I wonder what will happen?

As if everybody didn't know, except the characters in the book, all of whom were thick as two planks, except for the chef himself, who Melrose rather liked because he liked all that food he was fixing and, by the bye, giving out intricate instructions for making. That took up a lot of the thirty pages at the beginning, and Melrose meant to mark two dishes which he would ask his cook Martha to make.

He dozed or half dozed before the fire, with the flames shooting about as if seeking out their next victim, and that book looked damned tasty . . .

Melrose fluttered awake when a gentleman gave him a hearty "Hello" and his companion echoed the greeting.

"My word," said Melrose, sitting up smartly, "Colonel Neame and Major Champs! This is a pleasant surprise!" But why a surprise? These two old gents lived in the place, or seemed to.

Major Champs made a few gruff how-d'ya-do noises and they both shook Melrose's hand. They looked pleased as punch to see him. Yes, they had fought off sleep many's the time sitting in Boring's in their favorite chairs.

"Saw you at dinner last night with that attractive lady. You didn't see us; that dining room is so ill lit Young Higgins is always barking his shins on the furniture and spilling the soup."

Young Higgins would be doing that standing in the noonday sun of the Greek isles, thought Melrose, but didn't say so since Higgins was probably the same age as these two.

They had both taken chairs now and were looking about for one of the porters to bring them their whiskey. Major Champs was waving out a match he'd used to light tobacco in the bowl of his pipe. He said, "Now your friend, I thought she looked familiar, was sure I'd seen her and, lo and behold!" He held up the book he was carrying.

Polly's face looked out at the reader in a fearful way or an alarmed one, rather like Ruth Rendell expecting the worst.

"Marvelous yarn!" said Major Champs. "Neame's read it, keeps threatening to tell me who did it." He snickered. "Read all her books, every blessed one. I don't suppose"—he leaned closer to Melrose and into the firelight whose shadows carved even deeper hollows in his cheeks—"you'd introduce us?"

"Certainly, I would. I'll be seeing her in a week or two." Would two weeks allow time enough to read her book? Melrose looked at the bookmark in the major's copy. At least three fourths of the way through. Aha! thought Melrose, who said, "What d'you think about this poodle?" He tapped his copy. The poodle had wandered in around page twenty.

"Ah, that! The poodle. Never cared for them much myself, a prissy, mean-spirited, self-indulgent animal. She puts a lot of dogs and so forth in her stories. Last one was . . . a Labrador? Anyway, the dog finds the body. Damned clever. That's later, of course. Wouldn't want to give the plot away."

Oh, do. Please.

Colonel Neame put in, "And Hubert—"

Who the hell was Hubert?

"—the young lad, he's one of the few children in fiction I've found convincing."

Major Champs said, "We agree on that certainly."

They disagreed about other things and that was just splendid! Melrose fancied an argument that would offer up all sorts of morsels for him to file away before he saw her again. "In what way, precisely, do you find Hubert convincing?"

"Because . . . well, look at the way he responds to his mother's death and his father's suicide. Then the sister's falling from that cliff side—"

Melrose smiled slowly. He had no idea what they were talking about. "Yes, but did she really fall?" Of course she didn't. Had any victim ever "accidentally" fallen off a cliff—or for that matter, a chair—in any mystery?

Colonel Neame slapped the chair arm and said, gleefully, "Exactly, exactly! And did the mother really have a *heart condition*?" Wink, wink, nod, nod.

Melrose was picking up stuff. But it left him wondering about the chef and that dinner party at the beginning. What did all of these deaths in one family and the poodle have to do with that? Were all three of them reading the same book? Yes, the title of the one Major Champs held was quite definitely *The Gourmandise Way*. "Thing is," he said, brow knitted in puzzlement, "I've only gotten around, oh . . ." He was going to trap himself if he wasn't careful. (After all, he'd acted as if he'd read about Hubert.) "Well, I've not gotten terribly far, and I just wonder about the 'gourmand' idea."

"He's the father, isn't he? He's the chef." Major Champs gave Melrose a lowering look from under his thick eyebrows.

"Oh, the chef! Yes, of course, he's the *chef*." Melrose took a long swallow of his whiskey, commenting on how smooth it was.

Where did that damned poodle fit in? She'd asked him how he liked the Labrador, so she was certain to ask about the poodle.

"Evening, gentlemen," came a voice from behind Melrose.

"Superintendent!" said Major Champs and Colonel Neame in unison.

Jury made a slight bow and greeted Melrose Plant. "Back in the enfolding arms of Boring's."

"Delighted to see you, Mr. Jury, or"—Colonel Neame continued, sotto voce—"is there trouble afoot?" From his expression, one could tell he was hopeful.

"Not yet, anyway."

Major Champs said, "I hope a body doesn't turn up every time you do, Superintendent!"

"So do I."

They laughed at this and slapped their chair arms.

Melrose had beckoned to one of the porters as soon as Jury appeared. "Sit down," he said to Jury, making room on the leather sofa the unfortunate color of dried blood.

Jury removed his coat and sat as the porter (slightly stooped, but not as old as Young Higgins) came up to their group. Melrose said, "Whiskey all round."

Colonel Neame reminisced: "That death here was quite the most exciting and unnerving time I've had since the war. A real shocker, that was. To think the killer just walked in, stabbed poor Pitt and walked out again and no one the wiser."

Said Major Champs, "Just goes to show how dead we all must look in Boring's."

Jury laughed. "No, I really don't think so; what it shows is how shockingly easy it is for someone to commit a murder in a public place. Like this."

The waiter reappeared and set down their drinks.

"Cheers," said Melrose. They all raised their glasses.

"So you're not here on police business?"

"No, just to have lunch."

Major Champs *harrumphed.* "Well, I'm surprised someone hasn't killed the cook."

Melrose laughed. "That bad?"

"Lamb was tough. Still, food's usually decent enough. I expect even the cook can have a bad day now and then."

"But not as bad, let's hope," Melrose held up the book, "as Miss Praed's chef."

12

Young Higgins informed them that as there'd been a run on the lamb during this luncheon, he hoped the cold beef tongue would suffice. Or the stuffed portobello mushroom?"

Melrose raised an inquiring eye. "A *run?* But there's no one else here, Higgins." Melrose spread his arms in testimony to empty space.

"Don't be so dramatic," said Jury. "The mushrooms are fine with me, Higgins."

"Mush*room,*" said Melrose. "There's only one."

"What are they stuffed with, Higgins?"

"What is *it* stuffed with? Good grief," Melrose said. "Wiggins would know more about portobello mushrooms than you."

"If it was stuffed with a ground physic, maybe," said Jury.

"With what?"

"A ground-lamb mixture, m' lord," said Young Higgins to Melrose.

Melrose said, "Don't tell *me,* I'm not having them."

"It," said Jury.

Melrose gritted his teeth.

"I guess now we know what happened to the lamb!" said Jury with a manufactured gleeful smile.

Young Higgins joined in the revelry with a wrinkled smile of his own. "Yes, sir, and we also have a tomato-mozzarella salad."

Jury spread his huge white napkin across his lap. "Sounds good."

"Indeed, sir." Higgins bowed. "And you'll be having the cold tongue, m' lord?"

Melrose shivered. "No, I guess I'll have the portobello mushroom. We'll both have it."

"Them," said Jury.

Melrose glared.

"And we'll have the salad also?" said Young Higgins.

Melrose was tempted to say they would but was Young Higgins joining them? Higgins seemed to have adopted this Irish idiom of asking a question that wasn't a question and, in the bargain, including himself in. Instead, Melrose said to Jury, "We will, won't we?"

Jury nodded. "We will, yes."

The elderly waiter shuffled away.

"Young Higgins isn't getting any younger." Jury sighed as if this marked a stage in his own increase of years.

"He's not getting any older, either. He was probably an eighty-year-old teenager." Melrose opened the *carte du vin*. "The wine, the wine, the wine . . . Now what goes with portabello mushrooms?" He ran his eye down the list. "How about a nice little Merlot?"

"How about a nice big Merlot? Or maybe a Montrachet '66. All of the other '66s are over the hill. Undrinkable. But what I'd really like is a Bordeaux, say a Château Petrus? It's pretty pricey, but you can afford it."

Melrose shut his eyes. "Now, we've become a wine enthusiast?"

"I don't know about you, but I have. The bottle shouldn't be much over a couple hundred pounds."

"Really? Well, let's have a case if that's all!"

"Okay."

Melrose sought out one of the waiters, his eyes connecting with those of the (really) young ginger-haired one who came over snappily. Melrose gave him the wine order—the nice little Merlot—and the waiter sailed off.

This done, Melrose rested the wine list against the marble column by which the table sat. The columns were fixed at strategic places around the room, which was a handsome one, with its dark wood and vaulted ceiling and snow-white tablecloths. "Okay," he said again. "You have a story to tell me, you said."

Jury thought for a moment, but not about Harry Johnson. "Maybe that's what we live for, why we go on."

Melrose gave him a look. "You never got over the Henry James contest, did you? 'Why we go on,' indeed. Are you saying we live for stories?"

"Children do, don't they? Isn't that their favorite thing?"

"After beating each other up and tying firecrackers to their dogs' tails, yes, I imagine they like to relax over a good story. I expect you're making a point, but I don't know what it is."

"I'm not sure I do, either. The Henry James competition, remember: 'Man walked into a pub,' et cetera," Jury said.

"Ah. The master himself would put it perhaps as 'After a grave exchange with his interlocutor, Lord Joyner made his way to his dear old Pot and Pickle,' blah blah blah."

"Off the top of your head, damned good James."

"It's not easy being Henry James."

"No. Well, that's the point about this story. It begins in just that way. A man walked into a pub and told me this story."

"You're kidding."

"That's exactly what I said to him. Told him he was winding me up. Anyway, the pub's in the City. It's called the Old Wine Shades. I was there, sitting at the bar, glooming away, nothing special—"

"Special what?"

"For a gloom."

"Ah. Go on."

"A man walked in, clearly well off, clothes like yours—"

"This rag of a jacket?" Melrose pulled the collar down for a better look.

"—and sat down beside me. Somehow that sounds ominous."

"Yes, like Little Miss Muffet. Go on."

"He told me this story." Here Jury related the story to Melrose in great detail. Gödel. Niels Bohr. Wave function. It took him through the salad, the portobello mushroom, the pudding and now through brandy and coffee. "His name is Harry Johnson, did I mention that?"

"Yes. That's the strangest story I've ever heard," said Melrose, as he returned to the lighting of a cigar. "Not only because of the initial situation, but because it's a story within a story within a story."

Jury frowned. "What are you talking about?"

"It's four stories. Didn't you notice?" Melrose shoved his cup and glass aside and leaned toward Jury. "One"—he folded down his index finger—"is Johnson himself; he's the frame of the story. Two"—the second finger bent inward—"is the story of the disappearance of the Gault woman"—third finger ticked this off—"three is Ben Torres's story, and four"—fourth finger down—"is the story his mother told him."

Jury reflected. "I guess you're right."

"And in a way, it gets further and further from the first story. It's like those little Russian nesting dolls. Matryoshkas?"

"If it is, what's your point?"

"Well, that would certainly make me wonder if he's telling the truth."

Jury smiled. "You know that would somehow be the most outrageous thing of all. Is he? I asked him that during the first dinner and he asked why would he lie. To what end? Sergeant Wiggins thinks he followed me into the pub, that he knew who I was and told me the story."

"You're still left with 'why?' You believe him?"

"Not altogether. It becomes harder and harder the more he tells and yet easier and easier with his telling it."

"You mean we've not come to the end?"

"No, apparently not. He said that first night that there was no end. By that I expect he means no solution."

"Does he think perhaps you might be able to solve it?"

Jury shook his head. "I don't think so."

"Say he does know who you are. Sergeant Wiggins may well be right."

"I doubt it."

"Just *say* he does know you. What if this is not something that happened, but something that's going to happen."

Jury looked disbelieving at first and then amused. "How could it be—"

"Richard. You can listen to all this codswallop night after night, yet you can't entertain this theory? Admittedly odd, but then so's the whole story." Melrose rolled his cigar around in his mouth. "An event in the future."

"When did you take up cigars?"

"This afternoon. I knew it would annoy you to death."

"Thanks. Well, this theory of yours, can you take it out for a walk? Explain it?"

"No. Let me think. . . . If this is to happen in the future, it must be that Mr. Johnson is protecting himself or someone else. But how would it do that?" Melrose rubbed the back of his neck. "What if this Hugh—"

"Gault."

"—if Hugh Gault was trying to acquire this property for some reason—no, no, no. That's not what I mean. . . . A hypothetical: you investigate, you solve this mystery—"

"Not officially. I'm on leave, remember? CS Racer thinks I need a rest. What he really thinks is I need another job."

Melrose made a face and was silent.

Jury broke the silence. "You're theorizing that Wiggins is right, that Harry knew who I was, that he deliberately sought me out?"

"I expect that's what I'm saying, yes. I don't think it would suit his purpose to tell this story to just anybody. Hasn't your picture been in the paper, showing you as an example of police brutality?" Melrose grinned.

"Don't exaggerate." Jury sat back. "That is a point I hadn't considered. He might have recognized me, true." Jury frowned.

"And there's this shadow over your police record. You've 'shaken the very foundations of police work.' That's a quote from one of the rags."

"So I would be particularly vulnerable."

"Like that, yes."

"I have to admit I hadn't thought of that."

"It's still murky, of course. Say he wants to engage you, wants you as a witness. What I can't get my mind around is that Harry Johnson walked into—what's the pub?"

"The Old Wine Shades."

"Walked in with this dog Bingo—"

"Mungo."

Melrose nodded. "Walked in with Mungo and without knowing you, started in on this elaborate tale. What brought it up? What were you talking about?"

"Dreams. The belief of many researchers in the field that dreams have no real meaning. I said how do these dream experts get around the idea that there's always a narrative. A dream is a story. The scientific take on this is that the *dreamer supplies* the narrative. Well, I was talking I guess about narratives, about stories, and how all of us seem to want a story."

"Which is what you meant before."

"Yes. In any event, Harry said if I wanted a story he could tell me a story. And that was it. The Gault woman and her son vanished, along with the dog. The dog came back." Jury smiled.

" 'The dog came back.' Crazy. The dog was *brought* back, don't you imagine?"

"Yes, probably. But I like to think of Mungo's making this arduous journey back to London."

"Sentimentalist. But if the story is really a lot of codswallop, then why drag the dog into it? That the dog was with them and managed to get back from wherever they were is pretty fantastic."

"The whole damned thing's fantastic."

"Maybe your first instinct was right and he's just winding you up. But why?"

Jury shrugged. "Because he could?"

Melrose gave a short burst of laughter. "Yes, there's always that. Because he could."

13

It would hardly be called lively, but there were a few more customers in the Old Wine Shades the following night. Jury supposed
lunchtime was when the pub did most of its business. The City was
not a residential area, but a region of office blocks, financial institu-
tions, the Corn Exchange, Leadenhall Market, Monument and St.
Paul's. Although there were a few private residences, the heart of
the City beat in time to the making of money.

Jury posted himself in the same chair at the bar and ordered a
glass of Beaujolais (paying no attention to year or provenance,
which earned him no points with Trevor). He hoped that long talk
the night before with Plant hadn't tainted his ability to listen to the
rest of the story—the third installment—without prejudice.

Did Harry Johnson know who Jury was? Had he read about the
CID cock-up in the papers? It was interesting to speculate. And
while Jury was speculating, Harry walked in with Mungo on the
lead. Mungo was a dog who seemed to like routine; he sat looking
up at Jury until Jury reached down and rubbed his head. Then the
dog settled under his chair.

"I'm beginning to feel," said Harry Johnson, as he tapped a cigarette on his silver case, "a sense of déjà vu—a kind of trancelike
state. Are you?"

Jury smiled. "How many people have you told this story to?"

"No one." Harry's lighter clicked open, spurted flame, shut. He
examined Jury—

(Or so it felt to Jury.)

—through a brief scrim of smoke rising upward from his cigarette. "You're wondering why I'm telling you this, right?"

"I am, yes, seeing that I'm a perfect stranger."

"I suppose I wanted to tell someone who didn't know the people involved. You'd get a clearer picture, maybe."

"I don't know why you'd think that."

Harry Johnson smiled. "You still think I'm winding you up?" He ordered a glass of Pinot Gris Grand Cru ("'89, if you have it, Trev") and Trevor went off, smiling.

"Not that, necessarily, but whether you have some ulterior motive." That sounded like worn-out dialogue in a bad film.

"It'd be easy enough to check up on what I've told you. Call the agent; better yet, go to Lark Rise and *see* the agent and go to this Winterhaus and have a look round."

"But Gault's agent knows nothing of the history of the house."

"She knows Ben Torres."

"She knew only that he wanted to rent it, didn't she? At least that's what I gather from what you've told me."

Trevor set Harry's glass before him, poured a small amount of Pinot Gris into it. Harry thanked him and lifted the glass, sniffed it and rolled it around, making little waves. He sipped it. "Good. Excellent."

Trevor filled the glass, asked Jury if he cared for another drink, and, when Jury nodded, picked up the bottle of Beaujolais, which he clearly regarded as plonk, and poured some more, then walked away.

Harry didn't answer Jury's question about what the agent knew, but said, instead, "Shall I tell you the rest, though? I mean, do you want to hear it?"

Jury smiled. "Absolutely."

Harry drank the wine. "Then Hugh went to the house."

"To Winterhaus?"

"Yes. And the wood. The police had looked round, but after all it wasn't a crime scene, so they weren't about to spend time and manpower when as far as they knew, Glynnis Gault hadn't even been there."

Jury nodded. "I'm rather surprised they bothered looking in the first place."

"Well, perhaps there was not too much going on in Lark Rise, so they wanted to be helpful. I expect they saw how distraught Hugh was. The whole thing was crazy and it's possible they were intrigued, too." Harry stopped talking and drank his wine. "Um-um. This is good."

Jury waited.

Harry said, "Did it ever occur to you that what is unseen and unheard is more frightening than what we do see?"

"Oh, yes. Imagination can toss up things far worse than a John Carpenter film. It's the not knowing."

"Whatever is there, you get only the *sense* of. Hugh said he most definitely got the sense of something very scary."

"In the house?"

"In the wood."

Mungo came out from under Jury's chair and gazed up at him.

"What's up, boy?" Jury scratched his head. Mungo went back under the chair.

Jury went on: "But your friend Hugh was not in a state of mind where he would find otherwise. I doubt he would find the place benign, given what he thought."

"You think he was imagining things?"

"Of course. That's what we were just talking about."

"No, in this case, you're saying there was no basis for the imagining."

"Why didn't you go with him? Hugh, I mean?"

"Hugh didn't want me to. He wanted to be by himself. I didn't press him on that point. Anyway, the wood, he said, was very cold. At the edge of it, he found a sort of playhouse, you know, we call them Wendy houses. It was in a sorry state, probably hadn't been used in years. He thought it a strange place for one. What child would want it all that distance from the house? Besides, children are frightened by such places, aren't they?"

"Depends on the child, I expect." Jury was suddenly famished. "Let's have dinner."

Mungo stirred beneath the chair as Harry said, "Right," and finished off his wine.

They settled on an Indian restaurant called the Raj. The walls were painted a soft shade of pink and Jury liked the quiet of the place. They ordered curries and papadum. Jury smiled, thinking of Long Piddleton's own Trevor Sly of the Blue Parrot. Although Trevor didn't serve Indian food. It was something else, Arabic or something.

The waiter had brought them tall glasses of an Indian beer and now returned with their food.

Jury turned his glass round and round. "Tell me: is Hugh a reliable source?"

Harry looked up from his plate, surprised. "You mean was he lying?"

"No. But he is in this Stoddard Clinic, you said. His imagination could have been working overtime."

"Hugh's a scientist, don't forget. Yes, he's reliable."

Jury thought about this, then asked, "When you were in the house itself, how did you feel?"

"Feel? You mean did I feel there was a ghostly presence?" Harry smiled.

"Did you?"

"No, not really." He again smiled slightly. "But Hugh did."

"What?"

"That Glynn had been there. He thought he even recognized her scent, her perfume."

"Well, Hugh would've thought he felt her presence, wouldn't he? If for no other reason, the power of suggestion would do it."

Harry nodded.

Jury went on. "This old man who appeared to be issuing a warning that day, you never got a lead on him. Isn't there a village near? Or at least a pub? There's got to be a pub."

"There is; it's about a mile farther along the road. The Swan, if I remember correctly. Handsome building, half timbered, well kept up. Hugh asked the manager about the Torres house and had he heard anything odd about it. The barman—also the manager, I think—said he hadn't except that he knew it was for lease. Then he asked if he'd seen a woman in here, alone or with her son. Hugh pulled out his picture of Glynnis and the boy—here, I have this one." Harry drew a photo from an inside pocket of his jacket and handed it to the jury.

"Glynnis Gault?" It showed a pretty woman with short, lightish-brown hair and a lovely smile. "She's very attractive." He handed back the picture.

"Anyway," Harry went on, pocketing the photo, "the fellow in the Swan said it could be, for there had been a woman, a stranger, in who'd bought two lemonades, one for her son. Yes, he did recall that."

"Anyone else, other customers, who seemed to be interested?"

"No. Oh, they were *interested* all right. Imagine what a juicy bit of gossip to be going on with. A vanished wife and mum. Last them the whole year, wouldn't it? They probably thought the obvious— she'd have wanted to give this fellow here—Hugh—the boot." Harry signed to the waiter, and when he came asked for tea and brandy.

The waiter nodded and slipped away as quietly as Young Higgins, but considerably more upright.

Jury said, "It must have been very hard on Hugh, knowing they'd be thinking that."

"The only thing hard on Hugh was not knowing where his wife and son were. Everything else took a backseat: embarrassment, making a fool of himself—no, those things barely registered."

"He passed the photo around?"

"Yes. There were perhaps a dozen customers and Hugh said

they seemed to be *wanting* to recognize the woman in the picture. A couple of them said yes, they thought she'd been in the pub. One thought he'd seen a dog, noticed it because the dog reminded him of his own, that his had died. I think Hugh said some woman or other in the pub had driven by and slowed and asked if she needed assistance. Glynnis was stopped by the side of the road, across from the Winterhaus property, reading a map. Hugh ought to have gotten her name." Harry frowned.

Jury felt Mungo rearranging himself and in a second he'd stuck his head out from under the tablecloth. Jury scratched his head. He said, "You know I feel like Mungo here. You keep tossing things across my path as a sort of lure to listen, don't you?"

Harry laughed. "You think I'm stringing you along, is that it?"

"You do seem to have some agenda here that Mungo and I are not wholly aware of."

Mungo looked up as if he too were waiting for details, but then, hearing of the fate of the dog belonging to one of the Swan's customers, decided to pull his head back under the tablecloth, as if the details of dog deaths were better left unsaid and unheard.

Harry set down his brandy, smiling. "No agenda, really."

"Glynnis was reading a map?"

"That's what the woman said."

"Why?"

"Why what?"

"Reading a map. The houses were what? A half mile apart along that same road. Why would she have needed a map?"

Harry put down his brandy, untasted. "I don't know. I guess Hugh and I were so hell-bent on finding out where she was that we didn't pay much attention to what Glynnis was doing. Reading a map didn't sound so unusual in a place she'd not been to before." Harry paused, looking at Jury. "You're extremely observant. You don't miss a trick. Hugh should have put you on the case."

Jury closely observed Harry's expression as he said this. Was he being sardonic? He couldn't tell; Harry just took a drink of brandy. Jury said, "Not really. My advantage in this case is that it's all new to me; I don't know the Gaults. But when I asked why she needed a map, I meant, was she going someplace else? Not to Winterhaus but to a different place altogether off that road, or if not off it, then farther along—or, indeed, even *back* along that road? She might have made a call or received one that had her getting out a map. Or she might have seen another estate agent's sign along there and she was including it in her property search. Do you remember seeing anything along that stretch of road?"

"No, nothing. Which is not to say there *was* nothing. But I don't recall any property signs."

"It's just a thought. And this woman in the Swan might be wrong. Perhaps it wasn't a map." Jury thought for a moment. "Where was Robbie?"

"Well, we supposed he was in the car. Since Glynn was standing against the driver's window, Robbie wouldn't have been visible, would he? Or maybe the reason for stopping in the first place was Robbie needed to get out and have a piss. There was a dry stone wall along there and trees. He could have stopped behind one or the other."

"And whilst he was doing that, his mum takes out a map."

Harry nodded.

"Did you notice the roads that crossed the one you were on?"

"Actually, the wood"—roughly, Harry sketched a tangle of trees, rounded masses—"they might very well have been part of the Winterhaus estate."

"The agent didn't give you a plat or a property survey?"

"No. The trees began at some distance from the rear of the house. The more I think about it, the more I'm sure that was all Winterhaus property. Does it make a difference?"

"A difference who owned the woods? It might to an adult who'd keep clear of someone else's property. But it wouldn't mean anything to a child. I was thinking of that Wendy house."

Harry shook his head. "A child would hardly venture onto this property and into the Wendy house situated as it was."

"As of now, you can't really be sure Mrs. Gault was actually there. I wonder why she didn't call the estate agent after seeing it. She called about the cottage. She was like that, was she? Very definite about things? Decisive?"

"Yes, I'd say she was. I never gave it much thought before. But, yes, Glynn was quite firm in her opinions, though I wouldn't call her opinionated."

Jury drank his tea and wondered. As far as not giving much thought to it was concerned, Jury had an idea Harry Johnson had given a great deal of thought to Glynnis Gault. "So she has tea with the couple in the cottage, isn't too keen on their house, probably isn't too keen on *them* and calls Marjorie Bathous to tell her. But Mrs. Gault could simply have waited until she'd returned to Lark Rise. You're not sure if she called the agent about Winterhaus."

"You're suggesting they never got there?"

"That's always been a possibility, hasn't it? There's nothing conclusive about Winterhaus, except that it sounds like a hell of an interesting property with a strange history." Jury was thinking about Ben Torres.

"Glynn would have liked the air of mystery. Even liked the sinister, the ominous atmosphere."

"The agent would have gone through the house. What did she say about the furnished drawing room?"

"Remember, she'd asked Torres to do that to better show off the house. At least one room looked lived in."

Jury looked around the restaurant. The other diners seemed long since gone. "It looks like we're shutting down the place." He caught the waiter's attention. The waiter came up to their table with the bill and Jury quickly put his hand on it before Harry Johnson could take it. "My turn, surely."

Harry smiled and put away his money clip. "Very nice. Thanks."

"The bill probably isn't a third of the one in the Docklands place, so don't feel too thankful." Jury put down some bills and included an oversized tip.

They got up and headed for the door. Jury noticed the sitar music had still played for as long as they were at their table. Now it stopped. That the place would keep the music on as long as there were diners seemed to him a very civilized thing to do. It was the quietest restaurant he'd ever eaten in. The Raj. He would have to remember it.

Outside, Jury looked around at the quiet streets, felt the night air, cold for March. He smiled. "Is that all? Is that the end?"

Harry laughed. "By no means. You remember I told you it didn't end. It just reaches a point where I stop, when I've told you all I can." He pulled on his leather gloves, the color and texture of the crème brûlée they had had for dessert. "You know, you should really see that house."

"I might very well do that. Is the same agent handling it?"

"I think so. Anyway, it would be the same estate agency. It's Forester and Flynn. They're on the main street of the village. Lark Rise."

"I wonder what effect all of this had on the leasing of the house."

"Not much, I shouldn't think," said Harry. "It's not as if there'd been a murder there."

Jury looked away, then looked speculatively at Harry.

"What? Do you think there was? Christ, I can't begin to get my mind around that possibility." Harry shook his head and looked down at Mungo, who was swishing his tail on the pavement and looking from one to the other. "Good old dog, what do you know that we don't?" To Jury he said, "How in hell could Mungo here have got to Chelsea from effing Surrey?"

"Maybe Mungo didn't. Maybe he got there from Piccadilly or Sloane Street or West Ham. Why are we assuming that whatever happened, happened in Surrey? How do you know that Glynnis Gault and Robbie and Mungo didn't return to London?"

"But . . . Mungo's been gone for *months*. How could he be that near home and not show himself before now?"

"In a dozen ways. Someone could have found him on the Heath or in Green Park or wherever and taken him in. They might have put up flyers, tried to find the owner; or the RSPCA could have taken him in and eventually found a caretaker. He could have been dropped off in Chelsea. Although I'm not sure but what that raises another set of questions: the first would be another why. But this is the wildest speculation we're engaged in." Jury was trying to flag down a cab, all of which seemed committed to their ample, empty selves and chugged on by. "And maybe the answer is so glaringly obvious we'll wonder we could have missed it."

"I'd be happy to drive you home."

Jury shook his head. "No, you'd be going out of your way. I live in Islington. It's late. I don't mind a cab."

A cab finally pulled up to the curb and Jury stuck his head in to tell the driver he was going to Islington. "It's been, as always, fascinating."

"How about tomorrow evening?"

"Tomorrow evening?" Jury frowned a little. "I don't think I can make that; but what about the next evening?"

"Night after tomorrow, then? Old Wine Shades?"

Jury nodded, climbed into the cab and gave directions to his street. The cab swept on. Jury looked out of the cab's rear window to see Harry and Mungo growing smaller in the distance and looking strangely lonely.

Or was that just me? he wondered.

14

"It's none of my business—"

(Meaning, yes, it was.)

"Except I just don't understand—"

(Meaning, it was beyond the understanding even of Tony Blair.)

"Why you'd ever want to go to dinner night after night with somebody you hardly know at all instead of staying home like you usually do. I mean, if you want to go down the pub, well, there's the Mucky Pup hardly a fifteen-minute walk away." Carole-anne shrugged and went on flipping through the pages of some beauty magazine, stopping now and then, looking (she had informed Jury earlier) for a new hairdo.

To think any model's hair in those glossy pages could look better than Carole-anne's beautifully unkempt, easy-come, easy-go, ginger-gold hair was ludicrous. Jury said, "He's telling me a fascinating story and it's taking a long time to do it."

"It sounds like what's-her-name? Who was going to get beheaded if she didn't keep the king interested?"

"Scheherazade."

Carole-anne sat on the sofa in Jury's one-bedroom flat that looked out on the street and its oblong of park. Carole-anne's was on the third floor, and in between, on the second, was a flat of doubtful provenance, as it appeared to belong not so much to Stan Keeler as to Stan's dog Stone. Jury thought he heard Stone walking about up there.

Carole-anne wet her finger and applied it to a page, looking at it and then turning the magazine round to face Jury. The photo showed a ridiculous "do," the model's hair short and standing up in spikes.

"Hm. Sure, if you want your head to look like the Statue of Liberty's crown."

"Very funny. I just was thinking something short and neat."

"Stay out of hair-cutting emporiums. There's no way to improve on what you've got."

Narrowly, she looked at him, suspicious of his compliment. Then satisfied Jury had spoken honestly, she let the magazine lie in her lap and picked up another Jury-bashing topic. "What's going on about your job, then?"

"I'll be called in probably next week and my fingers whacked by the assistant commissioner and then made to stand in a corner." He drank his tea from the teacup resting precariously on the arm of his chair.

"So are you still suspended?"

"I'm not exactly on suspension. It's something else, some rarefied version of suspension while there's an inquiry. My guess is that our PR people—I'm assuming we must have one or more—think public opinion is so much in my favor suspension might be bad for the Met's image. To tell the truth, I'm rather enjoying my freedom."

Carole-anne sat forward so suddenly the magazine slipped from her lap and her turquoise blouse slipped off one shoulder.

That went well. Jury smiled.

"Are you saying you might just up and bloody *quit*?"

Here was a possibility far worse than all the storytelling dinners in London! It could mean that Jury was free, free to shake the dust of Islington off his shoes and go anywhere at all, *live* anywhere at all.

"Only if my two thousand shares of IBM and Microsoft split. Until that happy day, I'll be stopping here, as usual."

Relieved, she fell back against the sofa and took up her favorite I-told-you-so topic. "I told you, remember? That you shouldn't be going into that house without a warrant! I was sitting right here when I told you and Cody that."

"Actually, you were standing over there"—he nodded his head to indicate the kitchen doorway—"with a spatula in hand and a plate of sausages when you told me." He smiled. Clearly, no loss-of-memory disease had hit him yet.

Wearily she sighed. "Look what it's come to."

He waited a tick for her to tell him what it had come to, but she must have found it too bloody obvious to say. Apparently it had to do with Jury's getting sloshed every night in the Old Wine Shades with a stranger.

"I had to go into that house, warrant or no."

"No, you didn't. You ought to've used Correct Police Procedure."

He heard the capitals sounding in what had become her favorite phrase of late. "I *had* to." Why did no one except for DI Johnny Blakely and Melrose Plant understand this? "I didn't have a choice."

"Well, you're always telling me how a person has to go along with the system—"

Jury had never told her that in his life.

"—or otherwise we might just as well slip back into the Dark Ages."

"We have done anyway."

"Don't be daft. Now you're saying that Correct Police Procedure—"

Apparently, her all-time favorite.

"—might just as well pack it in."

Jury slid down in his chair and looked ceilingward. Pacing, back and forth, a tiny clicking of dog nails. "Why aren't you carting Stone around? Why is the poor dog wandering around up there all by himself?"

"I just was up there with him when you came in. I've got to take him out." She checked her watch. "Mucky Pup's still open. Fancy a drink?"

Despite the fact that he thought he and Harry Johnson had just drunk London dry, he said, "Good idea. We can take Stone with us."

The caramel-colored Lab accompanied them to Upper Street, stopping as they walked along every once in a while to investigate some tree or plant as if he were picking up clues, but finally finding nothing in the neighborhood much worth his notice. While they walked, Jury talked about Mungo.

"Well, fancy that!" Carole-anne was completely rocked by that intrepid hound's finding his way back to Chelsea all on his own. Jury didn't believe he had, but it sounded good.

Jury said, "Do you think if someone took Stone and dumped him somewhere else that he'd find his way back?"

"You do, don't you?"

"Oh, thanks."

15

Sergeant Wiggins was stirring his morning tea, not with a spoon, but with a long thin object that could have been a twig, a root or a finger dropped off by forensics.

Jury was training himself not to ask, and not succeeding, except he managed to get round a direct "What is it?" by making a comment. As now: "Yes, I'll have a cup, but I want a spoon to stir it, a proper spoon, and not that thing you're using."

This of course was tantamount to "What is it?" since Wiggins would have to explain. "It's vanilla bean, isn't it?"

"What? Why in hell would you be stirring tea with it?"

"It's been found to be good for the digestive tract."

Jury had draped his jacket, an elderly brown tweed, over the back of his chair and was rolling up his sleeves as if preparing to dive into a sea of casework. "Wiggins, your digestive tract has probably gone home to its mother. Does nothing stop in your stomach before it barrels right into your intestines? You've got enough digestive aids—black biscuits, herbs, roots and leaves—to rid an entire nursing home of irritable bowel syndrome."

Wiggins's sigh was long-suffering. "You seem a bit out of sorts today, if you don't mind me saying."

"Considering I might be out of work tomorrow, yes, I do mind you saying." Jury was opening and shutting drawers, looking for nothing unless it be Divine Intervention or at least Divine Explanation for his troubles.

"You exaggerate so much. Dr. Nancy called about that Soho shooting."

Jury smiled. "Did she want me to call her?"

"No, she wanted you to come to her."

Talk about Divine Intervention.

Wiggins added, "It's that shooting in front of Ruiyi? Danny Wu's place? In Soho?"

Jury shrugged into his jacket, wondering how many more questions Wiggins would ask to establish the geography. "In London?"

"What?"

"Nothing. See you."

Dr. Phyllis Nancy, in her green lab coat apron and pale-green plastic cap (looking as if she'd emerged from a beautifying sauna), looked up from the cadaver on the stainless-steel table and smiled.

"Phyllis." Jury smiled back.

"This was blunt trauma." She was speaking of the man who'd been downed by a gun outside of Danny Wu's restaurant. The one Racer claimed had been murdered by Danny. "I mean the blow that killed him, not the bullet, oddly enough. There's a heart bruise, which is like a heart attack. The bullet went straight through, nicked a few organs—trachea, esophagus—came right out the back. Do you think"—she pulled her apron over her head and the cap off it—"I could have another look at the crime scene?"

"Oh, indeed you can. The restaurant is just opening around now for lunch. Or did you bring your Betty Boop lunch box?"

"It's not Betty Boop. It's dinosaurs. Just hold on and I'll be back in two minutes."

She was, too. Phyllis was spot on time for an autopsy or for lunch. She was famous for her promptness.

Soho was as usual crowded enough to stop the Chunnel train. Phyllis, with her ginger hair, her brilliant smile and her ID, had the customers in line for Ruiyi parting like the Red Sea. Having cleared this pathway of air, she brought out a heavy-duty tape and measured that path from curb to inside the door, where the line of customers started. She wrote down the measurement, put pen, notebook and tape in her bag, smiled at them all and said, "Thanks."

Jury said, "Phyllis, what were you doing?"

"Nothing," she murmured, "but now we're at the head of the line."

Seated in a room filling up fast, their table was immediately visited by Danny Wu, the owner. "I don't know why people think a shooting's bad for business. The lines have been even longer than usual, and the MPD eating here also, well, that's almost as good as Bruce Springsteen. Almost."

"Thanks."

Danny Wu was, as always, impeccably dressed by either Hugo Boss or Armani. The restaurant hummed both upstairs and down. Little bowls of food appeared out of nowhere. From behind Danny's back—at least that's what it looked like—a clay teapot was plopped down, and, when Danny moved, little teacups were placed beside them by the hands that belonged to one of the owner's many cousins. They ordered sweet-and-sour shrimp and fish and several side dishes, including rice.

"And is Sergeant Wiggins keeping all right?" Danny asked.

"Brilliantly. Don't tell him we were here without him."

Wiggins adored this place. He was introduced to any number of health-promoting roots and shoots.

"How dapper," said Phyllis as Danny moved on. "He's very attractive, isn't he?"

"He is. He's also very suspect."

Phyllis poured the tea. "What do you mean?"

"Danny has his fingers in a lot of pies."

"You don't think he was the shooter, do you?"

"No, of course not. Had he been, the shot would not have been lying on his doorstep. Danny is not messy. No, the victim is probably some member of one of the God knows how many Asian gangs that operate here."

Phyllis sighed. "There you go, talking shop again."

The little black-haired waitress set down their various dishes, shrimp and fragrant rice.

"It's actually not my shop at the moment."

"Oh, lord. Are they still messing about with that? Maybe the next time a five-year-old child is shot in the back, we should drag the commissioner along. Give him a bloody taste of it." She speared a piece of sweet-and-sour shrimp as if she meant it. "Your victim here, though, he wasn't shot outside. My guess is he was in this room here and staggered back and fell onto the pavement."

Jury looked a question.

"Well, that measuring bit did tell me something."

He feigned sadness, his tone desolate. "So it's not me, after all. You weren't just making up a reason to come to lunch with me."

"Don't be such a baby." She studied the intricate bone structure of her unfileted fish. "How do I do this?"

"My God! You're our chief pathologist and autopsyest! And—"

"Autopsy*est*?

"—you can't sort that fish's spinal column?"

She removed the bones as cleanly as if she were unzipping a zipper.

Danny Wu was slipping about the room like a well-tailored wraith. He had that ability to turn up at your elbow and you not aware of him.

Jury told Phyllis that Danny's mother must have been a truly courageous woman; she had risked her life on many occasions to get him out of Beijing. Then Danny had risked his own to get out of Shenzhen. Maybe in the course of having to use your wits—or your power of persuasion—to break free of a place, a person picks up some bad habits. Like killing people.

"Or bad company."

Jury nodded.

"Has he ever been indicted?"

"No. He hasn't got form; he's much to adroit and clever for the likes of me."

"I seriously doubt that."

This had brought Harry Johnson to mind. "Let me tell you a story."

It lasted through the crispy fish, their glazed banana dessert, which Phyllis claimed was a miracle of tastes and textures, and was now working on her second order of it, and through the third pot of tea and a long line of Ruiyi fans who were coveting their table, willing Jury and Phyllis to leave. Jury couldn't have cared less.

Phyllis didn't take her eyes off him in all the time it took to tell the story of the Gaults. She had shaken her head a few times, obviously in near disbelief.

"So there will be another, if not the final, installment tomorrow night. What do you think?"

"I don't know what to think," said Phyllis. "Is this Harry Johnson reliable?"

"Seems to be. Of course I thought at first it was just a huge put-on, one of those man-walks-into-a-pub stories. I mean, really, 'The dog came back.'"

She smiled. "He's pretty good."

"Harry? Or Mungo?"

"Harry. You haven't heard yet from Mungo. It sounds as if he's just observing."

Jury laughed. "I must say after getting through three of those Old Wine Shades and dinner evenings, I think he's telling the truth, the truth as he knows it, of course."

"What about the husband, Hugh? Couldn't you speak to him?"

"He's in a place called the Stoddard Clinic."

"I know that facility. It's got an excellent reputation. The staff there is very good. Is this Hugh Gault psychotic? Or is he there more for mental exhaustion?"

"The latter, I think; I think Harry said he'd gone there of his own free will."

"So you could at least see him. I mean, just to see—"

"If he exists?"

She nodded.

Jury looked at his empty teacup. "I expect I could. Somehow, though—"

"You'd rather take the tale on its own merits. Or perhaps you'd rather not know." She smiled. "Well, it's a rather good story, certainly."

"You mean, I'd rather not spoil it?"

She nodded. "Maybe."

Jury was reminded of the boy on the train from Newcastle. "I had a bet with him that this was the train going to Swansea. He claimed London. Of course it was the London train. And the odd thing was, there were people he could have asked who would have proven him right. He avoided all of them: the porter with the tea trolly, the boy's own mother, the conductor who came through announcing the stops. He deliberately turned away from them."

"Did you ever read that Hawthorne story called 'My Kinsman, Major Molineux'? The boy comes to town looking for Major Molineux. It's never made clear *why* he's looking for him. He avoids asking the obvious people, such as the police. Instead he asks a prostitute, a drunk, a beggar. He wants to find Major Molineux disgraced, and when he does come upon a man tarred and feathered and being run out of town, he knows it's Molineux. The story's brilliant. Any psychiatrist would drool over it."

Jury propped his head on his fist and regarded her. "You're thinking I'm that boy?"

She bit into the hard coating of the candied banana. It sounded like thin ice cracking. She said, "If you're lucky."

That threw him and he laughed. "Lucky? Wait a minute: you think it's good fortune to be deceived by a stranger's story?"

"When did you decide this Harry Johnson was deceiving you? I'm not so sure, from what you've said. You met him what, four or five nights ago? Had dinner with him three times, but you've never checked up."

Jury felt defensive, as if he'd come under some revealing light. "Well, if you believe that—"

"I didn't say I believed it. But Harry, who's to say what he believes? He's the one telling the story."

"It's true I haven't checked up on the facts, but then it's really none of my business, is it?"

She held her teacup in both hands. "Is *that* the reason?"

"I just meant—" Jury didn't know what he meant. He shrugged. "Sergeant Wiggins thinks Johnson knew who I was that first night. Wiggins thinks he could have followed me to the pub and is pulling me in for some purpose I don't have a clue about."

"Why?"

"I don't know. I don't agree with Wiggins, though. Sounds too outlandish." Then Jury remembered Harry had asked him—if not asked, suggested—he visit Winterhaus. He told Phyllis this.

"Really? And are you going to?"

Jury thought about this. "I think perhaps I will. Tomorrow."

She looked at him for a long moment. She had the greenest eyes he'd ever seen, except for Melrose Plant's. "Take someone with you."

She bit into the glazed banana. Thin ice cracking.

16

Melrose Plant sat in his favorite club chair in the Members' Room with coffee, the *Times* and a book. As he waited for Richard Jury he drank his coffee and read his book, looking up now and again to see yet another chin drop on another chest while another snore rippled the edge of another newspaper. It was eleven A.M. but it might as well have been the Dawn of the Dead.

He frankly thought this little outing into Surrey was a wild goose chase, but he didn't mind at all going along with Jury. Soon, somnolence would overtake the whole of Boring's, not just the members, who were always dozing off, but also the porters, and even the occasional winged thing, fly or moth, suspend itself in a honeycomb of sunlight coming through one of the high windows. The very air was like a sleeping draught but Melrose resisted the temptation to take a nap—surely he had not reached that stage in life where napping was a commonplace.

It didn't help that he was reading *The Gourmandise Way,* in the hope of regaining Polly Praed's trust, although he wasn't exactly sure why he wanted it. After the eighth victim had been dispatched by poison in the foie gras, Melrose shoved the book between cushion and chair arm. He worked it out that the next murder would have something to do with mushrooms; mushrooms were always popular in crime fiction as a method of poisoning. Death's head mushroom or something like that. On the other hand, anyone in this book who had been around for eight murders and was stupid enough to eat his mushrooms on toast deserved what he got.

Melrose yawned. Well, he would just close his eyes for a moment . . .

"Taking a nap?"

Melrose jerked awake, his wild eyes scanning the room for the source of this question, even though the source stood directly in his line of vision. "What? What?" he bleated.

"You suit the place to a *T*," said Jury, looking pointedly at the gentlemen sitting around in pleasant states of doze, slipped down in their chairs, heads on shoulders.

"Oh, don't be ridiculous. I just had a very bad night. Couldn't sleep a wink." Except for the seven or eight hours of winks.

"I'll bet. The coffee, the *Times*, the fire, the chair . . ."

"You sound like Polly's Detective Plod. He lists things endlessly."

"Hell, at your age, I'd be napping every chance I got. May I have some coffee, too?"

Melrose held up his cup as a signal to the young porter walking through.

Jury sat down in the wing chair usually occupied by Colonel Neame. "It's rather nice, the freedom." He stretched out his long legs. The porter turned up not only with a cup but also with fresh coffee. Jury thanked him.

"You wouldn't last a week if you were free of that job."

"Ah, but I *have* lasted a week. Yes, that's just about right." Jury ticked off the days on his fingers.

"Look what you do with your so-called freedom. Report to your office and go out and find something to solve."

"It found me. So, are you ready? Or do you want to go up and lie down and get your strength back?"

"Oh, ha ha. Let's go."

17

They pulled into one of the slanted parking spaces outside Forester and Flynn Estate Agents, walked up the shallow steps to the raised pavement and went in.

Melrose said he'd hang about outside to look at all of the properties for sale stuck in the windows on cards. "If this thatched cottage is a quarter million quid, then Ardry End should pull in about three billion."

"Come on, you're the party who wants to lease Winterhaus."

"What? Since when?"

"Drag out one of those Earl of Caverness cards you carry around."

"I do not carry those around."

"Yes, you do."

"And why didn't you tell me your plan earlier?"

"Because I didn't want to listen to you whine all the way here. Look, you're interested in leasing this house. In the event this agent might decide to come along, don't let her."

"And how do I avoid that?"

"You pull rank. You're the aristocracy, after all. You should have pulling rank down to a fine art."

"Well, you're Scotland Yard CID. *You've* got a ton more authority than I have."

"Yes, but I don't want her to think that's the reason I came. Anyway, Lord Ardry has already called to make this appointment."

"Oh, really. Funny, I don't remember."

"You were asleep at the time. Come on." Jury held the glass door open. "Agent's name is Marjorie Bathous. Mrs., I think."

Melrose grumbled as they entered and walked to the other end of the room, where sat a middle-aged, still-pretty woman who was one of the three agents in the office and who seemed to be expecting them. Or him, at least.

Melrose extended his hand across the desk. "Mrs. Bathous?"

She smiled and shook hands. "You must be Lord Ardry. I'm Marjorie Bathous. I'm so happy you're interested in this property."

Jury thought that Marjorie Bathous, in her dark suit and white silk blouse, was the very template of the professional woman. She was probably born wearing navy blue. He smiled at her and her own smile slipped off Melrose and rested on Jury.

"How did you hear about Winterhaus?"

"From him." Melrose flipped his hand toward Jury. "He handles this sort of thing—" A foot descended on Melrose's instep.

Jury stretched out his hand. "Richard Jury, New Scotland Yard CID." He smiled brilliantly, and said, "But I'm not here in any official capacity, only accompanying Mr. Plant. I wanted a drive in the country."

Marjorie Bathous looked pleasantly astonished as she took his hand. The other hand went to her perfectly coiffed brown hair.

Jury's look at Melrose was telling him to take up the slack or they'd be bogged down in New Scotland Yard. Marjorie Bathous would have good reason to want to talk about that event a year ago at Winterhaus.

Melrose began his pitch as Jury looked around. It was an office filled with a great deal of dark wood—desks, paneling, coffee tables, twin sofas meant for clients. A sort of fence with a small gate much like that in a courtroom ran across the middle of the room. There were a couple of men, other agents sitting at two mahogany desks, one in front of the other. The man at the first desk had turned to the one behind him. They were talking, or one was, telling the other a story, perhaps. Jury could hear nothing of what they said. For an office that did a lot of business—and he could tell Forester and Flynn certainly wasn't hurting—it seemed so quiet. Jury took a

seat in one of the several wooden chairs that lined the agents' side
of the gate.

"I've been looking for a largish place, one with land around it."
Melrose hooked his wallet out of a rear pocket, opened it and withdrew one of his old cards. He ignored the beginning of a snicker behind him. He carried them in case of an emergency, though God
only knew why there'd be an aristocrat-needed emergency.

"And the countess?" Marjorie Bathous suggested.

Melrose took it as a suggestion that he might have forgotten the
countess. "Oh, well, there isn't one if you mean by that my wife;
there's just an old auntie who wants to live nearer London and insists
upon large rooms and trees. I shall probably visit at the weekend."

"Now, Lord Ardry . . ." She set about describing the property in
far less detail than Jury's secondhand description had done. "You
see Winterhaus hasn't been occupied for some time."

Jury said, "We heard something unfortunate happened there."

"Where did you hear that?"

Neither affirming and or denying. Perhaps she was afraid of
launching a full-scale investigation by New Scotland Yard. "I expect it's just a rumor. You know. And a friend was talking with the
owner—a Mr. Torres?"

"Mr. Torres, yes, well." But she said no more.

What Jury wanted was confirmation that a Mr. Torres was indeed the owner. Did indeed exist.

The first confirmation had been she herself. But, really, this
need for confirmation that these people in Harry's story actually
were—that was slightly obsessive, wasn't it? Would Harry Johnson
have told him *You should go there and see the house* had there been
no Marjorie Bathous, no Ben Torres?

Melrose nodded. "If you'd just give us your details on the
house—could the lease be done for five years? That long?"

"Yes, of course. Longer if you like." She drew the property information sheet from one of several stacks on her desk and handed
it to Melrose. "Right here."

She had not mentioned the Gaults, and no wonder. Worse to have gone into the house's history. Assuming that history had not been conjured up by Ben Torres's mother. "What I meant by 'strange history'—I was thinking more about the woman and her son who seem to have gone off in the process of viewing your properties."

Clearly, she didn't care for the link between the "going off" and viewing "her" property. Still, she was quite brave about it, quite matter-of-fact. "Oh, yes. You're speaking of Mrs. Gault and her boy. You know I did wonder about them. It was quite strange that she didn't come back. But there was no *certainty* she'd been to Winterhaus. I mean that had been her intention, to look in, but there was no way of knowing if she actually *had*. The boy was only eight or nine, I believe. But what happened, then?"

"We don't really know."

Marjorie Bathous shook her head, puzzled. "She was to look into two houses along that same road, and I know she'd stopped at Lark Cottage—she wasn't interested in it, though. 'Too quaint, too English' was the gist of what she said. It's also for sale. I thought, really, it would be just the thing as it's much smaller than Winterhaus, and there were only three in the Gault family, and I think it was just to be a weekend place. The owners are a lovely elderly couple—" She stopped talking and looked at Melrose. "I should have mentioned this place to you. Perhaps you'd like to view it?"

"No, I only—"

"Yes," said Jury, kicking Plant's foot away from his chair leg and saying to him, "you might as well." Then to the agent, "It's on the way, you said?"

"Only about a half mile between the two houses. I can call the owners and let them know."

As she turned away with her mobile phone, Melrose said, sotto voce, "Why see this cottage?"

"For the obvious reason: Glynnis Gault did."

"Oh. Well, she probably saw that petrol station we passed outside of town. Should we stop in there, too?"

Jury shook his head. "Remind me never to offer you a job."

"Okay. Never offer me a job."

Marjorie Bathous flipped her phone shut as she swung her chair around to face them. "They'd be delighted. I told them in about a half hour, which is plenty of time. You can get there from here in twenty minutes quite easily. Their name is Shoesmith." She was writing it down, together with the address, the phone number and directions, including a small diagram.

Estate agents were always so efficient. Maybe he should offer *her* a job.

Marjorie Bathous brought all of these items together and put them in a manila folder. She slipped in the property details of Winterhaus and Lark Cottage. She looked at the small picture of the house on the sheet. "It's quite a lovely spot."

"Yes," said Melrose.

She opened a drawer and took out keys with a little tag attached on which was a number. She handed these to Melrose. "Unless you'd like me to accompany—?"

The two agents came to the end of their ghostly conversation and laughed and returned to their work. Jury watched them for no particular reason. Parts of Harry Johnson's story came back to him. He felt it was by turns puzzling, sinister, sad, ominous.

They rose and thanked Marjorie Bathous and went back to the car.

18

It was one of those narrow roads bordered by hedges and dry stone walls, sheep off in the distance, recent rain with the trees still raining, a walker with a blackthorn stick and two Labs sniffing along and quick light on the white feathers of a rise of geese.

England. Melrose sighed.

"There's a wheelbarrow," said Jury. "And a cow."

Melrose was driving. "Oh, I wonder which is which."

"Just in case you didn't see them."

"You mean as they're taking up the entire road?" Melrose beeped his horn. "Ever seen a cow jump?" It didn't, but there was startlement.

"How childish," said Jury. "You really crave excitement, don't you?"

Cow and cowherd passed by, slowly, cow looking the more intelligent of the two—of the four, if it came right down to it.

"It's not much farther," said Jury, consulting the agent's map. In another minute, he pointed. "There it is—Lark Cottage."

Melrose slowed, pulled into the short drive. "Well, look at it: it *is* cute, isn't it? How very English."

The Shoesmiths—"I'm Bob and this is the wife, Maeve"—were delighted to make their acquaintance, especially Scotland Yard CID. That was too thrilling for Maeve, who was settling in with tea and biscuits on one of the several overstuffed dark-brown chairs with stiffly laundered antimacassars on the backs and arms. Jury looked around the room at the different patterns Maeve had chosen: the fleur-de-lis design of the wallpaper, the toile curtains crowded with old-English figures and the crushed roses in the carpet. Even the little wastebasket was decorated with vines and leaves. This mix of patterns Jury found poignant, for some reason, as if it reminded him of a home he didn't remember.

It took Melrose all of two seconds to hate the furniture. He hoped the Shoesmiths would fare better as he bit into a biscuit. Maeve was rattling on about Lark Cottage and its many advantages.

Bob said, "It's the old black beams that make it, don't you think? 'Course, we men, we got to lower our heads to keep from gettin' bashed by these lintels." As if it were really a joke, he laughed.

"Now, we've the three bedrooms, two up and one down," said Maeve. "The one down is en suite. But there's a toilet and bath upstairs, too." She looked from Jury to Melrose uncertainly. "Which of you—"

"That would be me, madam," said Melrose. "I don't require much room, or, rather my aunt doesn't; it's for her I'm looking. She wants a place nearer to London. And she wants a garden."

"Oh, well, our *garden* . . . you can see for yourself." Maeve made a sweeping gesture.

"Quite so," Melrose said, feeling himself growing stuffier by the minute. Pretty soon, you could toss an antimacassar on him and sit down.

"Kitchen's small but efficient," said Bob. "Got an Aga and even a newish dishwasher. One of those small ones that sits on the counter, you've seen those."

Yes, and they're ghastly, thought Melrose, makeshift and only big enough to wash a cat.

Jury said, "I recall a peculiar incident a year or so ago—woman and child who just disappeared from around here?" He smiled charmingly. "You'll have to forgive me, I'm not here in any official capacity, but when I heard about this house a mile or so on"—he inclined his head in that direction—"I naturally wanted to see it." Another charming smile.

Maeve was already smoothing stray brown hairs up into the roll in which she wore it. "Well, it was a bit peculiar, wasn't it,

Bob? Marjorie Bathous said she never heard from the woman again. Never did return the key, either. What was her name—Gall, was it, Bob?"

"Gault," said Bob. "A Mrs. Gault and her boy, he being about eight or nine."

"The Forester agent recommended that the woman stop here and see Lark Cottage. Indeed, Mrs. Bathous was quite enthusiastic. We were on the lookout for them, of course, and I would have tea ready, and when we saw the car out there parked along the road and her out and seeming to be using one of those mobile phones—"

"I thought probably she was calling Forester—that estate agency—to see if she got the right place, so I got out there quick as I could," said Bob.

"It says Lark Cottage clear as day; I don't know how she could've missed it," said Maeve, helping herself to a Caedmon biscuit.

Bob went on. "Nice woman she was and her boy was ever so nice and quiet. Well-brought-up lad. Even that dog of theirs had good manners." Bob chuckled.

"We showed her over the house and quite complimentary she was. I gave them a cup of tea. They lived in Chelsea, she said." Maeve passed the biscuit plate again.

"How did she seem, Mrs. Shoesmith?"

"Why, just pleasant, not tense or moody, not depressed or anything."

"How long were they here?"

"Oh, about a half hour, I think."

"No, Maeve. More like an hour, maybe forty-five minutes, but no less," said Bob.

Jury observed Bob Shoesmith. He would probably make a good witness. Jury leaned back and looked upward, studying the ceiling.

As far as Melrose was concerned, both of the Shoesmiths had forgotten their visitors' mission here. Make that three—Jury, free-lance copper. He was going on again about Winterhaus, asking who the owner was.

"Would we be knowin' their name, Bob? Was it Spanish or sort of Italian? Toro? Was that it?"

Bob closed his eyes to help him think, snapped them open again. "Torres! That's it. Torres."

Maeve said, "What with livin' a half mile away, we can't really count Winterhaus our neighbor. It does get lonely out here. It's why we're movin', see. But we can't do much about that till we sell up. Would you be wantin' more tea?" She held the pot aloft.

"Oh, no thanks. Then I guess you've never been inside?" said Jury.

"No." She poured herself a cup. "No, only from outside I've seen it." She colored a little and smiled. "Now, I must admit, since it's been empty I've walked around there. Even peeked in a few windows. And walked out back. Only to see why it was empty, I mean if there was somethin' could explain why, only that."

Jury sat forward a little, smiling. "And did you find any reason it should be?"

Maeve Shoesmith was thinking. "It's awful . . . desolate, I'd say. I mean, I guess Lark Cottage is out here in the back of beyond, but ours is different, so." She looked at Jury. "I can't say more'n that. Only, such a pretty place, or was. Of course the gardens are mostly gone now and it looks a bit rough. Then there's the woods, and the woods look awful cold to me." She rubbed her arm as if she'd felt a sudden chill.

Jury would have asked more except he didn't want it to appear this was the real reason they'd come to this place. He would have liked to get her to talk more; Maeve Shoesmith, unlike her husband, who was into details, she was into mood.

"And I'm thinkin'," said Maeve, "only would it not be too big for your aunt? Would it be too much to have the care of?"

"My aunt," said Melrose, "is peculiar in that regard; she likes big houses; she likes to roam."

"Isn't she going to look the property over herself?"

"She needn't. She trusts my judgment. I see this is an unusually wooded area. She doesn't really like trees."

The Shoesmiths looked blank. So did Jury.

"Doesn't like trees?" said Bob.

Melrose nodded. "Well, this has been most delightful!" He made signs of pushing off—slapping his thighs, rising, resettling his jacket. He looked at Jury, who appeared to have forgotten who he came in with. "We'd best be going," he said pointedly. *Remember? You're with me.*

Coming to his senses, Jury rose. "Thank you for your information about Winterhaus. It will come in useful, I'm sure."

Maeve rose, but Bob seemed still to have entered a little world of his own. He sat frowning, pulling at one of his thick eyebrows. Then he came back to the land of the living and with Maeve walked their two visitors to the door.

Said Maeve, "Well, in case your aunt would like to see Lark Cottage, we'd be most pleased to show her around, we would."

"Thanks so much, both of you." They shook hands.

"Good-bye, so." Maeve watched them walk to the old Bentley. She waved.

"Trees?" said Jury, dragging on the seat belt.

Melrose accelerated and backed up. "I was just trying to segue to the woods, for heaven's sake. Aren't the woods supposed to be sinister, or something?"

"Yes, but the segue turned out to be more interesting than the woods. I mean, what does one say about a person who doesn't like trees? It's a total conversation stopper. It's like saying she doesn't like flowers. Or grass or leaves or air. It brought everything to a full stop."

Put upon, Melrose sighed heavily. "Only trying to help is all. It was the first thing that popped into my mind."

A tattered field went by on the left. On the right was a low dry stone wall. "Really? It would be the *last* thing to pop into anyone else's. Indeed it would never pop at all." Jury raised his hand in greeting to a little boy with a burro. The boy did not return the greeting.

"I think you're diving right into this weird story as if you were a part of it. As if you were one of the elements reinventing itself."

"What do you mean?"

"I don't know. Sounds rather good, though, doesn't it?"

"No."

Melrose liked the sound of it anyway. "Consider Alice-in-Wonderland."

Jury made a strangling sound and slid down in his seat.

"Alice walking through that looking glass, finding herself in a world where none of the natural laws applied—"

"What about the first law?"

"What?" Melrose was annoyed at this interruption of his newly forming philosophical position.

"Alice is in the so-called real world at the moment before she steps in. So how does that work?"

Melrose sighed. "It's going *through* it that counts!"

"But to do that she has to go into it from reality's side. And on reality's side it's a natural law you can't do that—wait a minute." Jury was leaning forward, peering through the windscreen. "Isn't that the Swan up there?'

Melrose saw the sign. "Damn. We missed the house. We've gone too far."

"My fault. I was supposed to be lookout. Anyway, we both could do with a pint; we can go back after."

"I didn't see one single thing. And it's a big house."

"We were talking. When you're talking about walking through mirrors and not liking trees, you tend to miss things."

Melrose pulled into the Swan's small car park, parked and braked. There were several cars, a half dozen. "This place is to hell and gone and I can't imagine that road is a motorway. There's nothing around. Where do they get their custom?"

"From hell and gone, I expect."

They got out and walked up to the pub.

As at certain hours, the ones before Time is called, the denizens of any pub look more like part of the furniture than people, that was the case here; the some ten or twelve customers were stationed around as if it were a military installation, where the customers served as look-outs and suspicious-looking strangers were barred from entering. All pubs gave that impression at these slow times of day. Slow afternoons with nothing going for them but the drink and a line of chat.

When Melrose and Jury walked in, they were treated to an inspection that would have made a platoon proud.

"Pint of Foster's," said Jury.

"Same of Old Peculier," said Melrose.

"Ain't got that on tap. Bottled, though."

"Fine," said Melrose.

Jury nodded to a man as thin as a splint leaning against the old copper bar several feet away. The man returned the nod, joined by two others holding up the bar down a little farther.

Jury said to the barman, as he showed his identity card, "This is an old case, but I wonder if you recall about a year ago a woman disappeared from around here."

The barman nodded his head, looked thoughtful. "Ain't enough happens round here we'd be likely to forget that, right, Robin?" This was directed to the thin man who'd nodded to Jury.

"Shouldn't think so, Clive," said Robin. He gave a dry little cackle.

"No, can't say as I recall that."

"Police would have been round asking questions about her. You don't recall that?"

The barman shook his head. "Why? Something happen? I mean, to get Scotland Yard in on it?"

By now, three or four others had drifted up to the bar, hoping to get an earful.

"Any of you remember? She would have had a boy and a dog with her."

Heads were slowly shaken up and down the bar.

"Too bad Myra ain't here," said Robin. "She was talking about seeing them on the road somewhere."

"What did she say, exactly?"

Robin studied the air. "Now, let me think on that a minute."

Jury ran his eyes over the others in mute question. They shook their collective heads.

"All right. Where is Myra?"

There was a discussion about Myra's whereabouts, but no one knew for sure. "Usually, she stops in round about now," said Clive.

Jury said, "What's this Myra's last name?"

The barman looked blank; the other one who'd been talking tilted his flat cap forward and scratched his neck. "Now, I don't know I rightly ever heard her last name."

"Do you know where she lives?" asked Melrose.

That drew another lot of blank faces. The one in the flat cap offered, "Roundabout here somewhere. Maybe in Lark Rise?"

Jury took another drink, motioned to Melrose, who gulped down his remaining beer.

"Thanks, anyway. Let's go."

19

A mile or so later they saw that the stone wall on their right was higher and gated, though the gate was not only open but listing, as if sinking into the hard surface of the drive. A brass sign was embedded in the wall and hard to read. Had they not been watching for the property, they wouldn't have seen the inscription cut into the brass that said WINTERHAUS. They drove through the stone pillars and on up the rutted road to the house. It was Georgian, a gray façade, noncommital.

Melrose shrugged his overcoat farther up on his shoulders as they passed into a hall with a worn (but very good, Melrose pointed out) Persian carpet. The paneling in this hall was of a wood Melrose puzzled over. "It's not one of our common hardwoods," he said, running his hand over the wall like a blind man exploring the contours of an unfamiliar face.

There was, as Jury had been told, no furniture, except for what was in the drawing room. No portraits, no plaster or bronze busts in the several alcoves or niches that might have housed them. Nothing.

While Melrose talked, Jury didn't listen, but instead walked into a room to the right off the entrance hall. He stood looking at the windows—old leaded glass set in metal frames that looked too frail to hold the glass. They were casement windows and one was open, about a finger's thickness, so it was obvious the house wasn't at all secure. In his mind he suddenly saw another window, open not on a view of long lawns and dense pines and maples, but open to the sea—blue water, an intense blue, and a copper sun, heavy sunlight, hot sands. He did not recognize this landscape. Where had he seen it? A rogue memory of sorts. What had it to do with him? Slowly he shook his head several times, hard.

"What's the matter? I hate to say it, believe me, but you look as if you'd seen a you-know-what."

Jury half smiled. He pulled the window shut.

Melrose went on: "I'm surprised at you, messing up a secured crime scene. Fingerprints smeared, for instance."

"Oh? I didn't know it was one."

"Is this going to be one of those places that have people gibbering over evil forces?"

"I don't think it has anything to do with good and evil. Come on." Jury walked toward the next room.

Melrose had his arms clamped over his chest. "I'm cold."

Jury stood, his head tipped to one side like an older brother trying to hurry his younger one along. And another memory blanketed him. On the sand stood an older boy, arms crossed, impatient and annoyed and not really wanting to bother with him, Richard, and who opened his mouth and called. But there was no sound. Not from the boy or the waves, even though they were tall and crashing on the shore.

"You don't look so hot yourself, anyway."

Jury frowned. "I don't know, I seem to be remembering scenes from my childhood." He gestured for Melrose to follow him as he walked into the last room, the furnished one, the one where someone had served tea to someone else. He turned. Melrose was still fastened to the spot, arms crossed. "It's warmer in here."

Strangely enough, it was. The logs in the fireplace gave the impression they had just gone out, which of course they hadn't; they were rotted, crumbled ashes. There should be something in there, he thought, taking the poker from the stand—should be a note, a photograph, a letter, a notebook . . .

"What are you doing?"

"Looking around, obviously. Are you still cold?" Jury watched him trying to warm up his hands.

"Not as, certainly. I'm just blowing my frostbitten fingers back to life."

"You exaggerate everything."

"It's one of my talents. At least in here there's something to look at." Melrose's eyes traveled around the room—its wall of books, Adam fireplace, marble mantel. There was an elaborate bureau with silver inlays, a cream-colored Sheraton sofa faced two armchairs, also of Sheraton design, the three pieces sitting on a carpet that Melrose identified from his antique-appraiser-impersonator days up in Lincolnshire, as Kerman, somewhere in the ten-thousand-pound bracket. Against another wall sat a Regency commode, ivory and marquetry inlaid, above which hung a carved giltwood mirror, cousin to the larger mirror above the fireplace.

There were several paintings, oils and watercolor. Snow, winter light, windmills in this one with small figures skating and heavily dressed. Chill. This one was of a horse—only one—in snow up to his hocks and nothing but a few naked roots. Freezing. In this one, fog-covered ships, barely discernible and a winter sun setting behind. Not a shred of warmth in any of them.

The tea service sat on a silver tray on a handsome table. Melrose picked up one of the teacups, raised it to see its origin, noticed there was a trace of tea in the cup. How strange. He replaced it and picked up the teapot. He couldn't make out the stamp of the silversmith. "Someone's been having a tea party." He said this, he thought, to Jury, but Jury wasn't there.

"Hey!" Melrose felt absurdly anxious. *"Richard!"* Then he saw Jury coming through from the hall.

"I was upstairs. Totally empty, not a stick of furniture, not a bibelot."

"Well, this stuff's"—Melrose swept his arm to take in the room—"pretty valuable. That carpet alone would go for maybe ten grand. And that elaborate walnut bureau over there, God knows. That's from what I recall having been hastily schooled by Trueblood in my antique-valuer-days." He held up the cup. "The china is

Minton and someone's been drinking out of it." He showed Jury the cup with the dregs of tea at the bottom.

Jury remembered what Harry Johnson had said. He looked down into the cup as if he meant to tell a fortune, his own or Melrose's. "I wonder who? Marjorie Bathous? You know, it would be fairly easy to get into this house. Some of the windows aren't secured." He replaced the cup on the tray.

"Is all of this for anyone who chanced to be stopping? Prospective tenants, perhaps?" said Jury.

"Glynnis Gault?"

"And Robbie?"

"Don't forget Mango."

"*Mun*-go."

The French doors to the dining room stood slightly open. Jury had gone outside to stand on the narrow stone patio while Melrose looked again at the painting of the lone horse. Then he walked out to the patio.

"There's a child down there," Jury said.

"Where?"

"Off there." Jury pointed toward a little structure that must have been the Wendy house Harry Johnson had mentioned. "A little girl, by the Wendy house. Come on." Jury stepped onto a weed-choked stone walk and went down a grassy verge where there had probably once been flowerbeds.

Melrose followed. "We'll scare her."

Over his shoulder Jury threw back, "She scared me, didn't she?"

Melrose sighed and followed him.

The Wendy house was some distance from the main house, so she didn't see them coming; she was too engrossed in whatever she was playing at. When Melrose called out and waved, she stood up, but without haste as she pressed something to her chest, doll or stuffed animal, as if to protect herself, and yet she didn't seem anxious. Melrose was the anxious one. All he wanted to do was get back to Boring's and settle in with a Laphroaig whiskey. He could taste it.

This little girl was perhaps eight or nine and was probably too smart for her own good, or Melrose's, if the kids he had met up with were any example.

"Hello," said Jury. "My name's Richard. We were looking over the house."

Her brown-eyed squint was probably for Melrose, as if there were more—or better—to see. For Jury, the full-eyed treatment. "Are you going to live here?"

"I'm really looking it over for a friend."

"Oh. Is he the friend?" More squint-eyed appraisal.

Jury turned to look at Melrose with what was (Melrose could swear) the same expression as the one on the little girl's face. "No. The friend didn't come with me today."

Melrose was beginning to think they really were here to view the property.

Jury asked her, "Do you live near here?"

She pointed off in the direction of what might have been a crossroad. The direction she gave seemed to be through the woods.

"How do you get over here, then? Do you come through the woods?"

She nodded. "There's a kind of path."

Jury was sitting now beside her on the playhouse's single step. "Do you come here often?"

Clothing the bear she'd been holding in a yellow raincoat, she chewed her lip, but didn't answer.

"I won't tell anyone, promise."

"Okay, but you better not." She looked up at Melrose, who was still standing, and aimed that warning at him. "I come here nearly every day. Aunt Brenda doesn't want me to."

Melrose found a stump to sit on, presently occupied by a round-faced doll in a heavy-hooded coat. He picked it up.

She regarded him. "That's mine but you can sit there awhile."

Jury, Melrose noted, hadn't needed permission to sit on the step of the little house. He frowned at the doll.

"That's Oogli. She's an Eskimo."

Melrose looked more closely. "Inuit, not Eskimo." He was about to ask if she owned all the stumps around, but she turned back to Jury. "Aunt Brenda says this isn't our property and it's trespassing. I would have to ask before I came. But there's nobody to ask."

"So if there's no one to ask, what can you do?"

Her smile was a little thin—

(Stingy, Melrose would have said.)

—but it was more smile than they'd gotten so far.

Melrose couldn't resist saying, "But if you're gone that long and that often, doesn't this aunt ask where you've been?"

"Yes."

"What do you tell her? That you're taking a walk with that bear and Ugly?" He held up the doll.

"Oogli, not Ugly. No, I say I've gone to my friend Alice's." She tied the two strings hanging from the hood together under what chin the bear had. She adjusted the hood then.

"But doesn't your aunt ever call up Alice's mother to see if you're at her house?"

She shook her head. "Alice doesn't have a mother."

"What? Well, who does the poor child live with?"

"Nobody."

"But she has to sleep *somewhere*. She has to eat, for heaven's sake."

Jury stretched his legs out and said to Melrose, "Will you be through here anytime soon? Will you have Alice sorted?"

Melrose managed to look hurt. "I'm only trying to fill in the picture."

"No, you aren't; you're trying to show how smart you are," said Jury.

"He's not very." She said this with equanimity. She hummed a little in a self-satisfied way as she removed the bear's raincoat and went rooting for another outfit in her stack of little clothes.

Jury asked, "Have you been coming here a lot while the house stands empty?"

She nodded as she pulled a sweater over the bear's head.

"Have you ever seen people come here to look at the house? Like we're doing? Do you remember seeing anyone else last year?"

She looked off, thoughtfully. "Like who?"

"A woman and her little boy."

"Oh. Yes, I remember him; he was nice. He didn't talk, though. And he had a dog!"

This information was conveyed with more enthusiasm than she'd displayed toward Melrose certainly.

"He liked to bound around; he ran like the dickens, he did. Well, there's lots of space for running around here." She spread her arms wide. "We played and he gave me some of his candy. I mean the boy did. His name was—Robert? Bobby, I think. He didn't tell me; I only knew his name because his mum was calling for him. He gave me lemon sherbets."

"His mum, did you meet her?"

"No; I only saw her. She was at the bottom of the little walk calling for him. He didn't answer, and I told him he really should answer so his mum wouldn't worry about him. He just went off, back to the house."

"Did he say anything about the house? Whether his mum liked it or not?"

She shook her head. "Uh-uh. I told him there were ghosts."

Melrose snorted. "Ghosts!"

She nodded, not bothered by the scoffing.

Jury leveled a look at Melrose, then asked her, "Do you go up to the house, then, sometimes?"

She shook her head so vigorously, the very force of it said she was lying.

"Then," said Melrose, challenging her, "how do you see the ghosts?"

She gave him a look that was not unlike Jury's look. "In the woods." She had pulled a garment from the pile, a shirt covered with red hearts. She pulled off the sweater and held the shirt up to the bear.

"Have you seen anybody else here?"

She grew thoughtful. "There's a woman who I think takes care of things."

"The estate agent, maybe?"

She nodded. "Then a long time ago, last year I saw a man up there—" She pointed to the terrace. "But only for a minute."

"What did he look like?" asked Jury.

"I didn't see him good. He was tall. I guess he looked"—she glanced at Melrose—"like . . . you." She nodded toward Melrose.

She was making it up, for lord's sakes, thought Melrose. How could Jury listen to this drivel?

"Like Mr. Plant here?"

"Yes." She had Melrose in her sights and wouldn't give up, if she could help it. She was working the shirt over the bear's head.

"When was this? I mean, when last year?"

"Oh, I don't exactly remember. It was before my birthday—"

A Star Is Born. Melrose snapped a twig with his fingers.

"—and that's in July," she added. "I'm nine now." Her tone was a little puzzled, as though she mistrusted nine.

"About nine months ago."

"I guess."

"Are you afraid these people maybe would think like your aunt Brenda does that you're trespassing?"

"Yes. But there's nothing I can do about it."

Melrose's tone was sarcastic when he said, "You could not play here, that's one thing you could do."

"No. That's not going to fix things." She was quite certain on this point. And in the intensity with which she delivered this news, she didn't seem to realize she was punching out the bear's eyes. She breathed a world-weary sigh.

Melrose dropped his head in his hands and briefly considered punching out his own eyes. Didn't Jury *get* it? He was a detective, after all.

She said, "You don't understand. This is my favorite spot and I'm not letting people who don't even *live* here keep me away." Over the heart-littered shirt, she was buttoning up a moth-eaten little cardigan.

"That's very brave," said Jury.

"No, it isn't. I just don't have anywhere else to go."

The melancholy of that announcement made even Melrose sad. To have to inhabit a ghost world because there was no other place for you.

Jury looked up at the oyster-colored unpromising sky. "Do you come here in winter too?"

"Yes, I like it when it's snowing."

"It would be beautiful then."

She followed his gaze and both sat staring upward.

Now both their attentions were elsewhere, maybe he could take that spade from that bucket and bury Bruno.

In another minute or so the sky began to deepen toward night.

"I've got to go," she said, springing up from the porch. "Aunt Brenda doesn't let me be out when it starts turning dark."

"We'll drive you home," said Jury.

She seemed to take fright at the very suggestion. "No. I'll go my regular way." She pointed. "Along the path through the trees."

Melrose, delighted to be leaving, said, "I can imagine what auntie would say if she appeared with two strange men."

"Good-bye, good-bye," she called, having started for the path to escape people tinkering with her ritual.

Jury echoed her good-bye as she was swallowed by the trees.

"Well, that went well!"

They started their own trek back to the car and Jury said, "You know, if you'd pay more attention instead of needlessly arguing every little point—"

"Attention! I was hanging on every word."

"That must have been Harry Johnson whom she saw."

They had walked around the house instead of going through it. Getting into the Bentley, Jury said, "Try not to drive as if we're the only car on the road."

"Why? We are." Melrose let out the clutch and backed up.

Jury said, "My guess is she's gone into that house many times, but is keeping it a secret. Here's an old deserted house whose past she can freely make up. Make it be romantic, or unhappy or even fearful. Probably she doesn't want anybody coming around snooping."

"A child that age I'd think would be terrified of creepy things that go bump in the night—ghosts, ghouls, disembodied hands— that sort of thing."

Jury smiled. "Not her."

"Me, you mean, the so-called ghost who looked like me. It was all too transparent."

"I'm not so sure. You're tall, light-haired and today you're wearing that black coat. From any distance, one might think you were Harry Johnson."

"So *he's* been here."

"Of course. He came in Hugh's stead right after it happened. I mean right after Mrs. Gault disappeared. Maybe doing a spot of investigation on his own. Then he came back with Hugh. I told you all of this."

Jury watched the turning dusk, the trees, the fields, the farms, the richer ones whose crisscrossing white fencing spoke of horses, sleek and handsome racehorses. He thought of Nell Ryder and spoke of her to Melrose. Would he never come to terms with all that?

"Come on, Richard, Nell Ryder wasn't, well, she wasn't one of us, or at least not one of *me*. She operated in a whole different dimension."

"Strange thing to say."

"Look, she'd go along with us and our idiot ways until she saw something that needed her attention. In that case, those horses. They spoke, you know, her language. Or she spoke theirs."

They drove through Lark Rise, stopped at the estate agency and found it closed. Melrose slipped the key into the slotted box that said KEY RETURN and Jury looked at the shops, a few people in the local butcher's, the chemist drawing down his security blind.

Melrose said, "What is he keeping back?"

"Harry Johnson?"

"Yes."

Jury was silent, thinking. Then he said, "Perhaps that he was— is—in love with Glynnis Gault. That he would go to the place from which he thought she'd vanished, hoping he'd find some trace, some clue. I think that's possible."

Melrose waved that away. "You're ignoring a more sinister explanation."

Jury turned from the chemist's window to look at Melrose. "Such as?"

"What about his burying her on the property and returning, as we know all murderers do, to the scene of the crime?"

"Why?"

"Why? Well, it could have been as you said: he was in love with her. In a fit of jealous rage, he killed her and buried her in the woods. Together with her son."

"It strikes me as a strange place to do it, on a piece of property that might have tenants at any time and one that they have no connection to."

"But that's just it. Who would connect him with the crime? That man's rigged something; I can just feel it. I can't understand why you're not suspicious."

"Oh, I am."

"No, you're sold."

Jury laughed. "I'm *sold?*"

"Sold." Melrose fumbled a cigarette from a pack and jammed it in his mouth.

"You're not going to smoke in the car, are you?"

"I'll open the window." He buzzed it down.

"Have you become so slovenly in your smoking you don't even fill up your cigarette case anymore?"

"I've always been slovenly."

"Haven't you read about secondhand smoke? It's as bad—"

Melrose pounded the steering wheel. "I do *not* want a damned *lecture*."

"It isn't. It's only a comment."

Melrose tossed the cigarette out of the window. "I'll get the evil weed out of sight! Reefer madness threatens to overtake me."

"You always exaggerate things." Jury looked out of the window and up at the dense stars.

They drove in silence or in whatever version of silence one can on the A3 when Melrose punched the steering wheel again. "The dog! That damned Moonglow!—"

"Mungo," said Jury.

"Everytime I think I've got this mystery sorted, that damned dog turns up!"

"That's the easiest part of it." Jury yawned and slid down in his seat.

"Like Harry Johnson left him for dead, but the dog recovered and found his way back."

"No, actually I hadn't thought of that, brilliant deduction that it is. Are we going to have a drink at Boring's?"

"Yes. I'd sooner be chatted up by Major Champs and Colonel Neame than wonder about Mango."

"Mungo."

20

"Superintendent Jury! Let me get you a drink!" said Colonel Neame; this was seconded by Major Champs.

Getting one a drink was the first order of business in Boring's before anything else could proceed, including death.

"Thank you. I'm waiting for Mr. Plant." Or should it be Lord Ardry in here? Would one walk into Boring's without some sort of title? Some rank? Some number—the second, the third—appended to one's name? "Superintendent" worked well. "Commissioner" would have worked even better.

Colonel Neame had given the order to one of the porters and turned now to say, "You know, we've not yet gotten over that awful business in here a couple of years ago, have we, Champs?"

The "awful business" was the murder of one of Boring's distinguished members. A vanished love affair, the death of one's dog, the end of a war nonc could vic with a murder committed veritably under one's nose. No, nothing like murder as a springboard for nostalgia, a subject for reminiscence.

Jury's drink was delivered and he raised it. "To the good times, gentlemen."

And they answered by raising theirs.

Melrose appeared, hair damp, looking scrubbed as a three-year-old. He took his usual seat, wondering about having a usual seat. Was he getting as crusty as Champs and Neame? Well, he could think of worse ways of checking out—such as in his own living room across the way from . . .

"We should tell them," said Jury, "the story."

Melrose was surprised.

"It's not a secret. Go ahead." He looked at his watch and drained his glass. "I have to be going. I'm meeting Harry Johnson." He smiled, looked at Melrose. "Chapter four."

Nothing, thought Jury, could suit them better, nothing could be more welcome than a story like those bedtime stories that sustain us when we're children and that we listen to again and again, not bothered by the fact we know what's coming.

He thought about this in the cab taking its own sweet time on its way to the City.

You in a hurry, guv? the driver had asked when Jury climbed in. No, Jury had said; take your time.

The driver was whistling a little, in a good mood. Larking around, thought Jury, or something good had happened in his life. "I bet you get sick of it, don't you?" Jury said.

"Wha's that, guv?" He was searching in the mirror for Jury's eyes.

"Having to hurry. People wanting to go faster, faster."

The driver slapped the steering wheel. There was a lot of that going on today, for some reason. "You best believe *that.* It's the whole effing city, ihn't? And I want to tell them, it'll still be there—office, pub, wife—whether you get there in a minute or an hour."

They were driving along the Embankment—the long way round, Jury thought, but didn't care. Across the Thames were the fairy lights of the National Theater and the Tate Modern. Southwark always looked a little magical at night.

"Now, my girl, Minnie, strangest thing happened to her; right along here, it was—"

Jury sat back, thinking this might be the reason for the long way round.

"—said she'd just got outta her car when this punter rushes up to her, scares her half to death and o' course she thought he was going to mug her, but all he did was ask directions to Scotland Yard. 'Now *that,*' says Minnie, 'was a new pickup line if ever I heard one.'

"What he told her was he was being poisoned. So Minnie thought he was nuts, but she stopped there to hear him out. I tell her, 'Min, you never do things like that, love, *never.*' She says, 'But he looked so bad, Da, he looked to be on his uppers.' So she drives him to St. James's. And along the way he tells her he's from Brighton, where he's in the antiques business and for the last couple months someone's been slowly poisoning him. That he's getting sicker and sicker. No, it's not his imagination, and he's pretty sure it's his cousin.

"They get to New Scotland Yard and she pulls up in front of the main door and lets him out, whereas—"

Jury loved the "whereas."

"—there's a PC standing there, looks in through the passenger window, says, 'This isn't a hotel, miss. Move on.'"

Jury's cabbie again pounded his steering wheel.

"So then Min, she really wants to know what's going on inside and finds a parking place and goes in. The guy's sittin' there in the waiting area . . ."

Jury closed his eyes and listened or didn't listen by turns. He just let the words wash over him, imagining they were all there at Brighton beach—the driver and Min and the chap being poisoned, all watching the shingle to see what might turn up, the tide sliding in and leaving behind tiny shells, sea urchins, sea grass, sand dollars, a fag end, candy wrapper, plastic bottle—the detritus we all drop carelessly behind us like a trail of crumbs. Only we're not as clever or not as lucky as Hansel and Gretel and we don't get back. The tide comes in to wash it all away.

Jury was nearly asleep by the time they got to the City and Martin Lane. He got out, paid the driver, his ghostly companion across the Styx, and said, for he felt it was safe to guess, "She—Minnie—never found out the truth of it?"

The driver shook his head. "She got hold of a Brighton paper every week and she'd check the obits until one day nearly two months after it happened, there was this chap's picture. Well, the poor bugger up and died, right? He was fifty-three, pretty young, depending which side of it you're on, but the obit didn't give cause of death." He shook his head, took Jury's cab fare. Jury stepped out of the cab.

"Poor bugger should'a gone to the police."

"But he did, didn't he? Look where that got him." Jury slapped the top of the cab, and the driver was on his way.

21

Trevor, the barman, was happy to suggest something. "This"—he held up a bottle of Pinot Blanc—"is an absolutely glorious wine from Luxembourg, *Vin de Paille*. Pricey, but worth it."

Harry told him to pour. "How pricey?"

"This'll run you forty quid the half bottle."

"You certainly know how to spend my money, Trev."

"I certainly do." Trevor smiled and poured.

They were sitting that evening in their same bar chairs, with Mungo parked underneath.

Jury studied the wine bottle. A 1982. Was that a good year? Maybe for wine, but not for Jury. "Hugh Gault. What does his doctor say?"

"That he's overworked. Of course, the doctor doesn't tell me anything much as I'm not family."

"Denial, I'd imagine. Maybe it's what we all do at some point in our lives—deny. Or dive into work or booze to forget and keep forgetting. Hugh might have committed himself just to escape. He can sign himself out. Maybe he should."

"You could be right."

"If he had to slog through one day after another, it might help him; hell, it might even restore him. Do you see what I mean?"

"I do, yes."

Jury picked at the wine label. "He doesn't believe they're dead, does he?"

"No, he doesn't. They could be anywhere."

Jury wondered if he was to take that literally.

"Einstein distrusted quantum mechanics; he jokingly asked the question 'Is the moon not there unless I can see it?' "

"I'll drink to that." Jury raised his glass.

"No, no. The point is not that it *isn't* there, but that we can't *know* if it's there or not."

"The cat's alive, the cat's dead."

"Exactly. Nothing is real until you can measure it. And the act of measurement is part of the reality it's measuring. Look."

" 'Look'? I'd better or you'll disappear."

Harry laughed. Then he said, "Take a blood-pressure reading. The nurse can't know what it is until she straps that cuff around your arm and pumps. But the resulting pressure is that particular systolic and diastolic only in the act of measurement. Measurement means interaction. There is no way you can measure something without interacting with it. Measurement is not impersonal. It isn't an objective reality."

"The cat may be dead or the cat may be alive."

"You seem to be using this as a mantra."

"I think it's a good one. And I'm starving."

Harry checked his watch. "Dinner?"

Jury nodded, drank off the last of the wine. "We've got to drink the rest of this. I mean at forty quid, well . . ."

Harry laughed. "Thanks for reminding me."

There wasn't much left. He divided it between the two glasses, a long swallow each.

As Harry dropped some notes on the table, Mungo unsettled himself from under Harry's chair—from under both their chairs, really, for he'd stretched out under the two—and they left the pub.

They were sitting in a restaurant in Docklands, another dog-friendly one, or so Harry said. Jury wondered if the "friendliness" was occasioned by one big talking point, money, which Harry had clearly slipped the maître d'. The place was overpopulated with the up-and-comers and their mobiles. Nirvana, some of these places were.

"You were talking about Ben Torres. Go on."

Harry drank his water and then his wine. They'd been unadventurous and settled on a Burgundy. "According to Ben, his mother told him this person returned several times, always standing at the bottom of the garden at the end of the drive, simply waiting—or watching—she didn't know. She said she was working up the courage to walk out and ask him what in heaven's name he was doing—" Here Harry stopped and pulled out a small sheaf of paper, a few pages folded over. He opened them. "This story I have notes on; otherwise, I wouldn't remember the details."

Jury broke off a piece of a baguette. "You're doing pretty well at it."

"Finally, on the fourth or fifth night of it, not consecutive nights, for there were a few between for as long as a week, but on this night she was about to confront him, she opened the door to find he'd disappeared. Between the time she was inside the house, looking out and going outside, he vanished, he was gone. Couldn't have been more than thirty seconds, she said." He interrupted himself. "It sounds as if his mother was actually telling the story. But, of course, it's Ben's story." He stopped. "Is that important?"

Jury didn't think he expected an answer. He was asking himself.

When Harry stopped and took a roll from the bread basket, Jury thought that that was the end of it, all that Harry knew about the Torreses. He looked around the restaurant, into the shadows of its candlelit corners, as if they might contain the rest of the story.

"That was the end of it?"

Chewing, Harry shook his head, held up the pages. "Not exactly." He looked down at the paper.

Jury wondered why he felt relieved. "What then?"

"It was the end of this man's midnight vigils on the drive but not the end of his story. Shortly after that, perhaps a week after, one

night the gardener, who lived"—Harry looked down at his notes—
"on Laycock Road, was going home. There's a path through the
trees which he always took. About halfway in he heard something, a
rustling sound, which he took to be a fox or squirrel. But then he
heard a voice, only he couldn't make out any words. He walked a
little way into the trees, nearly stumbling over a man lying there in
great distress. The gardener, whose name was"—he turned a
page—"Cannon, William Cannon—was extremely frightened, not
of the man, but of the situation. He wanted to go for help, but the
man caught at his arm. Only just able to talk, he said, "Tell them to
leave this place." The words were so faint, Cannon had to put his
ear to the man's lips. "Cannon had been a gunnery sergeant in the
war and had seen so much of death, he knew the man would be gone
before he could even contact police or medical help."

Jury stopped munching. "Another story? I think this is number
four, or even five."

Harry looked puzzled.

"Well, the way I see it, we've got a story within a story within a
story within a story." He was recalling what Melrose had said and
was ticking these off on his fingers: "There's the story of Glynnis
Gault's disappearance; there's Ben Torres's story; there's his
mother's story; and now there's this man Cannon's story." On a
cocktail napkin, Jury drew four squares and said, "There's a fifth
one somewhere." He frowned.

Harry laughed. "I expect you're right. It gets further and further
away from the Gaults, I suppose."

"That's not what I was thinking." He remembered Melrose
Plant's comments.

The waiter had materialized before their table and launched
into that evening's specials. Jury ordered the Dover sole because it
was a marvel of simplicity, grilled, with butter. Harry ordered a
complicated fish, which had to swim through some serpentine
recipe on its way to the plate. Chilean sea bass, that was it. The
waiter departed to get their salads.

Jury asked, "Are you really so certain that Glynnis did not leave of her own volition?"

"Leave Hugh? No, I'll stick by that. They really loved each other."

It was heartfelt, Jury thought. It was also in the past tense. "Then possibly there was some other reason for leaving."

"The thing is, if leaving was in her mind, why in God's name would she take Robbie?"

"Or Mungo." Jury smiled as he felt the dog plop against his shoe. He looked under the table. Mungo returned his gaze. Jury thought he looked bored.

"Glynn wasn't like that—to walk out and take their son without any warning. She'd never have done that."

Past tense again. A bread bearer was back with another big, flat basket of rolls and baguettes. Jury took a roll, wondering if Mungo liked rolls. He broke off a lump and slipped his hand under the white tablecloth. There was snuffling and a quiet chomp.

"How was Robbie? How was he treated at home?"

Harry looked completely at sea. "You're not suggesting—you think Robbie was mistreated?"

The waiter had made a quick return and was setting down their salads.

"I'm not suggesting anything. It was a question." Jury cut off a bite of endive. "The thing is, you're determined that Glynnis Gault wouldn't take off because she was unhappy in her marriage. You're sure she wouldn't have disappeared of her own accord. Given, just for the sake of argument, she *did* disappear of her own volition, then what made her do it? She didn't want to leave her husband, so why did she? Robbie was okay, wasn't he?"

"Yes, insofar as I know." Harry frowned at his salad. Pears and walnuts. "Did I order this?"

"Yep." Jury had ordered the house salad.

"I must be drunk." Harry cut off a little bit of Stilton and topped off a bite of pear.

A couple dressed in Ferragamo blue and Armani gray glided into the chairs held for them by two waiters, who hovered for a few moments. Jury wondered who they were. Or what. The woman was wearing three rings on one hand. They were big enough to serve as brass knuckles, which would help when she got mugged.

The sommelier was back with a bottle of white, presenting it for Harry's inspection. Harry nodded. He and the sommelier exchanged a few words in French as the wine was uncorked, then poured. The sommelier then strolled next door where he had a lengthy conversation, again in French, with the handsome couple. The man spoke his French in a loud voice as if to signal to those near him that he did indeed speak it. Harry, on the other hand, had spoken it softly and far more swiftly and clearly did not mean to advertise his expertise.

Harry said, "The only thing I've ever heard them argue over was school. Well, I told you that. It's the reason Glynnis wanted a house near Lark Rise. That school is supposed to be very good. Autism can take a number of different forms; with Robbie, it was simply not talking, or speaking only minimally. Robbie had been doing just middling well at his current school, but Hugh didn't like the idea of uprooting him. It's what they argued about."

"Then Robbie wasn't given to fits of temper, excitability, violence?"

"No. Glynnis couldn't tell how he felt about school; she assumed he did only marginally well because he didn't like it, or wasn't interested or something like that. In any case, it wouldn't be cause for separation."

"Well, it certainly wouldn't explain what happened. Far from it. But he was okay with this excursion to Surrey?"

"Yes."

Jury still hadn't told Harry he'd been to the house, but he didn't know why. He asked, "Did you take Mungo?"

"Mungo was gone, remember?"

"Ah. Of course. So you haven't been there recently?"

"No." Harry shook his head, seemed to be giving his salad some thought.

"Do you think the dog could pick up some scent? I wonder if a retriever or a bloodhound could pick up something after a year."

"Well, Mungo isn't a bloodhound, that's certain. I'm not sure what he is. With those ears, though, he's certainly got hound genes. Hugh got him from a shelter."

"Good for him; he doesn't regard dogs as a status symbol."

Harry pulled up the tablecloth and looked, made some sort of *click click* noise.

Totally meaningless, Jury supposed, to an animal.

"Definitely not a status symbol." Harry laughed. "Glynn was never concerned with status, either. The right people, the right frock, the right address."

"She sounds nice; she sounds very likable."

"Oh, she was, she was."

"You keep using the past tense. Have you given up, Harry?"

"No. It's just that she's been gone so long now, she seems at such a distance."

"And Hugh? You said he didn't believe they were dead."

"Hugh thinks they're lost."

Jury frowned. "Lost? You mean amnesia? She's somewhere she doesn't know and can't find her way back?"

Harry drank his coffee and said, "No. Lost in another dimension."

Jury sat back. "What are you talking about? Or what's *he*? Is he really crazy, then?"

"No. He's a physicist. We only sound crazy. Hugh's main interest is string theory. Well, I told you that." He stopped and took another bite of his salad.

Jury stared. "Well, go on."

"It's a difficult concept to understand. String theorists argue that there are more dimensions than we experience. It's not four—three spatial and one time; it's *ten*—nine spacial, one time."

"Ten dimensions?"

"That's right."

Jury looked around—right, left, up, down. "Where are they?"

Harry laughed. "Where *are* they? Crumpled up, perhaps. So small you can't see them."

Jury gave him a look as he went on eating.

"Don't look at *me*, old man. I'm merely the messenger. However, if one believes, along with Einstein and Gödel, that time simply isn't real, that the past hasn't passed, it's not too difficult to accept."

Jury considered. "So there's no T. S. Eliot stuff—"

"What particular stuff do you have in mind?" Harry smiled.

Jury shrugged. "You know, the present and the past"—Jury inscribed a circle in air—"meet in the future—something like that. It's a circle. No, that sounds like Zen Buddhism."

"I don't know Eliot that well . . ."

"Neither do I, obviously." He speared a grape tomato from his salad.

"Gödel believed time is an illusion, in much the same way. Everything that happens—past, present, future—is laid out. Imagine tossing a box of puzzle pieces across the floor, turning them over, looking at them. They're all there without any relevance to past, present or future. . . . That, of course, is a terrible oversimplification."

"Don't not do it on my account."

"No one paid much attention to his incompleteness theory at first because they simply didn't understand what they'd heard when he delivered this as a paper at one of the conventions."

"Time! Here comes the fish."

Harry looked round to where the waiter—it always seemed to be a different one—was settling a tray on a stand. He whisked away their salads and put the sole and sea bass in their place. Harry's fish did not look as complicated as it had sounded, and the Dover sole was perfect.

"Incompleteness—"

Jury raised his hand, palm out. "Not yet. I'm still back there with the jigsaw puzzle. Look, if there's no time division, no past, present, future, then, if that's the case, someone could simply walk in from the past."

"The past doesn't exist—I mean as 'past.' Look at the idea of time travel. If one can indeed go back to a point in one's past, then that's to say the past is a fiction. But if you can rocket around in space, then you could do the same with time. Why not? The reference is spacetime. Einstein, again."

"So Glynnis and Robbie Gault may just turn up at some point?"

"Why not? It's amazing how physics and mathematics can free up our thinking, isn't it? The idea of ten dimensions is a whole school of thought. It's not just Hugh."

"But it's theoretical; it has no application to our day-to-day existence."

"Hugh would argue with you on that point, I'm sure. You don't think it's possible."

"How can I think one way or the other? How does all this relate to our actual living? We still bumble along using just the four dimensions. I'm sorry to be such a Luddite, but if it doesn't impact upon our four-dimensional selves—?" He shrugged.

"It would impact to hell and gone if you suspected your wife and son disappeared onto another plane of reality."

"There's a flaw in that reasoning." Jury smiled, then said, "Look, you don't think Hugh's gone just a little off the rails?"

"A little. I'm not saying I agree with him; I'm merely answering your question as to what Hugh thinks. Given there's been no explanation for what happened to Glynn and Robbie, and given Hugh's discipline—physics—from his point of view it's not crazy."

They ate for a while in silence.

Jury felt Mungo shifting around, either his paw or his head landing on Jury's shoe. He smiled. "What about Mungo? Mungo didn't go into one of those rogue dimensions with them. Why? I

should think it would be all of them or none of them. How does
Hugh explain that?"

Harry smiled. "That's a good point about the dog. No, Hugh
didn't mention the dog."

Jury wanted to laugh. "A 'good point'? A better point might be
that Hugh is into denial in a major way, don't you think?"

"Denial, maybe. He certainly sounds rational."

"I'm not saying he isn't, as you point out, string theory—"

"It would explain, you know, a lot."

"Hell, if it would only explain itself, I'd be happy."

"Why don't you come with me and meet him? I'm going to the
Stoddard Clinic tomorrow."

Jury looked at him. "So there really is a Hugh?"

"Of *course*, there's a Hugh." Harry laughed. "You still think I'm
winding you up?"

22

"Well, I don't see why you're having a meal with this person night after night," said Carole-anne, examining another lock of her ginger-gold hair.

Since it wasn't a female person, her annoyance level didn't hit the gong when she brought down the mallet.

"Because he's interesting." Jury smiled. Carole-anne, who, far from being asleep when Jury came in, was in beautiful disarray on his sofa in peacock-blue lounging pajamas and matching robe. She was doing inventory on her hair for signs of gray, she had said.

"I'm interesting too, but I don't see us out every night having a meal."

"No, but you do see us *in* every night looking for gray hairs."

"You've got some. But you needn't worry; you're a man. Gray looks distinguished on a man; on a woman it just looks old." Her old self sighed, then went back to pulling locks of hair around to assess the damage.

He had suggested she use a mirror but she didn't want to; she didn't want to see too much at one time.

She went on: "I don't understand why you've been suspended."

"I haven't been, exactly. I've been told to keep a low profile. Not blaze about working on cases."

"Didn't I tell you so? Didn't I tell you not to go into that house without a warrant?"

"More than once. *Many* more than once."

"Did you have to turn in your badge and gun? That's what happens on the telly."

"The telly's more interesting. I don't carry a gun."

"As far as I'm concerned you should get a medal, saving those poor little girls. Everybody agrees on that."

"Everybody" not to be taken as literal, since in this case it referred to Carole-anne and Mrs. Wasserman. "My superiors appear to disagree with you on that point."

"That bunch of old stuffed shirts."

Jury loved that. Police—including the chief constable—as stuffed shirts. "Do you want to hear this story?"

"What story?"

"Were you the template for attention deficit disorder?"

Carole-anne gave him one of her pouty looks, which meant she either did or didn't understand him. "Go on with your story, then," she said with an even deeper sigh, as if she were a long-suffering nurse to a ward full of babbling octogenarians.

"Okay. I met Harry Johnson in a pub in the City called the Old Wine Shades—"

"Is it nice? I hardly ever get into the City."

"Do you or do you not want to here this?"

"I said I did."

"Then don't interrupt. Harry Johnson told me of a friend of his . . ." And Jury capsulized the tale of the Gaults all the way through the tenth dimension. Carole-anne would tilt her head one way and then the other as if performing an exercise in thinking.

Jury stopped. "That's some story, isn't it?" He waited for the zillion questions she'd ask.

She didn't. "Well, you can bet he's lying."

Jury frowned. "Harry, you mean?"

"No, that other one—Hugh?—He's lying through his teeth."

He had expected Carole-anne to be entertained by this tale, not to supply a fresh directive. His (or Harry's) rather good story, he felt, was being brushed aside. First Wiggins, now, Carole-anne.

"You mean, lying about the ten dimensions?"

"No. That's easy enough to work out."

Easy? This so startled him that he shifted his feet from the coffee table to the floor and leaned forward, possibly with the intention of shaking it out of her. *Easy* enough?

"He's lying about everything else," she said.

Jury was puzzled. What was she making of this? "What else?"

She gave him a quirky smile. "You must have caught it from me, ha ha—attention disorder. He's lying about everything *but* those ten dimensions."

Jury was open-mouthed. His words staggered. "But . . . his wife *did* go looking at this property, *did* meet up with the agent, *did* go to Winterhaus and even her son *did* play with a little girl there. All of that happened; there are witnesses to it."

Carole-anne tossed back a tendril as if telling it to go to hell. (The devil would be delighted.) "Yes, but it happened because Hugh made it happen, see. I would think you, even though you're suspended, would see right through all that, smart detective that you are. Hugh murdered her—and maybe his boy too—and then set about with his mad act later, babbling about these ten dimensions and that superstrand theory of his."

"Super*string* theory." Jury just sat there with his eyes glazing over. He had expected a hundred breathless questions, and he chock full of a hundred dazzling answers. He had *not* expected her to trot out a solution. Especially one that he himself hadn't considered. He shook his head, trying to clear it. "Hugh is in a psychiatric clinic. I'm going to see him tomorrow."

"Good. Then you can talk to him and judge for yourself. Anybody can pretend to be crazy." She stretched.

"It's been nine months and police haven't found a body."

"Well, like you said, they aren't really looking, are they? They think she just did a flit. A body'll turn up. A body always does."

Jury sat there, his mind in just as much disorder as Carole-anne's hair. Of course, she was wrong, but it annoyed him that he couldn't immediately say why. Motive, what about that? "Why did he do it?"

"I don't know the man, do I? Probably he fancies some young

girl and the wife refused to give him a divorce. He buries the wife somewhere and then puts on this big act about trying to find her and being desperate and going bonkers. Then he comes out with this string bean theory. And after all, who knew she was going to look at this property? Him, of course. He knew she'd be there and the house was empty." Carole-anne shrugged.

"Before, you said that the ten dimensions were the easy part of it."

She slipped her feet back into her ornate slippers. The tops were littered with gold and silver embroidery and fake gems. They must have come from Ali Baba's cave in the Portobello Road. "It's been my experience that I'm always losing things, like an earring. I'll take it off so's to answer the phone. Then look for it one minute later and it's nowhere to be found. Nowhere. And it never does turn up. So there must be some place for it to go unless it grew little ear-ring feet and walked out on its own."

"It's obviously in your room."

"Then go up there and find it, Super." Here she punched her finger toward the ceiling several times.

"It probably just got wedged between a cushion and the arm of the chair."

Rising, preparatory to leaving, Carole-anne looked down at him and punched the finger toward the ceiling again. "I'm saying there must be a Lost and Found somewhere with our lost stuff in it. Maybe God runs a pawn shop, who knows? It's gone to the tenth dimension. Ta."

Jury sat there, chewing the inside of the corner of his mouth. Furiously.

23

Jury was still chewing at that corner of his mouth the next morning, sitting at his desk and watching Wiggins soaking tea bags in their blue earthenware mugs, a gift from his cousin in Manchester. Chewing and debating whether he should run this string theory by Wiggins. It would be a kind of test, wouldn't it, if the two least theoretically inclined people he had ever known—Wiggins and Carole-anne—were to agree that Hugh Gault's story was a pack of lies?

Of course, no matter what, he knew Wiggins's answer would be based on a trail of non sequiturs. He told himself *not* to ask Wiggins. The temptation, as usual, was too strong. "Wiggins, do you know anything about superstring theory? It's a theory in physics."

Wiggins was stirring his and Jury's tea and thinking about it.

"For God's sake, Wiggins, do you have to think about whether you *know* superstring theory or not?"

"Well, I could have known and then forgot." Delicately Wiggins tapped a spoon against the mug he had been sugaring up. Four sugars for him, one for Jury.

With his foot, Jury slammed shut the bottom drawer on which he'd been resting his feet. Sometimes you just had to do something physical, like beating up the furniture. "It was a *rhetorical* question, Wiggins. Of course you don't know about it; you'd almost have to be a physicist yourself to know about it."

"You know about it, don't you?" He rose with Jury's mug.

Jury bit his tongue as Wiggins set the mug of tea down on the desk. Returning then to his chair, he sat back and said, "Anyway, I wouldn't have to be a physicist to know about it. For example, I'm not in the 87th precinct, but I know all about that." To refresh Jury's memory on that score, he held up his Ed McBain novel.

"*No* one's in the 87th precinct, not Carrera, not Meyer Meyer, not even Ed *McBain*'s in the 87th precinct. It's *fiction*."

"I was just making a point."

What point? It'd be easier singing with whales.

"Enlighten me," Wiggins said, as he sat with his tea and his smug little smile.

Why were these people being so bloody condescending? You'd think their lives were fraught with theories that they were constantly sorting through as if their minds were blackboards chalked up with elegant equations. Jury said:

(You're going to hate yourself, mate!)

"String theory reconciles relativity and quantum mechanics." That didn't sound right. "String theory holds that there are ten dimensions, nine in space, one—"

Wiggins interrupted. "Well, see, that's where this theory is all wrong. There're three dimensions, or four, if you count in time. So this theory is off by six." Complacently, he sipped his tea.

(Told you.) Jury leaned across his desk as far as he could. "It's *theory*, for God's sake; that's what theories are. It's a hypothesis."

"A guess, you mean."

"Yes, but that's a very crude way of defining 'hypothesis.' A theory is something waiting to be proved."

Wiggins snickered. "It's in for a long wait, then."

Damnit, had everyone except him suddenly grown brains?

When his phone rang, jolting him, Jury clutched at it as if it were a parachute and found Fiona on the line telling him CS Racer wanted to see him. "He's not in a bad mood for once."

"That must mean he's been given the enviable job of relieving me of my warrant card and booting me out on the street."

She snickered, much as Wiggins had done. "He ain't in that good a mood."

Jury hitched his jacket from the back of his swivel chair. Here, at least, was someone for whom brains were never an issue. He gave Wiggins a dirty look and left his office.

It was merely an interim report on the progress of the investigation as no decision had yet been reached with regard to Jury's case; however, Racer took advantage of the process with yet another lecture on playing by the rules, team work, and not setting himself up to play the hero. It was this "hero" appellation which was causing the trouble: Jury and Detective Sergeant Cody Platt, who had gone into the house with him, were cast as heroes for saving the ten little girls. At least, that's how the media were playing it.

While Racer rambled on (now he was up and walking) Jury frowned over string theory. *Super*string. How did a physicist wrap his brain around the idea of a particle so small you would have to describe it as billions and *billions* of times smaller than the next thing up the list? An atom, maybe. *Billions.* Jury couldn't even think of it in terms of hundreds. How could someone like Hugh Gault use *billions* as if he were working clay? It must be something like those little Russian matryoshkas where you took out a smaller and smaller and smaller doll on into infinity until there came one so tiny you couldn't even see it. He thought about quarks. Charm quarks. He smiled and looked at Racer. Could there be charmless quarks, too? Why not?

"Jury! What the devil are you squinting over? What're you thinking about?"

"Quarks—I mean quacks. Yes, I was just wondering if that doctor I was ordered to go to isn't one. A quack." He smiled. Jury remembered that a police psychologist had been recommended, a recommendation he hadn't followed up on.

Racer enjoyed having any profession poor mouthed as long as he wasn't of it. "You keep going to that doctor, lad. Make it look good."

It was assumed that the experience in the Hester Street house must have been traumatic. It hadn't been traumatic. If anything, it had been liberating.

"Yes, sir." Jury's gaze was now fixed on the cat Cyril, who had been resting in the shallow curve of molding that hid the indirect lighting, little lights that traveled all around the ceiling. Cyril was sitting up, taking his victim's measure; that would be CS Racer, of course, who was pacing back and forth. Cyril had lately enjoyed leaping not on him, but flying straight over Racer's head and down. Cyril was revving up, but the door to the office needed to be open in order to escape. "Is that all? Sir?"

"What? Yes, yes." Racer waved him out.

Jury opened the door and Cyril, in an amazing display of aeronautics, flew directly in front of Racer, landed and made for the door and lickety-split slid right under Fiona's desk as a furious Racer marched into the outer office.

"Where is he? Where is that mangy animal? I'll kill him!" Racer looked wildly around the room, missing the tip of a tail sticking out from under the desk.

Cyril, Jury thought, was getting a mite careless. "He must've disappeared into the ninth dimension." Jury, like Wiggins and Fiona before him, snickered.

"You'd best keep on with that doctor, quack or not." Racer disappeared down the hall.

The cat Cyril popped out and up onto Fiona's desk and started in washing. The paw he had wetted raised, he looked at Jury as if he might be interested in more dimensions on which to operate—

"What do you know about Schrödinger's cat, Cyril?"

—and wasn't and, indifferent, washed the paw down over his face.

Jury had a couple of hours before meeting Harry Johnson at the Old Wine Shades, so he took a cab to Boring's.

Preprandial sherry and whiskey were in full swing when Jury entered the Members' Room. Melrose was sitting with Colonel Neame and Major Champs in the same chairs they had occupied before, looking as if they'd never left and were just as glad of it.

"Superintendent! How delightful; let's find a porter."

Rarely did a Boring's porter need to be found. One or another seemed always to be nipping by and now took the order for Jury's coffee.

"We've been working on your little problem, Superintendent."

There were so many little problems, Jury asked them which one. He had tossed his coat over the back of the sofa and sat down. "Come up with anything?"

Colonel Neame drew a folded sheet of stationery from his jacket pocket. "We have a question."

"Fire away," said Jury as the porter set his coffee on the table beside the sofa. Jury wished that he had had the comforting cup in his hand when Racer was jabbering at him.

Colonel Neame looked at Major Champs and was waved on. "Very well, now in this map"—here he unfolded the paper and wiped his hand over it. The Boring's crest was at the top—"here's the village. Lark Rise, was it?" It was represented by an assortment of little squares round a larger square. Probably, the little ones were meant to represent the buildings grouped round the square. "Ten or so miles on, you say, is the cottage that this Mrs. Gault stopped at— Lark Cottage. The agent received a call from the Gault woman, who said she thought the house was a bit too quaint. The second house was a half mile up the road, here"—he had drawn a larger square, with a long drive. "The agent didn't hear from her on that score. We presume she went inside—"

"No," said Melrose. "We know she went inside. There was a witness."

"Forgot that, yes. The child playing at the bottom of the garden. Anyway, next she called round at the Swan." He had drawn a square outfitted with a pub sign. He stopped and then went on. "Here's our question: How do we know that's the proper order? Why couldn't she at first have gone to the Swan? She might have called round there before looking at property. Then to look at the two properties, she'd be driving in the opposite direction, first coming to Winterhaus, then to Lark Cottage. The agent assumed Mrs. Gault was referring to Lark Cottage when she called; that would be natural, considering the location, because it was in that order one would come to them if driving from Lark Rise." Colonel Neame sat back.

Major Champs harrumphed a few times, pulling himself together to come in where Colonel Neame broke off. "Well, we know she and the boy had tea with the Shoesmiths—odd name, that, doesn't sound quite, you know, British." He paused, apparently wrapped up in thoughts about the name.

Melrose kept the story on track. "Look at how pleased they were that we happened along," he said to Jury. "Well, it could be that the Shoesmiths were the last people to see Mrs. Gault and her son alive."

That rather sinister statement hung in the air. Jury remembered the plain, pleasant owners of Lark Cottage and smiled. The notion of the Shoesmiths' doing away with Glynnis Gault and her son was a bit more than he could contemplate.

Major Champs said, "One wonders, you know, if something might have happened there. What sort of people are these Shoesmiths?" Again, he frowned over the name. "Don't strike me as quite the ticket."

"This comment she made to the estate agent," said Colonel Neame, "that the house was a little over the top—that depends what your 'top' is, I expect."

Melrose said, "That cottage is quite isolated, especially for an elderly couple."

"What are we proposing here?" asked Jury. "That the Shoesmiths added a little laudanum to the tea and then dragged the two of them out to the woods? That doesn't seem very likely. Couldn't this easily be cleared up by checking on the different times Glynnis Gault had appeared at Lark Cottage and at the pub, in addition to the time of her call to Marjorie Bathous at Forester's?"

All of them, Melrose included, stared at him as if he were some mischievous kid who'd stuck pins in their balloon. Jury, the spoiler.

Melrose said, "It's just a different tack to take."

"Yes, you're quite right." Jury signaled one of the porters and asked for a telephone.

"Don't you have a mobile phone?"

"Yes, but it's always running down. I hate mobiles. They should be outlawed except in cases of emergency."

"You're a *policeman.* What you get *is* emergency. If you'd had one back in December, it would have come in devilishly handy."

Jury nodded. "You're certainly right there." He had dialed and now said to the ghost at the other end, "Wiggins, I need you to do something. A couple in Surrey named Shoesmith, first names Maeve and Robert, near the village of Lark Rise. Nose around and see if you come up with anything, will you? Thanks." He hung up.

The three of them looked pleased now Scotland Yard was taking them seriously.

Which it wasn't. But Jury went on: "There are other possibilities. Mrs. Gault and her son could have lunched at the pub, then gone back to Lark Cottage and then to Winterhaus. There was a woman who saw them, we understand, saw Glynnis Gault standing beside her car, the boy presumably inside. If we could pin down a time there that would help in fixing the last place she was seen. That and the time they were at Lark Cottage—"

"And how do we fix the time if the Shoesmiths are *lying*?" asked Melrose.

"You're determined they were up to something, is that it?"

"No. I'm just allowing for the possibility."

What was Plant doing, aligning himself with these two? They were perfectly amiable, of course, and Colonel Neame was by no means stupid. (Major Champs's mental prowess, Jury wouldn't swear to, however.) It was as if they made a trio who shared the same ideas and insights. There Melrose sat, smoking one of Champs's cigars and giving Jury the same steely look that Colonel Neame was giving him, the only difference being the color of it: Colonel Neame's gaze was steel gray and Plant's, steel green.

"All right, we'll definitely take that into account." Jury shook his head, set down his coffee cup and listened to the grim bong of Boring's at noon. The longcase clock seemed to call to all of them here in this plague room to bring out their dead. Looking around, he thought there might be a couple of possibles. He slapped his chair arms and rose. "Gentlemen, good seeing you and thanks for the drink. I'd stay but I have a luncheon engagement."

"Power lunch?" asked Melrose.

"No. Pub lunch. That's about as powerful as I ever get."

All three, he noticed, were squinting at him, suspicious. Plant's look was squintier than the other two. Then Melrose sat back, puffing on his cigar, eyes still narrowed. This put Jury in mind not of a stinking rich, titled, estate owner but more of Humphrey Bogart in *Casablanca*.

"Something funny?"

"Not at all," said Jury.

24

Trevor's place had been taken by another barman, older, bar towel thrown over his shoulder, guttural North London accent. Jury wondered where Trevor was; perhaps this was his day off. He also wondered if this other one had Trevor's knowledge of wine. He doubted it. Few would.

Jury was early for his meeting with Harry and had a drink at the bar, a little worried about his midday drinking. He rarely did it, if, for no other reason, he hadn't the time.

There were more customers in the afternoon than in the evening. It was popular for stockbrokers, money managers, clerk typists. Somewhere he'd read that this pub was the only one left after the Great Fire, so it went back to the 1600s: that was in itself quite an accomplishment. The walls were covered in dark wood panels and featured advertisements of various wines and pictures of old London scenes. He wondered if any of the framed documents hanging on the walls attested to its history.

The place was crowded. Smoke hung in the air like a dropped ceiling. It really irritated Jury that inhaling secondhand smoke was just as unhealthy as firsthand. That was maddening, the smokers getting the pleasure of it while the ones who had suffered (and were still, if he was any measure of it, suffering) through kicking the habit—well, they might as well not have. He toyed with temptation for a while.

He dropped that way of thinking by going over what they'd said in Boring's. He should talk to the agent again. Perhaps she could be more precise about that phone call coming in from Glynnis Gault.

But Jury was quite sure the most obvious explanation was the right one in this case.

"Having lunch?"

Jury looked around to see Harry Johnson, wearing a different coat, camel hair this time, and just as expensive looking. "No, just this."

"They've a very good restaurant here upstairs."

Jury tapped the glass and then looked down. "Where's Mungo?"

Harry laughed. "In the car. I'm on a yellow line, so we'd better go, if you're ready. Sorry about lunch."

Jury nodded, left the glass half full and decided he wasn't really a midday drinker. He couldn't stand the thought of kicking one more habit.

Mungo positioned himself with his head out of the window.

"Why do dogs do that?"

"I don't know; maybe they're just breezing."

Breezing. It reminded Jury of the Ryders and horse racing. And Nell. What a bloody waste, oh, what a waste, he thought, as they maneuvered around a BMW, out for a lunchtime stroll on Upper Thames Street, and sped along the Embankment.

The Stoddard Clinic was Gothic and fiercely gated, stone lions atop the gray stone columns on either side. Cars had to stop and use the intercom embedded in one of the pillars. Harry pressed the button and a voice mixed with static asked his business.

"I'm here to visit Mr. Gault. Hugh Gault. My name's Johnson."

There was a silence except for the electronic stutter.

"Yessir, you Mr. Harry Johnson, then?"

"I am."

The gate pulled open and they drove in. The building, like the gate, was somewhat daunting. If this was a clinic principally for stressed-out people who had just a little too much on their platter, its demeanor was overkill. Decidedly medieval, with stone battlements around the roof and no chairs on the wide sweep of grass. No people in chairs on the grass either, although it was quite a pleasant day. It was all gray stone with a bell tower.

Jury said as they parked under a massive oak tree, "This strikes me as looking more like another sort of facility, you know, the sort that doesn't look kindly upon your signing yourself out and going home. If you know what I mean."

"Yes, I do. But it's not quite as forbidding as you think."

Jury nodded as they got out of the car, Harry petting Mungo and telling him they'd be back soon. Mungo made some throaty sounds, not, Jury was sure, to say he'd miss them, but because he thought freedom was at hand.

They walked around a smallish white bus with the name STODDARD painted on the sides—not CLINIC—perhaps to indicate that this place had been around for a long time and didn't need to be identified.

Harry said, "I had another friend here awhile back and she did leave. Her therapy was successful. Hugh's not a prisoner. Listen: sometimes Hugh wants to talk about what happened and sometimes not. At least he doesn't always bring the subject up. I let him take the lead on that score. You can imagine . . ."

Jury nodded, but certainly couldn't imagine. Nor could he imagine living with it, something like that hanging over his head.

Stoddard was quite as imposing inside as out. Inside, though, it had warmth as opposed to its cold exterior. The warmth came from its fireplaces, its flowered bronze wallpaper, its polished mahogany banisters. There appeared to be two drawing, or reception, rooms where one could wait, to the left and right of the large entry hall. A woman and two men were standing in the center of the room on the right, laughing. Jury wondered if one was the patient the others had come to see, and thought the group was a little boisterous. The woman bent to stroke the head of an Irish wolfhound, a dog that had always struck Jury as faintly ridiculous, though he couldn't say why.

When they walked in, Harry was greeted heartily by a nurse, whom he addressed by name—Mary, or Merle—and who walked to the receptionist's table with him, chatting. The receptionist, a bit of a fashion plate, with her elegant suit and bobbed black hair that edged her face like a helmet, appeared to be just as congenial as the nurse. Harry must have visited Hugh Gault often enough to have stirred up friendly feelings in the staff.

A man had come down the wide staircase and was standing in the hall looking from one room to the other. Jury wondered if this was Hugh Gault; the poor fellow looked utterly overwhelmed. A nurse came from around the reception desk and, smiling, led him into the other room, where everyone made a fuss over him, including the wolfhound, who nearly knocked him down.

So *this* must be Hugh Gault, walking into the twin of that drawing room now. He was tall and a little thin, but by no means looking as if his "condition" were responsible for the thinness. He greeted Harry, was introduced to Jury and sank down in one of the deep armchairs near the fire. Harry and Jury sat opposite in matching chairs. The room was dimly lit, which was pleasant. Some member of the staff apparently believed in ambient lighting. Jury wondered why. A better impression made? A softness conducive to more tender care? For whatever reason, it was extremely pleasant, even restful. These surroundings, with the flames leaping in the fireplace, looked quite glamorous, more the mise-on-scène of an expensive country hotel. Perhaps such appointments were considered therapeutic. Jury bet it cost a bundle.

"A detective *superintendent*? My word!" Hugh Gault nodded in Harry's direction. "Are we going to have to alibi each other? Me, I've been right here for eight months. Plenty of witnesses. Harry, on the other hand, I can't account for. He could be here, there, everywhere."

"Just a particle," said Jury, smiling. "That can't be identified because it can't be measured."

Hugh tossed his head back and laughed. "That's one of the

best descriptions of Harry I've heard. You're interested in quantum theory?"

"The little, the *very* little I know about it, yes, I'd say so."

Harry asked, "How's the book going, Hugh?"

"Still stumbling along. It might be easier if you'd give me back my damned notes." This was said not in anger, or even annoyance, but with good humor. To Jury he said, "Tell me, Superintendent, just how far along are you with proving this criminal conspiracy of ours?"

"Me? Not far. I'm stuck back there with Schrödinger's cat."

"Ah! Good for you!"

"Maybe. I'm not sure how good it is for the cat."

Again, Hugh laughed. "You're a quick study, Superintendent.

"No, I really don't understand the quantum world."

"Well, just remember that whatever governs behavior in our daily experience is wasted in the quantum world. Schrödinger's wavefunction was one of the revolutionary insights in quantum physics. Wavefunction."

Jury smiled at the way Hugh Gault rolled this around in his mouth like a delicious chocolate or single-malt whiskey. "It's a mathematical quantity. You have to solve Schrödinger's equation to get it."

"Schrödinger's cat. Alive and dead at the same—"

Hugh looked away and was silent. He looked back at Jury. "Sorry. I've taken a couple of blows and it's—" He sighed. "I miss my wife. I miss my son."

Jury could see how the ambiguity—no, more than ambiguity— of the cat might strike him as an analogy in this way. They were silent for a few moments, and then Harry stepped in to fill the vacuum. "You know, I can see how quantum theory might have a certain appeal to a detective. Things change as you look at them. So how does one measure? One thing becomes two things. Dead and alive simultaneously. Schrödinger was certainly pointing out one of the sticking points in superposition theory."

"Superposition? What's that?" asked Jury.

Back on track, Hugh said. "Take this: you've tossed pebbles into water, haven't you? And the result is concentric circles spreading out. Now throw another pebble in near the first one. Same thing: circles spreading out. But now the overlapping of those two configurations makes for a *third* configuration. And now you have a section of those circles being two things at once and, consequently, creating a *third* design. Superposition. You look skeptical, Superintendent."

"No, actually, I look dumb."

Both of them laughed. Hugh said, "Schrödinger's cat. Simultaneously alive and dead. It's the overlapping. You see, what's true on the microscopic level is in conflict with what we observe with our own eyes. The macroscopic level. The level of cats, for instance. The cat is tangled up with the decaying nucleus, and when the nucleus decays, the poison is released and the cat dies instantly." Hugh smiled. "Remember, as soon as you look you alter the outcome. "An aspect of Heisenberg's uncertainty principle is that the act of observation will ultimately affect the thing being observed."

Jury did not take this in. He was instead trying to track down something, something that Harry had said in the pub, but he couldn't put his finger on it. *Schrödinger's cat.* What Harry had said didn't seem to fit. Jury frowned. What was it?

". . . the incompleteness theory."

Jury shook his head as if to clear it. "I'm sorry. What were you saying?"

"Gödel. His theory of incompleteness. A proposition can be both true and unprovable."

"Oh. That."

Hugh laughed. "Not to worry. The brilliant mathematicians were lost. After all, that upsets the whole notion that mathematics is a gloriously closed system, provable from within its own borders. You can understand that: how can a proposition be *true* and yet be *unprovable*. And yet Gödel had worked out a proof of this."

Jury sat forward, his whole face in a frown. "You're saying this Gödel proved the unprovable."

Hugh smiled. "That's right. It appears to be a sort of double think, doesn't it? Gödel supported and subverted his theory. It was a work of art, really; it was pure genius. His solution lay in numbering. Gödel's numbering. But let's not get into that."

"Let's not," said Jury. "Let's get back to superstrings."

Hugh's smile was open and warm, the sort that could coax a smile out of anyone around him. "Good."

"How can you work with something that's a *billion* times smaller than the nucleus of the atom? Isn't that the size of one of your strings?"

"Close enough. It's actually a billion billion." Hugh held up two fingers.

"It gets to the point, doesn't it, where you're back to zero?"

Hugh sat back. *This is how he copes,* thought Jury, how Hugh Gault coped with the vanishing of his wife and son, by entering an abstract world.

"There is no zero," said Hugh. "A string is the last stop. And remember, what we're talking about is energy. Vibrating energy. The string is absolutely the last stop. The buck stops there." Hugh relaxed, as if, now he had explained this, it was safe to do so.

"How can that be? I can't get my mind round it. You're talking about something indivisible."

"Of course you can't imagine it. But you can work it out by way of logic." Hugh looked at him with something like doubt. "Why are you interested in this, Superintendent? I wonder that you would be since it's so abstract. You deal in facts, in proofs. You don't even like circumstantial evidence as proof, and that evidence at least is concrete. As you said—a billion billion—no wonder you can't get your mind around it."

Jury thought Hugh seemed eminently sane. But then there had been no question of his sanity. He had come here because he couldn't cope with the rug's being pulled out from under his life.

Jury wondered if he himself would be able to. Probably not, not living with all this uncertainty. But he went along, trying to hold up his end. "Abstraction doesn't run counter to facts, though. I mean, for example, say A refers to a fingerprint on a gun and B refers to the fingerprint of a suspect. The fingerprints on the gun, the ones of the suspect, hence the matter of who the shooter is—C—we can determine that the suspect is the shooter. Now, those fingerprints are salient facts. But to get from A and B to C, I have to make a leap— not a big one, but still a leap. That's an abstraction, that leap."

"Not exactly what we're talking about," said Harry.

"No?" Jury looked at him.

"Harry," said Hugh with a laugh, "thinks we're never talking about what we're talking about. He thinks it's double speak. We don't think alike, you know; we disagree on some basic points. That's why he absconded with my notes." Hugh smiled. "To see if he could understand."

Harry looked amused. "I understand, all right."

Jury wondered if they were competing and what they were competing about. It had occurred to Jury that Glynnis Gault might be part of it. It was obvious that Harry cared about her, but cared how much?

"No, actually, Harry disagrees with himself here. His idols are Bohr and Gödel. But Gödel didn't trust quantum theory any more than Einstein trusted it."

"All right, but how does all of this actually impinge upon your lives? If I say fingerprint A and fingerprint B are identical, I can also say C is the shooter. But I don't see how, for example, the theory of incompleteness translates into anything you'd be dealing with in your lives."

"I think that's what Harry meant when he said your definition of abstraction wasn't what we were talking about."

"Well, how many kinds of abstraction are there?"

"Mathematics is abstraction; numbers are abstract, fingerprints aren't," said Hugh.

Harry said, "That's not really an accurate description. I'm talking now about Gödel. Or *Hamlet*. Remember the play within the play of the traveling theatrical group? The actors in the 'play' being performed took on the characters, put on the masks of Hamlet's family. They poisoned the king in their skit as Claudius had poisoned the king in actuality, or, rather, in the play proper. It became self-referential. Actors commenting on the actions of their 'real' counterparts."

And Jury thought of Harry's story becoming a story within a story within a story. Had he been left knowing as little about the "real" events as he did about the uncertainty principle or the incompleteness theory?

In a way, it made him smile, without knowing quite what he was smiling about. Probably about that damned cat.

25

It suited Jury down to the ground to have this rest of the afternoon free to drive to Surrey and call in at the Swan in his unofficial capacity. Even in the absence of an official crime scene, he supposed the Swan's regulars would be pleased to see him, he having stirred their interest in this crime—if it was a crime. They had probably spent a fair amount of time talking about him and Melrose Plant and their appearance in the pub. And there was the woman who had seen Glynnis Gault. She would be able to tell him something.

He was driving through Slough when he suddenly felt saddened for some reason and was so caught up in this feeling that he drove the roundabout twice outside of an industrial park, of which Slough had many. It was a gray town, concrete and glass. Can one really imagine anyone reminiscing about "dear old Slough"?

Jury smiled and then the smile vanished as he stopped at a zebra crossing to let an elderly woman with a string bag full of groceries cross. He could even see the Weetabix and half loaf sticking out of the carryall and thought, yes, he could imagine her saying it.

Some driver behind him was honking. The woman, who appeared arthritic, was only halfway across the road, but to the driver behind him halfway was good enough. Jury waited until she reached the curb, sending the car behind him into a honking frenzy. Jury smiled and drove on.

He pulled into one of the parking spaces outside Forester and Flynn and went in. The two young agents were on their way out, probably for lunch together, leaving Marjorie Bathous to hold the fort.

She looked up from writing the particulars of a newly listed house, surprised. "It's Inspector—Jury? Is that right?"

They were all "inspectors," weren't they? "Close enough, Mrs. Bathous." Once again he showed her his ID. "I wonder if I could have another look at Winterhaus." It occurred to him then that he might revisit the neighbors. "And talk to the Shoesmiths, if they're available?"

Marjorie Bathous was already spinning her Rolodex. "I'm sure that wouldn't be a problem. They were quite thrilled about your visit the other day." She smiled at him as she waited for the phone to be picked up on the other end. One of the Shoesmiths answered and after settling on a time she hung up. "They'd be delighted; they can see you after you leave here. Now, about Winterhaus." She was opening and closing drawers. "Here we are." She handed him the key. "You don't mind going on your own? I could accompany you. I haven't a client to see until six—?" She was dimpling, her smile was so wide.

"Not at all, Mrs. Bathous—"

"Marj is what everyone calls me." The dimples again. "Well . . . are you, is Scotland Yard investigating that old business?" She apparently realized this subject called for gravitas, not dimples. "It's quite peculiar, isn't it?"

Jury rose. "It is, yes. Thanks very much." He held up the key. "I'll get this back to you." He said this with a promising smile. As he opened the door she was waving to him across the room.

He would see them first, the Shoesmiths, which would prevent their being elaborately ready with tea. Maeve Shoesmith was definitely a full tea sort of hostess.

"It's the Bill, Maeve!" bellowed Bob Shoesmith. "Better hide the swag!" He laughed enthusiastically at his little joke.

Maeve came quickly from wherever she'd been—kitchen, probably. She slapped at Bob's arm in a playful manner. "Aren't you awful! Come in, come in. Just walk through to the back parlor. You don't mind, do you? We've an electric heater and it's quite nice and snug. Here we are."

Jury thanked her and looked the room over, not noticeably different from the front room. The tea was here, waiting. A seedcake and some Carr's biscuits sat on the tray with the pot and mugs. Maeve Shoesmith was an uncanny judge of time.

"Your friend isn't with you today," she said, pointing out the obvious as she poured milk into three mugs. No cups and saucers today, for this was informal and friendly. "Has he found a house or is he still considering?"

"Still considering. Thank you," Jury said when she handed him a mug. "He was quite pleased with this one. He's gone back to report to his aunt on what he's found." But he didn't want to raise their hopes. "There's the distance from the town to consider. An elderly person might be nervous without a hospital or at least a doctor's surgery close by. I mean, if she's on her own, which she is. Very independent."

Bob nodded sagely. "There is that to consider, so. Still, you can't find a better deal than Lark Cottage, I'd say." Bob Shoesmith pounded on the whitewashed wall his chair was nearest to, as if the wall's not crumbling under the blow of his fist should be proof to the aunt she'd be wise to snap the cottage up. "Solid as a rock. And no damp, either. Dry as a bone—"

Jury interrupted this threatened flood of house details and clichés. "I was thinking about your meeting with Mrs. Gault."

"Yes, that was odd." Maeve furrowed her brow at the oddity of it. "Never did know what happened there, did we, Bob?"

Jury drank his tea, which was too citrus enhanced for his taste. (Even Wiggins, who never found a tea he didn't like, had commented on tea producers adding flowery bits and fruits and spices to tea: "It's got to the point you almost have to ask for black tea anymore, what with this decaffeinated, herbal fashion," Wiggins had said.) "Did Mrs. Gault actually say she was on her way to view Winterhaus?"

They looked at each other. Then Bob, brow creased, said, "Now

I'd have to think on that. I mean she did talk about the house . . . Maeve?"

"You mean was she going to see it or had she already been? The house 'farther on' is what she said. We must have been the first as we're on the way to Winterhaus. I recall she said it was rather large, but then she would've known that from the particulars they give you about a house, the photo and all."

"Her son stayed outside?"

"He did, yes. Played with the dog," said Maeve.

"Big kind of dog."

"I'd say medium sized."

They were going to make sure the details here were accurate.

"Flop-eared," she said. "The boy was tossing him sticks."

Jury said, "I'd been assuming Mrs. Gault stopped here, then went along to the bigger house and then to the Swan. But if the order was reversed, the pub would have been her first stop."

Bob's brow creased again. "Is it important?"

"To you? I'd say yes. If you were the last people to see her alive."

Bob blanched at that and sat back. "Well, we couldn't've been, could we? There'd have been whoever was around when she did a flit."

Maeve's anxiety over Jury's comment dissolved in the reasoning of her husband. She rocked and added to the drama, "Another man, that's what. She probably ran off with him."

Jury smiled. "Quite possibly. What time did she leave?"

Bob frowned in thought. Maeve said, "It'd gone two, half two, actually. And if she wanted to go, she'd better nip round there soon. We don't keep London hours here, and just as well, I always say. All the crime."

Jury liked that blanket comment, its lack of boundaries. "You can fix it at around two-thirty? You've got a remarkable memory," Jury said, "considering this was last year."

"I only remember because when she said something about the Swan, I remarked, well, it'd be closing in half an hour. That fixed the time in my mind."

"I wish there were more witnesses like you." Jury smiled.

She bathed in this display of approval. "Well, now." She tittered.

"Then that would mean this was the first place she stopped." Jury set down his mug. "Then Winterhaus, then the pub."

"Glad we got that straightened out!" said Bob. "No, we wouldn't have liked being the last place, I do assure you." He laughed.

"What did all of you talk about?"

Bob said, "Something to do with school, wasn't it?"

Maeve nodded. "Lark Rise Special School. It's a school especially for kids with disabilities, like, oh, what was it now?"

"Autism? Autistic?" said Jury.

"That's it. Lark Rise apparently specializes in that sort of thing. Her little boy"—Maeve leaned forward, voice lowered as if somehow not to jinx the lad by mention of it—"he was autistic. I took him out a biscuit and a cup of tea. He smiled and nodded, but didn't say anything."

"She was going to try to enter him in this school, was that it?"

Maeve nodded. "I don't think she meant the house to be a weekend house, do you, Bob? I think she meant them to live there while school was in session, maybe take their Christmas hols in the London house. That's my impression."

Jury thanked them for the tea, saying, "I'm afraid I really must be getting back there myself. Thanks so much; you've both been very helpful."

As they accompanied him to the door, Bob said, "You were asking about that dog. I'll say this, that was one smart ol' dog, from what I could make out. Looked like he might've been kin to things the rest of us aren't." Bob laughed.

"I'm with you there, Mr. Shoesmith." They shook hands.

26

The plain blank face of Winterhaus faced him. Jury left the car, unlocked the door with a big key that seemed more suited to some nightmare of vaults and crypts and went inside.

Echoes, also. As he walked from the wide hall into whatever room it had been—music? dining? morning room? Yes, a morning room quite possibly was it. Although upon reflection, Jury wasn't sure what the purpose of such a room was. But with the French window opening onto the terrace, it would be pleasant to sit in here, looking out into the rainy morning. So he decided upon that as the room's function.

It induced in him a reverie as it had done before, some mild hypnotic state in which he felt he was unable to move, or didn't want to move. He thought about Hugh Gault, wondering whether he found comfort in such stasis. He thought, probably, Hugh did. Winterhaus seemed not to have stirred up anything in Melrose, whom Jury would have thought to be far more susceptible to its atmosphere, the more fanciful of the two, more imaginative, more impressionable. He thought it an irony that he, Jury, dealing as he did in facts and figures rather than magic and spells, would be the one more susceptible. He felt the weight of the past pressing down on him, but it was his past, not the house's. Like a camera he seemed to be projecting images onto the blank screen of the wall, some of them real, most of them fanciful.

Disturbed by this, he moved a little to the left, where the French window gave him at least a present vista to gaze across. There was movement some distance away. Jury saw the little girl he and Plant had met, and he walked out and across the long sweep of lawn, along to the Wendy house.

Two dolls, one prettily dressed and one plainly, were in her hands. As he drew up, the plainly dressed gave the pretty one a fist right in the face. "Oh, hello," she said.

"Hello." He sat down on the wide stump Melrose had taken before as his chair. Jury nodded toward her Inuit doll, the one that had landed the fist in the other one's face. What did she call it? Not Ugly. "Oogli there knows how to punch. Who's she beating up on?"

"Caroline." She turned the one in the frilly pink dress so he could see exactly how things stood between her and prissy Caroline.

"Is Caroline anyone in particular?"

"She's my cousin and I have to live with her. I even have to sleep in the same room."

"Ugh!" said Jury, frowning.

Which she appreciated. " 'Ugh!' is right! I have to go to bed with Caroline and get up with Caroline and eat breakfast with Caroline. Caroline's everywhere."

Caroline sounded more like God than a girl.

"So that's why I sneak off and come here. If Caroline ever found this place I'd have to kill her, I guess." This happy prospect called forth a smile. "But she won't because it's too far away and you have to go through woods and she's too lazy. She gets all the fancy dresses"—attention drawn to the pink dress again—"and I get the plain clothes." She held the doll close to Jury's face for his scrutiny. Then she stepped back to give Jury a better look at her old jeans, an ankle's length too short, her white T-shirt and brown cardigan.

"But girls don't wear fancy dresses like that anymore. Caroline's completely unfashionable. Girls all dress like you do."

This stumped her. She looked down at herself. "They're *trying* to look awful?" She was thinking. "Maybe they all have Carolines."

This was so true, Jury had to laugh. In a moment, she did, too.

"But what about your mum?"

"I told you before. She's my aunt. Aunt Brenda. I told you when you were here with your friend."

She had, that's right. "Where's your mum?"

"Dead. I don't know where my dad is. He never came back for me."

The corners of her mouth dragged down and the plain doll gave the other one another wallop.

Jury tried to draw the talk away from dad. "Is that when you came to live with your aunt?"

Vigorously she nodded. "Caroline gets to go to parties. I don't. She's got friends, I don't, and gets to invite them to the house to play."

"At least that takes her attention away from you for a while."

She rolled her eyes at him as if he ought to know better. "No, it does not! All of them make fun of me then."

"That's awful, but"—Jury was back to the half-full glass again—"if Caroline spends most of her time trying to make you feel bad, doesn't it occur to you she's terribly jealous?"

The surprise in her face showed that it never had. "What do you mean?" Here, she came with both dolls to sit beside him on the stump.

This was definitely a sit-down topic.

"I mean, if a person's dead set against another person so that she has to belittle her all the time, usually it means the first person covets what the second one has."

"Covets?" Her eyebrows were a tiny scroll of puzzlement.

"Wants, wants to own, like one might want to own someone else's jewelry or clothes or house." Jury looked around at the monochromatic March landscape, almost artful in its blending of whites and grays and browns into a uniform backdrop for this Georgian house and its wood, dense and still.

"Remember the day last year the woman and her little boy were here?"

She pulled down the doll's dress and nodded.

"The boy—what was he like?"

"He was nice. I wish he'd come back. I wouldn't want them to actually live here, though. Because then I couldn't come here myself whenever I wanted to." She lowered her voice to a whisper. "I come here a lot. I'm not supposed to."

Jury lowered his own voice in keeping with the solemnity of that confession. "Did you ever see anybody else here? I mean besides the boy and his mum? And the man on the terrace?"

She nodded. "The lady who I think must take care of the house."

Marjorie Bathous. "The agent?"

"Probably." She nodded and picked at a broken button on Oogli's coat. "She comes and moves things around on the tea tray and changes the paintings sometimes, and sometimes moves a chair from one place to another. I can't imagine why."

She didn't realize she was admitting to spending a lot of time inside the house. Jury smiled. "Probably just wants to feel people live here. Estate agents must think of some of their listings as their own homes." He wondered if that was true; it struck him as poignant. Then he said, "Do you have tea inside sometimes, then?"

She hesitated, probably wondering if he could be trusted. "Well . . . I guess sometimes I do."

"Well, keep a sharp lookout for people around here, will you? I may need some more information."

She really smiled now. "I can keep a lookout, all right. From up there." She pointed to an elm tree with its entanglement of lower branches, offering a leg up to anyone who wished to climb it. Its moss-draped branches and thick leaves gave ample cover, too. It was higher than most of the other trees, maples and oaks.

"I like to climb it," she said, simply. Then, "I guess I have to go now."

"I do, too. It's been nice talking to you." And it suddenly occurred to Jury that he didn't know her name. "You didn't tell us your name. What is it?"

"Tilda. It's really Mathilda, but I'm called Tilda."

"How do you get home, Tilda?"

She inclined her head. "I go through the woods."

There once was a road through the woods.

"What's the matter?"

"Matter? Nothing. I just thought of a line of poetry, for some reason."

"I guess it's sad."

He nodded. "I guess so, too."

27

The regulars in the Swan remembered Jury. He was their enter-
tainment, their bit of cabaret come back for an encore.

"Oh-oh," said one of them. "This is getting serious, mates.
Clive, better hide that boatload you got from Belfast."

"Get on with it, Reggie," said the barman. "Pretty soon you'll
be stitchin' me up for that shipment what come for you the other
night."

Jury suffered this forced humor with a smile. "I'm not here
about your gun running, Clive. I'm looking for someone who remem-
bers seeing this woman, whom all of you, having gone temporarily
blind, know sod-all about." Holding the photo, Jury stretched his
arm out to scope it around. "With her son and her dog, too."

Clive peered at the photo, as if he meant to be helpful. He
shrugged. "Dunno, mate."

"Somebody must've noticed her."

A woman of late middle age set her empty glass on the bar and
said, "That would be me, I believe."

Clive said, "Myra—"

"Lady Easedale to you, you whiskey-diluting toad."

Jury turned. He was looking into faded blue eyes. Her expression was wonderful, as if she couldn't do enough for you. She looked
at the photo Jury carried with him of Glynnis Gault. "I saw her, at
least I think it was she. There was a boy with her, a child, and, I
think, a dog."

"That's quite definitely Mrs. Gault. What are you drinking?"
He smiled at her.

The barman threw the bar towel over his shoulder. "Ask her

what she ain't. If you can pour it, she'll drink it. Diluted, ha! Amount you drink, Myra, it better be." That drew some snickering up and down the bar as Clive stationed a glass under one of the optics where it stood like a good soldier.

"Never mind them. Come join me at my table."

"I will." He ordered a Foster's for himself before he followed Myra to a table in the corner. "Lady Easedale? Your husband was, what? Duke? Viscount? Honorable?"

"Duke of dreams, Lord Love-a-duck. The Honorable Nothing. My husband went over to Ireland and bought himself a title. You can do the same here, but there's a lot more red tape. Well, you'd know. About titles, I mean."

"Red tape, too."

"I don't call myself that; it's so pretentious, don't you think? Myra Easedale, that's who I am." She held out her hand.

Jury took it. "Richard Jury, detective superintendent with Scotland Yard. I'm happy to meet you."

"Now"—she said, dispensing with introductions, even taking as matter-of-fact the news that she was talking to a policeman. She leaned closer to him—"about this woman. I didn't make anything of it until you came round the other day, asking. Or Clive said you did. The people in here, well, they're not as unreliable as one might think at first. So I did wonder."

Clive was setting down their drinks. "He's not missing persons, Myra; he's CID. Homicides, that kind o' thing."

"Oh, and a lot you know about 'that kind o' thing.'"

Clive shrugged and walked back to the bar.

"Idiot," she murmured. "I heard the story from Marjorie Bathous—she's the estate agent—who said the woman had never brought back the key. Later she tried the number she'd got from the woman and nobody answered. For several days she kept trying. No answer."

"Mrs. Bathous didn't call the police?"

"Not as far as I know. Well, some people are awfully skittish about the police. I expect Marjorie Bathous thought Mrs. Gault would come back eventually. You see, people think that house is peculiar anyway. There were those who got a kick out of saying maybe that house swallowed them up. People are such ghouls, aren't they? The thing about that place is it's huge, it's isolated and it's vacant. Been vacant for some time. Was rented out some years ago, I recall. Well, most people don't want to rent a place out here in the sticks and not close to a mainline train."

"Getting back to when you saw Mrs. Gault—"

She reared back an inch or two, feigning shock. "My, you are relentless, aren't you?"

"Absolutely."

"When I saw her I was driving along this road, the one running by the Swan and the houses farther along. I'd come from Lark Rise, been doing a spot of shopping. When I was just coming up on Winterhaus, I saw her car and her standing beside it, reading a map. I stopped and asked her if I could help with directions and she said no, she was fine. So I drove on. The car was just opposite the Winterhaus driveway."

"What time was this?" Jury had taken out his small leather notebook.

"Oh . . . I'd say threeish, some time between three and four, in any case. Whether she was going to visit the house or had already done that and left, I couldn't say." Myra took a sip of her whiskey and looked doubtful.

"What is it?"

"It seemed an odd thing to be doing, stopping there to read a map. It just struck me later as strange. It's such a small point, though, I shrugged it off."

"Go on."

"Well, there was the driveway to the house—I mean you could hardly not see it from where she was standing. If she wanted to take out a map, why not stop in the driveway? She'd either be going *into* it or coming *out* of it, the same thing would apply, wouldn't it? Why not, in either case, stop somewhere along the driveway instead of leaving the driveway and pulling up across the road and getting out." She waved her own words away, as if their triviality embarrassed her. "It's such a small thing."

Jury smiled and raised his glass as if in a toast. "It's just such small things that could mean success or failure in solving a case. You'd make one hell of a witness." It's the same thing he'd said to Maeve Shoesmith.

She looked quite pleased by that compliment.

Jury asked, "And what did you think about her stopping where she did?" He saw her glass was nearly empty and signaled to Clive.

"Perhaps that she'd stopped to let the dog—or even the boy for that matter—out to, you know, relieve himself. But that presented the same problem. I suppose the boy might have said, just at the moment of leaving the drive, 'Mum, I've got to go!' But that seems most unlikely, doesn't it? Why leave the privacy of the property— there are so many trees and hedges there—to do something you don't want to be seen doing?" Again she seemed to wave the words away. "I do wish I'd been nosier and pulled my car up behind hers and seen—well, hindsight would save us all. Most of us, that is." She looked up at Clive, who stood with the bar towel draped over his shoulder.

"What's it to be, Myra, me old girl?" He smiled broadly.

"Two more," said Jury.

"Better watch your step there, Inspector; she'll have you for breakfast." Clive whistled his way off with the empties.

"Daft," said Myra.

"Let me ask you, if the car had been on the drive, would you have seen it?"

"I might have glimpsed it. The thing is, there's a heavy screen of hedge and tree there, so I'd only have caught a glimpse if I'd seen it at all." She sat back and studied Jury's face. "Are you saying she *wanted* to be seen?"

"It does look like it."

Myra just looked at him, frowning slightly. "The way it all happened, you'd think she wanted a witness."

Jury nodded. "But witness to what?"

The woman who came to the door was angular, but still nice-looking in her way, if her way hadn't been a surliness of expression, as if she were always gearing up for distasteful news.

"Mrs. Hastings? Brenda Hastings?" Jury showed her his ID. "My name is Jury; I'm with Scotland Yard CID."

Brenda Hastings's expression turned fearful. "What? What about? Has something happened to Caroline?"

"No, nothing at all like that."

She breathed a sigh of relief, and Jury waited a beat for her to ask about Mathilda. She didn't, at least not until Jury's prompt. "You have a niece, Tilda?"

"Oh. Oh, yes. Mathilda. We call her Tilda. Why? Is she in trouble?"

Interesting, Jury thought, that whereas Caroline might be in danger, Mathilda could only be in trouble. That was as far as her concern could take her.

"No, but she might—" Jury stopped. Why give away the little girl's secret. He had almost said she might be in danger, going to those woods, endangered possibly by some person who had come to Winterhaus. Endangered by a lack of supervision. Lack of interest; lack of love. He wondered what had happened to her parents. Why was he always running into motherless children? He knew what it felt like; he knew it went on forever. He knew it colored his responses to people. Look at him: barely in the door and he was already prepared to dislike Brenda Hastings. "It's not either of the children I've come about."

She brushed a pile of yellow hair back from her face—not blond, but yellow, harsh and yet faded, whatever shine had been there long since gone.

"It's really just information I'm after."

"Oh."

Jury nodded toward the uninviting parlor of this fussy little house. "May I sit down?"

"Yes. Just go through." She gave him a disconcerted smile.

Jury took an armchair covered in a cheap-looking material, rough feeling, with a pattern of monstrous sunflowers. The ruffled curtains at the two windows opposite were also printed with sunflowers.

Mathilda's aunt sat on the edge of the sofa, a dark, depressing gray. "Well, then—"

"You know Winterhaus?"

"That big place with all the woods? I've never been in it but yes, I know where you mean. Nobody lives there. I think they're trying to let it."

"You're about the closest neighbor, other than the Shoesmiths in Lark Cottage."

"Well, but I've hardly spoken half a dozen words to them over the years."

"It's not the Shoesmiths I'm interested in. It's Winterhaus."

"Oh? But I don't know anything about it. The family who owned it or maybe still owns it had a kind of Italian name—"

"Della Torres. Italian. The father of the present owner, that is. His wife was English, though. I assume that's the reason they bought that house. It's not about the Della Torreses that I've come. It's about the disappearance of a woman nine months ago—"

"Disappearance? Why, no, I don't know anything about that. Why? What happened?"

"A woman named Gault was last seen in this area. That was about nine months ago. The last people we know to have seen her are the Shoesmiths. Police would have been round asking questions—"

She sat up stiffly. "Not of me, they weren't. I don't know anything."

She was so adamant about her ignorance, Jury had to wonder.

"Anyway," Brenda Hastings went on, "it's been a long time, hasn't it, since it happened?" She raised her eyebrows as if wondering why Jury was so tardy.

"It might have been a kidnapping, Mrs. Hastings, but any information you might conceivably have—Do you recall seeing anyone back then? She would have been with a little boy and a dog."

She was shaking her head before the question was out of his mouth. "No, I never did." And she was handing back the picture he had brought out almost without looking up at it.

As he took the picture back he heard a door open and a little voice fluting, "Mum-my!"

The little girl's hair was nearly as yellow as her mother's, only brighter and lighter. The child crowded up to her side and gave Jury a wide blue-eyed look. Pleased as could be. Like the curtains, Caroline was ruffled. Even her play clothes: pink overalls and bright pink shirt had ruffles on the sleeves and at the bottom of the legs.

"This gentleman is a police officer, Caroline, so you'd better be good." The "good" was trilled around and the child wrinkled her button nose and giggled. Then she commenced giving Jury flirty glances. It was one characteristic of coming adolescence that he was always sorry to see already attaching its sticky self to childhood.

Jury asked, in a friendly way, in response to the charge of being good, "What do you do when you're bad?"

This threw both mother and daughter. Brenda Hastings looked suspicious and Caroline rather nasty, as if Jury had blown her cover. "I'm *not!*"

"No, not all the time, of course."

Caroline didn't know how to take this, so she turned on her flirty look again. "Tilda's the one that's bad." She said this with a measure of passion that rather surprised Jury.

"Tilda's your cousin?"

She did not verify this, eager as she was to get to Tilda's misbe-havior. "She goes into the woods all the time"—here she pointed in that direction—"and she's not supposed to. Mum told her never to go there."

Her mother stepped in. "Oh, now, love, she doesn't do that any-more."

"Oh, yes, she does! She's there now." This declaration was brought out with a measure of triumph.

"How do you know?" Jury asked.

"What?"

"How do you know?" It was doubly irritating to her that he sim-ply repeated the question rather than explaining it.

Then Caroline came away from her mother's side. "I-I-I knew she wasn't supposed to, so I followed her!"

"Never mind, Caroline," said the mother, giving her an indul-gent smile, which she then turned on Jury. Kids will be kids, won't they? the smile said.

"Caroline," said Jury, "do you remember seeing a woman, a stranger, at Winterhaus last year?"

Caroline rose to the challenge, "Maybe I did." Simpering, she went back and stood beside Brenda Hastings.

"Now you be careful what you say, my girl," said her mother. "No fibbing, now." But she said it with such indulgence, Jury thought she could look forward to many, many years of fibbing.

Caroline said nothing. She wound a yellow curl round her finger.

Jury laughed. "Come on now, Caroline. You didn't really see her, did you?"

With her arms crossed over the bib of her jeans, and her chin raised and that furrowed brow, she looked like a little old lady. This saddened Jury.

"Do you and Tilda play together, then?"

Violently, she shook her head. "No. She's stupid."

Her mother said, "Caroline! You oughtn't to talk about your cousin that way."

The reprimand was delivered in such a lilting tone—Brenda all but sang it—that it had no conviction or force. It was possible that Caroline was getting so many mixed signals, she did not know how or what to be.

Caroline went on: "All she wants to do is play with those stupid dolls and that bear, all by herself."

Jury said, "I expect Tilda doesn't mind being alone."

Definitely jealous of what she didn't understand.

Jury said, "One of those times you followed Tilda (and he bet she had done this many times), did you see a strange woman?"

She nodded, looking unsure of her ground now.

Brenda Hastings said, indignantly, "Well, if she did it was probably only somebody come to look at the property."

Jury ignored her. "Did she have a boy with her?"

Caroline crept a little closer, as if divulging confidences. "There was a dog. One of those *floppy-eared* ones. He was with that boy. He didn't pay any attention to him, though."

"The boy didn't?"

"No, the dog. He wouldn't come when you called or anything. He had to be on a lead or he might run away forever."

Meaning, Jury thought, that Caroline was also on a lead and suffering a similar fate. He imagined her there, hiding behind a tree or kneeling in the undergrowth, not daring to come out for that would mean an admission she wanted to be in Tilda's world of plainer clothes and fewer words and more imagination.

"Anyway, he didn't want to leave."

"No?"

"They had to practically pick him up and carry him. He was nice."

Her ordinarily heated vocabulary had cooled as she thought about this.

"Caroline," said her mother, "you know you're not to go over there! Neither one of you's allowed!"

Both Jury and Caroline ignored Mum. Jury asked, "Did you ever go into the house?"

Silence and then a small nod, avoiding Mum's eyes.

"What?" This nearly brought Brenda to her feet. "I've told you never to go—"

Jury's upraised palm shut her up. "What do you do there?"

Her answer was another shrug.

Brenda's mouth opened and shut when Jury looked at her.

"Did you follow Tilda into the house?"

Another nod, a bit stronger. "There's one of those glass doors that goes to the outside that doesn't lock properly. It was easy to get into."

"It was Tilda who set out the tea things, wasn't it?" He smiled about this.

His approval met with freely offered information. "She took them out of that cupboard, the teapot and cups and took spoons and napkins from a drawer."

Jury felt sad. There had been two cups, two spoons and two little plates for pastry. There should have been two little girls having a tea party. "But she wouldn't let you have tea, would she?"

Caroline said, frowning, "She didn't know I was there."

"You hid? Outside? Inside?"

"Behind the door or in that little closet with brooms. It was easy. Anyway, she sat that stupid doll on the sofa and she had a cup."

"You know, I bet Tilda would rather have company she could pretend with."

Shrugging again, Caroline said, "I don't know."

"Tell me: Did you like the little boy? His name was Robbie."

"He was okay." Now she was bouncing a bit of balled-up paper on the palm of her hand. "The lady was mad at him though, I think. She called and called from the terrace."

"Why would she have been mad?"

"Because he left the house and went to see what Tilda was do-ing. He just pretended he didn't hear her."

"It sounds like the boy and the dog were in the same boat."

Caroline turned her head to look at him. The smile was happy, and honest. It fairly glimmered.

Beneath the fake prettiness was the real thing.

28

"So what you're suggesting is that each of us put forward a solution to this little mystery," said Marshall Trueblood, as they sat in the Jack and Hammer running up a bar bill. None of them had come with money, or at least not folding, which was a laugh, considering the average income of each. Melrose Plant's and Vivian Rivington's were inherited. Diane Demorney's three divorces had been spectacularly fruitful. Marshall Trueblood (affluent antiques dealer) and Joanna Lewes (incredibly affluent writer) actually worked for a living ("or pretended to," was Joanna's assessment). One could say that Mrs. Withersby and Theo Wrenn Browne also worked for a living, but hadn't had any success with affluence. (Theo would not be happy at being grouped with Mrs. Withersby.)

Melrose had spent a good part of the afternoon in here reviewing what Jury had told him about the case. They were fascinated by it. They had insisted upon, and he had gone into, exquisite detail. Joanna Lewes (she being a writer) had importuned him not to leave anything out. Thus Melrose had slogged through quantum mechanics, string theory, the Stoddard Clinic and even what he knew about the mathematician Gödel. He was quite amazed at the way all of them (especially Marshall Trueblood) had drunk these details up, along with their beer, whiskey and martinis. But given that Long Piddleton was not exactly a destination village with a mellow-stoned, pricey country hotel; or a stormy coastline squawked over by scudding gulls; or a couple of restaurants that vied with Les Quatre Saisons (filled with some of Polly Praed's gourmandise); or a crumbling abbey; or a safari park—well, the disappearance of the Gault woman and son would understandably hold them in thrall.

"A contest!" said Diane, who judged a day's loss or gain only in terms of the amusement it had afforded her. She was occasionally entertained by earthquakes, fires, floods and twenty-car pile-ups on the M1, but they soon turned too grim because they had so little to do with her pursuit of amusement.

"It doesn't have to be a contest—" began Joanna Lewes.

"*I'm* in, bloody 'ell," yelled Mrs. Withersby, Scroggs's char, as she tossed a ten-p coin onto the table as if it were a poker pot. No one paid any attention to her.

"Why shouldn't it be a contest?" said Theo Wrenn Browne, who owned the bookshop across the street and who couldn't get a seat at their table unless he brought something to it before he sat down. (He claimed not to have brought money either, which was a lie; he didn't want to get stuck with the tab.)

Melrose couldn't stand him. None of them could stand him. Theo had tried like the very devil to shut down the library so he could make more money renting out books; he had sided with the defendant, Melrose's aunt, in the chamber pot affray; he caused little children no end of grief when they returned their rental books with so much as a thumbprint. No, he was not one of the group, not one of the team. He was the relief player on the bench who the skipper would send in only if all the other players were dead. The execrable corduroy jacket with the leather elbows he was wearing he claimed was Hugo Boss. Having donned this tobacco-brown jacket, he should never have sat next to Marshall Trueblood, who always looked like he *was* Hugo Boss or Armani.

Joanna Lewes, who had written two dozen genre novels in the fields of mystery, romance, horror or any combination of them, said, "You know, Leo—"

"*Theo!*"

She smiled. "As I was saying, you will know who wins when the police solve this case."

"That's not necessarily true. Police have been wrong. Even Superintendent Jury." Theo said this with such a sense of satisfaction, one couldn't help but ask him.

"When?" asked Trueblood. "When has he been wrong?"

Theo reddened. "Well, I don't—"

"Right. You don't." Trueblood went back to smoothing the raggedy edge of a fingernail with his little gold clipper.

Melrose said, "It's not, strictly speaking, a police matter. Jury is doing this kind of on his own, pro bono, you could say, because it intrigues him."

"We've got to have rules!" Theo Wrenn Browne smashed his femininelike fist on the table.

Diane stopped the martini on the way to her mouth (a sight seldom seen). "Put a sock in it, Theo."

"Can we just think out loud, then?" asked Vivian Rivington, looking beautifully calm in blue cashmere, "or do we go home and ponder and come back?"

"I'll ponder here, thank you. If I go home I'll have to mix my own." Diane raised her glass.

Mrs. Withersby announced, "Ya don't find me thinkin' out loud, not with you lot around. You'd steal the thoughts right outta me 'ead."

"Withers, old trout, I doubt any of us wants to go into your head, not even for a copyright." Trueblood pocketed his nail clipper.

"That's all you know, ya bloody wanker."

"Right," said Melrose. "Who wants to put forth a solution?"

Dick Scroggs, publican, had come to collect their empty glasses. "If one o' us has a good idea," said Dick, "will he use it? Mr. Jury?"

Melrose had heard idiotic questions put in here but this one had bells on. "Use it? Dick, this isn't one of your TV quiz shows. Who wants to start?"

Joanna held her pen in the air. "My money's on this Hugh Gault lying. He murdered his wife and son and is sucking in his friend

Harry Johnson—I admit I don't know why—and he's in this clinic just to throw everyone off, saying he's been driven crazy by his family's disappearance. Perhaps she had the money and he wants it. I dislike the idea of a parent killing his own child, but—" She shrugged and applied pen to paper. She had actually said once she could write entire books in here with everybody talking, including herself.

"I'm sure," said Diane, "Mrs. Browne gave the idea a whirl."

"Oh, funny!" said Theo Wrenn Browne.

Diane gave him a glassy smile.

Vivian said, "There's got to be an explanation of Harry Johnson's connection to the story."

Joanna thought for a bit. "Couldn't he just be acting out of pure friendship? Or perhaps Hugh is using him to test how much of this strange story a person could take."

Melrose nodded. "That's good, Joanna. Anything else to add?"

"Not at the moment."

Trueblood sucked in air and began, "I'm for the superstring theory, the parallel worlds. The Gault woman and the boy did step into another dimension." Happy with his solution, he lit a Sobranie cigarette the same color as his foam-green shirt.

They all stared at him, or glowered.

"You can't be serious," said Joanna.

Sniveling laughter from Theo Wrenn Browne.

"Have a martini," said Diane, sliding her glass toward Trueblood.

"Wanker." Mrs. Withersby plopped her wet mop from bucket to floor.

"Come on, now," said Melrose. "Hugh Gault apparently believes that and he's a respected physicist."

"But really, Melrose. People actually falling or disappearing into another world?"

"Why not?" said Marshall Trueblood. "Look around you." His

glance trailed round the room. "Anyway, you've experienced déjà vu, haven't you?"

"That's different."

"Why is the whole past not part of the present?"

"That's still different," said Joanna. "So you think the wife and son are wandering around in some godforsaken world—"

"Wait. Maybe *this* is the 'godforsaken' one and they're in the real one—"

Theo Wrenn Brown weighed in: "Well, my theory is that Hugh is in this clinic, isn't he? Far from his pretending to be nutty, he actually *is* crazy and this whole elaborate plan is the result of his fevered brain."

"But he's convinced What's-his-name?—"

"Harry Johnson."

"—that it's a true story," Joanna went on. "I get the impression that Harry isn't easily persuaded, that he's very intelligent and knows Hugh well. Surely, he'd know if Hugh was psychotic."

"Tell us again," said Diane, "about this clinic visit."

Melrose related Jury's story of that visit in detail.

Then, with renewed interest, she asked, "Does the place serve drinks?"

Melrose squinted at her. "Diane, this is a clinic we're talking about, not a lounge. Half the patients are probably alcoholics. It would be like ordering a rum collins from a church usher."

Said Diane, "I've often thought it would add to a hospital's ambience if it stocked a bar, not for the patients, of course; I'm not that crazy. But for visitors; you know, maybe right next to the gift shop. I mean, how many people have you ever heard say liked to visit hospitals?"

Melrose said, "Is this your theory?"

"No, it's my recommendation."

"I'll see it reaches the right ear in Commons."

"My *theory* is that Hugh's sending Harry on a wild goose chase because Harry is in love with the wife, maybe had an affair with her." Diane shrugged and reangled her cigarette holder. She was smoking one of Trueblood's, a shocking pink Sobranie. "Imagine how awful it would be if your lover simply vanished."

"But if she didn't, where is she?"

"Gone to some place like New York or Finland." Trueblood's brow creased. "I've never really seen the point of Finland."

Melrose said. "All right, let me recapitulate these solutions. One: Hugh is lying; he's murdered his wife and son and is feigning madness to throw people off the scent." Here he nodded toward Joanna, who gave an answering nod.

"Two: a parallel world into which they've vanished. The string theory."

"Superstring," Trueblood corrected. He had the quickest mind of the lot; he could vacuum up details like crazy.

"Three: Hugh is indeed insane and the story is a fantasy. Correct, Theo?"

Theo nodded.

"Four: Hugh's doing this to Harry as revenge for the affair with Hugh's wife."

Diane blew out a jetty of smoke and nodded.

"What I'd like to hear about is the fracas in the other drawing room," said Joanna.

Trueblood said, in the middle of blowing smoke rings, "Red herring." He blew a little smoke ring through a large one.

They all stared at him. "What the devil are you talking about?" asked Melrose. "What red herring?"

"It was done to draw the attention away from the people in the first drawing room. Where Superintendent Jury and Hugh Gault and Harry What's-his-name were talking."

Melrose passed his hand up and down before Trueblood's face as if he were a hypnotist making certain his patient was deep enough into a trance.

Trueblood went on blowing smoke rings.

Diane adjusted another cigarette in her sleek black holder. She waited while Melrose reached across the table and lit it. Then she turned to Trueblood, who sat there like a cat with a bowl of cream. "What we've been talking about isn't . . . a . . . story." She spaced the three words out in case his sanity or his hearing aid (he didn't wear one) were performing on a very low frequency.

He said, "Of course it is."

"No. It *happened*," Joanna broke in. "It actually happened!"

"Then," said Trueblood, "the red herring was 'actually' drawn across the drawing-room door."

"My *God*," said Melrose. "This is worse than the play within the play theory. The people were performing in a story no one had written."

"No," said Vivian. "It's *worse*: in the play within the play, the characters in the play proper are *still* actors. They're fictional. In this instance there's no fiction."

"We're not in it," said Trueblood, picking a mite of lint from his Armani silk-suited-sleeve. "It's fiction."

Melrose gaped. "But the fact that we're not in it doesn't mean *nobody's* in it. This story is *about* them. It isn't *them in the flesh!*"

Trueblood raised his perfect brows. "That's precisely what I've been saying."

Melrose winced. He brought his fist down on the table. "The people in the other drawing room are simply *the people in the other drawing room*."

Trueblood shrugged neatly. "Of course. That's the red herring part of it. See, we're supposed to be suspicious of them when there's nothing really to suspect. Richard Jury, Hugh Gault and Harry Johnson. Look." He took a gold pen from his waistcoat pocket and asked Joanna for a leaf from her notebook.

"You can have the whole thing. It's got my latest in it and scrap paper will be as good as it gets, I'm afraid."

Oh, if only Polly Praed had that attitude! thought Melrose.

"Thanks." Trueblood began to mark it up. "The play within the play." He drew two squares, a large one and inside it, a much smaller one. "Now, when the roving band of actors, the players, step out of their roles in the inner play—play two, we'll call it—and enter the play proper—play one—they're actors again. During play two the actors become Gertrude, Claudius and whoever happens by during play two. Just as Richard Jury becomes Richard Jury, police superintendent."

"Wait wait wait wait wait," said Melrose, breathless with objections. "It's *not* Jury's story!"

"Yes, it is. He's become part of it. He's become a police superintendent *acting* as a police superintendent, and consequently he changes the outcome. Anyway, he can't comment on himself as police superintendent."

They gawked and gaped. Theo Wrenn Browne, who'd been forced into silence by a total lack of understanding of any of this, but who saw where all the attention was going, said, "You know, I think he's right."

Diane gave him a look. "You don't think anything, Theo." Then to Trueblood: "You're crazy, Marshall. I mean, *anyone* who'd go to all of that mental effort, well."

Trueblood went on, tapping his diagram now and then. "That mathematician you were talking about—"

"Gödel?" Melrose couldn't understand a word of Gödel.

"That's the lad. Remember, sanity cannot comment on itself with respect to being sane or insane, because he has to do it within the system. Gödel says that *no validation of our rationality can be accomplished using our rationality.* So! Superintendent Jury has been unlucky here. He won't solve it, you know. He can't."

"Of *course* he will!" Melrose slapped his hand on the table.

Trueblood dribbled a bit of ash toward the metal tray. "Only if fate steps in and takes his side." He smiled.

Melrose could hardly remember what the argument was at this point. He shifted ground and said to Vivian: "We haven't heard from you."

Vivian had turned on the window seat and was looking out through the casement window at the walk edged with purple daphnes. "I don't have a theory yet. I have a question."

"Which is?" said Melrose.

She looked at him, frowning. "Why didn't they take Mungo?"

Why Didn't They Take Mungo?

29

It was about time somebody asked that question, Mungo thought. It was all so obvious, so incredibly simple, and if they couldn't work it out, why was it down to him to make the blind see? He sighed and stretched on the green sofa, belly up. Really relaxed.

Now, here came the cat Schrödinger, the color of thunder, who'd just had a flotilla of shiny little ones that she kept in the bottom drawer of a Queen Anne walnut bureau. The ormolu mounts brought it near enough to the floor to make it convenient. That's where she'd had them, and that's where they were staying. Little Mrs. Tobias, cook and cleaner-upper, just flapped her hand at the bottom drawer and said, oh, what difference did it make anyway, as the master hardly ever comes in here.

"In here" was the music room across the hall from the living room. The only reason it was called that was because there was a grand piano in it, upon whose keys Schrödinger liked to walk until Mrs. Tobias shooed her off.

Mungo enjoyed the kittens. He liked to take one out of the drawer and cart it about the room and hide it in different places. He had a good time watching Schrödinger look for them.

Well it was just something to do. It wasn't much different from walking around with a shoe in his mouth.

Mungo rolled over again to find he was staring into the yellow eyes of Schrödinger. You look like an owl. He sent her that message. Where is Elf? She sent him back a question.

Where's who? He feigned curiosity.

Don't pretend you don't know: Elf.

Anything that had to go around all its life with a name like Elf probably deserved his sympathy. But the kitten didn't get it. Pleased with himself, he let his eyes slew around to the fireplace. There was the coal scuttle, where a tiny, really tiny face rose over its rim, coming up like a dirt diver.

Schrödinger followed the direction of his glance. The cat gave Mungo's side a good claw and he yelped. Oh, didn't she look satisfied! Look at her nose in the air and Elf in her mouth.

Here she came, stalking back through filtered sunlight, and he wondered if it was dinnertime, and hoped he wouldn't have to put up with yet another smoke-saddled, drink-smeared, wine-sopping gin palace again.

She was sitting square before his damp nose, holding the pip-squeak like a lump of coal, then dropping the poor thing right on the sofa where it whined and blindly moved. You can see, you black sequin of cat. He sent this message and knocked Elf off the sofa.

He didn't, frankly, see how any of them managed to live through another dusk, another dawn, another day. I should have been a poet, he thought. I could go on and on and on in my simple-minded measure—

Schrödinger boffed him a good one on the nose, picked up the mewly kitten in her teeth again and slunk off to the bottom drawer.

Mungo played dead, feet frozen up in the air. If the cat was so dumb as to put it back in the same place, then she deserved to have them catnapped. Was that a word, though? Or did it just mean "sleep"? Had he been dognapped and for some reason didn't remember the event? What on earth the bloody point would be he couldn't imagine.

That Scotland Yard Spotter had been so close! Until he worked it all out Mungo would be lying under chairs in the Old Wine Shades and lumbering along to all of these different eateries.

How, wondered Mungo, could you tell this whole story to the five people in that pub in Northamptonshire, *and they'd none of them get it*? Except maybe the one who'd asked the question. She was closest.

I said it before; I'll say it again: it's not the bloody woods! Bodies buried in the woods, how trite. Now, the girl, the girl was something else again. She and the dreadful Caroline. Another clue that the nice one just might eventually pick up on. He calls himself a spotter?

Maybe people just want to be fooled. That's why it was so easy to fool them. Maybe it was an escape. We all needed escapes, so why not escape to Tuscany and ask this Torres fellow what's going on? Would he tell? Does he *know*? Maybe not. It would certainly make a change, though. San Gimignano What a name! And how that woman tossing back martinis had pronounced it! San Gimmi-*yanno*! *There* was a name for you!

He knew all about escapes. He stopped playing dead, bounced off the sofa and walked over to the bureau and its bottom drawer.

Leaving her question up in the air and unexplained, Vivian left the pub for an engagement she also didn't explain.

What the devil had she meant? "Why didn't they take Mungo?"

They had all sat there and gawked at one another, irritated as the devil that Vivian had gotten away without explaining herself.

And who was she meeting? Who did she have up her sleeve? They all knew one another's friends because they *were* one another's friends. Lord, thought Melrose. It's not another Count Dracula, is it? That engagement had lasted, what?, five years said Trueblood, five years of their working out ways to scotch that romance.

Joanna Lewes said it was too much for her; she had to leave to get home and finish writing her two chapters for the day. They all agreed Vivian's statement was indeed too deep, too—

Except Theo Wrenn Browne, who claimed to have a notion as to what she meant, but, of course, wouldn't say, for it was Vivian's idea. Then the lying little weasel of a bookseller had made an exit and it was the three of them left to mull it over. They had decided to go to Sidbury for a meal, although Trueblood had wanted to go to the Blue Parrot for laughs and Diane had plumped for London because she'd never been to that marvelous little restaurant Melrose had told them about called Snipers, which she thought sounded made to order for them; they were all such sneaks.

They had another round of drinks. Then it was after eight and too late for London, so they argued about the Blue Parrot and whether to go there as Trevor Sly served the most execrable food in Britain.

But then Trueblood said, "Ben Torres. He's a dark horse in this story, isn't he?"

"The story's full of dark horses."

But Torres was one whose story no one questioned and it was a bizarre tale in its own right.

San Gimignano, Diane had said again.

"That's where that torture museum is, right?"

"Marshall, you're the only person in the British Isles who could remember San Gimignano for its museum of antiquated torture artifacts."

"But it was fun."

Melrose stared at him. "I think I should have a little talk with Ben Torres; I think I'll go to San—" He paused, frowning a bit.

"Gimignano," said Diane, with her flawless pronunciation.

Trueblood sat up. "Oh, good. Get me some driving gloves."

Ben Torres. So finally you hit on the bloody obvious, good for you, Mungo was thinking as he made his way over to the bureau.

Schrödinger was in the kitchen, excavating for cheese or other bits of food, and Mungo was at the bottom drawer taking out Elf. He thought it would be especially irritating to Schrödinger if he kept hiding the same kitten all over the house. He could carry Elf in his mouth probably better even than Schrödinger could. He looked around, taking special note of a large jardinière by the bay window that held some sticklike little tree, all windblown out of shape, one of those trees the Japanese were so fond of. He trotted over there.

He dumped Elf in the empty space between the potted tree and the jardinière and ran back to the sofa, pretending to be asleep when Schrödinger slunk in and went to the drawer to count the kittens. She turned and let out a real raspy wail of a cry, like a cat-fighting cry, and then was all over the room, searching for Elf.

Mungo watched this pathetic search, this rooting around in bookshelves, looking in the coal scuttle again (would I choose the same place twice, for heaven's sake?), jumping up on chairs and nosing under cushions.

He watched and wondered about Ben Torres, why it was taking everyone so long (including even the Spotter, who was really okay and fed him scraps under the table) to get around to Ben Torres.

Schrödinger had her paws over the rim of the jardinière, but with no way of getting Elf out from that position, so she slid down into it. A lot of noise came out of it, meows and hisses and other cat sounds. Elf could get out by himself only if he scrabbled up into the dirt container that held the tree and from there to the edge of the jardinière and down to the floor. Mungo was tired of having to do everyone's thinking for them.

"I don't *know* what she meant," said Melrose to Jury, who was on the other end of the phone line.

"'Why didn't they take Mungo?' Well, if you stop to think—"

"I'd rather not." Melrose held the telephone receiver and picked at a bit of loose velvet on the chair in the hall of Ardry End. "I'm finished with thinking."

"When did you begin? If you stop to think about it, if Glynnis and Robbie were indeed abducted, it would be absurd to think the abductor would have taken the dog along."

Melrose said nothing and picked at the velvet. He'd called to let Jury know he was going to Florence.

"Florence? That's a lot of trouble to go to."

"You know me. Trouble's my middle name."

"Yes, sure."

"You don't need to be sarcastic."

"I don't need to be; I just want to be."

"Of course, Ben Torres might not even talk to me about all this."

"I don't see why not. He talked to Harry Johnson. It isn't as if it's a secret. All of it is in the past."

"Yes, probably. But who shall I say I am?"

"Well, you could try Melrose Plant or Lord Ardry."

"Funny. But what's my connection to be with Winterhaus?"

"You're helping out a friend, me, Detective Superintendent Richard Jury."

Melrose frowned. "But all of that's the truth."

"Learn to live with it. When do you leave?"

Melrose consulted the longcase clock in the hall. "It's too late to go tonight, so I expect I'll leave tomorrow morning."

"To Florence?"

"Well, of course to Florence. Do you think San Gimignano has a landing strip or a helicopter pad?"

"You just want to go to that glove shop again."

Melrose sighed deeply. That really annoyed him. Here he was traveling to Italy, to Tuscany, to help solve this riddle and Jury was trivializing his efforts. He said so.

"No, I'm not. You also want to go to the church to see the Masaccio murals. There's nothing trivial about Masaccio."

"May I remind you if it hadn't been for Masaccio's peculiar penchant for solitude, you might never have solved that case? Painful though the case was."

"I didn't solve it. I just got shot. You solved it. You didn't get shot."

Melrose thought there might be a compliment buried in there somewhere, but he didn't care for this juxtaposition of their separate fates. "Anyway, you'll have to give me Torres's address and phone number."

"Address? The man's lived in San Gimignano for years. I'd bet any of the Sangimiginanesi could tell you in a minute where Ben Torres lives."

"The what?"

"Sangimiginanesi."

There was a brief silence. "Since when did you learn to speak Italian?"

"I don't. I'm looking at *Time Out Florence*. Florence and surroundings. It's one of those guides written largely for the teenager who wants to find the best DJ place."

"Well, you certainly got that San-whatever off rather well. Spell it for me. I have a pencil."

Jury made some kind of noise. "S-a-n-g-i-m-i-g-n-a-n-e-s-i. It's the people there, as you might say 'Florentine' for the ones in Florence."

"Yes, 'Florentine' I can manage quite nicely. This one, though, I want to run by Diane, who seems to shine at Italian pronunciation. I mean, for someone who says, 'Let's all go there and sit around the piazza,' well. Anyway, what do you want me to find out about Ben Torres?"

"I don't know, do I? That's why you're going to talk to him. Since this queer story about the house and his mother got to me by way of another person, I wouldn't be surprised if something got omitted or changed."

"Sangimignanorines. How's that?"

"Oh, for God's sake," Jury breathed. "Don't forget your mobile."

"I don't have—" But Jury had already hung up.

Mungo sat up on the sofa watching Schrödinger dash from chair to table to bookshelf, trying to find the source of the mewling.

She missed the Trilby hat left on a table; Mungo had nosed up the brim and shoved Elf under it and now it was moving around. The moving Trilby. Mungo sighed.

30

Melrose had booked a room in the same little hotel he and True-blood had stayed in during their frenzied trip to Florence the year before. He loved this hotel, which occupied the upper floors of an old building and was reached by way of a cool marble staircase bathed in shadows. He had not discerned who or what occupied the ground floor. Probably no one did. The air was as undisturbed as it had been then.

The hotel was a refuge; when something moved here, it moved in padded silence. He thought the personnel, receptionist, waiters, manager went about in slippers instead of shoes. The floor was marble, but not the tap of a heel was to be heard. He had even asked for the same room; the management actually remembered it. Well, it hadn't been so long, only a few months since he had been here; still, there was so much for the Florentines to think about—the David, the Duomo, the gold, the gloves—that Melrose was quite astounded he himself was worth remembering. No, it was probably crazy True-blood they remembered, walking around in a trance with his Masaccio panels—or at least what he'd hoped were.

The little hotel was on a tiny cobbled street, but what wasn't once you left the center and the San Marco palazzo? It wasn't much of a walk to the Ponte Vecchio and that was where he headed when he went out.

The Arno, fretted with sunlight, moved so slowly it seemed almost still. The bridge was lined with little shops, mostly jewelers' and goldsmiths'. It was so pleasant to walk on old stone, to look at old gold, to breathe old air.

The glove shop at the other end of the bridge was as crowded this time as it had been the last; one could barely get to the counter or catch the attention of a shop assistant. These gloves were made of such creamy leather and in such misty or lustrous colors, the shop might as well have been selling rainbows and sunsets.

The spare little woman whose head didn't reach much higher than Melrose's elbow had no compunction about shoving it and the rest of Melrose out of the way, an unsuccessful effort that released a spate of Italian which could only be a string of invective.

Hundreds, even thousands, of pairs of gloves in plastic sleeves were nestled in little niches built all over the wall like an enormous letter box. Hot colors, cold colors, pale colors, bright colors—colors one doesn't see anywhere else except in sea or sunrise. The blues could be anywhere between the blue of the Aegean and the shadows cast on a snowy winter's day.

As he stood, contemplating this deluge of gloves sorted by color and size across the wall, the crowd had magically thinned out and he was actually being offered assistance. He asked to see the rose, the peacock blue, the sea blue, the winter blue. He purchased twelve pairs, enough to pay his hotel bill, and still felt he'd the best of the bargain. He watched the woman wrap his gloves; he loved the way the French and Italians did this, so carefully and prettily as if every purchase were a present.

One pair he asked to be left unwrapped, not to wear but just to feel its buttery softness. He left the shop.

Melrose walked back across the Ponte Vecchio, stopping every now and then to look at the Arno and its still passage. He held the gloves against his face, feeling comforted, and thought random thoughts of home.

31

As if the hilltop town in Tuscany was a fortress (and it probably had been), San Gimignano was surrounded by gated walls and graced by tower houses. In the twelfth and thirteenth centuries, the gates would have been closed and guarded in the night and the streets tied off with chains and the people under curfew. At least, Melrose imagined it had been that way. Feudal families built these towers, and probably all competed for the tallest tower. He imagined an early morning in winter, seeing the towers poking through smoke or fog, the whole little town floating above the hill it stood on.

Melrose parked his bee-sized car in the car park and undertook the uphill journey into the center of San Gimignano, if it could be said to have a center. This hike he was making could easily take the place of dueling at dawn, the winner the one who got to the top first.

He stopped in a little trattoria on the Via San Mateo for some *acqua minerale*. He drank a lot of it as it was one thing he could pronounce correctly. *"Acqua minerale"* he more or less flung out and was served without the waiter's asking him, with furrowed brow, to repeat himself. He left and continued his walk on the cobbled street to the landmark torture museum and past it and then looked for the house number that had been furnished by the trattoria waiters after they had a brief argument over Signore della Torres's house.

Ben Torres looked very English. He was dressed in flannel and a blue linen shirt, a man of medium height, with dark hair, long nose and eyes the blue of his shirt. He (blessedly) sounded English, too. His English was impeccable. Well, he *was* English, wasn't he?

It was just that one tended to think anyone who lived long in another country would assume its speech, its dress, its manner.

"Mr. Plant—?"

Melrose nodded and followed Ben Torres into a living room or library. Offered a drink, Melrose automatically said *acqua minerale* before he remembered Torres was English and then quickly changed the water to whiskey.

Torres laughed. "You know, I think I can identify an alcoholic as the one who asks for *acqua minerale*."

"Well, this one doesn't." Melrose held the chunky glass and looked round the room. It really was a sort of dream house for bibliophiles. There were books everywhere, on the shelves, on the floor, on the window seat, on the desk, where a few lay open, staggered across one another, as though Torres had been consulting them. They lay beside a computer.

"Odd to see that in a place like San Gimignano." Ben Torres said of the computer. "Strikes a discordant note, I think."

"Not if you're using it."

Ben Torres smiled. "You wanted to see me about the house in Surrey?"

"I've told your estate agent that I'd like to rent it. I'd actually like to buy the leasehold. The agent said no, that you weren't interested in selling it. But as I was in Florence, I thought it wouldn't hurt to come round and see you."

"Well, the agent is correct there. I could let you have it on a longish lease, four or five years, but I don't want to sell. Winterhaus is my childhood home; it's been in the family for nearly a century; I couldn't let it go." He paused and regarded his glass of whiskey, held up to the late-morning light. "Do you know anything about the house?"

"I'm not sure what you mean."

"It's a provocative place." Ben Torres's smile was slightly lopsided as if he meant to call the smile back. "Things happen."

Melrose smiled too. "They usually do. The agent told me the house had been vacant for some time."

"It's quite isolated. When I was a child I thought the place pretty spooky. All of that dark interior, those haunted woods."

"Haunted?"

"Well, as children do, you know, assign malevolence to certain places, I did that to the woods around the house. It's a good candidate for creepiness, don't you think? I had too much imagination and a place it could run wild."

Was Ben Torres on to him? After all, people who wanted to rent a property didn't ordinarily go to another country to discuss it with the owner.

He tried a different tack to pry the story out of him that Torres's mother had told him. "Does your family live in England?"

"They're dead, unfortunately."

"I'm sorry."

"Yes. My father and mother died only a few months apart. They were divorced, anyway."

"Did they share your feeling about the house? Its provocative nature?"

Ben Torres was thoughtful. "I think my mother might have. But she was highly imaginative, too."

Go on. Go on about the frightening figure on the path who scared her. Melrose realized—he had what he could only call a small epiphany—he wanted to hear it not just because he wanted to find out something to help them solve this strange case, but also to hear it because it was all such a damned good story. He was fascinated. "So they didn't see the woodland ghost? No lurking apparitions?" He wondered how close to the figure on the path he could take this without giving away his reason for coming.

"No ghosts or apparitions that I heard about. My mother did have a vivid imagination, though." He smiled and took a swallow of whiskey and didn't go on.

Melrose felt an urge to swat him. "How did that manifest it-self?" What a wooden question.

Ben Torres didn't seem to mind. "She didn't want me playing in the woods, I know that." He laughed as if pleased by this.

It's not the woods. It's not *the woods!*

Melrose looked quickly around. Where had that message come from?

"But didn't tell me why."

Hell. Torres had come up with a psychic for a mother and then dropped it. "Was there some sort of history of strange events in that house?"

"Not that I ever heard about. People are like that, aren't they? The isolated house, the banished garden, the deep woods. It's a kind of a mainstay of Victorian literature, isn't it? My mother was a romantic, I expect." He raised his glass. "Another?"

Melrose nodded, wishing his host wouldn't start and stop the way he was inclined to do.

Torres turned from the drinks table and said, "Do I detect in you a man who wants to believe a house is haunted?"

Melrose lurched a bit in his chair, then laughed a bit artificially. What he wanted was the rest of the mother's story. "Lord, I hope not. Was that what your mother wanted?"

Torres handed him his drink and sat down again. The drink was still a frugal finger. Torres wasn't cheap; perhaps he preferred small drinks to show himself he didn't drink much. It was hardly past noon. "I don't know, honestly, what my mother wanted."

There was just an edge to the statement, an edge of disap-pointment? Anger? But, of course, he stopped again, dropping the subject.

"When I was looking at the house, there was a child there, I mean, outside, at the bottom of the gardens, playing in a sort of Wendy house, I guess it's called."

"You must mean Tilda. Yes, she lives nearby. When I was last there, I saw her. I'm sure she's behind the tea in the cups that so puzzled the estate agent. I didn't tell her, anyway."

That answered one spectral question. Except they already knew this.

Melrose wished he'd get around to telling this story of the figure on the path that Torres had told Harry Johnson.

But there was a difference between him and Harry Johnson. Harry had come on a mission, to discover anything he could about the house as if the history might explain the awful business of Glynnis Gault's disappearance. He was standing in for poor Hugh Gault. Whereas Melrose himself had come only to ask if the house might be for sale. He had taken the wrong tack but, then, what other could he take?

"How about lunch?" asked Ben Torres. "The trattoria on the Via San Mateo is quite good. You probably passed it on your way up the hill."

Melrose agreed and they set off.

"I have a friend," said Melrose, "who's crazy about the torture museum." Melrose inclined his head in that direction as they passed.

Ben Torres laughed. "That's wonderful. Someone whose memory of San Gimignano is fixed on that museum. It's rather mad; or perhaps the person whose collection it is, is mad."

"Be an interesting spot for a murder."

Torres cocked his head at Melrose. "You're interested in murder?"

"Not beyond, you know, the usual." He was thinking of the gardener, and the man William Cannon, who had died in the Winterhaus woods so long ago. "Any in yours?"

"My what?"

"Your past."

They entered the trattoria, where Ben Torres was greeted in such a happy way, one would have thought he ate there every lunchtime. Perhaps he did. He certainly had no need of the menu, just ordered the calamari and suggested Melrose have it, too. He felt it would be ungracious to order something else. He knew at some point in his life he'd be trapped into eating calamari.

But when it came he found it was quite delicious. Done with currants, or something, and the garlic was so transparent it looked shaved. Tomatoes, olives and couscous completed the dish.

"I wish I could have my cook do this dish, I really do." Melrose was thinking mainly of setting a big plate of it—perhaps just the calamari—in front of Agatha when next she came to dinner, which he hoped would not be soon.

"Odd, but someone else was visiting me months ago and we talked about the house. Winterhaus. Someone I had known in a minor way. But I don't think he was interested in leasing it. . . ." Torres's voice trailed off and he drank some wine.

Harry Johnson. Go on go on go on! And then it suddenly occurred to Melrose that he was being a total dunce. That of *course* Ben Torres would not tell him the story his mother had told him, Ben. He'd want to lease the house, not turn people away, and a recounting of Winterhaus's strange history would be unlikely to attract a prospective customer. Well, nothing to be done about it now. They ate their lunch and drank their wine (which was superb) and talked for another hour, until Melrose left, stomach full, hands pretty empty.

He visited the Duomo; he strolled around the Uffizi; he went to the Accademia, or rather, sat in the piazza where he looked at Michelangelo's David, or rather the copy of it; they'd taken the real one away, which got Lou Reed's voice going in his mind.

> They've taken her children away
> Because they said she was not a good mother . . .

He sat in the piazza, stirring and stirring his tiny cup of espresso, and wondering why he was stirring, since he'd added nothing to it. He plunked in the mite of lemon peel. He stirred and gazed solemnly at the copy of the David and wondered how long it took to clean up a piece of sculpture. Lou Reed went on, singing about this benighted, drug-raddled woman. There it was: his highly developed aesthetic sense. Lou and Michelangelo.

The figure is not created but discovered. Michelangelo believed he was freeing the figure imprisoned in the slab of marble. Melrose liked that idea.

He stirred and went over his mental list, wondering if he had forgotten anyone. Vivian, Joanna, Trueblood, Agatha . . .

Mrs. Withersby!

He had forgotten Dick's char. Well, he'd just have to go back, wouldn't he? What a lovely prospect.

He stopped stirring and drank off his thimble of coffee, then rose and headed back over the bridge to the glove shop.

"Nothing," Melrose said to Jury the next morning, with the telephone receiver in one hand and his jammed-up croissant in the other. One of the staff had brought the phone into the little breakfast room for him. "Not a damned thing more than Harry Johnson already told you; indeed, there was a good deal less. I also got the impression there was much more, but that he didn't want to talk about it. But, then, could that simply have been me with my preconceived ideas?"

Yes.

Melrose looked around. Where had that answer come from? "Did you say something?"

"Me? No, I'm simply enjoying the silence of a transatlantic telephone call."

"Very funny. 'You won't solve it, you know.' I'm quoting Marshall Trueblood. 'Not unless fate steps in and takes your side.'"

"I'm sure he's right. Maybe this is too tall an order even for the stepping-in of fate. But how did Ben Torres strike you? Harry Johnson thought the man extremely agitated, even paranoid."

"Well, he didn't impress me as a man ready for the Stoddard Clinic. He seemed pretty calm. But then, of course, it's been almost a year since Johnson spoke with him, hasn't it?"

"Yes."

"I'm leaving this afternoon on the late side. I'll be back in London around seven or eight."

"You're stopping in Boring's?"

"Yes."

"At least the Florence trip wasn't a trip wasted."

"Why not? I didn't get anything out of Ben Torres."

"No, but you got the gloves."

32

"The same, Mr. Johnson?"

Harry nodded. "No hope of my venturing into the unknown, Trev."

Trevor smiled and looked at Jury. "You, sir?"

"Let me have a glass of red. Maybe that one I had before?"

Trevor looked pained at that "glass of red" appellation. "That was a Pinot Noir, sir. An '81."

"Oh. Well, it was quite good."

Trevor shook his head and went to fetch it.

"Okay, go on," said Jury. Under his chair, Mungo's warm nose seemed to be whiffing at Jury's ankle.

Harry nodded. "I could think of nothing else to do; the options had pretty much got down to zero. What was it Sherlock Holmes said? After you've eliminated the impossible, you take what's left, no matter how improbable? But nothing was left."

"Something was. Because there had to be. She—they—didn't vanish into thin air. Or another dimension, no matter what Hugh Gault wants to think," said Jury.

"You're right. You see, I honestly thought the house, Winterhaus, had something to do with it. That sounds spooky, but that's what I thought. I couldn't find evidence that it was the last place she'd been, but it appeared to be the last place she was seen, by the woman in the Swan who saw her by the roadside."

It occurred to Jury then, the business of the key. "If nothing had happened to her, wouldn't Glynnis have seen the agent when she returned the key?"

"There's a kind of letter-box thing at the agency to one side of the door that people can use to hand back a key. Probably that's what Glynnis did. In any event, Marjorie Bathous hadn't seen her. And the key wasn't returned to the agency."

"I keep going back to square one," said Jury. "If they left of their own accord—Glynnis and Robbie—they would have taken Mungo. But if they were abducted, it's unlikely the villain would have taken the dog too, isn't it?" Again, he heard Vivian's, *Why didn't they take Mungo?*

He told Harry about Vivian's question.

Harry said, "They did take him, though, didn't they? But he came back."

Jury felt the whip of Mungo's tail and looked under his bar chair. Mungo came out from under it and turned a wide-eyed look on Harry and then on Jury. Back and forth.

Harry smiled, "Talk about a look of devotion."

To Jury, it looked less like devotion and more like disbelief.

"If only you could talk, boy," said Harry, reaching down to ruffle his neck.

But Mungo avoided this by sliding under Jury's chair, where he put his paw over his eyes.

Their second round came, and Harry went on. "It sounds absurd, I guess, but having tried everything within reason, I decided to go beyond it and organize a visit to Surrey with someone who dealt in the paranormal."

"A psychic?" Jury set his replenished glass down. He'd meant to drink, but hadn't, now that they were dealing with other worlds.

"Psychic, medium, whatever they call themselves. I was almost ready to go in a tent and spend time with a fortune-teller."

"And she—or he—went to the house?"

"Yes. A Mrs. Chase from Putney. She was the picture of everyone's favorite auntie. Sweet face, gray hair, well-padded figure. I felt if she dabbled in the occult, the occult must be more down to earth than I'd ever given it credit for. Well, she stopped before the French door and stared out. I asked if there was something out there, or someone, but she said nothing, nor answered except to say, 'It's extremely cold in here.'

"Then we walked back to the furnished drawing room. She stood in the middle of it, looking around. 'This is not your house, is it, Mr. Johnson?'

"No, it belongs to a man named Torres."

" 'Of whom you spoke before. Where is Mr. Torres?'

"In Italy," I said, "near Florence.

" 'Do you know him?'

"I've spoken to him, yes.

" 'Did he tell you why he no longer lives here?'

"Too many unhappy memories.

" 'I shouldn't wonder. You don't feel it, do you?'

"What?

" 'The atmosphere.'

"She seemed to turn from comfortable nanny figure into some-one measured and exact. Hardly the medium dished out to us by the telly. I didn't expect Mrs. Chase to be struck by great waves of emotion, and she wasn't.

"She asked me, 'Now, why am I here? I mean, what is it I should be looking for?'

"It was then I told her about Glynnis and Robbie. She was not one for hasty answers, certainly. For some moments she thought about this.

" 'They were here, certainly.'

"And then?

"She looked at me for a while without saying a word. Then she said, 'I don't see the boy as clearly. Robbie? Is that his name?'

"I nodded; I couldn't believe what she was implying. 'You're suggesting that they met someone here?'

" 'Well, you could put it that way.'

" 'Could—?' I didn't believe what I was hearing. 'Mrs. Chase, this doesn't make sense.'

"At that, it was her turn to stare. 'Mr. Johnson, you didn't hire me to make sense. Quite the contrary, I think. She was murdered in this room.' Mrs. Chase directed her attention to his feet. 'You're standing on the spot where her body lay.'

"I stepped back, horrified. I couldn't take this in; I couldn't assimilate it."

"Did you believe her?" asked Jury.

"After another minute of blank fear, no, I didn't. I believed she was merely earning her five hundred quid."

"Lord, that's steep for a pleasant drive in the country. The trouble is with so-called psychics, their doubtful visions are difficult to disprove." Jury added, "As if I've ever known one."

Harry laughed. "As to proof, well, if indeed Glynn's body was to be found—"

He said this very quickly as if any stumbling or hesitation over the words would turn what he said to fact.

"You didn't report this to the police, then?"

Harry snorted. "Not bloody likely, I didn't. Tell the police a psychic says Glynnis Gault has been murdered?"

"And you didn't go over the grounds yourself?"

"All right, I did. Looking for freshly turned earth, for a grave, I did. I was ninety-nine percent sure this Chase woman was making it all up."

"Or, possibly, was telling the truth, but mistaken about what it was. There's always that."

Harry nodded. "There was that minuscule one percent. Always that small chance—and, anyway, looking for a grave there would probably be useless as the killer would have buried the body someplace else, don't you think?"

"Possibly, yes." Jury leaned his arm on the bar, his head propped by his hand. "It seems to me you're giving more than one percent credence to Mrs. Chase's theory, you know."

"Yes. I meant, at the time, I didn't believe her. But when I thought about it later I thought it was possible that someone could have followed Glynn from London, or at least known where she was going."

Jury smiled. "That puts Marjorie Bathous and Forester and Flynn in the frame."

"That I *don't* believe I was thinking of a person out of her past, an old enemy, an old lover, an old acquaintance—someone to whom she was a threat, someone who wanted revenge."

"So this Mrs. Chase might have been truly capable of calling up that image?"

"Hell, it wouldn't be the first time a psychic has made some discovery like that. I'd have to accept, obviously, that she is a psychic," said Harry.

"That, or a good actress."

Harry had been staring at his drink; now he turned quickly to look a question at Jury.

"Let's say either she herself was involved in the killing or someone hired her to tell you what she did."

Harry frowned. "What an elaborate ruse."

Jury drank off his wine and motioned to Trevor, who came down the bar with the napkin-wrapped bottle. Jury nodded to him and turned back to Harry. "Not necessarily elaborate. Say it was a job the killer didn't want associated with London. He chose this obscure house in Surrey that she was going to view. The Chase woman is hired to feed you this story, which further removes it from reality, and Glynnis and Robbie vanishing would shore up her so-called vision—"

"Wait a minute, though. How could anyone be sure that I'd contact this Mrs. Chase? I didn't know her."

"How did you find her?"

"A woman who knew someone who knew about his wife and son wrote to Hugh. He showed me the letter. She said—the letter writer—that Mrs. Chase had found her missing daughter."

"Then that letter itself could have been a plant. It would have been easy enough for someone else to write."

"It gets more and more complicated. The thing is, what on earth had Hugh to lose? Just a few quid."

"I don't agree. Hugh had a little more than money to lose. He had peace of mind to lose, hope to lose. But even if that's beside the point, well, what *was* the point? What was to be gained by introducing a psychic into the awful business? If Glynnis and Robbie—and she saw nothing of him—were murdered, why call attention to it? This was a month later. Anyone would probably think the wife had done a runner to get away from the husband, or to meet Mr. X, a lover, so why draw attention to it when it had died down?" Jury paused. "Unless—"

"Unless what?"

"Unless something was *going* to happen."

"Yes?"

Jury was thinking of what Melrose had said. *Some future event.* "Well . . . assuming that someone had indeed murdered Mrs. Gault, he or she or they had gotten away with it up to this point. But there might be a future event that would again call attention to it. Just as an example: What if work was to be done on the grounds? Excavation of some sort, digging around and digging up the body?"

"What good would it do the killer to have Mrs. Chase make her disclosure? A body would still be found."

"Yes, but now Mrs. Chase gets credit for preempting the discovery. If she knows there's a body, maybe she knows where the killer is."

"You mean she might direct the search away from the real killer? That sounds like the killer would be taking too much of a chance."

"It does. But remember, this would now be a crime that's nearly a year old when the police come to it. Anyway, all of this is posited on a future event; we have no idea what that might be, or if it even *will* be. I doubt it's the digging up of Glynnis Gault's body." Jury couldn't help but think of Carole-anne's prediction of several nights ago: *"A body'll turn up. A body always does."* He glanced at his watch. "It's eight o'clock already? I have to go. I'm having dinner with our police pathologist." Jury was stuffing an arm into his coat.

"That sounds a rare treat. Do you talk shop over the oysters?" Harry was straightening the collar of his black cashmere.

"Not if I can help it," said Jury, buttoning the coat. "If Trevor finds your body in here beneath the bottles, it'll be me that killed you for that cashmere coat."

Harry laughed and unwound the dog lead and gave a little tug and a *tck tck* sound, urging Mungo out from beneath Jury's bar chair.

He said, "Ah! I forgot to tell you. As Mrs. Chase was leaving Winterhaus, she turned to me and asked, 'What about the dog?'"

"Frankly, I was floored."

33

Mungo lay in his favorite spot—under the sofa in the music room, directly across from the living room. He didn't know why there was a music room. No one played the piano; it sat in a bay window, unused. He was tired of watching Schrödinger—whose nickname was Shoe—trying to get a fish to stop by batting the side of the aquarium with her paw.

He wanted to think. He wanted to think about the Scotland Yard Spotter who was beginning to be a big disappointment. The Spotter was playing dumb, surely. If he was really dumb, how could he hold down his job?

Mungo rolled onto his back and stared up at the muslin underside of the sofa, which got very boring, so he squeezed out from under it and saw that the cat must have grown tired of the fish always swimming beyond her grasp, for he thought he now heard her moving around the kitchen. Yes, there went the cheeseboard onto the tiles.

He trotted to the bottom drawer of the walnut bureau and saw this tangle of kittens sleeping all over one another. Elf was at the bottom of the pile, so he figured he'd be doing the kitten a favor by pushing away the ones on top and pulling Elf out. Of course, they were all hissing mad as they'd been having a nice sleep until he came along.

Mungo carried Elf around, looking for a likely hiding place. He'd used practically everywhere that could be a hiding spot in the music room. From the kitchen came the sound of something else thudding on the floor. He wondered if Shoe was at the cupboards again. He carried Elf across to the living room.

There were cubbyholes in the top of the desk where Harry kept papers. Mungo wondered if one of them was big enough to hold Elf. He climbed up in three stages: first, onto a footstool; second, up to the desk chair; third, up to the desk itself. He looked all over the surface, and at the cubbyholes and at the little desk drawers. For a closer measurement of kitten to cubbyhole, he let Elf down; Elf shivered and mewled, but Mungo didn't care as he saw something that made his brain come to attention.

It was a folder or brochure—actually there were several—of the place that Harry and the Spotter had gone into, leaving him sitting in the car. There were pictures of the front and the sides and the grounds and the feebly old.

He picked up one copy of the brochure and held it in his teeth as he clambered down the same way he'd got up. Then he crawled under a velvet love seat to think, not bothering with Elf. None too soon did he get under it, either, for he heard Shoe padding back. She'd obviously seen Elf up on the desk. The cat jumped up in one graceful swoop, and then all Mungo heard was a big *meee-oww* roiling around with a tiny *mee-ow.* And they were together again, Shoe carrying Elf back to the music room and the drawer.

Having this folder and making good use of it were two different things. He remembered being in the car and yapping himself nearly to death when Harry and the Spotter had gotten out. Fat lot of good that barking had done him. He lay there and thought some more, and thought of nothing that would help, so he slid out from under the love seat and went back to the music room, where Elf was just getting comfortable. Carrying the kitten around sometimes helped him think. Schrödinger had taken herself off to the kitchen. He deposited Elf in quite a good hiding place, then sat for a moment thinking about the brochure, which he had dropped when he picked up Elf.

If he tried to carry it to the pub, Harry would think it was just a piece of paper getting slobbered all over and take it and toss it in the trash. Mungo thought: Wasn't there one of those black Uniforms walking around this street? Didn't he get together with . . . wait a minute. There were cars of them. Turning blue lights and long drawn-out cries that reminded him of Shoe and the kittens. Hadn't the Spotter got out of one of these cars one evening? They were all part of the same club. They all must club around together.

They knew one another! They told each other things!

In another minute he was bounding to the kitchen with the brochure between his teeth and with Shoe hissing at him, he pushed himself through his dog door. Outside now, he ran around the side of the house to the pavement, then stopped and looked up and down the street. No Uniform.

Where were the Uniforms when you needed them?

Ah! At the bottom of the street one was rounding a corner.

Mungo dashed along the pavement, brochure firmly clamped in his jaws as he tried not to slobber all over it.

It was the friendly one, the one who even called him by name.

"Hey, Mingo!"

More or less. Mungo overlooked the error and dropped the folder at his feet.

"What we got here, mate?"

Mungo lowered his standards and barked.

The Uniform was down on his haunches, looking at Mungo, whose own eyes *bored* into the Uniform's. He picked up the brochure. "Stoddard Clinic, it says. What's that?" Still hunched down, the Uniform opened the folder, looked front to back, at each shot of the clinic and shrugged. "You got me, mate. What's going on here?"

Oh, God! Why were people so *thick*, so *backward*? If the cases had been reversed, he'd be in one of those blue-lighted cars careering around corners to that pub to give the Spotter this clue.

Now here came another Uniform, waved across the street by the first one. They wasted time ("Hullo, Kyle; Mac, how ya been keepin'? How's Greta and the little ones?" Blah blah blah.) Then the second Uniform, Kyle, was studying the brochure of the Stoddard Clinic, even reading bits of it aloud:

"An oasis in the middle of Fulham . . . !"

This called for laughs and comments, such as "SW 7 has an oasis? News to me, how 'bout you, Mac?"

Oh, how funny. Mungo allowed himself an angry bark.

"It's a clinic," said the first Uniform.

Mungo wanted to lie down with his paws over his eyes. *These are the people London looks to for protection? It's a clinic.*

Now they were both hunkering down to ask questions. "Somebody you know there, boy?" asked Kyle.

Yes Yes Yes Yes Yes! Mungo tried to bore into these men's minds with a look like an electric drill.

"Dunno," said Mac, shaking his head.

The pub the pub the pub the pub.

"What d'ya suppose? Somebody we're supposed to go and see?"

Mungo was nearly dancing now.

The Spotter the Spotter the Spotter.

Mac looked over his shoulder down the street. "Maybe Mingo's house? Maybe there's trouble?"

"Let's check it out." Kyle talked into a little black thing on his shoulder. "Okay, Bruno."

"No, his name's Mingo," said Mac.

"Okay, Mingo, lead the way."

Mungo was staying here until hell froze over.

"He's only just sittin' there," said Kyle.

"Okay, boy—" Mac was reaching out an arm.

Mungo could tell Mac was about to *pick him up.* No way. He started trotting toward the house.

The three moved up the marble steps and Kyle raised the brass dolphin knocker.

Who did they think was going to answer? Mungo wondered. Shoe?

But the door opened. Ah! He'd forgotten Mrs. Tobias! She was the shape of an apple, her cheeks nearly as bright red.

"Mungo!"

The Uniforms identified themselves, saying the dog appeared distraught and was everything okay at the house? Was it as it should be?

"Well, now, I only just arrived, but everything looks all right. Still, you might as well come in and 'ave a look round." She stood back from the door and the Uniforms filed in.

Mungo followed, as there was precious little else to do.

The Uniforms looked round the music room as if they were shopping—picking up one object after another, setting it down, as Mrs. Tobias watched from the hall.

Mungo was plopped down in the hall in a fugue state, head on paws.

From a corner of the music room came Kyle's voice. "Here, now, what's this kitten doin' in the piano?"

34

"What do you know about psychics?"

Dr. Phyllis Nancy put down her butter knife and said, "Not nearly as much as they know about me."

Jury laughed. Returning to his question, he added, "Would you believe one?"

"About what?"

"I mean, would it be possible for you to believe one?"

"That's the same question. Or, at least, it calls for the same answer: About what?"

They were sitting at a table in Aubergine, waiting for steak (Phyllis) and duck (Jury).

She was dressed in blue silk. It was the bluest blue Jury had ever seen, a riotous blue. It was deep enough to swim in. Jury entertained that image for a few moments.

"What?"

"Nothing, just thinking about your blue dress, which is gorgeous."

"Thank you."

"For example, what if a psychic told you you'd got cause of death wrong?"

She ate a bread stick, thought about this. Any other police pathologist would tell him to stop being ridiculous. A *psychic* questioning my diagnosis?

Phyllis said, "You know, that's an interesting idea." She thought some more and ate more of her bread stick. "I'm trying to think of an area in which I'd be more likely to be wrong. Poisons, poisonous plants? Something to do with poisons, anyway."

"So you wouldn't automatically discount the psychic's idea?"

"No, of course not. God knows there's enough room for doubt in police pathology. The drowned girl in the river for a month; the child murdered and dragged to the dark alley—no, there's a lot of uncertainty. I guess my point is that in pathology there's a lot of ambiguity and contradiction. There can be so many theories, all of which would appear to run counter to one another, it would be absurd to dismiss one that appears, on the face of it, unreasonable. You should know this if anyone should. Look at this situation: a woman and her son disappear—"

Jury smiled. "Correction: and their dog. People always forget Mungo."

Phyllis smiled as the waiter put down their food. "Believe me, I hadn't forgotten Mungo. Anyway, they vanish into thin air in the course of viewing property. At least, that's what you think. But they could have gone anywhere, couldn't they? What, in reason, would explain this disappearance? Did the woman walk out deliberately? Not only does her friend claim this is impossible, but she takes her boy, too. Perhaps the boy was being abused and she was protecting him."

"But what about the dog? Is it reasonable to believe that a woman bolting from her life is going to take a dog with her? Then there's the context: she's viewing property and talking to one person or another about it. Why would she leave her old life while doing this?"

"So the first explanation—that she ran out on her old life—is unacceptable. The second: they—mum, boy, dog—were abducted. Although I think this is a better explanation than number one, again, why would they take the dog?"

Jury thought about Vivian: "I have a friend who wonders why they *didn't* take the dog."

Phyllis cut off a morsel of her steak. "That's odd. How did he explain that?"

"She. She didn't." He took a fork to his roast duck on a bed of black cherry coulis. "If this tastes as good as it looks, I'm getting a doggy bag."

"You don't have a dog."

"I do, too. Well, he's not exactly my dog; he belongs to the chap upstairs. He's a very very *very* famous underground guitarist. Stan Keeler. Ever heard of him?"

"Yes. Don't you remember, you called me in when there was that shooting at the Hammersmith Odeon where the rock group was playing? I'm such a very *very* underground coroner. This is like coming up for air." She gestured toward the room. "My dinner is scrumptious. Where does that word come from? It sounds just like what it's describing. Scrumptious. You know, this is where the Americans can't get it right, reading all those diet books. They don't eat several courses of small portions over a two-hour period."

"Perhaps you're right."

"But the dog—"

"Mungo."

"Strange, how everyone forgets him."

"I don't. What's for the pud?" Jury picked up a small dessert menu, then put it down. "What you said a moment ago—'they could have gone anywhere.' It makes me think of Schrödinger's cat."

"Of what?" She was about to take a drink of wine, but stopped, looking surprised.

Jury smiled. "You mean I never told you? It's quite interesting." He explained the cat in the box analogy. "Only it's not an analogy; it's a theory: you can't know whether the cat's dead or the cat's alive until you open the box. I think the point is that the cat, as long as it's in the box and, therefore, *unmeasured*, has no reality. It's useless to ask the question 'Is the cat dead or alive?' No, not useless, so much as meaningless. The question has no meaning."

"That's rather extraordinary. 'Unmeasured'? What do you mean?"

"Quantum mechanics."

Phyllis looked at him in disbelief. "But you can't really mean that this Mrs. Gault is, well, *nowhere*, until you find her?"

"That's a good way of putting it, Phyllis. I think I do believe that. Because I'm missing something."

Jury said it again, "I'm missing something."

35

*A*t *last!*

It had traveled like an electric current from Aubergine in South Ken, along to Sloane Square, which it had circled several times before going on to Pimlico, and then backtracking to Belgravia.

In his excitement to hear the Spotter was finally on the right track, Mungo dropped Elf and let him run around until Shoe came in, saw Elf and rushed to pick him up.

But who was the one in neon blue who'd sent the message, anyway?

Talk about your *psychic*!

36

When Jury walked into his office the following morning, Wiggins handed him a message he'd just ripped from the pad.

"I don't know if I've got the name right—the woman just called. Something like Bath, Balthazer—something like that. Well, there's the number and as she appeared to know you I assumed you'd be able to work out the name."

"Right you are, Wiggins. Fortunately, I know a good psychic."

Stiffly, Wiggins asked him if he wanted a cup of tea.

"Not at the moment, no. Now, about this woman's name—you know you could have got her to spell it."

Wiggins sighed. "I would have done except she was so upset I didn't want to keep her lingering." "Lingering" was so idiotic even Wiggins gave up on it.

"Well, you're in luck; her name's Marjorie Bathous. Did she give you a clue as to what was upsetting her?"

"Not a peep. She just said it was urgent." Wiggins stirred the thick yellowish fluid in his glass.

Telephone receiver in hand, Jury told himself not to ask. "What's that?"

"A fruit smoothie."

The word itself should be enough to turn off anyone over eighteen months old. Jury tapped in the number. "It's one of those healthy drinks that have more calories in them than a Christmas pud—Mrs. Bathous? Superintendent Jury here." He had balled up the message and aimed it toward the wastebasket and missed. He was balling up a memo from Racer and stopped when she told him.

"They contacted me because of the Forester and Flynn sign."

Quickly, Jury said he'd be there, thank you very much, good-bye and hung up.

He rose and hitched his jacket off the back of the chair, jammed his arms into the sleeves and said, "I'll be in Surrey." He held up his mobile phone. "If you need me."

37

She was wearing the black suit, presumably the one mentioned by Harry Johnson, the one she'd been wearing when she left London on that day almost a year ago. She had been lying on the cream-colored sofa. Jury had seen her; they had taken her away.

"Traumatic asphyxia," said Dr. O'Reilly. "Almost certainly homicide." He was the forensic medical examiner for the Surrey police, or this part of it.

"You mean she was smothered?"

The doctor frowned. "Yes, but not in the sense we usually understand smothering. I mean, no pillow over the face, not that sort of thing. I'm talking about thoracic compression, which prevented her from breathing. You know, prevented the bellows effect." He put his wrists together and simulated bellows by opening and closing his hands. "Given the lack of bruising round the mouth, I'm inclined to reject the pillow over the face action." He yanked a silky pillow from the sofa and demonstrated. As if Jury and the chief inspector beside him needed a lesson in that brand of asphyxia. "No, it's the thorax—I mean pressure placed on it. Probably by a knee placed there and then all of the body weight pressing down. We'll see. That is, we *hope* we'll see." Dr. O'Reilly offered them his quirky smile and scooped up his bag.

"In any event," said Detective Chief Inspector Dryer, "if it's asphyxia, then we're out a weapon." He sighed. "We've ID'd the body on the basis of the estate agent's identifying her. I assumed since she was in here, she might have been having a look at the property and Forester's would know her. If she had a bag, it's missing. This Mrs."—the detective inspector glanced at his notes—"Bathous told us that you were inquiring about her. I've never seen this woman, but I take it you have?"

"No, I haven't." Jury thought of the dead woman who'd been lying on the sofa, whom Dryer had not permitted be taken away until Jury had seen her: cropped brown hair; the pale, almost delicate skin; the face which, having lost its animation, had lost some of its prettiness. "But there are several people who saw her here besides Mrs. Bathous. The Shoesmiths—" Jury gestured in that direction. "They live about a half mile down this road. They had her in to tea; they're selling up, also listed with the Forester and Flynn agency. And then there's a Myra Easedale, who saw Mrs. Gault on the road."

"Good. That seems clear enough. Assuming it is this Glynnis Gault, have you any knowledge of her family?" DCI Tom Dryer had retrieved the small notebook that he'd put down by the tray that held the tea service. The cups, the little sugar bowl struck Jury as infinitely sad, as if the tea had been laid on for a visitor, and the visitor arrived and now lay dead.

"I know the husband. Hugh Gault. At the moment, he's in a clinic in London. You said Mathilda Hastings found her?"

Dryer nodded. "Awful for a child to be the messenger, but that's what happened. She ran home and told her mum"—he consulted his notes—"no, aunt, Brenda Hastings. Then Mrs. Hastings rang police. Mathilda said she'd gone to the house for a drink of water."

Tilda had come in for a pretend tea, Jury bet, which is why she'd been in this room.

"The utilities—water, electric and so forth—are still laid on even though the house is not occupied. Waste of money, as far as I'm concerned, but as the agent is trying to rent it, I expect it makes a better impression." He sighed. "I don't mind admitting I'm stumped. And what's become of the boy? Her son was with her, the estate agent said."

Jury shook his head. "At least we know one thing."

"What?"

"What's become of the dog," Jury told him.

This proved to be of no particular comfort to DCI Dryer; indeed, it merely added to his dismay.

One of the crime scene technicians was still taking pictures.

Dryer said, "I'll need to show her picture to everyone who'd been likely to see her besides the estate agent, the occupants of this Lake Cottage—"

"Lark," said Jury.

"Oh, yes. Anyway, we've established identity, at least informally. A member of her family will have to make a formal one, of course. As I said, I tried to contact the husband. You say he's in some sort of clinic?"

Jury nodded. "The Stoddard Clinic. It's in Fulham."

"Yes, I've heard of it. It's a psychiatric facility, I believe."

Jury nodded.

Dryer ran a thumbnail across his forehead and looked contemplative. He spoke slowly and moved slowly; Jury wouldn't make the mistake of assuming that he thought slowly. Dryer's eyes had a flinty look. "This woman—first name"—he thumbed through some notes—"Glynnis Gault. About a year ago . . . no, less than that—and this is according to Mrs. Bathous—the Gault woman had been viewing property in this area in the company of her son, and—"

"Her dog, too."

Dryer smiled slightly. "I believe you're right. Mrs. Gault hadn't returned the key to this house, hadn't gone back to the agency and Mrs. Bathous hadn't seen her again. She thought this strange. When she called the phone number in London, no one answered. She tried several times, and still no answer. Then you came here and told her that Mrs. Gault and her son—yes, and her dog—had gone missing. This was the last place she'd been seen. That you told her—the agent, I mean—Glynnis Gault had been missing for nine months." Dryer flapped the notebook shut, looked at Jury.

Jury felt a curious unease, a fluttering of nerves. "Yes, that's correct." But hadn't Marjorie Bathous told *him* most of this? He didn't say this to Dryer.

"I asked Mrs. Bathous if she'd thought of reporting this to police and she said no, that she supposed Mrs. Gault had simply lost interest and returned to London. It's odd, in the circumstances, that no one was reported missing, don't you think?"

"But she was. The husband made the report to Surrey police." Jury frowned.

Dryer ran the thumbnail over his forehead again. "No, I don't think so. I'll check again, but I think you're wrong. Anyway, it's a most peculiar business."

Jury said nothing. That fleeting anxiety returned.

"Would I be far off the mark," asked Dryer, "to think the husband's going to this clinic had something to do with all this?"

"You'd be right *on* the mark. Hugh Gault signed himself into Stoddard Clinic when it got to be too much for him; he sank into depression."

"It would be too much for anyone."

"He's in very good shape now, I think. The clinic must be a good one."

"So you must have spoken to him."

"I did. I went there with a good friend of Gault's. Well, as I told you, the story intrigued me. Hugh Gault is a physicist."

Dryer was silent for a few moments, perhaps looking for a relationship between mysterious disappearances and physics. He nodded as if he'd found it, then said, "I'd appreciate your help in this case. You clearly already know a good deal."

Jury was surprised. Rarely did local police want the help of the Metropolitan police. Usually, the local police wanted the Met to get lost. It was all very territorial. Only one other detective (besides Brian Macalvie, that is) Jury had worked with had been as little on the defensive as Dryer; this was a senior detective up in Lincolnshire named Bannen. Bannen was one of the best detectives he'd ever worked with. Bannen, too, had seemed almost lethargic in mind, languid in movement. That was why Jury was making no assumptions about Dryer's alertness.

"I don't like to drop this on you, but I was wondering if you would tell Mr. Gault about his wife. Since you know him."

"Of course. I'd need more particulars, though. Hugh Gault would naturally want to know what police know. So anything you have—"

"Absent an autopsy, there's not a great deal more I can tell him. There's certainly a great deal more to know, question one being, why in the hell was she *here*?" Leafing through his notes, Dryer said, "This house is owned by a man named Benjamin della Torres, according to the Bathous agent. He lives in Italy, in Tuscany, in a little hilltop town with an unpronounceable name."

"San Gimignano," said Jury unable to resist trying it out.

"Good lord, you know that, too?"

Jury almost wished at this point that he didn't. "It's information coming from Hugh Gault's friend Harry Johnson." And from Melrose Plant, who'd filled in more details. "Torres doesn't want to sell this place, but wants instead to let it out. It's his childhood home and he has a strong attachment to it. The house has a strange, rather forbidding history, certainly an unhappy one—I'm getting this secondhand, you know—"

"From Mr. Gault's friend."

"Harry Johnson. He even traveled to Tuscany—"

"To San Jimmy-Jimmy—?"

"Gimignano."

"Ah."

"Johnson went there to ask Torres about the house. Over the years, there have been tales about the house, imagination working overtime, I'll bet. At any rate, Harry Johnson thought the house itself might have something to do with the disappearance of Glynnis Gault."

"Do you believe that? It sounds rather in the realm of the paranormal, wouldn't you say? Or paranoia."

"Yes. I'd have a hard time believing anything was at work here—"

"Except a knee applied to the thorax, possibly. I wonder if that's how it was done."

"Well, it's easy to *say* nothing strange was going on here, but then I didn't have a wife and son vanish into thin air."

"No, you're quite right," said Dryer.

"And the house surely does have something to do with the Gault woman's death, or she wouldn't have been murdered here. Nor would she have disappeared from around here. As far as an explanation goes, we're no closer to one."

"But as far as a body goes, we are." Dryer ran his thumbnail over his brow and looked deeply perplexed. "If this is true, what could have happened to the boy? I dread thinking that he's dead, too." He looked down at the markings. "You know, it just strikes me as so deliberate, you could say—" He searched for a word.

"Staged?"

Dryer frowned. "Yes, I think that's what it looks like. It's a bit hard to believe that the victim would have come back here instead of going straightaway to London. Home. This little girl—Mathilda—if she'd been coming here to entertain herself down in that toy house, might she have seen someone?" Dryer said.

"She did. She saw Glynnis Gault from a distance and the boy close up."

"Yes, she did tell me that."

Was this the way Dryer worked? wondered Jury. To let you think he doesn't know, when he does? It could be very unnerving. He himself felt a little unnerved.

"What if someone saw *her*, though? I think her parents would be wise to keep her away from this place."

"The parents aren't in the picture. She lives with an aunt—that's Brenda Hastings—but you know that. The aunt has told her any number of times not to play over here. It doesn't do much good. She still comes."

Dryer smiled. "You're a font of information, Superintendent."

Jury returned the smile. "The person you want to talk to is Harry Johnson. That's where I heard it."

"I certainly shall." Dryer glanced at his watch. "It's gone 2:00. Could we repair to the Swan before it closes?"

"Good idea."

"It's partly to have a drink, partly to see if any of the customers know anything. Actually, it's mostly to have a drink. I don't see hope of getting sod-all out of the customers."

The Swan's car park was crowded, considering this was midday.

As they walked across the gravel, Jury said, "Where do these people come from? There are practically no houses around here and the nearest town's Lark Rise and that's ten miles away, with its own compliment of pubs."

Tom Dryer laughed. "Come on, Mr. Jury, haven't you heard the old joke that if you were lost in the jungle with nothing but a bottle of gin and one of vermouth, a dozen heads would pop up in the bush and tell you how to mix a martini?"

Inside, the barman gave Dryer a most respectful hello.

"How you keepin', Chief Inspector?"

"Well, thanks, Clive. I'll have a pint of whatever's in those taps. Guinness. Good."

Jury asked for Foster's. Clive shoved two large glasses under the taps and pulled both. "Heard about that murder up at the big house. Nasty business."

"Already? It's only been a couple of hours since I heard about it myself."

"Yeah, well, you know how t'is." Clive stood with beefy arms on hips, waiting for the foam to subside and pulled some more. "It's all them police cars in front of the house, innit? Plus the mortuary van. All that's kind of a hint." Here he gave a gasping sort of laugh, like a swimmer surfacing for air, as he knifed the foam off the Guinness. He set the glasses in front of both of them.

"Well, I agree it's a nasty business."

"Strange, that. I can't remember we ever had a murder round here." Clive's deep frown suggested he really was trying to think of one, rather than trying to coax information out of DCI Dryer.

"I can't either," said Dryer, with a smile, before he and Jury went to a table.

Dryer said, "Mrs. Gault and the boy—"

"And the dog."

"—yes, what is all of this about a dog?"

"Mungo is his name. He was with Glynnis Gault and her son. A short while ago, he came back."

"Came back? What on earth do you mean? Came back to *London*? By himself?"

"I would imagine he was brought back."

Tom Dryer looked utterly confused. "Why? That's equally strange."

"I have no idea."

"That doesn't make sense." Dryer shook his head and drank his beer. "Now she's dead, and the boy still missing. And the dog—" He turned to look at Jury. "Are you quite sure you heard this right?"

"Talk to Harry Johnson."

"Why in hell would somebody keep the woman for almost a year and then murder her, and in that house she purportedly was taken from? I perceive, as Wallace Stevens said, 'the need for a thesis.'"

Jury nearly choked on his beer. "Stevens, the poet? Surrey police quoting Stevens?"

"What's wrong with Surrey? Wallace Stevens is very interesting."

"So is Arabic, but I can't speak it. Wallace Stevens is very *difficult*. I can't make him out."

"Oh, come now. 'She sang beyond the genius of the sea . . . Like a body wholly body, fluttering its empty sleeves; and yet its mimic motion made—'"

Jury interrupted. "You think that's easy to understand? I beg to differ."

Dryer said, "Well, even if it isn't it's quite beautiful."

Jury's attention was taken by Myra Easedale, where she was sitting at what must have been her table, talking to a young washed-out-looking woman with dingy hair. He said, "That older woman over there"—he inclined his head toward their table—"that's Myra Easedale. Have you spoken to her?"

"Yes. That is, one of my men talked to half a dozen people in here. She was one who'd actually seen Mrs. Gault and her son. That made the third time this woman was seen. There were the agent, the couple in Lark Cottage and she, the third person who actually saw her."

So Dryer had known all of this. Jury hadn't needed to fill him in.

"I thought she—Myra Easedale—made a very good point," said Jury. "She said she couldn't understand why Mrs. Gault, who'd either been or was going to Winterhaus, would park the car by the road directly opposite the Winterhaus drive and get out and consult a map. I could only assume she wanted to be seen. Which brings us back to the whole notion of staging."

Dryer turned his glass round and round. "You may be right."

Jury was thinking. "The body in that Stevens poem—"

"The sea is *like* a body, the body of the singer, 'fluttering its empty sleeves—'"

"The 'mimic motion.' Mimic. Look, I know this is way out, but that's how this whole business strikes me. It only appears to be real; it's actually miming an abduction and a murder."

Dryer looked at him, eyebrows raised. "I assure you, she's quite dead."

"Oh, she's dead all right. I just don't think she knew she would be. For her, the play turned real."

"You're saying the whole was, well, we did say 'staged.' We did indeed. From beginning to end? But to *what* end?"

"I don't know."

An hour later, Jury left for London, still not knowing.

38

Baffled, Melrose Plant looked at his goat, Aghast, who was quietly eating the primulas. He was not baffled by Aghast, but by the phone call from Richard Jury.

If Melrose couldn't work it out before Glynnis Gault was found dead, he certainly couldn't work it out after. Her murder presented fresh problems, one of which was, What had happened to the boy? Why wasn't he found dead, too? Or at least *found?*

Melrose gave Aghast a brief talking to about diet. Aghast just looked at him and slowly chewed. He was always chewing, whether he was eating or not. Melrose picked up the lead and took him back to his stall.

Then he went inside the house, pulled on his wool cap and set out for the Jack and Hammer.

"That there lady turned up yet?" asked Mrs. Withersby, who was smoking one of Trueblood's cigarettes while she leaned on her broom. When she saw Melrose Plant come in, she took up her station by the table in the window.

"If you're talking about the Gault woman"—he sat down between Trueblood and Joanna Lewes, the only ones at the table at the moment—"yes she has. Dead."

Mrs. Withersby could barely contain herself and slapped her leg as if this news were cause for celebration. "Tol' ya! Din't I tell ya?"

"No," said Trueblood, "you did not, old dustbin." To Melrose, he said, "Where?"

"Details, details," said Joanna Lewes. "Let's hear them!" Understandably, she was one to enjoy a good murder, if it was artfully done.

"I don't really have that much information beyond the basics. The body was found in that house in Surrey I told you about."

"The house she vanished from? And all this time later? This *is* spooky," said Joanna.

She said it, with a shiver Melrose thought she would have described as delicious. It even reached her mouth.

"Tol' ya," said Mrs. Withersby again.

"Oh, shut up, Withers," said Trueblood as he reached in his pocket and extracted his money clip. "Here, get yourself a drink." He took a five-pound note from the clip.

She grabbed it up smartly, saying, "I don't see you yobs waitin' on yerself, so why should I?" She fluted her order for a gin to Dick Scroggs, who paid no attention to her.

"You don't get waited on because you're the char, Withers."

"Ha! You fink you're better'n me?"

"No, I don't fink. I know I'm better'n you."

Mrs. Withersby gave Trueblood a killing look and sloped off to get her gin and argue with her employer, who had been enjoying a quiet read of the Sidbury newspaper.

"She was where in the house?" asked Joanna.

"The drawing room, the room that still had furniture in it. It was set up by the agent because a totally empty house is so lifeless. You know how empty a place can look. Anyway, that's where Mrs. Gault was found, lying on the floor."

"Blood?" asked Trueblood richly, as if he'd just hiked in from Transylvania.

"No. She was smothered."

"How?" asked Joanna. "A pillow?"

"Apparently, somebody pressing down hard on her chest."

"Who found her?" asked Trueblood. "Police?"

"No. There's a little girl who lives nearby who likes to play in an old Wendy house on the property. She went into Winterhaus for a glass of water. Then into the drawing room and found the body."

Joanna put her hand to her forehead as if this news were painful. "Poor tyke," she said.

"Not terribly tykish, she isn't. Still, I expect it was kind of awful. Anyway, she went rushing off to tell her aunt, and the aunt called the police."

"Staging," said Trueblood. "I mean, really." He gave a stunted sort of laugh.

"What?" asked Melrose.

"Well, as you said before, or as Superintendent Jury said, it looks—sounds—staged. I mean disappearing—mum, boy, dog—in the first place is funny enough. But to be murdered nearly a year later? And murdered *there*? That's choreographed to within an inch of its life, right?" He sipped his drink.

Melrose bit his lip. "I suppose so. Which only raises the question, Why?"

"Good lord, the entire thing's a 'why'; it's been a 'why' all along. And Richard Jury's no closer to an answer than he was. Rather the reverse, I'd say. All this murder does is cloud the issue. But, as I said before, he won't solve this; he's allowed himself to get stuck inside the system, and you know what that chap Gödel said."

"Gödel was paranoid. He thought someone was trying to poison him, so he starved himself to death."

Diane looked alarmed. "How dreadful. How *unspeakable*."

Trueblood went on: "That theory of his"—he shut his eyes, his face turned slightly upward to the ceiling, trying to drum up the theory—"incompleteness! That's the one: the theory of incompleteness. Clever notion—"

Oh, shut up. It irritated Melrose to death that Trueblood was sitting there working out the incompleteness theory.

Diane turned to Trueblood. "He might have starved himself to death. But he still took fluids, didn't he?" She raised her glass for a bracing sip of vodka.

39

Jury stopped at a light outside the South Kensington tube station, an extremely complicated little confluence of roads, lights, pedestrian crossings and small islands where one could safely cower to avoid being hit by impatient drivers coming from three—or was it four?—directions.

Stopping there, he was wondering how to tell Hugh Gault about his dead wife when Vivian's question came to mind again: *Why didn't they take Mungo?* What the hell did she mean?

Damn. He missed the light turning green until the car behind him tapped its horn. Jury jerked to and continued along the Fulham Road. He passed the Fulham/Broadway tube stop and another death-defying intersection and drove on up the Fulham Road. The night was black as tar, starless and cold.

He slowed a little as he passed the iron gates of Fulham Palace. Jury thought again of its gardens and what had happened there, and saw in his mind's eye the knot garden with its medieval herbs, the dead woman lying incongruously in a pitch of lavender. He saw the gorgeous grounds full of trees—silver lime, holm oak, chestnut, redwood—and wondered if he would ever have reason or nerve enough to walk through those trees and gardens again.

The elegant Stoddard Clinic gave off that same rather comforting sense of having removed itself from the demands of ordinary life, somewhat in the manner of Hugh's many dimensions and alternate worlds. For some reason, Jury thought of his delayed reaction to the light's changing in front of the South Ken underground: he intuited—and it was high time his intuition kicked in—that Hugh

Gault's idea of time was far more like that complicated arrangement
of lights and crossings than it was like tracks running parallel.

He had called already, and that and his ID had gotten him past
the gatekeeper. Now he sat there in the clinic's car park, under a
massive oak, trying now not to think. The whole thing was unravel-
ing like a frayed gown, and he didn't want it to come undone too
quickly. He turned the envelope holding the crime scene photos
Dryer had supplied him with around in his hands, feeling a lot like
he must have felt when he was a boy, slapping the book shut as the
end of the story approached, even though it was a book someone
had read to him many times before. He did not want the words at
the end spoken. This, he thought, was a very strange analogy and he
wondered what he meant by it. Instead of concern for the dead
Glynnis Gault, was he concerned about the end of the story?

He pocketed his key, got out and stood looking at the clinic's
complicated Gothic façade. Everything was complicated, he
thought. Everything. He smiled a little, thinking this whole case
would be solved not by he himself—Jury the dimwit—but by Wiggins, Carole-anne and Vivian.

And Mungo. Perhaps Mungo most of all.

Jury crossed the entrance hall to Reception and told the sleekly
suited receptionist with the black helmet of hair that he'd come to
see Hugh Gault. Of course she would already know this, having
been notified by the guard at the gate. Yes, he'd been here before.
Jury showed her his ID, and she swept her hand back over her
glossy black hair as if the warrant card were a camera. She wondered, Was something wrong? Not at all. He merely needed some
information from Mr. Gault.

"He'll be down in a minute anyway, if you'd care to wait?" With
a pen she pointed round to the same drawing room he and Harry
had waited in before.

Then Jury turned back to the receptionist: " 'Anyway'?"

"Pardon?"

"You said Mr. Gault would be down 'anyway.' "

"Oh, yes. He's already been told he has a visitor."

The visitor, then, was either the amiable woman with the fading good looks who glanced up from her magazine and gave him a quick smile, or the gaunt young man holding a sheepskin jacket in his lap who looked at Jury and away, his brown eyes incurious.

Jury had no time to pursue the question of who was who before Hugh Gault walked in and the woman stood up and they embraced. No, hugged was what they did, and hard; they seemed to be gathering warmth from each other.

Hugh released her and held out his hand to Jury. "You're Inspector . . . no, Superintendent Jury. It's nice to see you again." He turned back to the woman, introducing her. "My wife, Glynnis."

Things change as you look at them. One thing becomes two things.

He looked at Glynnis Gault.

He won't solve it, you know. . . . Only if Fate steps in and takes his side.

Fate just stepped in.

40

Jury reached out his hand to Glynnis Gault with a peculiar feeling (though oddly pleasant) that he was getting too much water up his nose and coughing from it, and would she kindly pull him out?

She had a sweet voice and a warm hand. "My goodness, what's Hugh been up to? I've been away for some time."

Indeed you have, Jury wanted to say. About nine months. But he was so surprised he could only gaze at her. Then after a few seconds of this, he said, "Mr. Gault's done nothing at all. I just wanted him to look at some police photographs." He was relieved that the reason for bringing the pictures would not now materialize, or worse, that he or DCI Dryer had come with the news that Glynnis had been found murdered before she herself had arrived here. It could so easily have happened.

"Let's have a look," said Hugh, motioning for all of them to sit.

Jury drew out the two photos of the dead woman and cautioned them that the subject was dead, had been murdered.

They—Hugh and Glynnis—were of that rare breed of witness who thought before they spoke.

Hugh shook his head. "No, sorry."

Glynnis also said no. "Who is she?"

"That's the problem. We don't know. She was found asphyxiated in a house in Surrey that's presently unoccupied. The woman had apparently disappeared nine or ten months ago, along with her son and the family dog."

Glynnis laughed. "I'm sorry, but, the family *dog*?"

Jury nodded and watched both of them sit back, making themselves comfortable, ready for the story. Jury told the bare bones of it, reserving for the moment the dead woman's masquerade as Glynnis Gault. And the boy's as Robbie Gault. And Mungo's as, well, Mungo. He was reserving this part of it—indeed, the most significant part of it—because the whole story was so incredible. Yet he had believed it, hook, line and sinker. "You're a font of information, Superintendent."

He said, wanting immediately to call it back: "The dog came back." He realized how strange the whole thing sounded. How *exceedingly* strange it sounded coming out of his own mouth, a Metropolitan policeman. A New Scotland Yard *detective*.

They looked at one another. Hugh repeated it: "The dog came back?"

"It's an account that was given me by Harry Johnson." He waited for Hugh to seize upon this piece of news. He did.

"Harry? You're saying *Harry* told you this story?" Hugh laughed.

His wife looked as if she thought it was too fantastic.

"He did, yes."

Glynnis laughed. "Please, Mr. Jury, this is some police trick, isn't it?"

Jury felt his mouth going dry. "No."

Hugh said, "I was more than a little puzzled when he brought you—"

Jury interrupted. "So that *was* Harry Johnson?"

"Yes, of course it was. The man is highly intelligent, he really is. It's too bad he can't channel it into something a little more productive than this obsession with quantum mechanics and me."

"He told me the two of you are collaborating on a book about it."

Hugh tilted his head as if in this position he could see more clearly into Jury's fevered brain. But of course it wasn't Jury's; it was Harry Johnson's brain. "This damnable book—is he still on about that? Harry's not writing a book, although I expect he thinks he is. *We're* certainly not writing a book together. I let him borrow my notes because they deal with the principle of complementarity. Niels Bohr, you know—with whom he has an endless fascination."

There was a silence, uncomfortable for Jury, but puzzled for the Gaults.

Hugh said, "May I make a suggestion?"

"Of course." It would not have surprised Jury at all if the man said, *"Why don't you check in here? I'm sure your work must keep you under terrific pressure."*

"The dead woman. She could, you know, have been doing this on her own, couldn't she? That is, she could have gone to the estate agent and simply asked to see property—"

Jury hated bringing it up, but he had to. "I'm sorry to mention it, but you had a son—"

Glynnis tried to be matter-of-fact. "We did. He drowned."

"The woman in these photos—she also had a son. Rather, there was a boy with her. The thing is, Mrs. Gault, the woman was using your name. She was impersonating you."

"What?" In her chalk-white face, her eyes widened.

"With a son named Robbie."

Hugh said, "Robbie died last year. It was why—" He didn't finish. "It was a boating accident. We were sailing on a friend's boat and things got rough and he was washed over the side." Hugh looked away.

Jury waited a few beats. He didn't want the question to seem rather cruelly frivolous. "Do you have a dog?"

"No. Hugh's allergic to them."

Jury nodded. "Does Harry Johnson have a dog?"

She looked at Hugh, puzzled.

Hugh smiled. "He does. I think his name's Mungo. He's smart, that dog. The clinic's very relaxed in that way. You can bring pets in for the patients to see as long as they're well behaved."

Jury stared. Then he knew. *Why didn't they take Mungo?* He knew the answer to Vivian's question. What she had wondered was why, if other dogs—like that Irish wolfhound—were permitted in the clinic, then why didn't they take Mungo in when the two of them went to visit Hugh? Mungo would have leapt in delight at seeing Hugh. A loyal dog, seeing his master after such a long time.

Because Mungo wasn't Hugh's dog. Mungo wouldn't have made the expected fuss over his master. Mungo wouldn't have done a damned thing. And Harry knew it.

He said to Glynnis, whose presence here he couldn't quite get over, "I believe you just got back—"

She nodded. "Yes, from the south of France. I was in Aix-en-Provence with my father." She faltered, looked down at the rug. "I was just devastated . . . I was. Sorry."

Jury had a million questions which he felt he couldn't ask at the moment. He rose, smiled. "Thanks for your help. I'm terribly sorry for your loss." But he was so relieved there hadn't been yet another one for Hugh Gault that the "terribly sorry" had little conviction. "I think I should be going."

"If we can help you more, don't hesitate, Superintendent," said Hugh, rising. "Although I don't think Harry's so far gone he'd really have anything to do with this."

He said this with the most sublime certainty.

Yes, Jury might be nuts, but Harry wasn't.

Jury was about to thank them and take his leave, but that comment stopped him: "So far gone? Harry?"

Hugh was standing now, having risen when Jury did. "I mean, since he checked himself in, as I did, he was free to leave, of course."

Can I be that stupid? Can I be that utterly, blindingly stupid?

"Harry was a patient here?"

Hugh registered surprise. "Well . . . yes. Harry was here for a little over a year. It's how I came to know him."

"This is where you met him?"

"Yes. I'm surprised he didn't tell you."

I'm not. Jury thanked him, both of them, and left.

41

Carole-anne was clopping her way down from the second floor as Jury was walking up to the first. Those dreadful shoes! What was she now? A Bruno Magli fanatic?

"I forgot your key," she said.

Jury put his own key in the door. "Usually, it's 'I forgot *my* key.'"

"Well, I didn't, did I? Just yours."

They both entered Jury's front room or, as Carole-anne would no doubt put it, *their* front room.

"And why this hunger to get into my flat?" he asked.

"I heard your phone. That answering machine's not very dependable. You look knackered." She plumped herself down on his sofa.

"I *am* knackered. Very knackered." Jury dropped his coat on the sofa and went to the kitchen, where he pulled a bottle of Foster's out of the frig. He took it back to the living room.

She said, "If you want a drink, let's go down the Angel."

Jury sank into his easy chair. "I don't feel like a pub."

"Oh, come on, Super." She flashed him a truly darling smile. "Everybody feels like a pub."

"I need to make a call. Will you excuse me?"

"Oh . . ." She grew anxious at his forays into privacy. But she got up.

She looked so sad, Jury had to say, "Don't leave. But don't listen."

Saved, she sat down again on the sofa and picked up a magazine, probably last year's issue of *Time Out,* and smiled again.

He shook his head. If only the stars shone so brightly.

Jury punched in the number for the Surrey police, though it was probably too late for Dryer to be in the office. Now where did he get that idea? As if provincial police kept regular hours, as London's slaved on through the trough of night.

A copper named Delancy with an accent to match answered. Jury asked for DCI Dryer. "If he's there. This is Superintendent Richard Jury of the Metropolitan police. I was with him earlier."

Jury could sense the very air in Surrey coming to attention.

"Just a moment, sir."

Jury heard Delancy bellow across the station room to someone else. Then he turned back to the phone. "Not here, sir."

"Would you see if you can get hold of him and tell him to call me. It's urgent." Jury gave his home number.

"Get on that right away, sir."

Jury hung up and took another pull at his beer. Carole-anne was now fully reclined on the sofa, the offending clogs off and on the floor. He said, "What's urgent is that the Surrey police found a dead woman in a house there."

"Pardon?" wide-eyed she asked.

"Come on, you heard me say 'urgent.'"

"I wasn't listening." Intrigued, she sat up. "Who is it? Where?"

"The who is unknown. The where is a house called Winter-haus."

"Oh, that."

"Yes, oh, that. Aren't you going to say 'I told you so'? You said a body would turn up. 'There's always a body,' is what you said. But here's the corker: the woman was indeed the one who the estate agent knew as Glynnis Gault. The same one a couple of other people identified as the Gault woman. Only, she isn't. When I walked into the clinic to see Hugh Gault, his wife was there. Mrs. Gault. Glynnis."

Carole-anne was interested enough to stop playing with her hair. She drew it back and twisted it, but it fell forward again. "Then he's wrong."

Jury was confused. "Who's wrong?"

"Hugh. He's wrong about the ten dimensions. His wife didn't go into one, like we thought—"

Jury loved the "we."

"—still, I haven't found my earring. So maybe he's not wrong. You sure you don't want to go to the Angel?"

Jury blinked at the maze of her thought. No, he wouldn't go to the Angel. He'd like to be sandblasted, though.

42

The next morning, Jury and Tom Dryer were on their way to Belgravia, Wiggins driving at the moment along the King's Road toward Sloane Square. Dryer was in back, Jury in front, turned toward him, his arm across the back of the seat.

"I'm assuming that Harry Johnson will know that I know the dead woman is not Glynnis Gault. Assuming, that is, that he knows the real Glynnis is back from Provence."

Dryer was hanging on to the strap as if uneasy that Wiggins would forget another zebra crossing was really for the sake of the pedestrian. "I imagine so, well, depending." He interrupted himself to say, "Sergeant, those three old ladies are not on skates." He was speaking of Wiggins's attempt to nose the car forward as the ladies tried to negotiate round it. This was near the Safeway and the old ladies had carryalls full of groceries. As soon as they'd crossed, the car jumped forward and continued down the King's Road.

Jury looked at Dryer speculatively. "Depending? Depending on what?"

Wiggins, living up to Dryer's expectations, sprang across an intersection outside of Peter Jones, forcing back several shoppers who had unwisely set foot on the crossing.

"Wiggins, watch it, for God's sake."

Tom Dryer, when he talked to Jury late last night, had thanked him for calling. Jury had said, "Well, it *is* your case, Tom." He also said that Dryer should have been with him at the clinic, but Jury thought it was going to be nothing other than a routine identification. Hardly routine for Hugh Gault, of course, but that Hugh would take one look at the police photos and say, yes, that's Glynnis.

"I can talk to the Gaults whilst I'm in London," said Dryer. "No harm done."

Jury was, actually, glad that Dryer had not been there; he had felt like an utter fool, given the reaction of the Gaults. "They didn't see how Harry could possibly have done what he did."

"Oh? Well, we've heard that before. Although, admittedly, the whole story is a little unbelievable."

Jury looked at him, but Dryer's expression was bland.

Wiggins drove round the square and pulled up in front of one of the handsome redbrick houses, this one with a couple of stone lions gracing the steps. "This is it, sir."

"Stay with the car, Wiggins."

Wiggins nodded. Jury got out of the front seat, and Dryer out of the back. Together they went up the steps, past the brooding lions. Jury rang the bell.

The door opened a few moments later and Mungo sat there in such a determined way, the dog might have opened it himself and would or would not grant leave to enter. But then a small woman appeared at the edge of the door, almost peeking around it, very unsure of taking this liberty. A housekeeper or maid or cook or char, Jury supposed. She was far more diffident than Mungo. Jury announced himself and Dryer and then reached down to ruffle Mungo's neck. They followed the little woman into a drawing room.

He could have slugged Harry Johnson, who rose with a smile, having discarded his reading glasses and newspaper and coffee cup. "Delighted to see you, Superintendent." He held out his hand to Dryer when Jury introduced them.

"Chief Inspector." Smiling, he shook Dryer's hand. "Surrey police? What can I do for you? Would you like coffee?" He reached his hand to the silver pot, nestled, together with cream and sugar, in folds of snowy linen.

They both declined.

Jury said, "This isn't a social call, Harry."

Harry waved them into dark leather club chairs, raising his

eyebrows and extracting a cigarette from a silver box. He offered the box to Dryer, who declined.

Mungo sat, raising one foot, then another, as if he couldn't wait to chase something.

"I saw Hugh Gault after I left the Old Wine Shades, Harry. Funny, but his wife, far from being dead, was actually there with him, very much alive and just returned."

"Ah! She's back from Aix, then. She's been gone for months."

Jury didn't like his matter-of-fact tone.

"She doesn't bear much resemblance to the dead woman, especially insofar as she's *alive,* you could say."

Harry put the cigarette in his mouth and picked up a heavy table lighter.

"Chief Inspector Dryer would love to hear your story, Harry. I told him it's a corker. I myself was, admittedly, rapt."

Harry flicked the lighter into flame, lit his cigarette, inhaled deeply and said, as he exhaled, "What story?"

43

Jury stared. He felt, oddly enough, as he had felt that night in the Old Wine Shades when Harry Johnson had begun his strange story.

Because now, he bet, there was to be another story.

"You know, Harry." Jury hated such a weak rejoinder, but he kept it up. "Beginning with the alleged disappearance of Glynnis Gault and her son—"

Mungo was gazing upward at Jury.

"—and her dog."

Or some future event.

Jury could have hit him for that sad little head shake Harry was giving. He never stopped smiling. "Superintendent, Glynnis Gault is very much with us as you yourself just told me."

Jury plowed on. "Hugh Gault, a man who lost everything— wife, son, even his dog. 'The dog came back' is what you said at the beginning." Jury inched his foot toward Mungo. "This dog, Harry."

"Mungo is my dog, yes; he's been here all along. You say 'the dog came back'?" His smile widened, as if to say, Oh, this is rich! "That's fascinating. That is, I admit, one hell of a beginning to a story. Only I never told it." Harry turned his blue eyes on Tom Dryer and shrugged.

What worried Jury at the moment was that Tom Dryer was looking not at Harry, but at *him*. He felt ridiculous—*"The dog came back"* . . . for God's sake! "Are you going to tell us now you've never been to a house in Surrey called Winterhaus?"

Mungo, sitting at Jury's feet, plopped, muzzle down, head resting between paws like a man throwing his hands against his ears, desperate not to hear what was coming next.

"I expect I *am* going to tell you that, Superintendent. Are you sure you won't have coffee?" He held up the silver-plated pot by way of invitation.

Jury's hand made an involuntary fist. He ignored the coffee offer. "The estate agent, Marjorie Bathous—"

As Harry looked a question at him, Jury realized that Marjorie Bathous had never seen Harry Johnson. She had seen only the woman calling herself Glynnis Gault. Indeed, who *had* seen Harry Johnson?

"What about Ben Torres?" Jury asked. At least *there* was someone who Harry couldn't deny knowing. Although Torres, according to Melrose Plant, had not actually named him, they could get confirmation one way or the other. No, wait. Jury delivered himself another little jolt. Ben Torres had told Melrose Plant exactly *nothing* to prop up this convoluted story. He had known Harry Johnson *in a minor way*. But the point was, he had known him before Harry had gone to Italy.

"Ben? Yes, I did visit Ben. He lives in San Gimignano. Near Florence," he added, as if Jury probably hadn't done his homework and Harry meant to help out.

"And you saw him during the past year. Coincidentally, you went all the way to Italy. That certainly was going to a lot of trouble."

"Is Italy ever a lot of trouble, Superintendent?" Harry's mouth twitched as if trying not to smile in the face of this paranoid police superintendent. "I'm not sure what you mean by 'coincidentally,' though."

Yes, you do. "That this trip to Florence was coincident with this unknown woman's going to Winterhaus."

"I do know that Ben has a house over here, but not where. We hardly talked about his house; we talked about quantum mechanics." Harry had stubbed out his earlier cigarette; now he lit another with the heavy table lighter.

"You took me to see Hugh Gault. He says you know a great deal about the subject—quantum theory and Niels Bohr and, of course, Schrödinger's cat."

Dryer spoke at last. "Whose cat? I'm coming in in the middle of things here."

Harry laughed. "It's a theory that tells us that since we can't know an outcome until we look in the box and see the cat, speculation is idle."

Dryer gave him a bleak smile. "Sorry I asked."

Harry smiled. "It does sound strange, I know."

Mungo got up and, nails clicking on the smooth floorboards, walked to the sofa and slid underneath. Again, he was like a person staving off bad news.

Tom Dryer cleared his throat and said, "We don't want to lose sight of the victim in this case, a woman who indeed was calling herself Glynnis Gault. This woman"—here he took the police photographs out of the envelope he was carrying and handed them across to Harry.

Harry took his glasses up from the silver tray and put them on. He looked at the pictures carefully before handing them back to Dryer. "No, I don't know her."

Dryer said, "She was seen by the estate agent, by an elderly couple in a cottage that the Gault woman was also viewing, by a woman who saw her standing by her car, and by a little girl who'd seen all three—woman, boy, dog"—Dryer looked at the sofa—"a description fitting your dog."

"What little girl?"

He was surprised, thought Jury. It's the first time something had surprised him.

"Just a child who likes to play in the grounds there."

"Ah. Well, as far as the dog is concerned, he's a hound, part bloodhound, Chief Inspector. They all look very much alike, though coloring of course would differ. You could arrange one of those identification parades and I'd be happy to bring Mungo along."

Hearing this, Mungo reappeared, or part of him did.

Why had Harry included Mungo in his plan? After all, it *was* damned peculiar that a dog looking like Harry's dog should be seen with Glynnis Gault's impostor. And then Jury thought he knew why: to drive his story into such an avenue of absurdity that it would be hard to imagine anyone believing it. Anyone in this case being the present company of Chief Inspector Dryer.

Mungo had slipped out from under the sofa to walk about, to pace almost. Back and forth, back and forth, as if this were all too much.

I tried to tell him, don't say I didn't try. Mungo skated on the slippery beechwood floor and was tempted to go across to the music room to calm down. Only Shoe was sitting in the bottom bureau drawers, keeping watch over Elf and the others.

Tom Dryer said, "Yes, I expect it would be difficult to swear to it that the dog with the woman was indeed your dog. Of course, there's always DNA, isn't there?" He gave Harry a little purse-lipped smile.

But Harry only smiled back. "Yes, there is that, if you could collect any of it from your crime scene." Then he nodded toward the envelope. "Let me see those photographs again, will you?"

Dryer reached the envelope over an abyss of very dark rug. There were several of these, interesting colors and designs, lying on the floor, sometimes overlapping.

Harry took up his reading glasses and fitted the pliable stems around his ears and took out the police photos of the dead woman.

What was he up to now?

Dryer said, with a seemingly casual interest in the whole thing. "Isn't this another coincidence, though?"

Harry looked with raised eyebrows at Dryer.

"I mean," said Dryer, "here is a lady going by the name of Glynnis Gault, the Mrs. Gault you do know. It's a little hard to believe that the woman in those photos didn't know any of you, that she wasn't acting in some capacity for the Gaults—or you or—let me rephrase it: that she had no connection with any of you. Seems unlikely, doesn't it?"

"Yes, it does seem unlikely. But that doesn't mean I know her. Now, Hugh . . . ?"

"Can you think of any reason why Mr. Gault would ask someone to parade around as his wife? Off hand, the only thing I can think of is that—and this is only a for instance—he needs an alibi, or needs to establish that his wife was indeed alive after he murdered her. But that doesn't work because the murder came later, long after the impersonation, not before it. Can you think of another reason? I mean as long as we're kicking possibilities around?" Dryer pulled at his ear lobe, at ease, unhurried.

Jury was only too happy to let Dryer do this.

Mungo had gone to sit between Jury and Dryer and looked from one to the other.

Harry slid down in his seat, also at ease. He smiled slightly. "Only, what makes you think that it's Hugh or his wife who instigated this masquerade? What about the dead woman herself?"

"Without your knowing?"

"Without *any* of our knowing."

"That's possible, of course. Acting, you mean, on her own. A woman calling herself Glynnis Gault, and with a boy calling himself Robbie and a dog—Mungo—makes appointments through an agent at Forester's in Lark Rise to view property. She makes an effort to be seen, to have people know that she's there. And then—*whoosh*—" Dryer made circles in the air with his hand—"she's gone, vanished, together with boy and dog. Now, that's very interesting, isn't it? Why she wants it to be thought that she's disappeared."

"It's fascinating."

"Hm." Dryer looked up and around the room, as if trying to pin down a vagrant thought. "That might be the whole point—the fascination."

Again, Harry smiled. He seemed to be thoroughly enjoying himself. "I'm not sure what you mean."

"Well, it's a bit like sexual allure, isn't it? I mean if a man is overtaken by a woman's beauty or sensuality, he's not really going to notice she hasn't a damned thought in her head." Dryer smiled quickly, then called it back. "In other words, he isn't going to try to make sense of her; he's only going to try to get her in bed."

Harry's smile was brilliant. "That's very good, Chief Inspector."

"Thank you." Dryer gave another quick little smile.

Jury said, "Smoke and mirrors, you mean?"

Dryer nodded. "Exactly."

"It's all rather confusing, then, isn't it?" said Harry.

"Extremely so, but, again . . . does she look familiar now, Mr. Johnson?" asked Dryer. "Have you changed your mind?"

Either Harry didn't pick up the sarcasm or didn't care about it. He sat thinking.

(Another story, thought Jury.)

"All right. Look," said Harry. "I won't deny I haven't been a hundred percent straight with you—"

Oh, *really*? thought Jury, simultaneously furious and fascinated. Having brought his story to what Jury concluded was a satisfactory end—for Harry, sitting there with one arm across the back of a love seat, continued to smoke and smile—Jury wondered what he was going to come up with.

Harry brought his arm down and leaned forward, all serious and solemn, and said, "I do recognize her. I said the woman in the photo, well, she wasn't Glynnis, true, but I also said I'd never seen her before. That isn't true. Mind you, the woman in Venice looked rather different in terms of the superficial things—hair, heavily outlined eyes, clothes—but cheekbones, nose were quite similar to your photo. Probably I didn't think of this Venetian woman because a face in death rarely looks the same as in life. It lacks expression to enliven it."

Jury knew the embarrassed shrug, the small boy smile were simply Harry's fabricated responses.

Dryer said, "So, you did know her, Mr. Johnson?"

"I did, yes. Her name is Rosa Paston. Actually, it's Pastoni, but she shortened it. She preferred something a little less Italian. Her father was Italian, her mother English—"

"Sounds exactly like Ben Torres," said Jury.

Harry ignored him and went on as he rose and moved over to his desk. "I met her in Venice—"

"You'd never been there before you met Ben Torres," said Jury. "Where?"

"Italy."

Harry shut his eyes against such thickness of mind. "No, Superintendent. I said 'there' meaning *Florence,* not the whole of Italy. Of course I'd been to Venice. Hasn't everyone? May I continue?"

With a half smile, Jury nodded. "Please do." He shook his head and looked down at the pattern in the carpet—intricate, ornate, but not nearly as much as Harry Johnson.

"I met her in Venice, as I said."

"And this was when?"

"A year ago. Last summer, late in June, I think it was."

"That would have been shortly before this Paston woman came to England."

"That's right." Harry leaned against his desk, tapping ash from his cigarette into a silver ashtray.

Dryer said, "You were involved with her, is that what you're saying?"

"Oh, no. I'd never met her before. I was there—to negotiate."

Jury pictured that scene at the Jack and Hammer, all of them talking about Henry James . . . and then the elderly con man walked in. "Like Lambert Strether."

"What's that got—" Dryer couldn't keep the annoyance out of his look at Jury's interruptions.

Harry just cocked his head and said, "Ah! A policeman who reads Henry James! No, not like Strether. He was quite deliberately American."

Dryer said, "Negotiate what, Mr. Johnson?"

Harry studied the coal end of his cigarette, his expression beautifully reflecting a man torn between something and something. Jury waited for Harry to fill in those blanks—blanks probably as much to Harry as to his visitors—torn between nothing and nothing. Harry's sigh was resigned, as if he, the lone keeper of the truth, now had to give it up.

Jury ached to hit him.

"Negotiating with Rosa Paston. For Hugh."

Bloody *hell!* thought Jury. He knew what was coming.

"It wasn't I, Chief Inspector, who was involved with her. It was Hugh. He had been seeing her for some time and he wanted to put paid to that. He felt incredibly guilty—"

"Bollocks," said Jury.

Dryer raised his hand in a gesture meant to fend off interruption. "Go on."

"Well, I tried, you see, to buy her off with a large sum of money. She laughed."

"I don't blame her," said Jury. He was making himself more and more unpopular with Tom Dryer, who shot him a look.

"She said she wanted Hugh, not money. That she had already made plans to go to England. And that she was pregnant."

"She clearly wasn't pregnant when she died," said Dryer. "The baby would have been born by now—*just.* So where's the child?"

Harry shook his head, smiling, as if he couldn't quite believe police would pose this question. "Chief Inspector, *I* don't know. Probably, the woman was lying in the first place."

"The autopsy will tell us, Harry. I'm sure you know that," said Jury.

"What? That she was lying?" Harry's eyebrows went up a fraction.

"She claimed the child was Mr. Gault's?" asked Dryer.

"Yes. On that point she was crystal clear. But what she meant to accomplish by this impersonation of Glynnis Gault, I can't imagine."

"It's all a bloody game, isn't it, Harry?" said Jury, teeth clamped.

Harry had just lit a fresh cigarette, and through a scrim of smoke, looked at Jury. "Apparently, to Rosa Paston, it was."

Jury's annoyance with Tom Dryer was growing. But then he remembered how plausible Harry Johnson sounded.

Dryer went on as if that brief exchange hadn't occurred. "Why would she go house hunting as Mrs. Gault? Did she think Hugh Gault would drop his wife and set up house with her?"

"I assume so." Harry shrugged.

Jury walked and Mungo followed him, clearly not liking being held responsible any more than Harry did. They walked over to one of the floor-to-ceiling bookcases standing on either side of a high arched window. Jury listened to Harry Johnson and ran his eyes over the books. He pulled one out called *Gravity Revisited.* A physicist's nod to E. M. Forster? The title, he imagined, was deceptive in its simplicity and its hipness. Hugh Gault was one of the three authors, the other two being a Charles Borman, an American, and a Sven Skagaared, a Swede. He gleaned this information from the short biographical account on the back flap. Hugh must be a heavy hitter, for his writing buddies had won the Nobel Prize. There was one book by Hugh alone, one by Skagaared and a compilation of articles on superstring theory, edited by Hugh.

Jury said, "Hugh's written quite extensively on quantum theory."

"He's the superstring theorist."

"Funny, but when I talked to him yesterday, he said he wasn't coauthoring a book with you, Harry."

Harry's pause was brief and untroubled. "He's probably forgotten."

"What? A man forgetting he was writing a book?"

"It hadn't got to the point of writing, Superintendent. We'd been kicking the idea around, taking notes, research, that sort of thing."

"I see. Hugh forgot he was kicking the idea around."

Harry sighed. "Look, Hugh's forgotten a lot. He's in serious denial because of his son's death and his marriage. It wasn't holding up under the weight of Robbie's death. Maybe it's all right now. Anyway, writing a book with me would hardly be uppermost in his mind."

"If we could get back to this Rosa Paston," said Dryer. "Why didn't you simply admit you knew who she was? And the circumstances under which you knew her? Did you think the police would suspect you?"

"You could do, but that wasn't the reason."

"What, then?" asked Dryer.

"Had I told you about this, I wouldn't be your prime suspect in this murder. Glynnis Gault would. I was trying to shield Glynnis, that's all." Harry smiled wonderfully.

Mungo crawled back under the sofa.

"The man's lying, Tom. He's a pathological liar!" They were walking down the steps to the pavement and the car.

"Still . . . you're sure you didn't mistake him?"

Jury was appalled. "Don't tell me you *believe* him."

Dryer fixed Jury with an amused glance. "You did."

44

"Mungo!" Melrose set down the knife he'd been using to butter his roll. "For heaven's sake, hire him! Melrose shook his head and picked up his fork. "He could be one of your sniffers, or whatever those dogs are called."

Jury smiled. "Mungo doesn't sniff. He thinks. Vivian's point was that if Stoddard *did* permit animals inside—witness the wolfhound—why didn't we take Mungo in to see Hugh?"

"Can I have Mungo after they put Harry away?"

"No. And I'm not at all certain we *will* be putting Harry away." Jury's tone was glum.

"Harry's own masquerade is over, in any event."

"For me, it is. I can't answer for Chief Inspector Dryer."

They were served their main course by Young Higgins. "Fish," said Jury. "I win again."

"Harry denies everything?"

"Everything."

"How did your Surrey policeman react?"

"DCI Dryer wonders if perhaps I misunderstood."

Melrose put down his fork. "You're joking?"

"He's not completely discounting that possibility. After all, that story is pretty unbelievable, isn't it? This, of course, is what Harry intended. Here I am, emotionally unstrung, insecure in my job. Dryer wonders if I didn't 'mistake' what Harry said. 'The dog came back'—for God's sake!"

"Harry's whole elaborate scheme was meant to give that impression."

Jury nodded. "That's the beauty of it: the elaboration. What fun for him." Jury speared a piece of halibut, ate it, then said, "Look: these people did indeed see a woman with a boy, but none of them had heard about a disappearance. Marjorie Bathous hadn't, the Shoesmiths hadn't and nor had Myra Easedale. One or more of them had heard that 'Glynnis Gault' hadn't returned to the estate agency and that Mrs. Bathous was extremely puzzled not being able to get hold of her. But there wasn't one person who had heard Harry's story, *except me.* I appeared to be supplying the details myself." Jury shook his head. "Beautiful, just beautiful."

"Why are you smiling?"

"I'm not."

Melrose didn't contradict him. He said, "You think he murdered her?"

"I *know* he murdered her. All of this has led up to that event. Remember? You yourself suggested that this might have been planned in view of some future event. Something in the future. And that wild story's meant to discount it." Jury speared some more halibut. "I mean look at it: I insist that Harry murdered this Rosa Paston but why would anybody take me completely seriously? Me, with my vivid imagination and me, emotionally unstrung, telling this wild story? Think about it: What did Marjorie Bathous actually say? That Glynnis hadn't brought the key back. And how strange it was that she, Marjorie, couldn't get in touch with her. She didn't actually *say* what Harry had said she did. She didn't refer to a police investigation, nor did anyone else. Because there'd never been one."

"Why go to all this trouble, though? Why not simply shoot this Paston woman as she's hanging out the wash, or in a dark alley, or toss her in the Grand Canal?"

"I just *explained* that," said Jury, a bit cantankerous now. "And maybe because there might be too direct a link between Harry and her. When Rosa Paston is investigated, I'm sure it will turn up a lover, but I bet it won't be named Harry Johnson. He's too much on guard. She was probably his lover. In any event, she was close enough to him to carry out her part. It fascinates me that a few of the story's components were true: the property search, the agent, the Shoesmiths, the woman who saw this alleged Glynnis standing by her car. Harry had instructed her to make herself seen, I'll bet, because he had to connect Glynnis Gault with Winterhaus. And Ben Torres. Harry did go to see him."

"Ben Torres. I don't know why it didn't click when I talked to him: it was what he left out; it wasn't what he *did* say but what he *didn't*. Harry *couldn't* tell Torres this elaborate story because if he had, well, then Harry couldn't deny it, could he? What Harry wanted to do was convince you. And now it appears there's another story, or another chapter: Hugh Gault's alleged mistress. This fellow really gets off on yarns." Melrose studied his wineglass. "Widening the list of suspects. It couldn't be Hugh as he's at the clinic. But his wife? She wouldn't have been pleased to find out about the mistress."

"No. If she believed Harry's story. They certainly found it hard to believe that Harry had told me what he did. Both of them, Glynnis and Hugh, found it laughable."

"So this Rosa Paston—Harry might have got the idea for the whole thing when he met her in Venice."

"What was his motive?" Jury thought for a moment and speared a new potato. "I'm not sure there is one."

"You mean Harry did it because he could?"

"Possibly. He's so bloody vain, I wouldn't put it past him. Make up a wild story to fool the police. Except there's a dead body at the end of the road. That's not fiction."

"What if he wanted to hurt Hugh Gault?"

"To do that he'd have had to abduct the real Glynnis, not her stand-in. But since there was never any abduction—"

"He had this story concocted a year ahead of time. But I don't see how this could have hurt Glynnis."

"If she's indicted for murder, I'd say that's plenty hurtful."

They ate for a minute in silence.

Melrose said, "Also, don't forget, there's you."

"Me?" Jury shoved his plate away and said, "What do you fancy for the pud?"

Melrose immediately switched gears and said, "Gooseberry Fool."

"I say fruit and custard. Now, what about me?"

"That he searched you out."

Jury frowned as Young Higgins shuffled over to take their plates and shuffled off again. "But he had no idea who I was and anyway I'd never been to the Old Wine Shades before. He could hardly have expected to find me there."

"You really believe it was an accident?"

Jury saw Melrose taking out his cigarette case. "You're not going to smoke?"

"You say that every time. I doubt Boring's ascribes to a no-smoking rule." Considering all of the cigars and pipes out in the Member Room, Melrose seriously doubted it. Boring's wouldn't dare.

"Can you imagine telling those two over there"—he pointed to a table a dozen feet away where two crusty old codgers were puffing a bale of smoke into the atmosphere—"being asked by Young Higgins to please douse their smokes? No. Boring's is still back there in the forties and fifties when my father was a member." He lit his cigarette just as Young Higgins was coming back with the dessert.

"Fruit and custard," said Jury cheerily.

Melrose stubbed out his cigarette and looked gloomily at the dish. "You win again."

"Harry Johnson searching me out. How did he know I'd be in that pub? He couldn't. How did he know what I even looked like?"

"How? Your face was plastered all over the paper because of that pedophile bust. As to where you'd be, I expect he followed you."

"To the City? That's a distance from Victoria Street. Anyway, why?"

Melrose's tone was irritated. "Don't be so literal. I simply mean arranged somehow or other to be where you were. And we always do butt our heads against that "why." You're a superintendent—a *vulnerable* superintendent, given all the publicity and the possible suspension. You're the perfect target."

"You mean no one would credit this wild tale coming from me?" He wanted to preempt an investigation that was sure to follow after he killed Rosa Paston. Bleakly, Jury smiled. "He was winding me up."

"Well, yes, but with a serious purpose. He knew when the fake Glynnis was found, you'd come round to him. He was prepared for that. Just think: a woman, her son and her dog disappear for a year. And the dog comes back." Melrose laughed. "That's a corker. He knows you know, but nobody else does. Superintendent, you're hallucinating. It's his word against yours—"

Jury grumbled. "Harry doesn't have a word. It's like Mary McCarthy saying of Lillian Hellman, 'Every word she writes is a lie, including "and" and "the."'" Jury thought about that. "What about the boy? The supposed son Rosa Paston took along on this venture? Police would certainly want to talk to him. Who was he? Where did she find him? He worries me."

"Why?"

"If Harry murdered Rosa Paston, what's to stop him killing the boy? The boy knew all this was an impersonation. Is he lying at the bottom of a quarry or drowned in a river somewhere?"

"Maybe it wasn't necessary to kill him," said Melrose. "Maybe he didn't know what Rosa knew."

"But I think he did. He knew about the impersonation itself." Jury finished off his dessert and pulled Melrose's over. "I don't think this woman was paid. I think she was Harry's woman— mistress. If it was payment, she'd be satisfied with the money and wouldn't be a threat, right?"

"No, wrong. She'd always be a threat. Blackmail, a dagger held over his head—always."

Jury nodded and spooned up some custard. "He knew it was going to end with murdering her. That's chilling. To think of her merrily larking about with this impersonation and then killed for her efforts. For her love. I think that's why this woman did it—for love."

"You're assuming a lot."

"But it makes no difference in the long run. Love or greed or ignorance, she's still dead."

"And the boy . . . Also, what about Tilda?"

Sharply, Jury looked up from his custard. "Tilda." He thought of Harry's question. *What little girl?*

"Well, she goes into the house all the time, and it's just possible she saw something," Melrose said.

"Possibly, but she would have said. After all, she ran home to tell her mother when she found the body."

"What if Harry was still there?"

"If she saw something—" Jury paused for a moment, then took out his mobile. "Does Boring's have a policy about these things?"

"Probably. They disrupt the general comfort level, so I'm sure they'd be outlawed. Anyway, if you're finished eating my dessert, we'll want coffee in the Members' Room." Melrose tossed down his napkin.

Jury went into the reception area to make his call while Melrose ordered coffee and brandy.

Jury came back and told him Tilda was fine and had strict instructions not to go onto the Winterhaus grounds.

"Ha! You know how much that means," said Melrose. "Although I'd think finding a dead body would be enough to keep a child away from a place."

"She's tough, though. She's been there by herself a lot and, frankly, that house rather spooks me." Jury swirled his brandy, liking the way it caught the reflected flames of the fire. Liking the fire, too.

"You're such a wimp."

"Right. Thanks for the brandy. And the dinner."

Melrose raised an eyebrow. "This is all my treat? Even though you won on all the courses?"

"That's right. Ah, hello, Major Champs."

"Thought we saw you over here; the backs of the chairs are so high it's hard to make out anyone." He chuckled.

"Where's Colonel Neame?" asked Melrose.

"On his way. He stopped in the dining room to have a word with Young Higgins. Now, I don't mean to pry, but how are you getting along with your case? Developments—" he whisked out the *Daily News,* opened it and pointed to an item, a follow-up relegated to the inside pages, which wasn't a follow-up so much as a rehashing. The conclusion was that police knew nothing more. They had contacted the owner of Winterhaus, Ben Torres.

"Ben Torres," said Melrose. "We left Ben Torres out of the roster of suspects."

"Well, if he'd left Italy, the police will certainly find that out."

"San Gimignano." Melrose sighed. "I'd never leave it."

45

He had tried the jardinière but the only way to get Elf into it would be to stuff him in and Mungo didn't think he should do that. He looked around the living room. Most places had already been used. . . . Ah! The window seat was propped open with a couple of books, for some reason. Could he reach up there? No. Anyway, someone might let the top down and he wouldn't be able to open it again.

There was that big copper thing that people once used to spit in. It was low enough that Shoe would be able to see Elf's ears, but it would do; Mungo was weary. That thin, stringlike *meewwww* was getting on his nerves. And his nerves were not in good shape at all after that affair with the clinic folder and the Uniforms. If he'd wanted to get that Spotter to the clinic, he couldn't think of any other way of doing it. He could hardly *tell* the man he was not Hugh's dog (worse luck). Well, even some kids had it bad there, too. That boy he'd spent the afternoon with a year ago—

What an afternoon! He couldn't remember when he'd had one so wonderful. Playing ball, running with his stride as far out as it could go, running across that land, ears flying, tail flying, he himself nearly flying, as the wind whistled and the trees glittered to where the girl was, running back, running forward. And he had liked that woman, Rosa, and now she was dead.

He thought sometimes of running off. But if he ran, who'd look after Elf and the others? He plunked Elf in the copper pot and stood back to look. Yes, you could just see the ears.

Even dogs should have a plan instead of running around just stirring up air. Mungo now had a plan. It was better than suddenly putting himself at the top of the stairs just when Harry was stepping down. Too crude. No, his plan had started just this morning.

On Harry's desk were the notes he prized so much. He was always going over them, *talking* over them, as if the notes could answer back. Harry was smart, extremely smart, but not quite as smart as Hugh. He was far more inventive, though. Why couldn't people be satisfied with what they were? Harry was forever going to the bookshelf to drag down one book or another of Hugh's and pore over it in the little pool of light the desk lamp shed on the pages.

First, Mungo had to push the silver paperweight that held them down and kept them from fluttering apart in a breeze. He shoved the notes off the desk and watched the pages scatter all over the floor. Then Mungo barked. When Mrs. Tobias didn't come, he barked again.

She came. "Whatever are you barking about? What are you doing on the desk?" She drew closer and stopped, seeing the pages of notes all over the floor. "Oh, my, oh, my, oh, my, you naughty dog. Oh and won't he be just furious?" She bent down. "I'll never be able to put these in order; there's no numbers on the pages!"

Right.

"All of this math, all these signs and numbers—I can't tell what's what."

Right.

Poor Mrs. Tobias was down on her knees gathering up the pages. She got up and tried to neaten them by tamping them on the desk until all the pages were even. Then she put the pile where she thought it had been.

Paperweight paperweight. Mungo nosed the paperweight around and stared at her.

"What now? Oh, yes." She put the weight back on the pile. She stood back and surveyed the notes. "Looks as if they never was touched. Only, they're all out of order. He'll wonder."

He'll wonder, thought Mungo.

* * *

The next morning, as Mungo was transporting Elf to the copper basin, he heard Mrs. Tobias shout. He put Elf down in the middle of the rug and raced to the kitchen.

"Oh, look, oh, look what I went and done!" She held up her hand, bleeding profusely from a cut along her thumb. Mungo raced around, wanting to help, but not knowing how. Except he had seen bandages in the downstairs loo. He raced to it and saw the gauze up on a little shelf that he couldn't get to. So he jumped up on the toilet seat, grabbed the end of the toilet paper in his mouth and then jumped down and trailed it into the kitchen where he set it in her lap.

Mrs. Tobias had to laugh at this effort. "Good dog! Good! Thank you. It'll make do for the moment." She wrapped and wrapped it round her thumb and hand. "That'll have to do for now. I think it looks worse than it is. I'm calling Mr. Humphries." Mr. Humphries was Harry's doctor. Mrs. Tobias went out to the telephone.

There was quite a lot of blood, a pool of it.

Mungo looked at it. Then he tore out of the kitchen, raced upstairs and grabbed Harry's slipper, a lightweight leather one. Back to the kitchen he went.

Mungo placed the slipper over the blood, messed the sole about, then ran back upstairs with the bloody slipper. Then he dropped the slipper on the floor of Harry's bedroom, pressed it down with his paw, picked it up again, dropped it a little farther along, pressed it down. And so on. The blood lasted a surprisingly long time, through six impressions.

Bloody footprints. Not bad. The prints looked just like the sole of the slipper. He considered taking the second slipper.

Mungo looked around the room at the Art Deco wall sconces. He sighed. Oh, for some gaslight. Mungo liked old movies.

Things had a way of working out, if you were patient.

46

Hugh Gault was settled into the same chair he had occupied two days before, looking again at the same police photographs. Then looking at Jury. "You're joking."

"No."

"My mistress? That's what Harry said?"

Jury nodded. "His own, more than likely. She lives—or lived—in Venice; he probably spent time with her in Florence when he went to see Ben Torres, who, according to Harry, he knew. The police there will question Torres to find out what exactly went on, but I have no doubt it will be pretty much what Harry told Chief Inspector Dryer."

Hugh handed back the photos. "And I thought Harry was quite harmless."

"Harry's not."

"But that whole story he told *you*—"

"Oh, Harry's flat out denying it, of course. Not all of it; he was careful that the various people he named did exist, Ben Torres, for one; the estate agent actually did deal with the woman calling herself Glynnis Gault, whom we now know was Rosa Paston. There had to be enough verification of his story that I'd believe it, but not so much anyone else would believe what I told them. The Surrey police were never contacted, for instance."

"But, why? Why did he do this?"

Jury laughed. "You really don't know Harry, Mr. Gault. Harry's got a massive ego. One reason I think he did it was because he wanted control over at least part of your life. I wonder if he resented your wife—"

"Glynnis? Why?"

Jury shrugged. "I don't know. Maybe she was an obstruction, something he had to get round to get to you."

"So he murdered her stand-in? That's mad."

"He didn't asphyxiate Rosa Paston because of her, let's, say, symbolic role; he killed her to get rid of her. Then he saw a way to get your wife in a world of trouble. But again, that was merely—shall we say—one of the 'perks' of the operation. My guess is that Rosa Paston was killed because she was giving Harry trouble. She was a nuisance and he wanted to get rid of her. When he hatched this plot, I don't know, but I imagine it was when she began to be too much of an inconvenience."

Hugh shook his head. "I'm lost."

"Here's a woman who is masquerading as the real Glynnis Gault. How long did it take DCI Dryer to get here and question both of you? Not long. But particularly Mrs. Gault, since you were covered for that afternoon. You're always here. But your wife had no alibi for that afternoon."

"Wait. Are you telling me that Glynnis is a suspect?"

"Not now she isn't. But Surrey police might well have had her down as a suspect. And remember, making your wife a suspect wasn't Harry's main reason for killing this woman—indeed, I could be dead wrong. Perhaps it didn't even come into it."

"Her name was—what?"

"Rosa Paston. Maybe she wanted him to marry her; anyway, she was someone who was probably causing him trouble. Harry doesn't like trouble; he doesn't like any threat to his illusory world. Or perhaps I should say 'delusory.'" Jury thought about this.

Hugh laughed. "You make him sound mad as a hatter, Mr. Jury."

"Oh, he is." He regarded Hugh. "And you're looking quite skeptical, Mr. Gault. Which is, of course, just the way Harry would want you to look."

"This whole wild plot simply to get rid of a woman—well, I'm sorry, that sounds awfully callous, but you know what I mean."

"Yes, I do. Harry is an incredibly clever man. He probably impressed you as quite rational in the months you knew him here. In spite of the fact that he *was* here."

"But like me, he committed himself, you know."

"That's what he told people." Jury shrugged.

"His doctor, Santiago, who's also mine. He'd know. Have you spoken to him?"

"No. I'm going to see him when I leave you." Jury hesitated, looking down at the pattern in the rug. Camels, howdahs, clever-looking monkeys. "Mr. Gault, I'm sorry to bring up what must be a painful subject, but your son, Robert, how old was he—at the time of the boating accident?"

Hugh covered his eyes with his hand, as though light were hurting them. There was no light outside of what was cast by the dimly glowing lamps with fringed damask shades. It was one reason the room was so restful. Through the high windows the night was clear enough to count the stars. In the fireplace, a log fell and sparked, flaming up in unearthly blues and greens.

"Robbie was nine. He was our only child. Not that his death would have been easier if we'd had a dozen children. After the accident, Glynnis and I could hardly—well, this sounds terrible—but we could hardly bear each other's company. That was when Glynnis went to France. Her father lives there. I thought we were finished, you know, as a couple, but, fortunately, no—" He shrugged. He smiled as if he'd pulled off a wizard trick.

Jury slipped forward to the edge of his armchair to close some of the distance between them. "Mr. Gault, there was also a young boy involved last year, that is, at the beginning, on that day a year ago when Rosa Paston was looking at property. The boy was seen by the same witnesses as had seen her. He played the role of her son. I imagine Harry wanted this to make the whole thing even more convincing. Did Harry know Robbie?"

"Oh, no. Robbie died over a year ago. I didn't know Harry until

I came here and that's been about nine months. What is it about this boy?"

"We don't know who or where he is. No child was reported missing back then, so the supposition is he went back to his life. But we don't know what that life was."

"Who could he be?"

"He must have been important to Harry, because now he has another witness. Did you talk to Harry about Robbie?"

Hugh nodded. "I think I talked to *everyone* about Robbie."

"Harry would have wanted the boy to be as much like your son as possible. Is there anything about Robbie that might help us find this other boy?"

Hugh was silent for a moment and then once again he covered his eyes with his hand. He looked at Jury sorrowfully. "Did you know that Robbie was autistic?"

Jury nodded. "Harry told me."

"Robbie's was a pretty severe case. He spoke very little. But he was very sweet. He'd been to several experts in the field, but it didn't help much."

Jury wondered. If this stand-in child *was* autistic, he was probably still alive. Somewhere. He couldn't be chatting up his mates with stories of this superadventure, for which he had been paid. Had it been Rosa Paston who'd contacted the boy? *"Would Robbie enjoy an outing, Mrs. Smith?"* or Jones or Brown. *"It's ever so nice a day, the weather holding. And there's a hundred quid in it—"*

No, too much. Or no money changing hands at all. Wouldn't want the suspicion that Robbie would be involved in something illegal. *"A couple hundred pounds my friend will pay to have Robbie as a model for some pictures."* No. There would be other approaches, and it wasn't important how he'd been enticed.

Jury got up and thanked Hugh for talking to him.

After he left Hugh Gault in the drawing room, Jury got on the phone to Tom Dryer.

"If the boy's autistic, then he might not present a threat to Harry Johnson," said Dryer. "It might have been the reason he was brought into this venture."

"Not altogether. I think the reason was his resemblance to Robbie Gault."

There was a silence. Was the same thought running through Dryer's mind as his own? It was:

"But Robbie Gault is dead."

"That's right. An accidental death. A boating accident. It's that he *is* dead that bothers me."

Tom Dryer let out a long breath. "Then I'd better get my skates on, hadn't I?"

47

Dr. Santiago did not so much occupy his office as grace it. Wearing a beautifully tailored charcoal suit, he was handsome, cool and calm—a presence he no doubt had had to master in view of the vulnerability of his patients. Jury thought he must fill his female patients with both hope and despair, that he was at once so accessible and yet forever inaccessible. Transference must have hit the patients like a hammer. Men, too, but they'd be more likely to experience hostility—both that they hated him, but also that they couldn't be him.

The name suggested a partly Mediterranean background, or ancestry, Spanish or Portuguese, perhaps. But in his looks was something English, something of the rosy skin that makes Englishwomen look so fresh, so just washed, just dried in the sun.

The wall behind the doctor's desk was covered with framed degrees. He seemed to have earned his degrees everywhere: Switzerland, Seville, Oxford and more.

Sitting behind his wide rosewood desk, Dr. Santiago said, "I'm happy to help you as much as I can, Superintendent, but I can't really go into Harry Johnson's sessions with me."

Jury said, "I'm not actually asking for a psychological profile. You see, I know him. We've socialized. We've had drinks and meals together several times."

"Harry's a very charming man, as I imagine you've found." The doctor smiled his world beater of a smile.

"Harry's a liar and a manipulator, as I imagine *you've* found. He's got a hell of a Narcissus complex. All of the people, all of the faces he sees seem only to reflect his own."

Dr. Santiago looked both disturbed and surprised. He went dead serious, leaned forward in his swivel chair, elbows on desk. "That's a fairly good statement of Harry when he came here. I thought a lot of that had been resolved. I thought, to tell the truth, I'd done rather well."

"You didn't." Jury weighed in with a world-beater smile of his own, wanting to take the sting out of that comment. "Which simply attests to Harry's incredible ability to deceive everyone."

The doctor shook his head. "I think I meant 'well' in relative terms. Certainly not 'cured.' Had it been up to me, I would have kept him here longer. Actually"—Dr. Santiago rolled up the end of his tie and shook his head—"Harry wasn't anything."

Jury looked at him, puzzled. "What do you mean?"

"You say he's a liar and a manipulator—" The doctor shrugged slightly and straightened his tie. "I think that's just the surface."

"You think that's the *surface*?" Jury half laughed. "You mean that deep down Harry wouldn't hurt a fly?"

With his liquid brown eyes, Dr. Santiago regarded Jury. "I mean that there is no 'deep down' when it comes to Harry."

"A strange thing for a psychiatrist to say. Is it possible that there are people who are all façade? That's what you seem to be implying."

"It's possible. Merely another way of saying 'shallow,' isn't it?"

Jury thought about this, then said, "Well, shallow or not, Harry's a loose canon, doctor."

"That's true, in a way, but . . ." He left it unfinished.

"Are you going to tell me his childhood was rotten?"

Dr. Santiago smiled. "Oh, everybody's childhood was rotten. Whether it was or not, we're all fated to think that. It's a matter of degree, isn't it?"

Jury thought of his own and didn't answer.

"Please, Superintendent, you're not one of those reactionaries who think Freud was completely wrong, are you?"

He didn't answer that, either, but asked instead, "How long was he here, can you tell me that?"

"About a year, a little more." The doctor looked perplexed, sat back, again rolled his silk tie up from the bottom.

Jury smiled; that tie was a tell. "Hugh Gault. How long?"

"Over eight months." He dropped his tie, smoothed it out.

"And are they, were they, indeed, good friends? For I know Harry claims they are."

The doctor shook his head. "No. I shouldn't say this—"

"It's important. Very important. I appreciate your professional ethics. Consider these exigent circumstances. If a patient is a danger to himself or others, that would override ethics, I believe. Believe me, Harry is a danger." When the doctor didn't respond, Jury said, "Look: I could get a warrant." No, he couldn't.

Santiago nodded. "Hugh Gault was an obsession with Harry."

"Why?"

Santiago frowned. "The source of it I don't understand. Possibly his having such a fractured childhood. Between parents, between relations. But certainly one of the reasons is that Hugh Gault is brilliant in his field. Physics. Quantum mechanics, some part of it."

"Superstring theory."

The doctor smiled. "You seem to have some knowledge of this."

Jury shook his head. "Not at all. I've had a lot of conversations with Harry, and I picked up a little. Believe me, I don't understand it. But Harry's field was quantum mechanics, he said."

Dr. Santiago laughed. "Harry doesn't have a field. He's never worked, as far as I know. He's wealthy. Family money."

"Yet he talks about it quite knowledgeably."

"I didn't say he wasn't smart. He absorbed what Hugh Gault said and he did some research. Certainly read Hugh's books. Harry is a very intelligent man. Make no mistake about that; it could cost you."

"It already has." Jury's tone was acidic.

"So he's still putting on the physicist's hat, is he?"

"Yes. Tell me, how did Hugh Gault take all of this so-called friendship?"

The psychiatrist gave Jury a long look, debating. "Hugh's still a patient here."

Jury said, "I'm not asking you to repeat what Hugh Gault said in his sessions with you. Only what could have been observed by any of your staff." Jury remembered how friendly the nurse, the receptionist had been to Harry. Of course, they would be; they knew him.

The doctor nodded. "Hugh appeared to humor Harry. I think Harry's fantasy of the book they would write—"

"He was going to coauthor a book with Hugh Gault, he said."

"It was an elaborate fantasy, Superintendent. They'd win the Nobel Prize. His idol—Harry's, that is—was Niels Bohr."

"The physicist."

Santiago nodded. "Quantum mechanics." He held up his hands, palms flattening the air between them, as if to preempt Jury's objections, and smilingly said, "Before you say anything, let me assure you I know nothing about quantum mechanics. I had to read up on it a bit to talk to Harry. This is part of the little I know about the subject." He leaned forward again, as if to bridge the distance between them. "What Harry especially liked was complementarity. Bohr's theory."

Jury searched his mind. "You can see one part of something or another, but not both at the same time."

"Exactly. Like the well-known picture of what might either be a vase or the profiles of two people. You know. One could say Bohr was Harry's God and Hugh was some sort of ministering angel." The psychiatrist grinned. His face was astonishingly boyish when he did this. "Harry was also fascinated by the theory that you can't speculate about where something is until you measure it. It's a lot like the tree in the forest thing. Or the existence of the moon. If you're not in the forest to hear it, no tree fell. If you can't see the moon, it isn't up there."

Jury thought about this. "But that isn't exactly it. Isn't it more that the question is meaningless because the subject *can't* be measured?"

"Very good. You learn quickly."

"Not quickly enough, Doctor. He had me fooled. But if you believed that the tree wasn't there, you'd have no trouble rearranging time and space, right? Because Harry insisted that Hugh believed his wife Glynnis stepped into another time, or spacetime, another dimension—that sort of thing."

Santiago laughed. "Sounds like Harry." He started rolling up his tie again, staring down at it. "It's *Harry,* not Hugh, who believes that theory. That's where he thinks Niels Bohr is—on or in a different level of spacetime." He dropped his tie again, smoothed it and drummed his fingers on the edge of the desk.

Again, Jury smiled at the mannerism. The tie was definitely a tell.

"After the death of his son—" said Dr. Santiago.

"Robbie? I understand the boy was autistic."

"He was, yes. I think Hugh and his wife disagreed about how best to handle this, at least in the matter of schools—well, I'm saying too much here, perhaps. But the fact is Robbie died in a boating accident. One of the sails came round and hit him and he went over the side of the boat. Of course the Gaults blamed themselves for the boy's even being *on* the boat; he was so young and knew nothing about boats. He drowned. Hugh and Glynnis—" He stopped, knowing he could be breaching a confidence. "Let me put it this way: Hugh came here under the crushing weight of the boy's death. His wife, Glynnis, went away to stay with her father in the south of France, I believe. They handled the tragedy separately. It's unfortunate when that happens, but it happens more often than one would think, more often than the couple finding strength in one another." Dr. Santiago was saddened by this. "Which I think is the saddest of all. What is marriage for, anyway, if you can't share such a tragedy?" He sighed and sat back. "But, then, I expect one is so overwhelmed by the event, one hasn't room for working on anything else."

They were silent for a moment.

Then Jury said, "Mrs. Gault, I take it she's only recently back?"

"That's right. Only a few days, actually. I'm glad they seem to take comfort in each other now."

Jury digested this information and said, "To Harry, her disappearance could easily have meant that she'd gone over some space-time edge."

"Yes, I expect it could."

"To Harry, a very satisfactory explanation. Then, of course, one might want to get rid of the evidence?" Jury rose.

Santiago rose, too. "I don't follow that."

"I mean that if a man believed that the tree only fell and the moon only shone in his presence, he might get rid of anyone or anything that proved he was wrong. He might get rid of whatever gave his reality a kick in the pants."

"Neils Bohr might have agreed." The doctor smiled. "I must say, Superintendent, you're a quick study. You appear to have picked up a lot regarding quantum theory."

"Not quick enough, Dr. Santiago. Harry took me in."

Dr. Santiago shrugged slightly. "You're not the only one." He looked at Jury. "Is that why you're so angry?"

"Angry? I'm not angry." Jury frowned, feeling the anger spread almost like a blush and was irrationally irked with himself.

"Hm. But you are, Superintendent."

Jury shook his head. "No."

Dr. Santiago ignored this. "I don't think it's because he took you in. I think it's because you like him. And that, Superintendent, must be infuriating."

48

Marshall Trueblood held up one of the London dailies, a sala-
cious rag, but then weren't they all? "This?" he asked, tapping an
item in that paper. "Do you mean this?"

"That's it, yes," said Melrose.

"Rosa Paston," said Trueblood. "That's her name. Paper says.
Well, this is a development!"

> "The victim has been identified as Miss Rosa Paston of
> London and Venice, Italy. Previously, she had been looking
> at property near Lark Rise in Surrey, presenting herself as
> Mrs. Glynnis Gault."

"That's interesting," said Diane, crowding her head into Trueblood's viewing space.

"What?"

"The Forester's agent—this Marjorie Bathous—identified her
as Mrs. Gault, saying it was the suit she'd been wearing when she
first came to the agency. A black suit. Marks and Spencer. Hm."
Diane sat back, smoking and considering. "So this woman"—said
Diane Demorney—"what's her name?"

"Rosa Paston," said Melrose, remarking that Diane had the attention span of a flea.

"Rosa Paston could've been the man's lover."

"Could've been a lot of things," said Trueblood.

"Although I find it hard to believe a woman would do this for
love. Money, yes. Probably he paid her."

"Maybe she did it as a fling," said Joanna Lewes, marking up a page of her manuscript. "Where's your sense of humor?"

"In the toilet," said Diane. "No, I doubt fun had much to do with it, not with her wearing a suit from Marks and Sparks. That means either love or money. If there's enough of either in the world to make one wear a suit like that."

"You've a damned strange way of assessing value," said Joanna with an abrupt laugh.

"Melrose, you see that jacket you're wearing?" said Diane.

He held out an arm, fastened his eyes on the brownish-green wool and nodded. "I do indeed see it."

"That cloth is one of the premier Donegal tweeds. The cut is clearly that of the sharp little tailor who's done for your family for a hundred years. Now, would you have the gall to walk into his rooms in a jacket off the Army and Navy rack?"

Melrose squinched up his eyes and looked at the ceiling in a pretense of thinking. Then he said, "No. You're right. I wouldn't."

"Of course you wouldn't. It would be like me wearing pink jeans."

"Is it possible you two are missing the point of all this?" Trueblood rattled the paper, jabbed his finger at the news item.

Diane wasn't troubled by the point of all this. "Of course it could be that she didn't want to get her Dolce and Gabbana messed about. The problem isn't hers now. She's dead as a doornail. What about this boy who masqueraded as her son? What happened to him? Or may be going to happen?"

Joanna struck out half a page and raised her eyes to look at Diane. "Good lord, Diane. It almost sounds as if you care."

Diane brought her silky eyebrows together, as if she were weighing the words. "Well, not care, *exactly*, but it goes against the grain to see one so young in danger. He was part of it. Of course, he could have been a friend of the killer. I mean, part of the conspiracy. But why were they doing it? I must admit it is an intriguing little problem." She sipped her martini. "Ah, well, Superintendent Jury will sort it."

Marshall Trueblood, still with his eyes on the paper, said, "Not unless fate steps in. I told you."

"But fate," said Melrose, "apparently has."

49

The boy's name was Timmy. He had seen her picture, the dead lady's, in one of the newspapers lying on a table in the lounge and had no idea what to do or if he should do anything. He remembered her, of course he did. He wasn't stupid. And he wasn't deaf, either.

Timmy sat on the edge of his cot after he'd made it, pulling the rough brown blanket tight and tucking it in. Most of the others couldn't make their beds; all they could do was yank and pull. There were five other cots in his room. They all looked unmade or stirred up. His things were in a small trunk at the foot of his bed. Being orderly and neat made him feel safer.

He looked at the woman's picture again. When she'd come here to take him out she'd been wearing fancy sunglasses and had the lightest hair, long to her shoulders. But then she'd gotten rid of the sunglasses and changed the hair. He wanted to ask her why she'd done this, but of course he couldn't. She had smiled and said her name was Rose or Rosa and that this was all a huge trick, a game they were playing.

And all this time later, inside that same house, somebody smothered her or something. Why? Why was she there again? Why hadn't she come to take him along? If she had, would he have been dead now, too?

It was terrible now, to think about that day, for now fear had attached itself to it. Now, it was dangerous. It had been such a wonderful day. Especially running down through the untended gardens behind the house to where that girl was playing. And that dog. That dog would always be his favorite. Even if he were to get his own dog, no, that dog was the best. Not that there was much hope he'd ever have one.

He stood up and, with the paper under his arm, went in search of help.

Not that he had high hopes of finding that, either.

"I see two possibilities," said Tom Dryer. "One is a small school for autistic and deaf and dumb children. I mean hearing- and speech-impaired children. We can't even say that anymore—'impaired'; now we have to say 'challenged.'"

"We can't say much of anything anymore," said Jury.

Dryer laughed. "No. Another place is a family who takes in handicapped children. I understand a few have been autistic, so it's possible the lad might have come from there. If you're right about this. Why don't you take the school and I'll take the family?" He tore off the notebook page on which he'd written the address and handed it to Jury.

"The Lark Rise Special School, isn't it? This is the one Harry Johnson told me about. One of the reasons Robbie's mum wanted a house there. Why she was looking. Not just a weekend getaway place. Not that that makes any difference anymore," Jury added, ruefully.

"There's a Mrs. Copley-Sutton in charge."

"Have you talked to her?"

"No. I thought it would be better for one of us to simply turn up unannounced."

"So you're thinking if someone came along—someone being Harry Johnson's girlfriend—and wanted to take out one of the boys, Mrs. Copley-Sutton would permit this?" said Jury.

"If the visitor claimed to be some relative or even friend of the family. Yes, I think she would. Especially if a sizable donation to the school came along with the family friend. This headmistress has a reputation for being a bit of a wide lady, so to speak. Nothing

terrible, of course; she's very nice to the children, but still—"
Dryer shrugged. "Do you have your mobile?"

Jury said he hadn't, feeling as if he were letting down the wired
world.

"Here, take this." Dryer pulled open a drawer, got out a mobile
phone, tossed it to Jury. "I hate the damned things. I've got a whole
rap on instant access. Cells, Internet, computers. Yes, I know one
must have one for emergencies, still, something's gone out of life
with all those things. Suspense, maybe."

Jury smiled. Suspense. He liked that.

"We have time for a sandwich," said Dryer. "Let's go to the Bird
on the Wing. It's the nearest, also the fastest service. But what a
silly name for a pub. I prefer they all be named the George or the
Rose and Crown."

The school's maintenance man, Mr. Purdy—he called himself
"janitor," not one for dressing up mops and brooms with ribbons
and bells—was also reading the paper. This woman that got
murdered—something about her looked familiar, but he couldn't
put his finger on it. He sat on thinking for a moment, then got on
with his work.

It was Mr. Purdy Timmy came upon first.

The janitor was returning a mop to his maintenance room, his
little fiefdom. Purdy was quite proud of that room, like an office, it
was, and a place to escape to when Mrs. Copley-Sutton was on the
prowl, looking for things to complain about. It was a place to sit and
have a drink, too. He looked around when he felt the tug on his
sleeve.

"Why, hello, young Timmy, how are you keeping?"

Purdy was surprised, actually, that Timmy had made it all this
way down the long hall. The outside wall was a row of windows.
Timmy always got stuck on one or another of them, forever looking
out, from one to the other he'd go, stopping, as if they gave on different prospects. Yet each one had the same view of the car park

and the front of the school off to the right. There was a little arched entryway of gray stone that jutted out like a canopy. It was a pretty building. The school would be all right, it would be fine, if only there had been more sports for the kiddies, more equipment.

Timmy held up the newspaper and pointed to the picture.

"Ah. Just let me get me specs on, Tim." Purdy got the eyeglasses out of their heavy case that snapped like an animal when he closed it. "Ah, yeah, read about that poor woman. It's a mystery, that is."

Timmy pointed back and forth several times, from the paper to himself.

Mr. Purdy frowned. "There's something about her looks familiar. Is it somebody you knew, then?"

The boy, ordinarily not as noisy and excitable as some of the others, was nodding his head and at the same time bouncing back and forth from one foot to another, as if getting the whole engine going would make Mr. Purdy understand.

"Okay, now, Timmy, now what do we do?"

The boy was near to crying with all of this effort and the importance of it.

"Well, let's go see the head, then." Mr. Purdy had never much cared for Mrs. Copley-Sutton, but he didn't know what else to do for Timmy, to try to help him out. He took the boy's hand and they went off down the hall.

Mrs. Copley-Sutton was sitting at the desk in the large foyer, a long, polished table positioned so that it faced the entryway. There was a brass plaque on it marked RECEPTION. She wasn't, of course, simply the receptionist, but she did take over the desk from time to time, careful to position there another brass plaque, this with her name and HEAD in smaller letters below it. It all looked sort of elegant, Mr. Purdy thought, with the exception of the head herself.

"What is it, Mr. Purdy? Why have you brought Timmy? Hello, Timmy." She smiled.

"It's to do with this paper, madam."

"And what's that, then, Mr. Purdy?"

He put the paper on the desk, folded so that she could see the photo. "It's this woman. Timmy seems to be upset by the picture."

"Really. Well, I don't believe I know who she is. It's most unfortunate for the poor woman, but I don't see—is it because somebody killed her, Timmy?"

For Timmy, this was an impossible question. If he nodded yes, then she would think it was the killing that bothered him; if he shook his head no, then she wouldn't realize it was the woman herself that was the problem. So he indicated neither answer, hoping maybe that she'd put the question differently.

"I don't see the problem, then, Mr. Purdy." She smiled again at Timmy, and wished she was fonder of children.

The janitor thought it was like Father Ryland with his go-thy-way-and-sin-no-more dismissal. Now there was a priest God could have done without. "I just think madam."

"Mr. Purdy, please go back to your duties and leave the thinking to me."

Purdy nodded, and, taking Timmy's hand, whispered they'd find another way. Timmy was very agitated as they walked across the foyer. "Now, why don't you go outside for a bit? There's Brian and Peter still here and a couple others—and I saw them a moment ago kicking a football around."

Timmy had no desire to kick a football around, and even less desire to do it with Brian and Peter, but he thought he would like to go outside and sit by the frog pond. So he nodded to Mr. Purdy and walked over to one of the doors in the rear and stepped out onto green lawn.

Timmy really didn't much like Brian or Peter or most of the others who were down at the other end of the garden doing what Mr. Purdy had said, kicking a football around. Most seemed to have families who sometimes came to take them out—dad or mum or uncle—to take them off for the Christmas hols or Whitsun or even just out for the day. But then he remembered what the dad or mum had been like and decided maybe he wasn't so unlucky after all. Adults were so stupid around kids like him, talking loud as if you were deaf, or down as if you were stupid. No, some of those relations he'd seen he wouldn't want to have.

It was the reason he'd so much liked Rose or Rosa, for she had been like family, and Peter and the others had been envious because she was so pretty. An aunt who'd just got back from traveling the world and lived in Italy. Imagine.

They had gone, the three of them (for Timmy counted the dog Mungo as a third party), to an IceDelite between the school and the village, where he had eaten a double Razzberry Blitz and where she'd gone into the ladies and come out looking quite different. Looking like someone else. Her long pale hair was now glossy brown and short. The sunglasses had been exchanged for eyeglasses, smart looking, narrow with a metal frame. The bright red lipstick was changed for a softer, milky rose shade.

It was all to be a marvelous trick, she said. They were going to look at property, a few houses, and it would only take a couple of hours. Then they could stop somewhere for dinner before she took him back to the school.

His name, just for the day, was to be Robbie; hers, Glynnis. Robbie was what she would call him around other people, if they ran into other people and in case anyone should ask him. (Not that asking him would do much good.) She had even given him ten pounds. He kept the note in his shoe, more as a souvenir than for safekeeping.

Yes, it had been a marvelous trick—although he never had discovered the trick of it—and a marvelous day.

Timmy sat on the stone bench thinking about her and about that day. So lost in thought he was about what to do, he hardly registered the car sitting on the other side of the wall, part of whose hood he could see through the iron grating of the fence. It was a narrow side road that cars didn't usually venture up. He was curious and got up and started toward the gate, a little distance away.

It was then he saw the dog, who started circling around and then squeezed under the gate and ran, big ears flapping, off and back and off again and back.

Mungo!

Mungo jumped up on him, nearly knocking him down and Timmy laughed.

But Mungo ran in the other direction, away from the gate, and turned and waited for Timmy.

Come on come on don't get in that car!

The man called, "Timmy!"

Mungo barked. *Run away, run away!*

Timmy sensed something; he smelled something, as often he did, picking up a scent almost as well as a dog. But he couldn't get a picture of it in his mind.

"Timmy! Mungo!"

Timmy did not see the man who belonged to the voice. He was on the other side of the wall. So Timmy went through the gate, Mungo reluctantly following.

He had only two seconds to wonder why this big black car was parked here by the side of the school, when someone behind him quickly wrapped an arm around his neck, pulling him back.

"Open your eyes."

In the Bird, a dandyish pub with a lot of chintz and window seating, Jury and Dryer were both having cheese salad sandwiches.

"What about that little girl," said Dryer, munching lettuce, "the one who found the body?"

"Tilda." Again Jury heard Harry's voice in the house in Belgravia:

What little girl?

Tilda saw the car coming up the drive. She was in the drawing room having tea with the Queen (the Queen's role here performed by Oogli, her Inuit doll) when she heard a car and ran to the window.

Tilda ran back, plucked Oogli from the silk sofa and raced from the room and then from the house. When she got to the Wendy house, she was out of breath, but all right. She was not sure, even, why she was afraid, running, but she was. So she supposed she ought to be.

Timmy did not want to get out of the car.

When he'd opened his eyes again, he couldn't see. He wasn't blind; it was just that his vision was blurred, as if he were looking at objects through rings of water.

He knew it was the same house, even if he couldn't see it sharply, couldn't make out the details or see the edges. It was the house that Rosa had taken him to.

He did not want to get out, but he would have to; in another minute he would be pulled out by this man, this stranger, whom he couldn't see except as a tall blurry figure.

Mungo had scrambled out when the man who'd been driving got out and locked the doors. Timmy could make out Mungo when he looked through the car window. He was sitting there on the gravel in front of the house. When Timmy put his face up against the window, Mungo made a few scampering forays forward and backward—

Which puzzled Timmy.

—and then took off like a shot running toward the house and then running back.

What was the dog trying to do or say? He wanted Timmy to get out of the car.

Now.

Tilda didn't see him, didn't hear him, didn't know he was there until he grabbed her from behind, hard. Somehow he must have found a path through the wood. He came up behind her.

"Open your eyes," he said.

The arm wrapped round her neck grew tighter. The temptation was to seal her eyes shut as if that would help her. The hold grew tighter; he'd choke her to death. She opened them. A fluid, several drops of it, was forced into each eye. She blinked, tried to blink it away but she couldn't. Tilda shook her head several times, eyes closed.

He wasn't hurting her, just holding her tightly against him as if his life depended on it. Tilda found this almost funny, that somebody's life depended on her. That she was that important.

He held her that way for what seemed like a long time; she guessed it was only minutes. But they stood locked together until his arm eased up just a little.

With a force, a strength she had no idea she possessed, she broke away, suddenly, when his arm relaxed just a little.

He yelled. She *hurtled* herself into the woods. If he was thinking not being able to see clearly would stop her, must stop anyone running through woods, well, he was wrong. She knew this place too well. Blind, she would almost be able to find her way through these trees. And she knew exactly which tree she wanted. She darted from tree to tree. She zigzagged.

She heard him, and then he must have stopped.

After feeling over the collection of buttons on the inside of the car door, the driver's door, Timmy finally managed to hit the right one; he unlocked the door, pushed down on the handle and was out of the car.

Timmy could see the white blur of Mungo, rushing toward the house.

When Timmy hesitated—he wasn't sure what to do—Mungo rushed back, forward, back forward, as before.

Timmy followed, slowly, then quickly. He could see the front of the house and then Mungo, more visible, less visible, running to the other side.

He ran, and now so did Timmy.

The man yelled at both of them, yelled something Timmy couldn't hear and Mungo paid no attention to.

* * *

Tilda heard them coming—dog and boy. From what she could see, squinting in her partial blindness, they were racing each other.

The dog got there first—the woman who'd come that day long ago had called him Mungo, hadn't she, when she was calling for the two of them to come? Mungo was running a circle round the bottom of the tree. She really liked him and would have laughed if it all wasn't so frightening.

"Can you see? Can you see properly?" she asked him.

Nothing. No reply. But she could tell he was trying to, motions of his head and hands.

She remembered, then, he didn't, or couldn't, talk. He made a keening sound. She bet that whatever the man had used in her eyes, he'd put in the boy's, too.

Tilda put her hand on his shoulder, ran it down his arm and found his hand. "If you can't see squeeze my hand." He did, hard.

She heard a shout and looked toward the house. A figure moved on the patio and down the steps. He seemed in no hurry walking down the wide lawns. He was whistling.

Timmy heard him even at this distance. Timmy heard everything. It was hard, hearing everything.

The dog grabbed Tilda's sock with his teeth and pulled. At the same time the boy grabbed her hand and yanked her.

The three of them took off deeper into the woods. At first, Tilda thought maybe they could go to her house. But when she looked toward the wide lawn through the trees, she could see he was moving a little faster and there wouldn't be time.

She made it to the big oak and said, "You can climb, can't you?"

Timmy (who'd never climbed a tree in his life) got hold of her hand, squeezed it hard, yes.

Tilda blessed this tree she was climbing and blessed herself for knowing it so well she could climb it without seeing it properly. Well, she'd climbed it in the dark, hadn't she? She knew how high she could go and the best branch to sit on. Another branch and another. She looked down; the boy was coming. He was coming up quickly, like a monkey. But she guessed being followed by someone this dangerous could turn anybody into a monkey.

Another branch, another branch, and she stopped. The boy caught up, almost completely out of breath. She motioned for him to sit on the branch just below her.

What about the dog Mungo? He had started up barking again and for a moment she was afraid he was at the bottom of their tree. But no, he'd gone somewhere else.

The man had come into the woods. He was calling the boy. His name was Timmy. Tilda had forgotten his name. Now, the man was whistling for the dog Mungo.

Mungo sounded farther away than he had a minute ago. The man had stopped right beneath their tree, but now walked off, in the direction of the bark, which grew a little fainter still. Tilda blessed the dog; he was leading the man away from this tree.

She calculated it was almost five minutes since he'd followed the dog's barking. They might be able to get down from the tree and get home through the woods if the dog had led the man off in a whole different direction. She put a foot on Timmy's branch and whispered for him to go down. He scrambled off, lowering himself to another branch.

Squinting her eyes did no good, they were too cloudy. They felt like rain. But she'd be able to separate a moving figure from the rest of the woods, and as she set her foot on each new branch, she could tell there was no one moving around. When they reached the ground, she heard Mungo's bark coming closer. She grabbed onto Timmy and whispered to him to follow her.

Timmy didn't move. Mungo's barking was getting closer, sounded almost what she'd call hysterical (if her aunt had been doing it).

Tilda pulled on the boy, but he stood fast.

Then she knew he was waiting for Mungo. He wouldn't budge without the dog.

In a few seconds, here was Mungo bursting through the trees, probably in one last attempt to get them out of this place.

Of course, it was too late, for here he came. The tall figure stood over them sounding as pleased as if he'd found some secret hoard of treasure. Tilda found Timmy's hand, and Mungo just stopped.

"Well, that was fun, kids."

Funny, but he sounded friendly, not at all dangerous.

That was how, Tilda bet, the most dangerous ones sounded.

50

Twenty minutes later, Mrs. Copley-Sutton was still at reception and musing over the delights of Upper Sloane Street, then turning her mind to improvements sorely needed at Lark Rise Special School.

Suddenly the door opened and a man, a stranger, walked in and up to the desk.

He showed her identification. New Scotland *Yard?* What on earth . . . ?

"Superintendent Richard Jury. Are you Mrs Copley-Sutton?"

Hand smoothing hair again, she answered, "Yes. I'm the head. May I help you?"

He showed her the local paper, the item and picture of Rosa Paston. "Do you know this woman?"

Again, here was this dead woman being brought up. She frowned, took the paper to look at the photo more closely, but still couldn't place her. "No, I've never seen her."

"Is there anyone else who might have?"

It was then Mr. Purdy appeared. "Madam, something's bad, something's wrong—"

"Mr. Purdy, can't you see I'm busy here? This is the police."

About time, Mr. Purdy thought. "You remember that woman come for Timmy last year?"

Hermione Copley-Sutton knew, she had suspected at the time, that day last year—*knew* this would come back to haunt her. She worked her mouth in nervous silence, delaying. "Let me think, now . . ."

"We believe she was interested in one of the children here. One of the boys," said Jury.

Mrs. Copley-Sutton frowned. There was no reason not to tell the truth, was there? She hadn't committed any crime. "But she looked so utterly *different* then. Yes, you're quite right—she came here to collect one of the boys. I believe she was his aunt . . . ?" She believed nothing of the sort. There had been a donation to the school. She was wearing part of it, the Sonia Rykiel dress, purchased at one of those shops on Upper Sloane Street and still smart after a year. That was the thing about really good clothes, they simply didn't wear out their welcome.

"What was the boy's name?"

"Oh. Timmy. Timmy Radcliffe."

"She took Timmy out, did she?"

"Why, yes. He was gone most of the day I think."

"Excuse me, madam, but I was lookin' out t'window. Timmy and that dog, you recall that dog—"

Timmy had liked that dog. She said this, and the policeman seemed to stiffen.

"What dog?"

"Same one as was here before. Timmy went with him."

"Where are they?"

Mr. Purdy shook his head. "All I know is, Timmy was playing with that dog"—he pointed toward the back of the building—"and next I looked, they was gone."

"How long ago?"

"'Bout twenty minutes, I'd guess."

Such a short time. Jury was furious, more with himself for spending those twenty or so minutes in the pub than at her for allowing her charges to be checked out like coats.

In another moment, knowing words would simply waste time, he thanked her and walked out. He got into the car, slammed the door and let the engine idle. Where would he take the lad? Winterhaus? London? Anywhere. Anywhere he damned well wanted to.

While he maneuvered the car along the drive, the mobile phone Dryer had given him in one hand together with the scrap of paper with the numbers of the station and the house Dryer was going to. He tried the station. Dryer was back. Jury told him what he'd found.

"Buggered off to London, I shouldn't wonder," said Dryer.

Jury said he was going to Winterhaus first.

"When I get done here with some work . . . ring me if you find them at that house."

Jury said he would and flipped the phone shut.

It took another twenty minutes to drive to Winterhaus.

The empty house filled Jury with a kind of dread. It seemed for a moment bent with the sadness of recent vacancy, as if it had seen its occupants leave for the last time.

When he'd seen no car in front of the house, he assumed that Harry must have gone to London. Or had he been here and gone? Just now?

He went out to the patio and looked down the lawn. No sign of Tilda. He walked to the Wendy house. Nor here. Jury was looking, fruitlessly, he knew, for some telltale sign of their having stopped here. Why he wasted minutes doing this, he didn't know.

Harry, he was sure, would include Tilda as part of his cleanup, for Tilda might have seen him, might even have been in the house when he and Rosa Paston had been here. And Tilda, unlike Timmy, could talk up a storm.

What little girl?

That had been the only fault line Jury had seen in Harry Johnson's defenses—if he believed there was even a small *chance* that Tilda had seen him, well . . .

He thumbed through his small notebook, found Brenda Hastings's number, called. He listened to the telephone ring in the empty house. Then he called Surrey police again and asked Dryer if someone there could check with Brenda Hastings to see if Tilda was home.

Jury climbed into the car once more, drove fast down the drive and headed for London.

51

Three hours later, Harry came to the door of his Belgravia house and smiled upon seeing Jury. "Richard! Or should I say 'Superintendent,' as we appear to be at odds these days?"

Jury forced a smile. "Harry."

"Come in, come in."

Did the son of a bitch have to be so expansive? Jury walked into the drawing room and sat down in one of the armchairs. "We finally tracked down the lad, the one masquerading as Rosa Paston's nephew. Timmy Radcliffe."

"Oh?"

"So did you, Harry."

"So did I what?"

"Track him down."

Harry looked puzzled. "What are you talking about?"

"I'm talking about the Lark Rise Special School, the boy you took away from there just a few hours ago."

As if light had honestly dawned, Harry's eyes glittered. "What boy?"

It echoed so closely Harry's earlier question, *What story?*, that Jury could hardly sit there, outwardly calm, inwardly seething.

"You know what your trouble is, Harry?"

"No, but I bet you're going to tell me." Harry grinned. There was just enough of the sly child in it to turn the smile to a grin. "Care for a drink?" He rose and went to the cabinet where he kept the liquor.

Jury sighed. "No, I don't want a drink, Harry. Where are Tim and Tilda?"

Harry turned from the bottle and glass. "Tilda? Who the devil is Tilda? Are you going to hold me responsible for every missing child in Surrey?"

Jury looked at him. "I didn't say child; I didn't say missing; I didn't say Surrey."

"Wow!" Harry whirled around in mock wonder. "That was one of your trick questions that police try out on suspects! Please, Richard. If this Tilda is mentioned in the same breath as Timmy, she's clearly all three."

Harry's logic was, as usual, both flagrant and flawless. Damn. It was hard to think anyone who was as quick as he was could at the same time pretend to the extent that he could. Or maybe it was all imagination or madness.

Harry went on: "I'm disappointed in you to think I'd fall for something like that. Sure you won't have that drink?" He held up his own finger or two of whiskey in a squat tumbler.

"Yes, I'm sure. Mind if I have a look round?"

"My *house?* Don't be absurd; of course I mind." Harry lowered himself into the deep cushions of an armchair.

"I can get a warrant."

"To search the house? I don't think so, otherwise you'd have come with one."

"What have you got to hide?"

"It has nothing to do with hiding. It has a lot to do with my civil liberties."

"Hell, yes. We certainly want to protect those. Two kids aged eight and nine—what about their rights?" Jury knew this was stupid talk. You didn't argue with the Harry Johnsons of this world. You didn't lock horns with sociopaths. You either walked in and took what you wanted or you didn't go in at all. There were some expert safecrackers who believed that, too.

"You know, I recalled something you said about Mungo in the pub. Something to the effect that he'd 'always been like that.' Had always hated your cat. It was a comment no one but an animal's owner would make. I should have seen that." Jury shook his head.

Mungo could not go down into the basement. The door was locked and bolted. So he lay down outside the door and thought about the situation.

They couldn't yell for help because their mouths were pulled shut by that tape. They couldn't use their hands, either, as they were tied together behind their backs.

And here they were, down there, with the Spotter actually sitting in the living room, sitting almost *over* them, talking.

Life just wasn't fair.

This was not something Mungo had just discovered.

According to Chief Inspector Dryer, there had been no report to Surrey police about a missing person—or persons—and dog. That's what really gave the police a chuckle, one of the things that would keep anyone from believing there'd been a kidnapping. "You kept a lot of plates in the air, didn't you, Harry? I must say the juggling was first rate."

Harry drank his whiskey. "No."

"Oh, come on, Harry. You're not going to tell me that none of this happened? None of that story you told me over those evenings in the Old Wine Shades?"

Harry looked as if he were truly considering this story. "Well, some of it must have happened, I expect, since a woman was indeed murdered in that house, but none of it has anything to do with me." Harry flashed Jury a smile.

"Rosa Paston. You did know the victim."

"Of course. I simply mean that I have no idea what this woman was doing in that house. Or why she pretended to be Glynnis Gault."

It was with an effort that Jury rose. "I'll be off then."

"But you just got here. I'm enjoying your company."

You would, wouldn't you?

Harry said, "I'll be going over to the Shades tonight, if you care to join me." Harry smiled. "Around ninish. You know." Harry took a swig of his drink.

Sitting there with the most sublime confidence Jury had ever seen. Not a care in the world, have you, Harry? Jury supposed he'd just have to keep trying. Harry would keep on smiling, but he might let something slip. "I might just do that."

Jury looked at him while Harry finished off his whiskey and, even though he knew there was nothing personal in what Harry was doing, felt oddly betrayed.

"Good-bye, Harry."

52

Jury left Belgravia and went to see Johnny Blakeley at West End Central. Johnny headed up the pedophile unit, here where he spent a good three fourths of his time. He was the most dedicated detective Jury had ever known, except for Brian Macalvie, in Devon. Johnny had been suspended once and very nearly twice. He had broken into a run-down house in Earl's Court where some kids, just teenagers, were using a camcorder to shoot dirty films. It was what they knew, wasn't it? Their "stars" were three kids between three and seven. No warrant. Johnny had nothing by way of probable cause; he knew he couldn't make a charge stick, but—what the hell?—he tried charging them with kidnapping and reckless endangerment all the same. Still, Johnny had gotten the little kids to what he hoped was a safe place.

The solicitor for the oldest boy, who had been operating the camcorder, laughed the charges right out the door, along with his client.

The client hadn't been laughing, though, not in Earl's Court, not after Johnny smashed the camcorder and started wiping the floor with him. Johnny could scare these amateurs to death. Professionals, too, if he could get them alone long enough.

After Jury told him the story, Johnny looked at him, half smiling. "What would I do? Rich, if there's one person you don't need advice from it's me. But you're right; there's no way you've got probable cause. This is even worse than the Hester Street business, when it comes to getting a warrant. You won't get one."

"Well, it won't hurt to try. I'm still going to try."

Johnny was thinking. Then he said, "Can you get this man Johnson out of the house? If he lives alone—" Johnny shrugged.

"Oh, I can get him out of the house. He's out of the house this evening. Invited me to have a drink with him, which I'm going to. He's going to give something away sometime. Me, I'm just going to keep after him. No, the problem is *keeping* him out of the house to give me time to have a look round."

"Because if you could, and those kids are there, who's to know? What's to prove you were there?" Again, Johnny shrugged.

"Harry is anything but stupid. As long as he's got me in the pub, he knows where I am."

"What's to keep him from disposing of these kids right now?"

"I don't think killing them is what he has in mind. I don't think he'd do that. Otherwise, why bring them to London? If that's what he intended to do, he could have killed them right there in Surrey. No, I think he wants to scare them into silence. Well, Timmy Radcliffe is silent, anyway. He's autistic."

"Then why bother kidnapping him at all? Unless, of course, the Radcliffe kid might have other means of communicating—"

"I've got a man watching his house."

Johnny leaned forward, said, as if in confidence, "Look, you get him out of the house and I—"

"No." Jury was emphatic. "Absolutely not, Johnny. You can't touch it."

Johnny sat back.

"But thanks. Thanks a lot for the offer. I'll think of something." Like what?

"Listen, on a more cheerful note, Linda—she's Social Services—told me that the two you especially wanted to stay together have been placed in the same home."

"Rosie and Pansy?"

"Yeah, I think so." Johnny dived a hand into his desk drawer and came out with a list of sorts. "Yep, they're in the same place."

"Where?"

Johnny was copying off the information onto a page of his note-book. "You know I can't divulge that information." He tore off the page where he'd written the address and handed it to Jury. "Here."

Jury took it, smiled. "Thanks, Johnny. You're the salt of the earth."

Johnny nodded toward the page, saying, "The thing is, though, if you turn up at that house, they're going to know someone leaked the information and maybe complain. Remember, I don't want to get in bad with Social Services. They trim a lot of corners for me, espe-cially Linda."

"That was nice of you and Linda. Tell her I appreciate it."

Johnny looked back at the paper again. "Rosie's even going to infants' school."

"My lord, that was fast."

"Well, it's a public school, so it's easier to bend the rules." Johnny took back Jury's notebook page and wrote on it. "I think Linda said it was right round the corner from where the family lives, in Chelsea."

The Piccadilly and Green Park tube stations were equidistant from Hatchards bookshop and Fortnum & Mason. He took the Jubilee Line to Green Park, only one stop but he didn't feel like walking or taking a car; driving around Piccadilly was merely frustrating. You could troop off to the Outer Hebrides in the time it takes to get around Piccadilly Circus in a car.

Jury had always felt something akin to affection for Fortnum's, though he couldn't say why. It was not a venue in which he ordinar-ily shopped; it was too expensive for a CID man's pay. But its win-dow decorations employed more imagination and its arrangement of tins and fruit and sweets were given to more artful staging than a West End theater. Look at those pears and plums in their cata-strophically expensive produce section! Or on the other side of the floor the fowl and fish, a smoked salmon sliced so thin it fell away in folds, like the skirt of a pink silk gown, transparent slices of

cucumber neatly tucked into the folds. And that perfect hell for di-
eters, the pastry counters. You could eye those little meringue
swans filled with strawberry chiffon, or that devilish chocolate
mousse dusted with cocoa and frills of more chocolate and make
your salivary glands weep. It looked rich enough for a lifetime of
desserts. There was a rum cake that leaked its liquor onto the plate,
a coconut cake adorned with thin shavings of white chocolate, a
lemon tart that glowed as if lit from within.

He had never seen food so hypnotic in his life. He could taste
every single thing in those glass cases. From a little whippet of a
salesperson, Jury bought one of the meringue swans and a more
pedestrian cream doughnut.

As he walked back through Fortnum's out to the street, he
doubted if there was a better pastry shop in Vienna or Paris or
heaven. He stopped to eat his cream doughnut and look in Fortnum's windows, where the mannequins looked electrified either by
his looking at them or by their handsome outfits. The designer
dresses they'd been clothed in won.

Next he went to Hatchards, a bookshop that leaked learning the
way that rum cake had leaked rum. No matter how many customers
there were, this bookshop always had a sort of hush to it, as if the air
were padded with cotton or clouds. He held this cloud fancy in his
mind as he walked down the circular stair to the children's section.
There he looked up the Maurice Sendak books, pulling out *Outside
over There* and the one he particularly wanted, *Really Rosie.* He
leafed through it . . . well, more read it standing there. Then he put
Rosie under his arm and read again about the ice baby in *Outside
over There.*

Did anyone understand children better than Maurice Sendak?
Psychologist? Teacher? Social worker? He sincerely doubted it.

Chelsea was about as far from Hester Street in spirit as it was in distance. In place of seediness and drabness, here was a sort of elo-
quence, a paean to upper-middle-class values. Snobbish, too, it

could be, but he didn't think that would influence Rosie or Pansy. They'd seen too much awfulness to be impressed by the pretensions of society.

The address Johnny had given him was one of the mews cottages which he stood now regarding. Artfully arranged little dwellings that so pleased foreigners. It was an old stable block: it was funny, really, how there was such cachet in living in a stall that once had housed a horse. But it was so lovely that Rosie and Pansy were living in a dollhouse: ivy, climbing roses, pots of bright zinnias. All of the doors were painted in pastels.

The school, Johnny had said, was near—around the corner—and he came to it in less than five minutes. It was a building of old brick and wide marble stairs. Gathered at the bottom of the stairs were a number of women, parents, probably. Others were getting out of BMWs, Mercedeses and fancy smaller cars. He wondered if Rosie's new foster mum was among them. The women all looked sleek, whether they were wearing Liberty linen or old jeans.

He looked through the fence at the little playground where the children were now lined up and ready to move, double file, into the school and then out again to their mothers. He looked hard for Rosie among them, but couldn't find her. With their blue and gray uniforms, the children all bore a curious resemblance to one another. A few had apples and one tiny girl a pear, which she was mashing all over her face, trying to eat it.

"Sir, are you a parent?"

The young woman seemed to have sprung up before him on the other side of the fence. A teacher. She looked uncertain, yet not wanting to insult him if he were.

"I? No, no I'm not. I was just looking for—" But Jury remembered Johnny's warning and said nothing more.

Her eyebrows raised, but still slightly smiling, as if there were something about him that kept her from thinking the worst.

For which he was grateful. He shifted the books from under his arm, again remembering that he shouldn't do anything to let the foster parents know that someone had given out their information. He saw her glance move to *Outside over There* and felt the book rendering him harmless. But he heard in his inner ear a kind of cracking or splintering, reminding him (oddly enough) of the other night and Phyllis biting into the glaze of her dessert. As if the ice baby were breaking.

"Perhaps it's the wrong school. Yes, it must be. Sorry."

He could feel her eyes on him as he made his way through the collection of parents and the school bell sounding the end of the day.

53

It was a real plum for Chief Superintendent Racer, a real opportunity to showcase his response to the kind of question (in this case Jury's) that came along once in a lifetime, and if you couldn't give it your best shot, well, that was it, mate. Never another chance.

Racer didn't really have a best shot, though, so all he could do was lard up his response to Jury's request for a warrant with as much sarcasm as he could muster. "A warrant. Ah, yes, a *warrant*." Fake laughter here, while Racer got up and wandered around his desk to lean on the front of it with his arms folded. He said it again: "A warrant, a warrant."

It put Jury in mind of that child's rhyme: "To market, to market." The next line just slipped out, under his breath, but not way under: "To buy a fresh pig."

Racer stared. "Taking this whole business pretty lightly, aren't you, Jury? Considering there's three kids involved?"

"Two." Jury couldn't resist holding up two fingers.

"You said three."

"No. The third one's a dog."

"Oh, I see! You need to save a *dog*! Well, that's *different*, Jury! Why didn't you say that in the first place?" Here Racer gave an acerbic little smile, as if even the name were an entry in the ironic sweepstakes. "Jury, since when do *you* need a warrant? Since when have you ever bothered with a *warrant*? Why, as I recall, you managed to batter your way into that house in Hester Street, you and that cowboy of a policeman from Devon. You did this without being blessed with a warrant. So I expect you'll find a way into this Belgravia house without a *warrant*, too." Racer couldn't repeat the word often enough to please himself, as it had been part and parcel of Jury's recent trouble and what had nearly resulted in his being made redundant (not to put too fine a point on it).

Racer would never let it go, Jury knew. "These two kids' lives are at stake, guv." He never used this appellation unless he wanted something from Racer, and that was rare. Jury lifted his gaze to the bookcase where the cat Cyril was flattening himself against the top. Waiting.

"Well, you should have thought of this before you stormed into that Hester Street house," Racer said, with his usual illogic. "Evidence, Jury! Let's see some evidence that these children are being held there. Let's see some evidence of probable cause, if it's not too much to ask." Racer moved around to stand behind his desk with arms braced and hands flat on it so that he could glare at Jury like some Fleet Street publisher letting off steam at one of his reporters.

"There's the head of the school who can certainly testify that Timmy's missing. There's the little girl Mathilda's aunt who'll tell you her niece hasn't come back, either." Neither of these would work as evidence without more time passing, and even then would not implicate Harry Johnson. But Jury put it out there, anyway. "And there's the dog. The maintenance man and probably some of the other children out there in one of their games can testify that the dog ran onto the grounds and up to Timmy. The same dog—" Jury sighed, walking right into it.

Like a pitcher winding up for the pitch of the year, Racer worked up his expression into such a fulsome display of scorn he could hardly find words to match it, so settled on one. "A dog. A *dog*. You're asking for a warrant with the doings of a *dog* as evidence. Oh, well"—Racer flung out his arms in mock acceptance of this idea—"in *that* case, we see no problem in issuing said warrant." Racer got his face up close to Jury's: "Now you listen to this, laddie. You're not to go within a thousand yards of this Harry Johnson's house." He trotted out police harassment. "So, far from getting a *warrant*, you'll get a hell of a lot more than a slap on the wrist *this* time around. It's no use pleading exigent circumstances that your hotshot barrister used to get you out of the mess you were in. There's not even the whiff of the exigent circumstances you managed last time around. No, that won't fly again!"

Speaking of flight, Cyril gathered himself together and took aim.

As the cat came down, Jury got up. Cyril dived toward Racer's desk in a graceful arc and made a three-point landing on Racer's shoulder. Yes, the guv'nor yelled at that!

Fiona came in through the door that Cyril ran out of.

Jury smiled. You wouldn't catch Cyril sticking at a warrant.

Jury was in his office, feet up on his desk, leaning back in his swivel chair, hearing only snatches of Wiggins's views on the evils of robotics. It was a subject Jury had not, "funnily enough" (he told Wiggins), thought of as a terrible threat.

He was irked with himself for letting Harry Johnson know that he, Jury, was certain that Tim and Tilda were somewhere in that house. That was an unbelievably stupid thing for him to have done. This might only precipitate some action on Harry's part sooner, rather than later.

Wiggins had shifted his peroration to cloning. "They're cloning animals and not just sheep, but family pets. Dogs and cats."

Since Jury was big on dogs these days, Wiggins's voice filtered through. The world, thought Jury, could use another Mungo. Many, many Mungos.

Wiggins went on. "What's happening here is like that business of freezing yourself, so when medicine comes up with a cure for what killed you, you can come back. It's like nobody really dies."

"Doesn't it strike you as ghastly, Wiggins? DCS Racer coming back when we thought we were finally rid of—" Jury stopped suddenly. He brought his chair forward with a thud. He sat thinking for a minute while his smile broadened. He looked at his watch. It had just gone 4:00.

What the hell? It might just work. If it didn't, nothing lost. Jury rose and unhooked his coat from the stand. "If you need me, I'll be at Boring's."

"You be careful, sir, you never . . ."

Wiggins's voice trailed after him down the hall. What was he to be careful of? Was it the Day of the Robots or the Night of the Clones?

54

Jury made a stop at Foyles Bookshop in Charing Cross Road. It was out of his way, but Foyles was the biggest bookshop in London. Waterstone's might outdo it for square footage but Foyles had the most exhaustive inventory. He told the clerk (were they called that anymore?) what he wanted and was directed to the third floor.

It was a bookshop one could literally get lost in, which Jury thought was to its credit. It put him in mind of a small dusty shop in a London by-lane, which had grown bigger and bigger like a child's Lego structure. He found what he thought would do, paid for it and left.

With his book in hand, he stood outside of Foyles looking up and down Tottenham Court Road, but did not see what he wanted. A #10 bus was coming along, and he thought a better vantage point to see the shops would be gained, and more quickly, by looking out of a bus window. When it came to a wheezing stop, he climbed aboard. Less than three minutes later, he saw the little shop called Pigtails (how he loved that name!) down a side street and got off at the next stop.

Pigtails. What whimsical mind had thought that one up? Jury walked through the door with its tinkly little bell and stood there for an unbothered minute—the receptionist having left her post—and thought he knew why women favored these places. Pigtails was calming, like a sanctuary, even with all of the hair blowing and chattering.

"Do something for you, love?" said the receptionist, a plump girl with a hairdo that struck Jury as old-fashioned, the way the hair bobbed about her face in dark ringlets.

"Oh. Yes, you can." He took out his ID and surprised her to death. "We're needing one of your stylists for an important job."

Round-eyed, she looked at him. "Which one?"

"The stylist? Doesn't make any difference. The job won't take more than an hour or two. And of course we'll pay twice the usual tariff." He smiled. How could Pigtails lose?

The receptionist looked around the shop. Jury noticed there was a kind of uniform, not in design or cut, but in color. This was a coppery color, a brownish red. They were all wearing it in some guise or other. There were nine or ten stylists. "Lucy's free, I think." She raised her hand and spoke the name.

Putting down her magazine, Lucy did not walk so much as drift toward them like a pile of russet leaves. She had golden-gingerish hair that matched her dress, worn long to her shoulders, pale, pale skin, luminous light brown eyes. Her whole person, as she came languidly toward him, seemed weightless, insubstantial, like an etherialized Carole-anne. Lucy was quite beautiful.

Jury told them what was needed. He needed to have a job done; it was an important police matter. He repeated that he would pay twice the usual cost of the service. But as circumstances prevented this person's coming to Pigtails, well, Pigtails would have to go to him. Would she?

Lucy and the ringleted receptionist exchanged glances. Yes, she would. What exactly did he want in terms of color? Jury told her an ordinary brown and Lucy smiled. From some list in her head, Lucy ran down all of the brown possibilities. Jury settled on one and she said just a tick, she'd be right back. Then she drifted away.

Back she came in five minutes with her long loose hair caught in her coat collar and carrying a tote-bag.

Jury had in the meantime gotten a cab, which now waited at the curb, meter quietly ticking over. He gave the address and they sailed off, if "sailing" was any kind of metaphor for threading a car into London traffic. But that's how it felt to Jury, caught up in this little fantasy.

Lucy's smile matched his smile, as if she were in on the joke.

Although he was terribly troubled by the fate of these two little children, he still could smile over his plan. He loved it, a love undiminished by knowing Melrose Plant would hate it.

"No," said Melrose, rattling his *Daily Telegraph* back in front of his face and picking up his drink.

Melrose had driven up to London just that afternoon, and had been here barely an hour when Jury walked into the Members' Room. Melrose wanted only to relax with his paper and his afternoon drink, but that wasn't the reason for his refusal. He was refusing because it was the dumbest thing he'd ever heard of, an opinion he was happy to share with Jury.

"Here's a book to read," said Jury, handing Melrose his purchase from Foyles. "You don't have to read the whole thing, obviously, but just pick out a few salient points and make yourself very familiar with them. It's got pictures, too."

His paper lowered, Melrose saw that Jury had paid no attention to the no and nor would he. Jury was intent upon this harebrained scheme, the harebrained part to be performed by Melrose. He pointed out that Jury was not the one who was expected to carry out this plan. Oh, no. As usual, that would be Melrose's job. "It took me a *week* to learn about flowering mead and enameling and that was just *gardening*. How in the devil do you expect me to master this"—here Melrose held up the book in a wobbly way—"in an afternoon?" Then he held up his glass in the same way for Young Higgins to get him another drink.

"Do what Diane Demorney does. Diane's so-called intellectual prowess is based on nothing more than her picking out some all-but-unknown fact about a subject and then finding out everything she can about it. You remember the Stendhal syndrome thing. She knows nothing at all about his books, but she knows everything about his fainting while looking at art. It's a brilliant idea, despite Diane's being anything but brilliant."

"I was considering going into dinner in a few hours."

"You don't have time for dinner. I'll have dinner and bring you something back."

"What an excellent plan! If you think I'm skipping dinner for this, you're crazier than I thought. And that was pretty crazy." Melrose sighed. "You know this will never work. It's completely outrageous."

"You seem to forget. Harry Johnson is insane. So that gives us an edge."

"Who's that person you parked out in the lobby? What's she all about?"

"That's Lucy. She's from Pigtails."

Melrose shook his head hard to see if he could clear it. "Pigtails? *Pigtails?*"

"Right. Wait here. I'll just get her."

Wait here? Where the devil did he think Melrose could go? Grumpily, he waited, polishing his eyeglasses. Without them, he looked across the room to where Jury was coming with someone in tow when Melrose could describe only as, well, *gossamer*—the airy clothes, the diaphanous skin, the gauzy veil of hair. Good lord. He hoped some of this would be rectified when he put on his glasses.

Which he did, in a hurry.

No, that's pretty much what she looked like. He stood up.

"This is Lucy from Pigtails." Jury grinned.

She could have been Shirley from Sheepshorn or Betty from Cowbell as far as Melrose was concerned.

"Hello, Lucy. How long will this take?"

As if he cared.

55

One of the narrow windows in the basement didn't shut properly. Through this window Mungo had watched Harry force Timmy and Tilda down into the basement. That is, when he realized Harry was taking them down to the basement, he'd practically flown out the rear door and through the garden to this window. He could not make out exactly what was going on because the window was grimy, but he knew it wasn't good. There was a lot of shuffling about, as if the children were trying to get free. But they didn't scream or shout because their mouths were taped.

When things were still again, and Harry had left the basement, Mungo went back through his dog door into the kitchen and sat wondering how to get into it. He had stayed by the basement door for a long time, part of it taken up by listening to Harry and the Spotter talking in the living room. The Spotter had left some time ago.

By now, it had gone from light to dark, day to night. He was outside again. Mungo had never been good at opening things—doors, trunks, cabinets—with his paws. He could pry things open with his nose sometimes, but this window was nearly even with the ground and he couldn't get his nose into the opening. He turned in circles and whined, something he rarely did.

When Shoe appeared around the corner of the house, he whined harder and butted the window, whined and hit the window again. Shoe stalked over, not trusting Mungo, but she was curious. She crept to the window and peered in. It was pitch dark in the basement so that she had a hard time making out the children. Had she not been blessed with cat's eyes, she never would have seen them.

Shoe sat back and watched Mungo circling and whining and

hitting the window. She yawned, enjoying the fact that he wanted something from her that she could either grant or refuse. She started washing a paw, which really got Mungo mad. Now he was bouncing against the window, back and forth.

He wanted to help the kids down there. Well, now, that was different. She belly-crept close to the window, as if she had to make herself invisible, something she was used to doing. The window was open enough for her to get her paw round it and pull.

They couldn't speak because their mouths were pulled shut by silver duct tape. They couldn't use their hands to tear it off because the hands were tied behind their backs. He had also made them put on these thin latex gloves. They could, however, move around, as Harry hadn't tied their feet. But he had looped the two of them together so that one couldn't move without the other.

When they heard the commotion outside, the two of them looked at each other. At least, he had removed the blindfolds. Shortly before they got to this house, he had pulled over and parked and put more stuff in their eyes. This time he had also blindfolded them, even though their vision was still cloudy. She supposed it was to make sure they'd have no chance of seeing what they passed—streets, buildings, lights—where they were in the city. It was quite definitely the city; you didn't have to see out the windows to know that.

But down here in the dark, he'd removed the blindfolds. After a while, whatever he'd put in their eyes had finally worn off. They could see now, and they moved together to the window, to stand beneath it in time to see a branch being pushed between the window and the sill.

They looked wildly at each other and would have cheered or, at least smiled, except for the tight tape over their mouths. Somebody was out there trying to help them, trying to fix a way out. They couldn't shout; they couldn't clap their hands; but they could jump up and down as long as they jumped together. They kept falling against each other, then scrambling up again. But they were so buoyed by their feelings of relief they went on trying. And they both grunted *uh uhh uhhh* as loud as they could.

Something—a snout?—was working its way now into the window's's opening. Mungo! Timmy and Tilda jumped again and fell again, jumped and fell.

Mungo shoved his head between window and sill, then his body. He dropped down. The basement floor was a little farther down than he'd have liked, but it didn't hurt much as he'd fallen on something that wasn't, at least, cement hard. Indeed, he dropped gracefully, considering the difficult angle of the window and sill.

Shoe stuck her head through the window, but then withdrew it, unprepared for heroic measures. She sat back and started washing.

Mungo circled round the children, knowing they couldn't tell him what to do. Anyway, the boy couldn't have told him even if his mouth had been free. Mungo wondered if this trouble Timmy was in now wouldn't shake some words loose in him.

Well, it was down to Mungo and he'd better work it out and do it fast. He wanted them to sit down; all he could do was yank on Tilda's dress. Finally, they sat down. Now he could get to the rope, which wasn't very thick, he was glad to see. All it would take was getting the rope loose on one hand, any hand; he chose Tilda's.

Mungo chewed. He chewed and chewed, wrestling one bit free and then chewing again. He couldn't chew through the knot, which would have made it easier. Where had Harry learned that trick? His long stint in the merchant marines? Right. Don't make me laugh.

Mungo sat back, his jaw really tired from this effort and meditated a moment about how he'd ever come to belong to Harry. Had it been some misfortune as a puppy? What Harry needed was some slick and silky dog he could sport about—

Grunts. *Uh! Uhh! Uhhh!*

Mungo stopped woolgathering and started quickly chewing again. This time he managed to chew through the final threads of one part of the rope on Tilda's wrist and free one of her hands. She did not remove the rope from her other wrist; she ripped the tape from her mouth, winced with the pain and, having got her mouth free, left the rest where it was. She did not peel off the gloves. All of this was in case he suddenly decided to check on them. If that happened, she wanted to be able to retape her mouth and at least make it appear her hands were still tied. Tape dangled, as did the rope.

"Mungo!" she said, throwing her arms around him while Timmy kept on grunting. It was short work for her to loosen the rope around Timmy's hands. He pulled away the tape, his eyes tearing with the pain of it, as hers had. It hurt too much to tear away and, anyway, it made no difference, especially for Timmy. He started to remove the gloves.

Tilda said, "Leave it, Timmy! If he comes down we'll want to be just as he left us or he'll know."

Timmy did as she said.

But footsteps above them shut her up. Someone was in the kitchen and Tilda held her breath. This was what she had feared and she put the tape back over her mouth, clamped a hand over Timmy's (as if he'd give the show away, anyway). She held to that pose until the steps grew fainter, moving away from the kitchen.

She sighed with relief and whispered, "We can get out if we can just reach it." She was looking up at the window.

Timmy, though, was already shoving a wooden crate, empty of its wine bottles, but still solid with packing material. Tilda found a smaller one and stacked that on top of the wine crate. She whispered, "Mungo, you go first!"

First? He hung back. Of course he wouldn't go *first.* But he knew he had to get back through his dog door before Harry went out.

"Mungo? Oh, okay. Timmy, you're first."

Timmy climbed up on the first wine crate and then up again to the smaller one. From there, he had enough purchase to force the window open a little wider. He pushed it farther open, shoved himself through it. Then he held it wider still for Tilda, scrambling up and out, then reaching the branch down as far as she could for Mungo. He couldn't climb like Shoe (who was watching this operation), but with the help of the branch he managed, with a short lunge, to get up to the window.

Then all three were out. They would have whooped and hollered for joy had it not been dangerous.

Shoe stopped washing for a few seconds and watched Timmy hugging Mungo and then Tilda doing it again. Hugging that dog. Shoe went back to her grooming.

Tilda grew sober. "Now what? Now what?" She had her hands in a tight grip as if they were still tied with rope. Now she peeled off the gloves and looked around the dark garden. No light from the windows showed.

"Maybe he's gone someplace." She looked through the darkness, saw nothing but the shapes of the trees, heard nothing but the swish of a car go by, was afraid that before he left he would go down the basement stairs to check on them. "Timmy! We've got to get out of here!"

Timmy looked at her, waiting for direction.

Money. Timmy sometimes forgot he kept the bill in his shoe, he'd gotten so used to the feel, it seemed like part of his foot. He knelt down and untied his shoe and, like pulling a rabbit out of a hat, pulled the ten-pound note out of his sock.

Tilda was dazzled. It was like watching some magician pull a coin from behind her own ear. "That's enough to get us somewhere! It's enough for bus fare to somewhere. Even to just another part of the city. Somewhere!"

Timmy was glad he could offer this money; "somewhere" sounded like paradise.

Mungo saw them start for the front of the house and headed them off. He rushed up to pull at Timmy's sleeve.

"What?" said Tilda.

Mungo ran off to the side, down a slight incline toward the

pavement, then rushed back again, meaning for them to follow. He was afraid that if they went to the front of the house Harry might come out of the door and see them.

They followed him.

"Mungo, thanks, thanks." Tilda gave him another hug.

They ran off toward Sloane Street and Mungo ran after for a little bit, knew he could do no more and sat on the dark pavement and watched until they'd disappeared, two children, into the London night, as if they were the last act in a magic show.

56

When Jury walked into the Old Wine Shades at 9:15 P.M., Harry was sitting at the bar talking to Trevor. They were talking about the bottle of wine Trevor was holding, napkin wrapped. Trevor, Jury knew, only wrapped napkins around serious bottles of wine. Harry greeted Jury as if they'd just met and hadn't an hour's worth of trouble between them. Or at least as if whatever had passed was all water under the bridge and they were still mates.

How the hell, wondered Jury, does he do it? That is, as if he *hadn't* done it? "Hello, Harry, Trevor."

Mungo had been sitting under the bar chair next to Harry and unwound himself to ease out and get his neck scratched by Jury. When Jury sat down, Mungo returned to his place underneath the bar chair.

"Trevor's breaking out the real stuff tonight," said Harry. "Look at this Hermitage. Very rare, very scarce. Have some," he said, as if they'd come here for a wine tasting.

In an acrobatic motion, Trevor flipped a glass from the shelf at his back, turned it up and set it on the counter. Then he poured an inch into the glass and hung fire.

"Go ahead and fill it up, Trevor; I trust you."

"Come on, come on," said Harry. "Just taste it, go on."

Jury smiled because they both were looking at him with an expectation that suggested he had to do this before they could assess the true provenance of this bottle. Jury held it to his nose, swirled it about, tasted it. It was superior, but then to Jury it was all good in here, including the house plonk that ran like a river between the stalls.

What killed him was that they both looked so serious. He felt himself drawn into this fabulous setting, this wine fable, these racks and racks of bottles, and beguiled by Harry Johnson as if it were the first time, so much so that Jury might have dreamed up everything that had happened in the last week.

"Wonderful. Delicious."

They both frowned and looked like twins with the frowning. As if momentarily disappointed, as if Jury should say more, or be more precise, more exact, as if his answer should come on little wine feet, as to the wonder of it.

"Best wine I've ever drunk." He smiled; he couldn't help it, looking at both of them frowning in concert.

Harry finally broke the spell by pushing his glass forward. "Another measure, Trevor."

Trevor poured the Hermitage into Harry's glass, ignored the deadbeat Jury's, nodded, walked off down the bar with the napkin-wound bottle.

Harry sat smoking a fragrant cigar—or perhaps to Jury all smoke was fragrant, redolent of the past.

"So tell me more, Harry."

"More what?"

"The ten dimensions. Because a friend of mine dropped an earring and it's vanished."

Harry laughed. "You know, there's a refinement of string theory that says there are eleven; it's called M theory."

"No! Don't give me another dimension to deal with, for God's sake. I just want to know where the other six are, the ones I can't seem to lay hands on." He beckoned to Trevor. Jury was beginning to feel as if he owned the place. "Where are they hiding?"

Harry smiled behind a plume of smoke. Trevor reappeared and filled Jury's glass.

"Oh, did you think I meant—?" Jury's eyebrows shot up. "No, I don't mean *them*. I mean the dimensions. And really, what good is it if we can't see them?"

"You're joking? You don't believe that only what you can see has any relevance for you. Other dimensions might explain the whole makeup of the universe."

"Harry, I just want them to explain the makeup of *me*. Or better yet, *you*. I can get a mental image of the three we mortals slog through every day. Maybe even the fourth—time—I just can't get at those other six."

Harry sighed. "Arrogant, aren't you?"

Jury loved the charge of arrogance, especially considering who it was coming from. He laughed.

"You're not supposed to get a *mental image* of everything in the universe. However, perhaps this will help." Harry tore off a little bit of a bar napkin and crumpled it up. He put this tiny bit behind his glass. "Like that." It was minuscule, hidden by the base of the glass. "Another dimension. A loop, perhaps."

"Possibly. But is this just wishful thinking on Hugh's part?"

Harry frowned. "I'm not getting it."

"I'm talking about Robbie. Doesn't Hugh believe that given those dimensions we could have a complete misconception of spacetime and that Robbie could come back? That's all I meant by wishful thinking."

"Come on. Hugh's a scientist. He's an advocate of string theory, hence the other dimensions."

"How about you?"

"Me? I believe *anything's* possible." He picked up his glass and Jury reached over and picked up the crumpled bit of paper. He looked into Harry's eyes, looking for some clue perhaps, for some sign of madness. All he saw was life, and it shone quite brightly.

"For you, Harry, it probably is. God knows you're inventive enough."

Harry turned, smiling. "Am I wrong or do I hear the bugle tap of retreat in that?"

Jury laughed. "Until I can get a warrant, there's not a damned

thing police can do. I might as well just sit here and drink this superior wine."

As if he'd heard his own bugle tap, Trevor appeared. This was a
different bottle he held, a Haut-Brion, a '75, from a château whose
name Jury didn't make out; it was very expensive, but "Mr. Johnson," Trevor claimed, could afford it and it looked as if the two of
them were celebrating. This brought laughs from both of them and
Harry said, go ahead, pour, pour, pour.

Trevor did, after the little whiffing, tasting, routine.

Jury was looking in the mirror—had been, for a little while—
waiting for the pub door to open. Just at the moment of Trevor's
pouring, it did.

Melrose Plant's hair was a rather attractive shade of brown, and
his green eyes were fairly well hidden behind the lightly tinted
glasses. He wore a three-piece suit, quite elegant, but not over-
whelmingly so. He walked up to the bar and sat down, without fan-
fare or invitation, beside Harry, who, of course, turned curious eyes
on him.

Even Mungo was interested and came out from his lair beneath
the tall bar chair.

If a dog could be said to look suspicious, that's how Mungo
looked, peering up at Melrose Plant, who held out his hand to
Harry, and said, "You're Harry Johnson, aren't you?"

Harry looked at the hand, looked at the man and said, "I am,
yes. And you're—?"

"I'm Niels Bohr."

Mungo crawled back under the chair and put his paws over
his eyes.

Dog walked into a pub . . .

57

It was a dead cert.

Until he found it wasn't.

This time, Jury had said, there were eyewitnesses, two of them—except as it turned out, there weren't.

"We never saw him," said Tilda, reddening, then looking away, looking at anything but Jury, as if she'd let him down, as if her not having seen the man's face had been unforgivably careless of her.

Timmy sat and stared at Jury and nodded at everything Tilda said. He too wore an expression of failure.

Jury told them they had been very brave, had shown an ingenuity he wished all of the Metropolitan police had. Then to Jury's question, had they been blindfolded or something?

Tilda said, "It was our eyes. First, he put something in them and everything was blurry. No, it didn't hurt; it's just that everything was so blurry we couldn't see what his face really looked like. He blindfolded us too, but not for long."

(Phyllis Nancy had said, "Dilating drops, the kind that ophthalmologists use on every patient up to a certain age. The drops dilate the pupil. You've had them, haven't you? Simplest thing in the world, except you have to wait for a time until they take effect.")

"He just stood in back and kept us from turning around and blindfolded us. He took the blindfolds off in a little while, though, but we still couldn't see, right, Timmy?"

At sometime before 11:00 that night, Tilda and Timmy had presented themselves at New Scotland Yard near the St. James's tube stop and said they had to see Mr. Jury and would they be safe in here? "I mean if we have to sit and wait?"

They were assured they would be safe.

"Okay, then, come on, Timmy." Tilda had led him over to a long bench to sit.

Superintendent Jury had gotten off an elevator less than five minutes after they walked in.

Tilda was surprised when he walked over and hugged her, really *hard*. It was as if he'd missed them.

He did not hug Timmy, and that was probably the right thing to do, as boys like to think they're grown up and beneath hugging. Jury shook Timmy's hand and praised him for being so brave and resourceful.

Timmy was not sure about "resourceful" but he knew he was being complimented. You didn't need to talk to be brave and resourceful, which was good news.

Now, how had they gotten to New Scotland Yard?

"We were running along a street, I don't know which one. When we left the basement, we just ran. It was a busy street and we just got on a red bus and sat on top. Timmy'd saved some money in his shoe. We got off that and got on another. In case we were being followed. We rode and rode. That was fun, wasn't it, Timmy?"

Timmy nodded vigorously.

How was it kids could turn some part of a hair-raising experience into fun?

Jury had gotten back to his office a half hour before the kids had arrived. Sergeant Meek, who'd been watching the house, had gone in with Jury to search for them. Jury hadn't asked him to, of course he hadn't. He'd told Meek there was no warrant and he could land in a world of trouble.

Meek had said, "Two little kids, I got kids of my own, boss. If they were in this spot I'd hate to think they could've been found if only some copper hadn't waited on a warrant."

The most likely place was the basement and the door down to it was both locked and bolted from the kitchen side. Meek, whose uncle (he liked to tell people) had been a first-rate safecracker until "an unfortunate affray," had his own special tool for locks. And this lock wasn't a very good one to begin with. The sergeant had it open in five seconds.

It was really a wine cellar—shelves, rows and rows of bottles. So Harry was a connoisseur. Jury thought he had known a little about wine, but only a little. Harry, Jury was disposed now to think, had a hard time telling the truth about anything.

No. Harry was a rotter. He was a self-aggrandizing, vain, fraudulent—not to mention dangerous—sod. A very, very clever sod.

There was nothing in the basement—no kids, no evidence they'd been there.

Where had he moved them? Because Jury knew Harry had them.

"Come look at this, guv," said Meek.

Jury left the wine racks and went over to where Meek was standing. Wine crates, upended, stacked.

"That window? It's open," said Meek. "Not very big, but it wouldn't have to be. That's it, innit?"

Jury laughed. That was most certainly it.

Jury's mobile chimed with a horrifying sweetness. A tiny tinkling of bells. He pulled it out, spoke.

Melrose told him that Harry had just walked out the door. "When he realized you were gone, he collected Mungo and left. Didn't seem upset, actually. I guess he thought I was worth it. In case you want to know about complementarity, well, I'm your man. Wonderful conversation we had, me being back from the dead. Somehow, I don't think he quite believed it."

Jury ended the call, said, "Those crates, Sergeant, grab the small one and let's get out."

It was the smaller of the two crates, but big enough to be awkward. Sergeant Meek managed, even laughed. "Those kids." He laughed. "Pretty cool customers."

Jury smiled. "The coolest."

The crate went straight to forensics.

"Sorry, guv. No prints."

Jury talked to one of the print experts. "But there have to—I mean, it was the kids who shoved those boxes to beneath the window; it was they who stacked them. How could there not be prints?"

"Two things: first, that crate's undressed wood. It wouldn't pick 'em up. Second, the kids maybe were wearing gloves."

"Why would they be wearing gloves?"

"Maybe they were made to. You said they put the crates underneath the window and crawled out. Or that's what it looked like. Well, they would have left prints on or around the window. Couldn't hardly help doing that."

"Not with gloves on," said Jury.

"Depends what kind. A print might've gone through a glove, if the glove was thin enough. Find any latex gloves lying about?"

"No. If I had, I'd've picked them up, wouldn't I?"

"Sorry, guv. Just you get us to go over that window frame, you'll see."

Yes, and I can also see immediate suspension—for me, for Sergeant Meek and also for you, if you care to join us with your kit—as we don't have a rat's ass worth of a warrant. He did not say this; he did say, "Nothing to be done about it. Thanks."

So Harry had even considered that. He didn't want them leaving prints anywhere, so he'd made them wear some kind of glove. He said this to Wiggins; they were in the office the next morning. But there'd be prints in the car. Jury doubted Harry had tied their hands in the car, for the same reason he'd removed the blindfolds: it would be too attention getting.

"God, is there *anything*," said Wiggins, as he stirred his tea,

"Harry didn't think of?" Wiggins, who had never met him, still felt on a first-name basis.

"Yes." Jury hooked his jacket from the back of his chair. "There's one thing."

"What's that, sir?"

"I don't know." Jury stood in the doorway jingling change in his pocket. "Yet." He walked out.

58

It was her father who came from Manchester to collect the body.

Albert Bly's face wore the permanent stamp of sorrow, deepened, Jury thought, by the death of his daughter.

"Pastoni was her married name. She met some Italian bloke there and married him and divorced him. Rosie could never stick with anything for long." This was said not in a critical tone, but merely to convey information.

"I'm truly sorrow for your loss, Mr. Bly."

Albert Bly looked down at his cup of tea. "Nothing to be done about it, I expect." He sighed deeply, sitting in the café Jury had taken him to after the father had ID'd Rosa Paston's body.

Finding the family had taken a bit of looking, as the police knew Rose Bly only as Rosa Paston.

"It's the wife it'll be a bit hard on."

A bit hard. Jury sometimes marveled at the British ability to understate. Yes, he could well imagine her daughter's death would be "a bit hard."

Albert Bly went on: "Even though Rosie hadn't been to see us in more'n a year—no, two, more likely. You know how it is with kids."

Rosa Paston—Rosie Bly—had stayed on in Italy, in Venice, after the divorce and got herself a job. "The place suited her, I don't know why. All those canals, all that water, can't even drive your car. You wouldn't catch me in one of them boats—what'd'ya call 'em?"

"Gondolas." Jury smiled.

Mr. Bly made a face and drank his tea. "Nice caff, this is." After carefully returning his cup to its saucer, he said, "Have you got the bloke did this?"

"Not yet. We've got a suspect, though."

Albert Bly's shoulders seemed to slump farther.

"Mr. Bly, did Rosie keep in touch? I mean, did she write to you and her mother? Did she mention any man she'd met? One that she was fairly serious about?"

The wife might know more about that, but he doubted it. Rosie didn't write much, and never did tell them much going on of a personal nature.

There had been a man. That information had come from Rosa's flat mate. She'd told police Rosa "had a fellow" and they were going to get married. She'd left Venice for London sometime around mid-June. Last year.

And had Rosa given her friend any clue as to who this "fellow" was?

No. But he was handsome and rich.

Weren't they all? thought Jury, sadly.

Venetian dreams.

They would, of course, talk to the mother. But Jury knew he knew more than either of the parents. Finally, they left the café and Jury went with Albert Bly to his small B&B. He took down the information they'd need for the eventual return of Rosa Paston's remains.

"We'll get him, Mr. Bly. Make no mistake about that."

It wasn't much of a comfort.

Epilogue

It was 7:30 in the Old Wine Shades and Harry was sitting at the bar talking to Trevor. Or, rather, Trevor was the one talking, leaning over the bar as if he had many secrets to impart.

"Hello, Harry," said Jury, pulling out a chair. It being the one Mungo was stationed under, the dog came out, looked at Jury—

("Bemused," Jury would have said.)

—and then slipped back under the chair.

"Richard! I haven't seen you in nearly two weeks. What've you been getting up to? Listen: you've got to try this." Harry tapped his glass. "Barolo Monprivato, this is."

"Your Italian is very good."

"Oh, no question. That was so hard to say."

"I bet you have no problem pronouncing the name of that Tuscan hill town—you know, the one near Florence."

"San Gimignano?"

"Perfect." As Trevor set down a glass for him, Jury said, "I bet you even speak it. Italian, I mean."

"Not hellishly well."

"Enough to pick up girls and so forth."

"Probably." Harry snickered.

Trevor had poured and now Jury drank.

Harry said, "Don't *gulp* it, for God's sake! Trevor here will have a stroke."

Trevor was leaning against the bar, happily waiting for Jury's reaction.

It was as if their raison d'être—the three of them—were lodged in the Old Wine Shades and this bottle of wine.

"Great," said Jury. "Fat and full, as Trevor would say."

"I wouldn't say that," said Trevor. "Fruity, sensual. It's a Château Latour, this one is."

"He'll make sommeliers of us yet," said Harry.

Us. That was nice. "You're one already, Harry. I bet there's enough in your cellar to open up a bar."

"*My* cellar? Richard, have you been snooping around?"

"Wow!" exclaimed Jury. "That's one of those trick questions suspects ask to trap the dimwitted policeman! I'm assuming anyone who likes wine this much is going to have a wine cellar."

Harry laughed. He took it all absolutely happily. What amazed Jury was that he apparently didn't feel in any danger. The kids had fled, after all. They could be talking to police a mile a minute. Talking away. Identifying Harry. "Yes, he's the bloke that had us prisoners." Pointing to a picture: "That's him all right. We'd not forget him, not bloody likely."

Jury's fantasy. Except there was no picture, no identification. Was Harry one of those people—seldom seen, in Jury's experience—who would stonewall until the bitter end, until the wall completely crumbled?

"You're just too bloody clever, Harry."

"I? *I'm* clever. No, I'd say the cleverness crown definitely goes to you. And that friend of yours. Niels Bohr, for God's sake. Niels *Bohr*. I'll say this for your friend. He had me going for a while. He had a grasp of the principle of complementarity almost as good as Hugh's. He's quite brilliant, your friend. We went back and forth, through a bottle of Bordeaux"—Harry tapped his glass again—"not this, but an excellent Château Margaux, right Trev?"

"Right. That cost you," said Trevor, with a huge smile. Trevor was fascinated. He stood behind the bar polishing the glasses, which he would then hold up to the light to check for smears.

"Anyway," Harry went on, "we went back and forth, back and forth. It was like a game of chess, really." He smiled, remembering.

"Who got checkmated?"

"Oh, we didn't get to the end after I realized you'd just slipped away. Where did you go?"

"I had a date." Jury leaned toward him, lowered his voice. "What were you going to do to them, Harry?"

"Them who?"

"Timmy and Tilda."

"Oh, lord, are we back to *them* again?" He checked his watch. "Dinner?"

"No, thanks. I've got to be some place." Jury got up, finished his glass of wine.

So did Harry finish off his. "Well, I'm starving. So I guess it's to be just Mungo and me."

Mungo came out, looking (Jury would have said) jaded (if that was possible for a dog), world-weary, dead tired, knackered. Jury reached down and gave his head a rub. Jury hadn't taken off his coat, so he didn't need to put it on.

After Harry got into his black cashmere and dropped some enormous sum of money on the bar, they walked out. Harry stopped outside to light up a cigarette.

"Give me one of those, will you?"

"What? A cigarette? You stopped smoking." Harry held out his cigarette case. "Well, I hate to be the cause of your starting up again."

"I bet you do. Harry, I'm going to dog your footsteps."

Mungo looked sharply up.

"Sorry."

"Think nothing of it."

"I wasn't talking to you, Harry."

Harry laughed. "Good, we can meet regularly right here for a progress report. Right now, I'm starving. Night." He walked off, whistling, turned around and waved.

Mungo turned around, too.

Jury was glad he couldn't see his expression.

He put the cigarette in his mouth, patted his coat up and down, frisking himself for matches, knowing he had none. But it was a pleasant reminder of what he used to do.

Jury smiled.

It wasn't for the smoke.

That, he tossed in the gutter.